Praise for George Pel[...]

SOUL CIRCUS

"Clear any breakfast meetings off your calendar—you're gonna be up late reading this one."
—Jonathan Miles, Men's Journal

"*Soul Circus* serves up what George Pelecanos's fans have come to expect, and once again, the effect is sharp and satisfying: a richly textured tapestry, a quirky plot, a large, multicolored cast of lawbreakers, law enforcers, misfits, malfeasants, and innocent bystanders....The novels of Pelecanos are passionate, vital, and vigorously demotic. If they have sense, historians will plumb them for evidence of how men and women lived, feared, and coped in the war zones of everyday life: not only when they preyed on each other, but when they talked, loved, listened to music, or just wasted time."
—Eugen Weber, Los Angeles Times

"In the realm of crime noir, few contemporary writers connect criminal acts and the society that spawns them as efficiently as Pelecanos. His writing in his eleventh novel is as polished and as exquisitely honed as the guns that wreak havoc in the neighborhoods where his novels are set. You'll want to reread scenes of violence for the beauty of the language and the cinematic quality that pushes readers to envision urban evil in all its forms."
—Carol Memmott, USA Today

"George P. Pelecanos covers Washington, D.C., like a police-beat reporter. He attends trials, rides with cops, burns shoe leather, keeps his ears open....*Soul Circus* may be his most moving venture yet."
—Zach Dundas, Willamette Week

"Pelecanos's most satisfying Derek Strange novel."
—*Entertainment Weekly*

"Last year Pelecanos hit the bestseller list for the first time with the critically lauded *Hell to Pay*. His latest, *Soul Circus,* is a worthy successor, because Pelecanos has the first-rate writer's ability to entertain you and break your heart on the same page. His storytelling keeps you turning pages to determine the guilt or innocence of a drug lord on death row.... Derek Strange is one of the realest creations in contemporary fiction, whether he's solving a crime or worrying about getting a haircut. Just for the record, he's an admirable guy too. The only unbelievable thing about this powerfully affecting character is the notion that Pelecanos made him up."
—Malcolm Jones, *Newsweek*

"Like Walt Whitman in 'Song of Myself,' Pelecanos plays 'not marches for accepted victors only'; he also plays 'marches for conquer'd and slain persons.' And what eloquent literary 'marches' they are, swelling with the music of Philly soul, rap, the soundtracks from spaghetti Westerns, and a bit of Springsteen.... Pelecanos writes with intelligence and complexity, as well as with a sober recognition of the evil at large in the world. His latest novel, *Soul Circus,* may be his best yet—but I've been declaring that clichéd judgment about a lot of his novels ever since I've been reading him.... *Soul Circus* grapples with some of the Big Questions, along with the relatively mundane ones that Strange and Quinn are hired to investigate. The American racial divide, the existence of God (and, especially, a God that would allow harm to children), the meaning and transience of life—they're all on the board here. What's so brilliant about *Soul Circus,* and Pelecanos's novels in general, is that he raises these questions not only in meditative passages but also in scenes of the rawest violence."
—Maureen Corrigan, *Washington Post*

"Pelecanos balances several stories with amazing skill. Tension and outrage build as the pages fly by.... Thanks to Pelecanos's insight and talent, readers will agree that they can't wait to see what happens next."
— Michele Ross, *Cleveland Plain Dealer*

"Pelecanos is fascinated with the way things work, and he takes apart the gun trade like an urban anthropologist, fitting the pieces into the drug business and the gang culture with an exactness that is breathtaking—and depressing. At the same time, he treats his criminals like human beings, talking their talk, driving their cars, listening to their music, getting into their world with something that can only be called sympathy."
— Marilyn Stasio, *New York Times Book Review*

"When George P. Pelecanos began his current series featuring an unlikely pair of D.C. private investigators, he told readers he intended to make a trilogy. Well, *Soul Circus* is the third of these novels, and it is such an outstanding effort that the author will no doubt be hearing howls of protest as people plead, 'Don't stop now!'... *Soul Circus* should both solidify Pelecanos as one of the best crime writers working today and boost his sales into the bestseller regions."
— John Clutterbuck, *Houston Chronicle*

"Pelecanos expertly constructs both a gripping thriller and a tense internal drama. As always, his deeply textured portraits of the victims of poverty and violence add an almost Dickensian breadth to the novel. Throw in a shocking conclusion with far-reaching ramifications for the series, and you have one more superb installment in what has become a remarkably revealing portrait of urban life and the most intimate matters of heart and mind."
— *Booklist* (starred review)

SOUL CIRCUS

A Novel

GEORGE PELECANOS

BACK BAY BOOKS
Little, Brown and Company
New York Boston London

Back Bay Books / Little, Brown and Company
Hachette Book Group
237 Park Avenue, New York, NY 10017
www.hachettebookgroup.com

Originally published in hardcover by Little, Brown and Company, March 2003
First Back Bay paperback edition, March 2011

Back Bay Books is an imprint of Little, Brown and Company. The Back Bay Books name and logo are trademarks of Hachette Book Group, Inc.

The characters and events in this book are fictitious. Any similarity to real persons, living or dead, is coincidental and not intended by the author.

The publisher is not responsible for websites (or their content) that are not owned by the publisher.

Library of Congress Cataloging-in-Publication Data
Pelecanos, George P.
  Soul circus : a novel / by George P. Pelecanos. — 1st ed.
    p. cm.
  ISBN 978-0-316-60843-5 (hc) / 978-0-316-09941-7 (trade pb)
  1. Private investigators — Washington (D.C.) — Fiction.   2. Washington (D.C.) — Fiction.
3. Drug traffic — Fiction.   I. Title.
PS3566.E354 S68 2003
813'54 — dc21   2002016207

10   9   8   7   6   5   4   3   2   1

RRD-IN

Printed in the United States of America

To Michael, with gratitude

MAY

1

THE chains binding Granville Oliver's wrists scraped the scarred surface of the table before him. Manacles also bound his ankles. Oliver's shoulders and chest filled out the orange jumpsuit he had worn for half a year. His eyes, almost golden when Strange had first met him, were now the color of creamed-up coffee, dull in the artificial light of the interview room of the D.C. Jail.

"Looks like you're keeping your physical self together," said Strange, seated on the other side of the table.

"Push-ups," said Oliver. "I try to do a few hundred every day."

"You still down in the Hole?"

"You mean Special Management. I don't know what's so special about it; ain't nothin' but a box. They let me out of it one hour for every forty-eight."

Strange and Oliver were surrounded by Plexiglas dividers in a space partitioned by cubicles. Nearby, public defenders and CJA

4 • GEORGE P. PELECANOS

attorneys conferred with their clients. The dividers served to mute, somewhat, the various conversations, leaving a low, steady mutter in the room. A thick-necked armed guard sat watching the activity from a chair behind a window in a darkened booth.

"It won't be long," said Strange. "They finished with the jury selection."

"Ives told me. They finally found a dozen D.C. residents weren't opposed to the death penalty, how'd they put it, *on principle.* Which means they found some white people gonna have no problem to sit up there and judge me."

"Four whites," said Strange.

"How you think they gonna find me, Strange? Guilty?"

Strange looked down and tapped his pen on the open folder lying on the table. He didn't care to take the conversation any further in that direction. He wasn't here to discuss what was or was not going to happen relative to the trial, and he was, by definition of his role as an investigator, uninterested in Oliver's guilt or innocence. It was true that he had a personal connection to this case, but from the start he had been determined to treat this as just another job.

"The prosecution's going to put Phillip Wood up there first," said Strange.

"Told you when I met you the very first time he was gonna be my Judas. Phil can't do no more maximum time. Last time he was inside, they took away his manhood. I mean they ass-raped him good. I knew that boy would flip." Oliver tried to smile. "Far as geography goes, though, we still close. They got him over there in the Snitch Hive, Strange. Me and Phil, we're like neighbors."

Wood had been Granville's top lieutenant. He had pled out in exchange for testimony against Oliver. Wood would get life, as he had admitted to being the triggerman in other murders; death had been taken off the table. He was housed in the Correctional Treatment Facility, a privately run unit holding informants and government witnesses in the backyard of the D.C. Jail.

"I've been gathering background for the cross," said Strange. "I was looking for you to lead me to one of Phillip's old girl-friends."

"Phil knew a lot of girls. The way he used to flash . . . even a bitch can get some pussy; ain't no trick to that. Phil used to drive this Turbo Z I had bought for him around to the high schools, 'specially over in Maryland, in PG? Drive by with that Kenwood sound system he had in there, playin' it loud. The girls used to run up to the car. They didn't even know who he was, and it didn't matter. It was obvious he had money, and what he did to get it. Girls just want to be up in there with the stars. It's *like* that, Strange."

"I'm looking for one girl in particular. She swore out a bru-tality complaint against Wood."

"The prosecution gave you that?"

"They don't have to give you charges, only convictions. I found it in his jacket down at the court. This particular charge, it was no-papered. Never went to trial."

"What's the girl's name?"

"Devra Stokes. Should be about twenty-two by now. She worked at the Paramount Beauty Salon on Good Hope Road."

Oliver grunted. "Sounds right. Phil did like to chill in those beauty parlors. Said that's where the girls were, so he wanted to be there, too. But I don't know her. We went through a lot of young girls. We were kickin' it with 'em, for the most part. But we were using them for other shit, too."

"What else would he have used a girl like Devra Stokes for?"

"Well, if she was old enough, and she didn't have no priors, we'd take her into Maryland or Virginia to buy a gun for us. Vir-ginia, if we needed it quick. We paid for it, but she'd sign the forty-four seventy-three. What they call the yellow form."

"You mean for a straw purchase."

"A straw gun, yeah. Course, not all the time. You could rent a gun or get it from people we knew to get it from in the neighborhood. It's easy for a youngun to get a gun in the city. Easier than it is to buy a car. Shoot, you got to register a car."

Strange repeated the name: "Devra Stokes."

"Like I say, I don't recall. But look, she was workin' in a salon, chance is, she still doin' the same thing, maybe somewhere else, but in the area. Those girls move around, but not too far."

"Right."

"Phil's gonna say I killed my uncle, ain't that right?"

"I don't know what he's going to say, Granville."

Oliver and Strange stared at each other across the desk.

"You standin' tall, big man?" said Oliver.

Oliver was questioning Strange's loyalty. Strange answered by holding Oliver's gaze.

"I ain't no dreamer," said Oliver. "One way or the other, it's over for me. The business is done. Most of the boys I came up with, they're dead or doin' long time. One of the young ones I brought along got his own thing now, but he's cut things off with me. Word I get is, he still got himself lined up with Phil. Shoot, I hear they got two operations fighting over what I built as we sit here today."

"What's your point?"

"I feel like I'm already gone. They want to erase me, Strange. Make it so I don't exist no more. The same way they keep poor young black boys and girls out of the public's eyes today, the same way they did me when I was a kid. Warehousin' me and those like me down in the Section Eights. Now the government wants to bring me out and make an example out of me for a hot minute, then make me disappear again. And I'm a good candidate, too, ain't I? A strong young nigger with an attitude. They want to strap me to that table in Indiana and give me that needle and show people, that's what happens when you don't stay down where we done put you. That's what happens when you rise up. They want to do this to me bad. So bad that they'd fuck with someone who was trying to help me to stop it, hear?"

You left out the part about all the young black men you killed or had killed, thought Strange. And the part about you poisoning your own community with drugs, and ruining the lives of all the young people you recruited and the lives of their families. But there were some truths in what Granville Oliver was saying, too. Strange, following a personal policy, did not comment either way.

"So I was just wondering," said Oliver. "When they try to shake you down — and they will — are you gonna stand tall?"

"Don't insult me," said Strange. "And don't ever let me get the idea that you're threatening me. 'Cause I will walk. And you do not want me to do that."

Strange kept his voice even and his shoulders straight. He hoped his anger, and his fear, did not show on his face. Strange knew that even from in here, Oliver could have most anyone killed out on the street.

Oliver smiled, his face turning from hard to handsome. Like many who had attained his position, he was intelligent, despite his limited education, and could be a charming young man at will. When he relaxed his features, he favored his deceased father, a man Strange had known in the 1960s. Oliver had never known his father at all.

"I was just askin' a question, big man. I don't have many friends left, and I want to make sure that the ones I *do* have stay friends. We square, right?"

"We're square."

"Good. But, look here, don't come up in here empty-handed next time. I could use some smokes or somethin'."

"You know I can't be bringin' any contraband in here. They bar me from these meetings, it's gonna be a setback for what we're trying to accomplish."

"I hear you. How about some porno mags, though?"

"I'll see you next time."

Strange stood.

"One more thing," said Oliver.

"What is it?" said Strange.

"I was wonderin' how Robert Gray was doin'?"

"He's staying with his aunt."

"She ain't right."

"I know it. But it's the best I could do. I got him all pumped up about playing football for us this year. We're gonna start him in the camp this summer, comin' up."

"That's my little man right there. You're gonna see, that boy can jook. Check up on him, will you?"

"I get the time, I'll go by there today."

"Thank you."

"Stay strong, Granville."

Strange signaled the fat man in the booth and walked from the room.

OUT in the air, on the 1900 block of D Street in Southeast, Derek Strange walked to his car. He dropped under the wheel of his work vehicle, a white-over-black '89 Caprice with a 350 square block under the hood, and rolled down the window. He had a while to kill before meeting Quinn back at the office, and he didn't want to face the ringing phone and the message slips spread out on his desk. He decided he would sit in his car and enjoy the quiet and the promise of a new day.

Strange poured a cup of coffee from the thermos he kept in his car. Coffee was okay for times like this, but he kept water in the thermos when he was doing a surveillance, because coffee went through him too quick. He only sipped the water when he knew he'd be in the car for a long stretch, and on those occasions he kept a cup in the car with a plastic lid on it, in which he could urinate as needed.

Strange tasted the coffee. Janine had brewed it for him that morning before he left the house. The woman could cook, and she could make some coffee, too.

Strange picked up the newspaper beside him on the bench, which he had snatched off the lawn outside Janine's house earlier that morning on his way to the car. He pulled the Metro section free and scanned the front page. The *Washington Post* was running yet another story today in a series documenting the ongoing progress of the Granville Oliver trial.

Oliver had allegedly been involved in a dozen murders, including the murder of his own uncle, while running the Oliver Mob, a large-scale, longtime drug business operating in the Southeast quadrant of the city. The Feds were seeking death for Oliver under the RICO act, despite the fact that the District's residents had overwhelmingly rejected the death penalty in a local referendum. The combination of racketeering and certain violent crimes allowed the government to exercise this option. The last execution in D.C. had been carried out in 1957.

The jury selection process had taken several months, as it had been difficult to find twelve local residents unopposed to capital punishment. During this time, Oliver's attorneys, from the firm of Ives and Colby, had employed Strange to gather evidence, data, and countertestimony for the defense.

Strange skipped the article, jumping inside Metro to page 3. His eyes went to a daily crime column unofficially known by longtime Washingtonians as "the Roundup," or the "Violent Negro Deaths." The first small headline read, "Teen Dies of Gunshot Wounds," and beneath it were two sentences: "An 18-year-old man found with multiple gunshot wounds in Southeast Washington died early yesterday at Prince George's County Hospital Center, police said. The unidentified man was found just after midnight in the courtyard area behind the Stoneridge apartments in the 300 block of Anacostia Road, and was pronounced dead at 1:03 A.M."

Two sentences, thought Strange. That's all a certain kind of kid in this town's gonna get to sum up his life. There would be more deaths, most likely retribution kills, related to this one.

Later, the murder gun might turn up somewhere down the food chain. Later, the crime might get "solved," pinned on the shooter by a snitch in a plea-out. Whatever happened, this would be the last the general public would hear about this young man, a passing mention to be filed away in a newspaper morgue, one brief paragraph without even a name attached to prove that he had existed. Another unidentified YBM, dead on the other side of the Anacostia River.

River, hell, thought Strange. The way it separates this city for real, might as well go ahead and call it a canyon.

Strange dropped the newspaper back on the bench seat. He turned the key in the ignition and pushed a Spinners tape into his deck. He pulled out of his spot and drove west. Just a few sips of coffee, and already he had to pee. Anyway, he couldn't sit here all day. It was time to go to work.

T WO house wrens, a brownish male and female, were building a nest on the sill outside Strange's office window. Strange could hear them talking to each other as they worked.

When Strange was a child, his mother, Alethea, had held him up to their kitchen window on mornings just like this one to show him the daily progress of the nest the birds made there each year. "They're working to make a house for their children. The same way your father goes to work each day to make this a home for you and your brother." His mother had been gone two years now, but Derek Strange could recall her words, and he could hear the music in her voice. She still spoke to Strange in his dreams.

Late-spring light shot through the glass, the heat of it warming the back of Strange's neck and hands as he sat at his desk. The wedge-shaped speaker beside his phone buzzed. Janine's voice, transmitted from the office reception area up front, came from the box.

"Derek, Terry just came in."

"I'll be right out."

Strange glanced down beside his chair, where Greco, his tan boxer, lay. Greco looked up without moving his head as Strange rubbed his skull. Greco's nub of a tail twitched and he closed his eyes.

"I won't be gone long. Janine'll take care of you, boy."

In the reception area, Strange nodded at Terry Quinn, sitting at his desk, a work station he rarely used. While Quinn tore open a pack of sugarless gum, Strange stopped by Janine's desk.

She wore some kind of pants-and-shirt hookup, flowing and bright. Her lipstick matched the half-moons of red slashing through the outfit. It would be like her to pay attention to that kind of detail. Strange stared at her now. She always looked good. *Always.* But you couldn't get the full weight of it if you saw her seated behind her desk. Janine was the kind of tall, strong woman, you needed to see her walking to get the full appreciation, to feel that stirring up in your thighs. Like one of those proud horses they marched around at the track. He knew it wasn't proper to talk about a woman, especially a woman you loved, like she was some kind of fine animal. But that's what came to mind when he looked at her. He guessed it was still okay, until the thought police came and raided his head, to imagine her like that in his mind.

"You okay?" said Janine, looking up at him with those big browns of hers. "You look drunk."

"Thinking of you," said Strange.

Strange heard Lamar, seated at Ron Lattimer's old desk, snicker behind him. For this he turned and stared benignly at the young man.

"I ain't say nothin'," said Lamar. "Just over here, minding my own."

Strange had been grooming Lamar Williams to be an investigator as soon as he got his diploma from Roosevelt High and took up some technical courses, computer training or something like it, at night. In the meantime, Strange had Lamar doing what he'd been doing the past couple of years: cleaning the office, running errands, and keeping himself away from the street-side boys over in the Section 8s, the nearby Park Morton complex where Lamar lived with his mom and little sister.

Strange looked back at Janine, then down to the blotter-style calendar on her desk. "What's my two o'clock about?"

"Man says he's looking for a love."

"Him and Bobby Womack," said Strange.

"His *lost* love."

"Okay. We know him?"

"Says he's been seeing our sign these last few years, since he's been 'frequenting an establishment' over on Georgia Avenue."

"Must be talkin' about that titty bar across the street. Our claim to the neighborhood."

"Georgetown's got Dunbarton Oaks," said Janine with a shrug. "We've got the Foxy Playground."

Strange leaned over the desk and kissed Janine fully on the lips. Their mouths fit together right. He held the kiss, then stood straight.

"Dag, y'all actin' like you're twenty years old," said Lamar.

Strange straightened the new name plaque on the desk. For many years it had read "Janine Baker." Now it read "Janine Strange."

"I didn't have it so good when I was twenty," said Strange, talking to Lamar, still looking at Janine. "And anyway, where's it say that a man's not allowed to kiss his wife?"

Janine reached into her desk drawer and pulled free a Pay-Day bar. "In case you miss lunch," she said, handing it to Strange.

"Thank you, baby."

Terry Quinn stood, a manila folder under his arm. He had the sun-sensitive skin of an Irishman, with a square jaw and deep laugh ridges framing his mouth. A scar ran down one cheek where he had been cut by a pimp's pearl-handled knife. He kept his hair short and it was free of gray. The burst of lines that had formed around his green eyes was the sole indication of his thirty-three years. He was medium height, but the width of his shoulders and the heft of his chest made him appear shorter.

"Can I get some of that Extra, Terry?" said Lamar.

Quinn tossed a stick of gum to Lamar as he stepped out from behind his desk.

"You ready?" said Strange.

"Thought you two were gonna renew your vows or something," said Quinn.

Strange head-motioned to the front door. "We'll take my short."

Janine watched them leave the office. Strange filled out that shirt she'd bought him, mostly cotton but with a touch of rayon in it for the stretch, with his broad shoulders and back. Her man, almost fifty-four, had twenty years on Terry, and still he looked fine.

Coming out of the storefront, they passed under the sign hanging above the door. The magnifying-glass logo covered and blew up half the script: "Strange Investigations" against a yellow back. At night the light-box was the beacon on this part of the strip, 9th between Kansas and Upshur, a sidearm-throw off Georgia. It was this sign, Janine's kidding aside, that was the landmark in Petworth and down into Park View. Strange had opened this business after his stint with the MPD, and he had kept it open now for over twenty-five years. He could just as well have made his living out of his row house on Buchanan Street, especially now that he was staying full-time with Janine and her son, Lionel, in their house on Quintana. But he knew what his visibility meant out here; the young people in the neighborhood had come to expect his presence on this street.

Strange and Quinn passed Hawk's barbershop, where a cutter named Rodel stood outside, dragging on a Newport.

"When you gonna get that mess straightened up, Derek?" said Rodel.

"Tell Bennett I'll be in later on today," said Strange, not breaking his stride.

"They got the new *Penthouse* in," said Quinn.

"You didn't soil it or nothin', did you?"

"You can still make out a picture or two."

Strange patted his close-cut, lightly salted natural. "Another reason to get myself correct."

They passed the butcher place that sold lunches, and Marshall's funeral parlor, where the white Caprice was parked along the curb behind a black limo-style Lincoln. Strange turned the ignition, and they rolled toward Southeast.

3

ULYSSES Foreman was just about down to seeds, so when little Mario Durham got him on his cell, looking to rent a gun, he told Durham to meet him on Martin Luther King Jr. Avenue, up a ways from the Big Chair. Foreman set the meeting out for a while, which would give him time to wake up his girl, Ashley Swann, and show her who her daddy was before he left up the house.

An hour and a half later, Foreman looked across the leather bench at a skinny man with a wide, misshapen nose and big rat teeth, leaning against the Caddy's passenger-side door. On Durham's feet were last year's Jordans; the *J* on the left one, Foreman noticed, was missing. Durham wore a Redskins jersey and a matching knit cap, his arms coming out the jersey like willow branches. The back of the jersey had the name "Sanders" printed across it. It would be just like Durham, thought Foreman, to look up to a pretty-boy hustler, all flash and no heart, like Deion.

"You brought me somethin'?" said Foreman.

Durham, having hiked up the volume on the Cadillac's system, didn't hear. He was moving his head to that single, "Danger," had been in heavy rotation since the wintertime. Foreman reached over and turned the music down.

"Hey," said Durham.

"We got business."

"That joint is tight, though."

"Mystikal? He ain't doin' nothin' J. B. didn't do twenty years back."

"It's still a good jam."

"Uh-huh. And PGC done played that shit to death." Foreman upped his chin in the direction of Mario. "C'mon, Twigs, show me what you got."

Mario Durham hated the nickname that had followed him for years. It brought to mind Twiggy, that itty-bitty model who was popular from back before he was born. It was a bitch name, he knew. There wasn't but a few men he allowed to call him that. Okay, there was more than a few. But Ulysses Foreman, built like a nose tackle, he sure was one of those men. Durham reached down into his jeans, deep inside his boxers, and pulled free a rolled plastic sandwich bag containing a thick line of chronic. He handed it across the bench to Foreman.

Foreman's pearl red 1997 El Dorado Touring Coupe was parked on MLK between W and V in Southeast. Its Northstar engine was quiet, and no smoke was visible from the pipes. Foreman didn't like to tax the battery, so he was letting the motor run. He sat low on the bench, his stacked shoulders and knotted biceps filling out the ribbed white cotton T-shirt he'd bought out that catalogue he liked, International Male.

Across the street, a twenty-foot-tall mahogany chair sat in the grassy section off the lot of the Anacostia Medical / Dental Center, formerly the sight of the Curtis Brothers Furniture Company. The Big Chair was the landmark in Far Southeast.

"This gonna get me up?" said Foreman, inspecting the contents of the bag.

"You know me," said Durham. "You know how I do."

Foreman nodded, glancing in the rearview. A Sixth District cruiser approached, coming slowly from the direction of St. Elizabeth's, the laughing house atop the hill. Foreman never worried. If he didn't know the beat police in this part of town, then he could name-check some of their older fellow officers, many of whom he had come up with back in the late eighties, when he had worn the uniform himself in 6D. Being a former cop, still knowing existing cops, it was usually worth a free pass. Leastways it stopped them from searching the car. The cruiser went by and was soon gone from sight.

Foreman reached under the seat and produced a Taurus 85, a five-shot .38 Special with a black rubber boot-shaped grip and a ported barrel. He handed it to Durham butt out, keeping it below the window line. Durham admired it in the morning sunlight streaming in from the east.

"It's blue."

"For real. Pretty, right?"

"Damn sure is."

Durham turned it in the light, the barrel now pointed at Foreman. Foreman reached out and with the back of his hand moved the barrel so that it pointed down at the floor of the car.

"It's loaded?" said Durham.

"You got to treat every gun like it's live, boy."

"I hear you. But is it?"

"Yeah, you're ready."

Durham nodded. "When you want it back?"

Forman weighed the plastic bag in his hand. "I say you rented about five days of strap right here."

"That's a hundred worth of hydro in that bag. I coulda *bought* a brand-new three eighty for, like, ninety dollas."

"You talkin' about a Davis? Go ahead and buy one, then. But give me back my *real* gun before you do."

"That's all right."

"There you go then, little man. You want to ride in style, you got to pay." Foreman pushed his hips forward to slip the bag into the pocket of his jeans. "What you need the gun for, anyway?"

"Need to make an impression on someone, is all it is. Why?"

"I can't be fuckin' with no murder gun, hear? You plan to blow someone up behind this shit, I got to know. 'Cause I can't use no gun got a body attached to it. We straight?"

Durham nodded quickly. "Sure. Do me a favor, though. Don't be tellin' my brother about you rentin' me this gun."

"Why not?"

"He might say somethin' to our mother. I don't want her stressin' over me."

"I can understand that. We don't need to be worryin' your all's moms."

Foreman had already decided that he would tell Dewayne Durham that he had rented a gun to his half brother, Mario. Dewayne might not like that, but it would be better if he knew up front. Foreman figured, what harm would it do? This miniature man right here wouldn't have the courage to use the gun anyway. Foreman would have it back in five days, and he had some free hydro to smoke in the bargain. Didn't seem to be any kind of problem to it that he could see.

They shook hands. Durham ended the ritual with a weak finger snap.

"Let me get on back to Mer-land where I belong," said Foreman.

"I got an appointment I got to get to my own self."

"You need me to drop you somewheres close?" Foreman had no intention of driving Mario Durham anywhere, but he felt it made good sense to be polite, go through the usual motions and ask. Foreman's business relationship with Dewayne Durham was on the rise.

"Nah, I'm just down there around the corner."

"Awright, then," said Foreman.

"Aiight."

Durham dropped the pistol into the large pocket of his over-size jeans and stepped out of the car. He walked down the hill and cut left. Foreman watched him, wearin' a boy's-size Redskins jersey, a slip of nothing in his Hilfigers, hanging like some sad shit on his narrow ass. "I'm just down there around the corner" — that was some bullshit right there. Twigs didn't own no car, or if he did it wasn't nothin' but a bomb. Most likely he was headed for the Metro station to catch a train to that appointment he had. Must be a real important date, too. Foreman had to admit, though, Mario Durham always did have some good chronic to smoke. Dewayne, a dealer over in Congress Heights, advanced him however much he wanted.

Durham walked toward the Metro station in Barry Farms, passing hard-eyed boys on the sidewalk, thinking how different it felt when you had a gun in your pocket. Different on the physical tip, like he'd grown taller and put on fifty pounds of muscle. Lookin' in those young boys' narrowed eyes, thinking, Yeah, go ahead, fuck with me; I got somethin' right here gonna make your eyes go wide. Having that .38 just touching his leg through the fabric of his Tommys, it made him feel like he had four more inches of dick on him, too.

He'd catch a Green Line train and take it over the river to the Petworth stop. The man's office, he'd seen the sign out front with the magnifying glass on it all those times he'd been to that titty bar they had across the street from it, on Georgia. His office, it wasn't far from the station stop.

Durham wondered, could the man in that office find Olivia?

Because his kid brother wasn't gonna wait much longer without taking some kind of action his own self. Sign out front claimed they did investigations.

Strange Investigations.

That's what it said.

c h a p t e r

4

"THERE it is right there," said Quinn, pointing to the in-dash cassette deck in Strange's Chevy.

"He said 'hug her.'" Strange sang the words: "'Makes you want to love her, you just got to hug her, yeah.'"

"'You just got to *fuck* her,'" said Quinn. "That's what the man's sayin'. Rewind it and listen to it again."

They were on eastbound H Street in Northeast, where the sidewalks were live with pedestrian traffic, folks hanging out, and deliverymen moving goods from their curbed trucks to the shops. They passed a Murray's Steaks, several nail salons and hair galleries, and a place called Father and Son Beer and Wine. Strange turned right on 8th and drove toward Southeast. He rewound the tape and the two of them listened again to the line in question.

"There it is, man," said Strange. "He said 'hug her.'"

"He said 'fuck her,' Dad."

"See, you're focusing on the wrong thing, Terry. What you

ought to be doing, on a beautiful day like this, is groovin' to the song. This here is the Spinners' debut on Atlantic. Some people call this the most beautiful Philly soul album ever recorded."

"Yeah, I know. Produced by Taco Bell."

"*Thom* Bell."

"What about those guys Procter and Gamble you're always goin' on about?"

"Gamble and Huff. Point is, this is pretty nice, isn't it? Shoot, Terry, you had to have —"

"Been there; I know."

"That's right. You take all those slow-jam groups from that period, the Chi-Lites, the Sylistics, Harold Melvin, the ballad stuff that EWF was doin', and what you got is the most beautiful period of pop music in history. It's like America got their own . . . they finally got their own opera, man."

Quinn turned up the volume on the deck. He chuckled, listening to the words. "Derek, is that what you mean by opera, right there?"

"What?"

"'Makes a lame man walk . . . makes blind men talk about seein' again.'"

"Look, the song's called 'One of a Kind (Love Affair).' Ain't you never had the kind of love that could rock your world like that?"

"When I was bustin' a nut, maybe."

"That's what I can't understand about you young folks, Generation XYZ, or whatever you're calling yourselves this week. Y'all ain't got no romance in you, man."

"I had plenty in me last night."

"Oh, yeah?" Strange looked across the bench. "How's Sue doin', anyway?"

"She's fine."

"Yeah, and she's *fine*, too."

On M Street, Strange cut east. They took the 11th Street

Bridge over the river and into Anacostia, bringing them straight onto Martin Luther King Jr. Avenue.

The welcoming strip in this historic part of town was clean and carefully tended. Merchants swept the sidewalks outside their businesses, and the cars along the curb were late model and waxed. Commercial thinned out to residential as the Chevy began to climb the hill in the direction of St. E's. Strange and Quinn drove by the Big Chair without remark. Farther up, on the left, Strange mentally noted the nice lines on a pretty red El Dorado parked along the curb. He loved the beauty of big American cars.

"'I Could Never Repay Your Love,'" said Strange, upping the volume on the deck.

"Thank you, Derek," said Quinn.

Strange ignored him, settling low on the bench. He smiled as the vocals kicked in. "Just listen to this, man. Philippe Wynne really testifies on this one here."

❐

STRANGE found Devra Stokes on their third stop. He had first gone to the Paramount Beauty Salon on Good Hope Road, where no one claimed to remember the girl. Strange checked his files, located in the trunk of his car: Janine had located Devra's mother, Mattie Stokes, using the People Finder program on her computer. Strange found her, a tired-looking woman in her late thirties, at her place in the Ashford Manor apartments, down by the Walter E. Washington Estates off Southern Avenue. She informed Strange that her daughter was working in another beauty parlor on Good Hope Road, a block east of the Paramount.

Quinn stayed in the car while Strange entered the salon. He went directly to an oldish woman, small as a child, whom he figured to be the owner or the manager. He told the hard-faced woman that he was looking for Devra Stokes and was pointed to a young lady braiding another woman's hair. A little boy, no older than four, sat at the foot of the chair, playing with action figures

and making flying noises as he moved the figures through the air.
When the older woman told Devra that a man was here to see her,
she glanced at him with nothing telling in her eyes and returned to
her task at hand. Strange had a seat by the shop-front window and
flipped through a copy of *Essence* magazine. The miniature woman
he had spoken to was looking him over as if he had just come calling on her granddaughter with flowers, chocolates, and a packet of
Trojan Magnums. He tried to ignore her and studied the photos
of the models in the magazine.

Ten minutes later Devra Stokes walked over to Strange and
sat down beside him. Time and her environment had not yet
bested her. She had almond-shaped, dark brown eyes and a wide,
sensuous mouth.

"You lookin' to talk to me?"

"Derek Strange." He flashed her his license. "Investigator,
D.C."

"This about Phillip and them?"

"Yes."

"Knew y'all would be along."

"Will you speak with me?"

"I can't today. I got appointments."

"But you will?" Devra looked away. Strange gently touched
her arm to bring her back. "You filed a brutality complaint against
Wood."

"That was a while back."

"When the time came to take the stand, you changed your
mind."

Devra shrugged and looked in the direction of the little boy,
still playing beside the chair. Strange was certain that Phillip
Wood had paid her to stay away from court. It was possible, also,
that Wood had fathered her child. Wood would be put away forever, and with him any money he could provide to Stokes and her
son. Strange was counting on her awareness that she'd been permanently dogged out. He hoped it burned her deep.

"I just need some background information," said Strange. "Chances are you won't have to testify."

"Like I say, I can't talk now."

"Can I get up with you here?"

"Where else I'm gonna be?" said Devra, looking down at her shoes.

"What time you get off today?"

"About five, unless my clients run over."

"Your little boy likes ice cream, right?"

"He likes it."

"How about I see you around five? We'll find him some, and we'll talk."

Devra's eyes caught light and her mouth turned up at the sides. She was downright pretty when she smiled. "I like ice cream, too."

Course you do, thought Strange. You're not much more than a kid yourself.

❏

AT the Metro station Strange idled the Caprice while Quinn passed out flyers to Anacostians rushing to catch their Green Line trains. The flyers were headed with the words "Missing and Endangered" and showed a picture of a fourteen-year-old girl that Sue Tracy, Quinn's girlfriend, had been hired to find. Tracy and her partner, Karen Bagley, had a Maryland-based business that primarily took runaway and missing-teen cases. Bagley and Tracy Investigative Services also received grant money for helping prostitutes endangered by their pimps and violent johns. Quinn had first met Tracy when he agreed to take on a case of hers that had moved into D.C.

Strange watched a cocky and squared-up Quinn through the windshield, the only white face in a sea of black ones. Quinn was drawing fish eyes from some of the young men and a few double takes from the older members of the crowd. Strange knew that

Quinn was unfazed by the attention. In fact, he liked the challenge of it, up to a point. He was, after all, a former patrol cop. As long as he was given the space he gave others, everything would be cool.

But it often didn't happen that way. And when Quinn was shown disrespect, the kind that went down with a subtle eye sweep from a black to a white, it got under his skin, and baffled him a little bit, too.

Something was said by a couple of young males to Quinn as he began to walk back to the car. Quinn stopped and got up in the taller of the two's face. Strange watched Quinn's jaw tense, the set of his eyes, the vein wormed on his forehead, the way he seemed to grow taller as the blood crept into his face. Strange didn't even think to get out of his car. It was over without incident, as he knew it would be. Soon Quinn was dropping onto the bench beside him.

"You all right?"

"Guy *told* me to give him a dollar after he called me a white boy. Like that was gonna convince me to pull out my wallet. God, I love this town."

"It was the *boy* part got your back up, huh?"

"That was most of it, I guess."

"Think how it felt for grown men to be called *boy* every day for, I don't know, a couple hundred years before you were born."

"Yeah, okay. So now it's my turn to get fucked with. We all gotta have ourselves a turn. For some shit that happened, like you say, before I was even born."

"You don't even want to go there, Terry. Trust me."

"Right." Quinn breathed out slowly. "Look, thanks for stopping here. I told Sue I'd pass some of those out."

"Who's she looking for, anyway?"

"Girl named Linda Welles. Fourteen years old, ninety-nine pounds. She ran off from her home in Burrville last year, over near Woodson High, in Far Northeast? Couple of months later, her older brother recognizes her when he's with his boys, watching one of those videos they pass around."

"She was the star, huh?"

"Yeah. It was supposed to be a house party, freak-dancing and all that, but then a couple of guys start going at it with her back in one of the bedrooms, right on the tape. Not that she wasn't complicit, from the looks of it."

"Fourteen years old, complicit got nothin' to do with it."

"Exactly. The brother recognized the exterior shot of the street where they had the party. It was on Naylor Road, up around the late twenties, here in Anacostia. That was a while back. The girl's just vanished, man — nothing since."

"So, what, you gonna go deep undercover down here to find her?"

"Just passing out flyers."

"'Cause you're gonna have a little trouble blending in."

"But I feel the love," said Quinn. "That counts for something, doesn't it?"

They drove back to W Street, passing the Fredrick Douglass Home, then cut up 16th toward Minnesota Avenue, where they could catch Benning Road to the other side of the river and back into the center of town. They passed solid old homes and rambling bungalows sitting among tall trees on straight, clean streets, sharing space with apartments and housing complexes, some maintained but many deteriorating, all surrounded by black wrought-iron fences. Many of the apartment buildings, three-story brick affairs with the aesthetic appeal of bunkers, showed plywood in their windows. Hard young men, the malignant result of years of festering, unchecked poverty and fatherless homes, sat on their front steps. Strange had always admired the deep green of Anacostia and the views of the city from its hilly landscapes. It was the most beautiful section of town and also the ugliest, often at the same time.

"You can't find one white face down here anymore," said Quinn, looking at a man driving a FedEx truck as it passed.

"There's one," said Strange, pointing to the sidewalk fronting one of the many liquor stores serving the neighborhood. A cock-eyed woman with a head of uncombed blond hair and stretch pants pulled up to her sagging bustline stood there drinking from a brown paper bag. "Looks like they forgot to do their head count this morning up at St. E's."

Strange was hoping to bring some humor to the subject. But he knew Terry would not give it up now that he'd been stepped to.

"Bet you there's some down here, they'd tell you that's one too many white people on these streets," said Quinn.

"Here we go."

"You remember that loud-mouth guy they had in this ward, ran for the city council, Shazam or whatever his name was? The guy who wanted everyone to boycott the Korean grocery stores?"

"Sure, I remember."

"And?"

"And, nothin'," said Strange.

"So you agreed with that guy."

"Look. People down here got a right to be angry about a lot of things. They talk it out among themselves, in the barbershop and at the dinner table, and when they do they talk it out for real, the pros and the cons. But one thing they don't do is, they don't go shittin' on that guy you're talking about, or our former mayor, or Farrakhan, or Sharpton, or anyone else like that to people like you."

"People like me, huh?"

"Yeah. Black folks don't put down their own so they can feed white people what they want to hear."

"This guy ran his whole election on fear and hate, Derek."

"But he didn't win the election, did he?"

"Your point is what?"

"In the end, in their own quiet way, the majority of the people always prove that they know the difference between right and wrong. What I'm saying is, there's more good people out here than there are bad. Once you get hip to that, that anger you're carrying around with you, it's gonna go away."

"You think I'm angry?"

"Look at the world more positive, man." Strange reached for the tape deck, looking for some music and some peace. "Trust me, man, it'll help you get through your day."

5

I SEE you're a 'Skins fan," said Mario Durham, nodding at the plaster figure with the spring-mounted head on Strange's desk.

"I see you are, too," said Strange, his eyes passing over the Sanders jersey Durham wore as he sat slumped in the client chair.

"I do like Deion. Boy can play."

"He couldn't play for me. Biggest mistake the 'Skins ever made, gettin' rid of a heart-and-soul player like Brian Mitchell for a showboat like Deion. Mitchell used to get that whole team up, man. That's what happens when a new owner comes in, doesn't understand the game."

"Whateva. You a longtime fan, though, I can see. This right here must go back to Charley Taylor and shit." Durham reached out and flicked the head of the plaster figure. Greco, lying belly down on the floor, raised his head and growled.

"Watch it," said Strange. "My stepson painted that, and it's special. Money can't replace it."

"That dog all right? Animals and me don't get along."

"You interrupted his beauty sleep," said Strange.

Durham shifted in his chair. "So anyway, like I was sayin', I'm lookin' for this girl."

"Olivia Elliot," said Quinn, seated beside the desk.

"Right. I was knowin' her for, like, two months, and I thought we was gettin' along pretty good."

"Where'd you two meet?" said Strange.

"I was tryin' to hook up with this other girl, see, worked at this nail and braid salon in Southeast. I went in there lookin' to date this girl, and I see Olivia, got some woman's hand in her lap, paintin' it. Y'all know how that is, when you get a look at a certain kind of woman and you say, uh-huh, *yeah,* that right there is gonna be *mine.*"

"You had a lot of girlfriends, Mario?"

"I ain't gonna lie to you; I been a player my whole life," said Durham. He smiled then, showing Quinn and Strange two long, protruding front teeth surrounded by space. "But this was different right here."

"And then she left," said Quinn.

"She just *up* and left, and I ain't heard from her since."

"You two have an argument, something like that?" said Strange.

"We was cool," said Durham, "far as I know."

"Where was she staying when she disappeared?"

"She had this apartment, stayed with her son, young boy. They stayed in this place they rented off Good Hope."

"Her son's name?"

"Mark."

"Same last name? Elliot?"

"Uh-huh."

"And he's in school?"

"Elementary, down in that area they was stayin' in, I guess, but I don't know the name."

"You try her mother, any other family?" said Strange.

"She never spoke of any kin," said Durham. "Look, fellas, I'm worried about the girl."

"Why hire private cops?" said Quinn.

"What my partner means is," said Strange, "you suspect some kind of foul play, what you need to do is, you need to report it to the police."

"Black girl goes missin' in Southeast, police ain't gonna do shit. But it ain't like that, anyway. Olivia was the kind of girl, it was a cloudy day or somethin', it would bust on her groove. She'd be, like, cryin' her eyes out over somethin' simple like the weather. I'm worried in the sense that she's sad, or got the depression, sumshit like that. I just want to know where she is. And if we do have some kind of problem between us, then maybe we can work it out."

"All right, then," said Strange. "Give Terry here the details on what you just told us. Addresses, phone numbers, all that."

Strange went out to the reception area while Quinn took the information. He phoned Raymond Ives, Granville Oliver's attorney, and left a message on his machine informing him that he was making progress on the gathering of countertestimony against Phillip Wood. When Strange returned to his office, Mario Durham was standing out of his chair. He wasn't but five and a half feet tall, and he couldn't have weighed more than a hundred twenty-five pounds.

"We all set, then," said Durham.

"Just give my office manager out there your deposit on your way out," said Strange, "and we'll get going on this right away."

"Fifty, right?"

"A hundred, just like Janine told you when you spoke to her on the phone."

"Damn, y'all about to bankrupt a man."

"It's a hundred. But this shouldn't take too long. Our rate is thirty-five an hour, and if it comes out to be under the hundred, then you're gonna get what we didn't earn back."

"Put a rush on it, hear? I can't even afford the hundred, seein' as I'm in between jobs right now. I'm just anxious to see my girl."

Durham began to walk from the room. Greco got up and followed him, sniffing at the back of his Tommys as he walked. Greco growled some, and Durham quickened his step. Greco stopped walking as Durham passed through the doorway. Quinn shut the office door.

"Animal doesn't like you," said Strange, "must be a reason."

"We don't usually ask for one-hundred-dollar deposits, Derek."

"I made an exception for him."

"It's because he's black, right?"

"It's because he's a no-account knucklehead. That hundred's the only money we're ever gonna see out of him. He's got no job, wouldn't even give Janine a fixed address. Said if we needed to get him we could look up a friend of his called Donut in Valley Green."

"Donut, huh? You can bank that."

"And his only phone number is a cell."

"You think there's something funny about his story?"

"Course there is. Somethin' funny about half the stories we hear in this place. Maybe she owes him money, or he's just tryin' to find out if she's shackin' up with someone else."

"You don't think a woman would leave a prize like him for another man, do you? That'd be like, I don't know, driving across town for a Big Mac when you got filet mignon cooking on the grill in your backyard."

"Was it just me, or was that man butt-ugly?"

"Playa hater," said Quinn.

"Almost feel like pressing his money back in his hand, giving him the phone number to a good dentist."

"Last time I saw two teeth like that, they were attached to

somethin' had a paddle for a tail and was chewin' on a piece of wood."

"Well, a hundred dollars is a hundred dollars. If any of that information he gave us is accurate, I'll find that girl this afternoon."

"Quit bragging."

"No brag," said Strange, "just fact."

"*Guns of Will Sonnet,*" said Quinn. "Walter Brennan."

"Damn, boy, you surprise me sometimes."

"You need me," said Quinn, "I'm puttin' in a few hours at the bookstore today."

Strange said, "I'll call you there."

6

STRANGE went back down to Anacostia and had a late lunch at Mama Cole's. Its sign claimed they served "the best soul food in town," and if that wasn't enough, the cursive quote on the awning out front added, "Martin Luther King would have eaten here." Strange didn't know about all that, but the food was better than all right. He ordered a fish sandwich with plenty of hot sauce, and when he had his first bite he closed his eyes. That pricey white-tablecloth buppie joint on the suit-side of town, claimed it was South authentic, didn't have anything this good coming out of its kitchen.

"How you doin', Derek?" said a man at a deuce as Strange was making his way toward the door.

"I'm makin' it," said Strange, shaking his hand. The man was an assistant coach for the football squad that played their home games at Turkey Thicket, but Strange could not remember his name.

"You gonna be ready this year, big man?"

"Oh, we got a few surprises for you, now."

"All right, then."

"All right."

They shook hands. Quinn would say something now, if he were here, about Strange running into someone he knew in every part of the District. It was true, but Strange never found it surprising. He'd lived here, and only here, for over fifty years. For its permanent residents, D.C. was in many ways still a small town.

Strange got into his Caprice. He was full and happy. He pushed in a mix tape and found "City, Country, City," the War instrumental that he always returned to when he was under the wheel on a fine spring day. He drove to the nail salon where Mario Durham had first met Olivia Elliot and entered the shop.

The owner of the place, a youngish woman who looked like she had a ropy bird's nest set atop her head, hadn't seen or heard from Olivia in a long while. She didn't ask why Strange was looking for Elliot, and he didn't bother to invent a ruse. She had marked him as a bill collector, most likely, an assumption he did not confirm or deny. If Elliot had left her job on bad terms, then this would work in his favor.

"You have no idea where she's working now?" said Strange.

"I don't believe she could hold a job for long," said the owner.

"Girl was keepin' bad company, too," said another woman, unprompted, from across the shop.

"She didn't know Jesus," said the owner. "So how could she know herself?"

Strange drove toward the complex where Olivia Elliot had lived. He passed Ketchum Elementary and wondered if Olivia's son, Mark, was a student at this school. But it wasn't like this was the only grade school in the area; Strange had noticed another one, and another still, just in the small distance he'd covered since leaving the shop. There was no shortage of babies being made in this part of town.

He parked in the lot of the Woodland Mews, a grouping of several tan brick units surrounded by the ubiquitous black iron fence. The grounds were on the clean side and the parking lot, half filled on this workday, was mostly free of trash. Strange wrote down the name of the complex's management company, posted with a phone number under an "Apartment Available" notice hung on the fence. He called this in to Janine and asked her to check with the company to see if Elliot had left a forwarding address. If she had put a security deposit down, he reasoned, she would be looking for them to send it to her.

Strange crossed the lot, going by two young men standing beside a tricked-out Honda. An old Rare Essence track came from the open windows of the car. The young men's conversation halted as he passed. Strange wore his cell on a holster, along with a Leatherman Tool-in-One looped through his belt. He wore his Buck knife as well when he felt he had the need to show it, but had left it in the office today. He carried a spiral notepad with a pen fitted into the rings.

Strange walked as he had taught Lamar and the kids on his football team to walk when they were out on the street. Chin up, shoulders square, at a steady clip but not too fast. The effect was confidence and, in his case, authority. Among those who were acquainted with the traits and mannerisms that are common to police, Strange would always be made as a cop, even though he had not worn the uniform for thirty-some-odd years. The young men resumed their conversation as Strange made his way into the stairwell of a nearby unit.

The stairwell's interior walls were the usual dull cinder block. The words "Mews Crew" were spray painted on the wall, artlessly, along with several nicknames. "Black," that most popular of D.C. street names, was among them. Strange had become acquainted with most of the gang names down here in the course of his long investigation related to Granville Oliver, but he had not heard this one mentioned. He figured that the wall tag was just the work of hopeful kids.

Strange knocked on the apartment door where Olivia Elliot had lived. No one answered, but there was music behind the door, and Strange knocked again. A girl opened the door to its chain length and peered out. He could smell marijuana through the opening, and the girl's eyes told him she was high. Strange caught a glimpse of an older boy, shirtless above the waist, backing into the hallway of the apartment.

"I'm looking for Olivia Elliot," said Strange.

"I ain't know her," said the girl.

"Is your mother at home?"

"At work."

"How long have you been living here?"

"We only been stayin' up in here, like, a month."

"What —"

"Bye."

She closed the door. Strange was accustomed to having doors closed in his face, and he wasn't about to knock again just to get the same response. Anyway, he had the feeling that this was a dead lead. The management company was the way to go. But he figured he'd upturn all the stones he could while he was here.

Strange knocked on another door, then tried a third. He walked back down the stairs to the open air. A man in the parking lot, smoking a cigarette beside a Dumpster, stared him down. Strange looked him over and walked on. With his cell holstered to his belt and his pen and pad, Strange was obviously some sort of official, cop, or inspector. He didn't feel the need to explain himself or acknowledge the smoker in any way. Besides, Strange had sized up the man and decided that if it came down to it, he could kick his ass. Didn't matter how old you got, there was always some kind of satisfaction for a man in knowing that.

He walked around the unit to the back, where the apartment's balconies faced a small playground holding rusted and broken equipment. Strange studied the balconies. He noticed a boy's bicycle in the 20-to-23-inch range chained to a rail on the third floor. That size bike would belong to a child who was somewhere between seven and twelve years old. He counted the apartments and where they were in relation to the stairwell, and he returned to the front of the building and took the steps to the door he thought he was looking for. He knocked on the door and soon it opened.

A dark-skinned, unkempt woman whose facial features had begun to collapse stood in the frame. Hung on a chain around her mottled neck was a large wooden crucifix that lay on a threadbare housedress. The furniture in the room behind her followed the lead of the dress. A piece of rug art, a brown-and-white pony standing in a field of black, was tacked to the wall over a shredded sofa.

"Yes?"

"Yes, ma'am." Strange softened his eyes. "I'm trying to get up with Mark Elliot, little boy lives here, down on the floor below you. Trouble I'm having, the phone number I had on his mother, when I dial it I get a recording, says it's been disconnected."

"Well, that's because they moved out."

"I was afraid it might be that."

The woman looked him over and crossed her arms beneath her sagging breasts. "And you are?"

"Excuse me. My name is Will, uh, *William* Sonnett. I've got a football team I coach every fall over in Turkey Thicket, run it through the, uh, church group. We do this camp in the summertime, kind of ease the kids into their conditioning, if you know what I mean. I was hoping to recruit Mark into the Pee Wee division. I heard from some of the neighborhood boys that he could play."

The woman's features untightened and she let her arms fall at her sides. "Mark would have liked to have played, if he still lived here. He's a good little athlete. He played with my grandson all the time when he was living here."

"That so."

"Yes, they rode their bikes together day and night."

Damn, thought Strange, I am good. His blood ticked the way it always did when he was getting close. He'd like to see Terry's face when he told him that, just as he had predicted, he had found the woman in one afternoon.

"You don't know how I can get in touch with Mark or his mother, do you?"

"No, I'm sorry. They left without a word."

"And she hasn't called you or nothin' like that."

"No. *She* hasn't."

"What's that?"

"Well, Mark has called. He calls my grandson 'bout once a week or so. I think he must be lonely, wherever they're stayin' at."

"So your grandson, he must call him back."

"I don't allow Daniel to call out on our phone."

"Oh."

"But I think Mark called here a couple of days ago. Maybe I still have the number on the caller ID."

Strange smiled. "I sure would appreciate it if you'd check."

In the small kitchen the woman handed Strange a cordless phone. He pressed the directory button and thumb-wheeled through the record of calls printed out, one by one, on a lit yellow screen. There were thirty old calls listed in the directory.

"I never think to erase them," said the woman.

"Neither do I," said Strange.

Strange found a number with the name Olivia B. Elliot printed above it. He copied the number onto his pad.

"Thank you," said Strange.

The woman, ugly by anyone's standards but with a peculiar bright-eyed energy to her, looked up at Strange with admiration.

"You're doing the Lord's work helping these kids like you do, Mr. Sonnett. Praise God!"

"Yes, ma'am," said Strange, unable to meet her eyes. "I better be on my way."

◻

IN the car Strange phoned Janine.

"Derek, I didn't have any luck with the management company. Apparently she moved out without giving them any notice and she left no forwarding address."

"That's okay. I got a phone number on her. You ready?"

Strange gave her the number. Over the years, Janine had cultivated contacts all over town. But her contact at the phone company was the most valuable. Strange sent Christmas cards out to all the people he did business with. A few of these cards contained gift certificates. At Christmastime, Strange sent Janine's contact at the phone company a Tower Records certificate along with a crisp one-hundred-dollar bill.

"I'm going to meet Devra Stokes," said Strange. "Call me on my cell when you get an address."

Strange's cell rang as he parked in the lot of the strip center on Good Hope Road. Janine was on the line with Olivia Elliot's address. Strange wrote it down, thanked her, and cut the connection. Then he phoned Quinn.

"Terry, can you get out for a while?"

"I think Lewis can handle the shop."

"Yeah, what else is a cat like Lewis gonna be doin' with his time? All right, write this down. Just need you to verify that she's at the address."

Quinn took down the information. "That's up around Lincoln Heights. Northeast, right?"

"Yeah, it's on the north side of East Capitol."

"Took you, what, two hours to find her?"

"Some of it was lunch. And most of the rest was drive time."

"You are one macho motherfucker."

"And I drink the bad dude's brew."

"Gonna make beaver boy happy."

"He's gonna get some change back, too."

"Why can't you take care of this yourself?"

"I got some more work down here in Anacostia. The character wit I called on today, on the Oliver thing."

"I'll take care of it," said Quinn.

Strange hit "end" on his cell.

He looked through the window of the hair salon. Devra Stokes's little boy was holding on to her pants leg as she gathered up her things. Even his timing was on today. Sometimes, Strange thought, everything just goes right.

c h a p t e r

7

DEWAYNE Durham checked himself in a full-length mirror
hung crookedly on a nail pushed into a bullet hole in a plaster wall.
He wore a new pair of jeans his mother had pressed for him and a
Nautica shirt with a black-and-beige Hawaiian print. He wore a
pair of black Jordans, the Penny style, on his feet, which picked
up the black of the shirt real nice. He looked good and he looked
strong. A little on the thin side, but that was his fun-house reflec-
tion in the cheap mirror, which one of his boys musta bought from
Target or someplace like that. He'd have to talk to that boy. Wasn't
no such thing as a bargain; you had to spend money to get nice
things.

Trick mirror or no, he'd have to watch his weight, make sure
he didn't go in the direction of one of those sad-sack motherfuckers, had no ass and got no respect. Like his half brother, Mario,
had to be the saddest, most okeydoke-lookin' motherfucker in

Ward 8. Mario'd be dead by now, picked off just for sport, if it wasn't known that he was kin to Dewayne.

"Your brother's out by your car," said Bernard Walker, a.k.a. Zulu, Dewayne's next in command.

"Aiight, then," said Dewayne, patting his hair, shaved nearly down to the scalp, one last time in the mirror before walking from the room. There was a mattress in the room, the mirror, and nothing else. Walker followed him down a narrow hall.

The house, a duplex on Atlantic Avenue in Washington Highlands, near 6th, was unfurnished except for some folding chairs and a couple of card tables where Dewayne's boys bagged up and bottled up their shit. Plywood filled the window frames. The house had radiators but no gas, and the electricity and water had been shut off long ago. The 600 Crew, Dewayne's outfit, used the house during the day to conduct their business, and also used it as a place to cut up, roll dice, play cards, and hang.

They passed an open door to the bathroom, where excrement, urine, and paper clogged the toilet and filled half the tub. Dewayne's crew peed in the bathtub and sometimes they shit in it, and on occasion they hid their airtight, weighted bundles of marijuana and cocaine underneath the mess. Dewayne had figured that no police would stick his hand down in there, and he was right; the last time they'd been raided, the uniform had stood there for only a couple of seconds, hardly looking into the bathtub, gagging while he was shaking his head, and then walked out. Later, Dewayne would let some young boy with ambition fish out the product. The stench in the house didn't bother him or any of the fellas. Got so now they didn't even notice it.

Four boys were bagging up some chronic at a table in what used to be the dining room as Dewayne and Walker came down the stairs. Dewayne's New York connect had made a delivery the night before.

Walker had to bow his head at the foot of the stairway, since the ceiling there was kind of low. He had gotten the name Zulu partly because of his skin color, which was close to black, but mainly because of his height and build. He was six and a half feet tall and could throw a scare into Charles Oakley on a dark street. Walker was a feared enforcer down here in Anacostia. He was an unhesitant triggerman, but it was known that he could also go with his hands. It was said by Dewayne's rivals that Zulu Walker was the long hair on Samson's head. You cut it, and Dewayne Durham wouldn't be shit.

"Y'all gonna have it ready to go for the shift tonight?" said Dewayne.

"We good," said a medium-skinned, handsome boy named Jerome Long, a.k.a. Nutjob, seated at the table. He made eye contact with his boy Allante Jones, a.k.a Lil' J, who was beside him. The two, equally tall, had come up together in Stanton Terrace. Both were fatherless. With one mother on a slow junk-ride down and another in and out of jail, they had been raised by Long's grandmother until she could no longer handle them. To this day they were rarely seen apart.

An electronic scale sat on the table along with boxes of zip-lock bags of various sizes purchased at Price Club. Pounds of marijuana rested at the feet of the boys in grocery store paper bags. A beat box, running on batteries and playing an old North-east Groovers go-go PA tape, sat beside the table on the floor. Another boy stood by the window frame at the front of the dining room, looking through a quarter-size hole punched out of the plywood, checking the street for police.

"My troops," said Dewayne, giving them the verbal pat on the back he felt they needed but meaning it in his heart, too. Dewayne was only twenty-three and hadn't gone past the tenth grade, but he felt he knew more about business instinctively than those who went to those kind of schools had ivy growing up the walls. One thing he did know: A man, however big he believed himself to be, wasn't nothin' without his employees.

"We'll roll on back in a little while," said Dewayne.

Jerome Long watched them go down a hall and through the kitchen. When he heard the back door open and shut he head-motioned to Allante Jones and the two of them got up from the table. They went back to the kitchen and looked out the window over the kitchen sink, the only window in the house that had not been boarded up.

"Check them out," said Long, looking past Dewayne and Walker, on the concrete walk now, to the Yuma Mob members sitting on the back steps of a house on the other side of the alley.

"All bold and shit," said Jones.

"I'm tired of sittin' at that table."

"So am I."

"You ready to make some noise, Lil' J?"

"Drama City." Jones elaborately shook Long's hand. "'Bout time someone in this town remembered our names, too."

Long forced a smile. He felt he had to talk this way sometimes, so his friend and the others would believe that he was hard. But he wasn't hard for real. He didn't want to kill no one, and he didn't want to die.

☐

GOING out the back door, Dewayne and Walker went down a concrete walk split with weeds cutting a small yard of dirt. Past the alley, where Mario stood leaning against Dewayne's Benz, Dewayne could see the fenced backyards of the street that ran parallel to Atlantic. About three houses down, on the back steps of another duplex, a group of boys sat drinking out of bags in the late-afternoon sun, listening to their own box, passing around a fat one and getting high. These were members of the Yuma Mob, headed up by Horace McKinley, who had risen under Granville Oliver, Phillip Wood, and them. Crazy boys, 'cause they were trying to make a rep, the worst kind. Especially those two cousins, the Coateses, who had come up from the South. Dewayne briefly locked eyes with one of them, because this was what he was expected to do, then kept walking toward his car.

Dewayne didn't sweat behind the competition. He expected them to be there. Shoot, you didn't go openin' no *Mac*Donald's, then get surprised when a Burger King moved in across the street. There was business enough for everyone down here, just so everyone knew their place and kept to it. That is, if you stayed on your strip. Once in a while, at night, if anyone was still down here, his boys would fire off a shot in the Yuma Mob's direction to let them know they were still around, and they'd fire one back. Turf etiquette: We're down and there's peace if we stay behind our imaginary lines. Even the square motherfuckers lived on these blocks, had payroll jobs and kids and shit, got used to the sound of occasional gunfire. Long as those boys didn't come into your house and start shittin' on your bed, then everything would be cool.

"Little brother," said Mario, stepping off the car.

Dewayne shook Mario's hand, hanging off a wrist you could circle with your thumb and pinkie, then pulled his older brother in for the standard half-hug. To say Mario was thin was to say that Kobe had a little bit of game. Mario was famine-in-Africa kind of thin. You saw a photo of him, you'd start sending money to that company on TV, claimed they could feed kids for eighty-nine cents a day.

"Zulu," said Mario, "how you been?"

Walker allowed him a nod. "Twigs."

It hurt Mario to hear Walker call him that name, but he managed to hold a friendly smile.

"What's up, son?" said Dewayne.

"Wanted to get up with you, D. Let you know I'm gettin' close to finding the girl."

"Yeah?"

"Uh-huh. Hired me one of those private investigators to do it."

"Okay. And what you gonna do then?"

"I'm gonna make it right."

"You find her, you let me know where she at, *I'll* make it right."

"Nah, man, this here is me."

"'Cause you can't be lettin' no bitch do you like she did, and I don't care how good that pussy was. She took me off, too, and I can't *have* none of that."

"Said I'm gonna square it."

"Don't tell me. *Show* me that you will."

"We're kin," said Mario. "I won't let you down."

Kin. Who would know it? thought Dewayne. Boy looked like a water rat ain't had nothin' to eat for, like, forever. They shared the same mother; that was true. Mario's father, a nothing by all accounts, had died in a street beef when Mario wasn't nothin' but a kid. He must have been one ugly man. Dewayne had never known his father. His mother, Arnice Durham, had claimed that he was handsome. He was doing a stretch, last Dewayne had heard, in some joint in Pennsylvania. Didn't mean shit to Dewayne anymore, if it did mean something to him to begin with. Whateva. Anyway, he had promised his mother he'd look after Mario, and there wasn't anything Dewayne wouldn't do for his moms.

Dewayne looked down at Mario. He reached into his pocket and pulled out a roll of bills. He handed a couple of twenties to Mario.

"Here you go," said Dewayne. "Go out and buy you some new stuff, don't look like last year. Shit's hangin' off you, boy. And Deion ain't even with the squad no more."

Mario held up the bills. "I'm gonna get this back to you, too, soon as I get myself situated with a job."

Mario slid the bills into his pants pocket, alongside the Taurus, thinking, now I got some of the hundred back I gave to that Strange in Petworth, and it's right here next to my gun. It feels good.

"Okay, then. You need a ride somewhere?"

"Nah, man, I got my short right up there at the end of the alley."

"I don't see no car."

"It's down the street some."

"Holler at you later," said Dewayne.

Mario turned and walked away. Dewayne watched him hitch up his Tommys as he went down the alley.

"That boy ain't got no whip," said Walker.

"I know it," said Dewayne. "I don't know who's more stupid, a man can't afford no car or a man who'd rather walk than admit it."

Some kids on bikes had been circling them in the alley, not lingering but keeping within Dewayne's sight. They all knew who Dewayne Durham was. They were hoping to catch his eye in some way, get noticed. They were hoping, someday, to get in with him if they could.

"Hey, D," said one of them, riding by, "when you gonna put me on?"

Dewayne didn't answer. The one who had asked was bold on the outside but was hiding his insecurities and his fears. Dewayne had noticed how this one always backed down when someone called him on his words. The kid standing on the pegs of the back of the bike, that was a kid to look out for. He didn't speak too much, but when he did the other kids listened. And they stepped out of his way when he was walkin' toward them, too. He wasn't but eleven or twelve, but in a couple of years Dewayne would start him out as a lookout by the elementary school, across from the woods of Oxon Run, where he moved product at night. Give him the opportunity to rise up above all this.

"Yo, little man," said Dewayne to the kid riding the pegs. "Move that shit out the head of the alley so we can roll on out of here."

The kid nodded and gave directions to the one steering the

bike. They rode to the T of the side street and moved some old tires and trash cans placed there to discourage the police from entering the alley. Then they rode back and continued to circle the car. Dewayne held out a five-dollar bill to the kid on the pegs as he made a pass. The kid refused the tip with a short shake of his head. Another thing Dewayne liked about this one: He was looking toward the future. He was smart.

"Better go see Ulysses," said Dewayne, head-motioning Walker toward his car. "Told him we'd be out."

Dewayne got under the wheel of the Benz, and Walker got in beside him. They drove slowly down the alley, the kids on the bikes following their path. Walker got PGC up on the radio. Soon he grew tired of the commercials and scanned down to KYS. They listened to the song, that Erick Sermon joint that sampled Marvin Gaye. Marvin was a D.C. boy originally, and anything had his voice in it was all right. Least they hadn't played this cut out, the way they liked to do.

"You think Mario's gonna fuck up?" said Walker after a while.

"Maybe he won't this time."

Dewayne kept his eyes on the road and tried not to show that sick feeling he'd been having inside his stomach these days. Running a business was easy. Dealing with family, that was hard.

◰

HORACE McKinley stood in the back window of the house on Yuma and watched Dewayne Durham's Benz roll out the alley. McKinley, large like Biggie, looked even heftier today in his warm-up suit. He wore a large crucifix on a platinum chain that hung outside his shirt. He wore the latest And Ones on his feet. A four-finger ring, spelling YUMA in small diamonds set in gold, was fitted on his right hand.

McKinley's body filled the window's frame. Kids around the way called him Candyman when he was coming up, not from that horror movie but from that big fat actor whose heart went and blew up in his chest. McKinley was fat then, and he was still fat, but no one called him Candyman anymore.

He had been watching Dewayne Durham talking to that sad-ass, no-job-havin', retard-lookin' brother of his across the alley. If Horace had a brother like that he wouldn't claim him. But Dewayne was soft that way. That soft spot was gonna get him dead someday, he didn't look out.

Truth was, Dewayne didn't seem to have the fire no more to keep up what he'd got. McKinley'd seen the way Dewayne had cut his eyes away when one of the cousins, out on the back steps, had stared him down. It was cool not to look for trouble, but sometimes you had to give a little attitude just to wake up the troops. Bottom line was, these boys were in this shit to begin with for the drama, like the way boys used to be all eager and shit to go off to war. That's what most folks didn't understand. But Horace McKinley did. Once in a while you had to feed your boys some conflict, just to give them something to do.

A cell phone rang behind him. He heard his man Michael Montgomery, a.k.a. Monkey Mike, talk into the phone. Then Mike was beside him by the window, hitting the "end" button on the cell.

"That was Inez over at your hair shop," said Montgomery.

"He came back?"

Montgomery nodded. "She say he looks like some kind of police. Drivin' a police-lookin' car, anyway. He's been sittin' in the parking lot waitin' on Devra. Look like she's fixin' to meet up with him, sumshit like that."

Horace looked over at Montgomery, his arms longer than shit, his hands hanging down around his knees. How he got the name Monkey, Horace suspected. But he never had asked Montgomery to confirm it. Didn't serve no purpose, other than to rile his ass up. Monkey was loyal, but when he was fierce he was fiercer than a motherfucker, like someone went and crossed the wires and shit inside his head. At the same time, there was something soft behind his eyes, too. McKinley had never been able to figure that part of him out.

"Better keep an eye on her," said McKinley.

"I'll get a couple fellas from out back."

"Get the cousins," said McKinley, and Montgomery went to the back steps, where James and Jeremy Coates were with the others, getting high.

McKinley mopped the sweat off his forehead as he watched through the window. Montgomery was out there now, telling the Coateses to get up and come with him. The two of them, had the same last name 'cause their fathers were brothers, stood like they were on springs. That's what McKinley liked, how ready those two always were. Course, they *were* a couple of stone 'Bamas, only having lived up here for the last two years. And they drove a 'Bama car, one of those Nissans, the 240SX, trying to be a Z but wasn't even close. But you didn't want your boys driving whips as nice as yours, anyway. They needed to see what you had and want it bad enough to work for it their own selves. Want it bad enough, up to a point.

Horace McKinley understood a lot of things about running a business. He had learned them, mostly, from Granville Oliver, and he had learned some from Phillip Wood. Granville Oliver wasn't comin' out, and maybe Phil wasn't either, but if they put Oliver down with a needle, that left Phil alive.

So he'd put his chips in with Phil. Stayed in contact with him, got him cash and cigarettes, and passed him messages through the guards at the Correctional Treatment Facility, the ones who took money to look the other way. And he kept an eye out here for those who could undermine Phillip Wood with regard to his upcoming testimony.

McKinley believed in staying on the winning side. Like every leader who had come to terms with the long-range prospects of being in the life, he knew this was going to end for him in one of two ways. Either he'd be got by one of his rivals or he'd go to prison. He might be doing time his own self someday, and if he was, he might be lookin' to Phil Wood for protection.

He had told all of this to Mike Montgomery when Mike had asked why they were going through all this trouble. Mike couldn't really see why they were looking after Wood when it was damn near certain that he would be in forever. The way McKinley explained it, Mike almost seemed to believe it. Almost. Anyway, Mike followed orders. He always had.

There *was* a good reason for McKinley's protection of Phil Wood, and it did have to do with McKinley's well-being. But he'd been told not to give Montgomery, or anybody else, the full, true story. Just like he'd been *told* to track Phil Wood's enemies while the Oliver trial was in effect. And you couldn't fight the ones who was doin' the tellin'. McKinley never did have much school, but he was smart enough to know that. Smart enough to do as he was told.

One thing he did know, and that was that Granville Oliver was as good as dead. So, regardless of his motivation, there wasn't no upside to gettin' behind Oliver. That was the other part about being a good businessman: You had to know who to stand with when things started to come apart.

8

ASHLEY Swann stood on the back deck of the house she shared with Ulysses Foreman, dragging on a Viceroy, tapping the ash into a coffee mug set on a wooden rail. In her other plump, pink hand was a glass of chardonnay. She wore a pair of silk pajama shorts, salmon colored with a matching top, and leopard-print slides on her feet. Her hair had a streak of black running through the part, but the remainder was blond with an orangish tint. There was a little bit of green in it, too, but that was from the chlorine in the Dream Dip, what they called the indoor pool at this cheap motel she and Ulee had stayed at in Atlantic City. Thank God the green was finally starting to fade.

Having a smoke with her white wine on the back deck was one of Ashley's true pleasures. She preferred to smoke outside rather than in the house, especially on nice days like this one, where she could listen to the birds and look into the woods that bordered their backyard. It reminded her of the tree line on the edge of her father's soybean farm down in Port Tobacco, where she had been raised.

Hard to believe that they were within a mile of Anacostia, just over the District line in Maryland, off Wheeler Road. Once you crossed that line there was even a country store, telling you, abruptly, that you'd left the city behind. Right past a Citgo gas station, not too far from the country store, was their place.

Ulysses had been smart, like he had been smart about so many things, when he'd bought this house right here, set back like it was in a stand of trees. Close to his business but protected. Made you feel like you were far away from the drama. You could even hear crickets chirping on summer nights, though those sounds were sometimes mixed with the occasional crack of gunshots riding up from Southeast, if the wind was right.

Even when she'd first got to know him, when he'd been a patrol cop and she'd been a dispatcher in 6D, Ulysses had talked about having a house in the country. All right, so this wasn't exactly the country. But he'd had ambition, unlike most men she'd known, including her husband, who was happy working on small motors and such. For Ulysses, the ambition was more than just talk. Since she'd met him, he had always got close to what he'd set his sights on. She loved that about him, that and his size. A woman could feel secure with a big, driven man like Ulysses Foreman.

He was coming through the rambler now, toward the back deck. She could hear his footsteps, large as he was, and now she was thinking, You should've changed up out of these pajamas, girl; he's gonna say something first thing.

"Damn, Ashley," said Foreman, coming out into the open air. "You ain't dressed yet?"

"Thought I'd ease into my day."

"Well, you better ease your fine ass inside and get into some street clothes. I got a business meeting out here any minute."

Ashley made a half turn, blowing out an exhale of smoke

and smiling, giving him a look at her ass cheeks hanging out the bottom of those shorts.

"Don't you like the way I look in these, Ulee?"

Foreman took her in and felt his mouth go dry. Her hindparts were bigger than most, but that was the way he liked them. And with those dimples and wrinkles and shit, it looked like someone had thrown oatmeal onto the back of her thighs. She had some veins on her, too, like blue lightning bolts, back there. But you didn't see all that when you closed your eyes. Same thing went for her belly, and the shotgun-pellet-lookin' marks on her face, and her little upturned nose, didn't even look large enough to let the air in, to tell the truth. That switch on the bedside lamp was what he liked to call the Great Equalizer. You could excuse a lot with a woman who could buck like Ashley.

Lord, she had a set of big, full lips, too. Woman could suck a man's dick without touching her teeth to it, the way a dog gives love to a porterhouse bone. Okay, she wasn't fine by any stretch, nothin' you'd want to march around in front of your best boys. But there were things she did he'd never go looking for anywhere else. Black women loved you like that for a night; a white woman, though, once you gave her some of that good thing? They'd love you the Heatwave way: forever and a day.

"I do like those jammies on you, baby, you know I do." Foreman pointed his chin toward the back door. "But hurry up on in there, now, and get dressed."

Ashley stubbed out her Viceroy in the cup. She had another sip of wine and hustled herself inside. Foreman found himself grinning. It was hard to get mad at her, and he was still up, anyway, having burned some of that hydro Mario had traded him. That smoke was nice.

Foreman checked his watch. Dewayne Durham would be showing up any minute.

He didn't care to do business here, what with the risk. But he made an exception for those who headed up the various factions in Southeast, especially the leaders of the largest ones. What with Granville Oliver gone, there were plenty of players vying for the action now. Dewayne Durham, from the 600 Crew, and Horace McKinley, holding the Yuma Mob together, had to be the top two. They expected to be treated right, to have their meets down in his basement, sitting in comfortable chairs, having a sip of something, instead of in some car parked out on the street. Having them over the house was worth the risk. Business was good.

Oliver had been his first hookup. He'd started taking payoff money from Oliver when he, Foreman, had been a cop. It was about then that Foreman had seen a way to make big money for real. His years as a police officer had given him insights into the criminal mind, and he'd learned the mechanics of illegal gun sales, straw buys and the like, the same way. Oliver had been his first customer, and his best up until the time the Feds busted him on those RICO charges.

But even with Oliver and his boys put away, there would always be a market down here. This new breed of hard boys comin' up, they all wanted shiny new guns, the same way they wanted nice whips. And the turnover was high, on account of you couldn't hold on to any one crime-gun too long. Long as there was poverty, long as there wasn't no good education, long as there wasn't no real opportunity, long as kids down here had no fathers and were looking to belong to something, then there was gonna be gangs and a need for guns. This textbook he'd had called it supply-and-demand economics. Foreman had learned about that during the one semester of courses he'd taken at the community college over in Prince George's County.

So he'd quit the force, citing the burnout effect of the job. Six months later, Ashley Swann, who he'd been doing since he met her, resigned from the MPD as well. She left her white-boy husband, a lawn mower repairman, no joke, and moved into this house with him. Ashley hadn't worked a day since.

She didn't need to work. She didn't need to get out of those pajamas or put her wineglass down, she didn't want to. Foreman was making good money moving guns around, and he worked about twenty hours a week as a security guard on top of that, just so he could show something to the IRS come tax time.

Course, he wasn't the only dealer in this part of the city. But he was the quality man. He didn't sell Davis or Lorcin or Hi-Point or Raven, none of those cheap-ass guns project kids bought on their first go-round. He carried fine American, Austrian, and German pieces, pistols, mostly, and occasionally special-order stuff the young ones had seen in the gun mags and the movies, AKs and Calico autoloaders, carbines, and the like. He customized some of the guns himself. You could still buy a Hyundai down here, you wanted to, but he was the Benz dealer in this part of town. His goods were marked way up, but he had no problem moving them. Shit, the high price tag was a badge of honor for these kids, like bragging that you had spent a couple thousand on a Rolex watch or a clean grand on a set of rims.

Foreman had a couple of boys working for him. These boys rounded up young girls, just old enough and with no priors, to do the straw buys in the gun store over in Forestville on the Maryland side, and in Virginia, in these shops they had way down Route 1. They used junkies and indigents, too, long as they had no record. You had to be careful with the junkies, though. The 4473 had a question, asked if you used drugs, and if you got caught lying on a federal form after the trace, that was a felony. Filing off the serial number, that was another amateur play right there, something Foreman would never do. Another felony, good for an automatic five. It was the way police squeezed testimony out of suspects and got them to flip. As far as solving cases went, shaking down suspects to give up other suspects worked better than ballistics and forensics every time.

Another of Foreman's boys was a student at Howard who had been raised in Georgia. He made the 95 South run in his trap-car once a month to his hometown, where family and friends made purchases in the area on his behalf. This boy was putting himself through college with what Foreman was paying him. It was true that D.C. had a handgun ban, but its good neighbor states, especially those to the south, did not. So there wasn't no thing to getting a gun in the District. Simple as buying a carton of milk. And you didn't even need big money to do it. You could rent a gun or trade drugs to get one, or the community could chip in to buy one. What they called a neighborhood gun. In many of the Section 8s there was a pistol buried somewhere, could be got to quick, in a shoe box. Most everyone knew where that shoe box was.

It was an easy business to be in and manage. Situation wasn't getting any better for these kids, so there would always be a need, and the money continued to flow in. So why was Foreman feeling those burning pains in his chest? Had to be the start of an ulcer, or what he imagined an ulcer to be. It was because he had been a cop, and in that time he had learned something about criminals, and being a criminal himself now, this is what he knew: His time was gonna come. No one in this game, be he gun dealer or gang leader or dope salesman, lasted forever. It could be the police or someone younger, stronger, or crazier than you, but the fact remained that someone was going to take you down.

It was kinda like playing the stock market. You had to know when to sell, not let greed make you stay in too long. He knew he had to get out, and get his woman out the clean way, too. The question was, how?

Foreman heard some heavy bass as a car pulled off the road, came down his long asphalt entrance, and slowed, arriving at the circular drive that fronted the house. That would be Dewayne Durham. Prob'ly had that big-ass sucker they called Zulu with him, too.

Foreman slipped back into the house and went down the stairs off the kitchen. He hoped Ashley had got herself dressed by now. She could show Durham in, and his personal giant, too.

◗

FOREMAN had spread out several pistols on the felt of his pool table down in the recreation room of the rambler. He had bought a ring once for Ashley, and this was the way the jeweler had presented it to him, on a square of red felt. When Foreman had chosen his pool table at that wholesale store he went to, he had gone for the red, remembering how he had been sold on the ring. This was the way he presented all his goods.

Five guns were set in a row, turned at a forty-five-degree angle to the line of the table. Above them were boxes of ammunition, "bricks," the contents of which fit the guns. A Heckler & Koch 9mm automatic was at the head of the row. A Sig Sauer .45 was next, followed by a stainless steel Colt of the same caliber, then a Glock 17. The Glock was the MPD sidearm and, Foreman knew, was always a sure sale. The young ones wanted what the police carried, nothing less. At the end of the row was a Calico M-110 auto pistol, a multiround, 22-caliber chatter gun. It was generally ineffective and hard to conceal but had recently gained popularity on the street due to its round capacity and exotic look.

"That's pretty right there," said Dewayne Durham. He was pointing to the Colt .45 set between the Sig and the drab plastic Glock. Foreman had placed the gun there strategically, knowing it would stand out.

"You like it, huh?"

"What kinda grips you got on there?"

"That's rosewood," said Foreman. "The checkered style. Ordered them from Altamont and put 'em on my own self. Looks good against the stainless, right?"

Durham picked up the gun, felt its weight in his hand. He racked the slide and dry-fired at the wall. He placed the gun back on the table.

"Pretty," repeated Durham, Foreman knowing right then that he had made a sale. "That's like that gun you got, right?"

"Same gun," said Foreman. "Only I got the ivory grips on mine."

"You had it long?"

"Just came in. Got bought at a store down in Virginia and changed hands once since. Never even been fired."

"How you know?"

"Smell it."

"Okay, then. I'm gonna take that Glock, too, if it's clean."

"You could eat off it, dawg."

"Aiight, then."

"What about that?" said Bernard Walker. Foreman had been watching the tall man's eyes and knew he was talking about the Calico.

"Brand-new," said Foreman.

"Where the bullets come from?"

"Right up top there, why it's long like it is. They call it a helical feed."

"What you need that for, Zulu?" said Durham. "Shit ain't even, like, practical."

"I guess I don't need it," said Walker. "I was just askin' after it, is all."

Durham said to Walker, "I'm buyin' you the Glock." To Foreman he said, "How much for the two?"

Foreman closed his eyes like he was counting it up. He had already decided on a price.

"Sixteen for the both of them is what I'd normally charge. With those grips and all, price got up."

"Sixteen hundred for two guns?" Durham made a face like he had bitten into a lemon. "Damn, boy, you gonna make me pay list price, too. What, you see me pull up in my new whip and the price went up? Or I got the word *sucker* stamped on my forehead and nobody done told me."

"I said it's what I'd *normally* charge. I'm gonna make it fifteen for you. And I'll throw in the bricks."

Durham looked down at his Pennys. He had made up his mind, but he was going to let Foreman wait. They both knew it was part of the process.

Durham looked up. "You got anything to drink up in this piece?"

Foreman smiled. "I'll throw that in, too."

Foreman got them a couple of beers from the short refrigerator he kept running behind his bar and opened one for himself. He brought them frosted pilsner glasses he stored in the fridge for his guests. They sat in leather chairs grouped around a leather couch studded with nail heads, a glass-topped table in the center of the arrangement. Italian leather on the couch, Durham guessed, soft as it was. Foreman did have nice things. Why wouldn't he, with the prices he charged?

The room was paneled in knotty pine. Foreman had always wanted a room like this, a room that he imagined a secure man would own, and now he had it. To him, the wood had the smell of success. There was the pool table and a deep-pile carpet, wall-to-wall, and a wide-screen Sony with a flat picture tube, the best model they made, with a DVD player racked beneath the set. His stereo, with the biggest speakers they had in the store, was first-class. He had a gas-burning fireplace in here, too, and the bar with the imitation marble top. He was all hooked up. He'd rather sit down here and catch a game than go out to the new football stadium or the MCI Center, matter of fact. He'd rather sit down here and chill than do just about anything else.

Durham took a taste of beer. He had a look around the room. Looked like some old man, wore his pants up high, owned it. Foreman was playing some old-school stuff on the stereo, Luther Vandross from when Luther could sing, had some weight behind his voice. Music from the eighties, that fit this place, too.

"Saw your woman," said Durham, after enjoying a long sip of beer. "She looked good."

"Thank you, man," said Foreman.

It made Durham kinda sick just to think about her. Why it was, he wondered, that black men who went for white women always went for the most fugly ones. When a white boy had a black woman she always seemed to be fine. You could bet money on that shit damn near every time.

Foreman's woman, she had come to the door in some JCPenney's-lookin' outfit, no makeup on her face and wine breath coming out her big mouth. Looked like she just dragged her elephant ass out of bed; must have remembered that it was feeding time, sumshit like that. Talkin' about, "How you two be doin'?" A big-ass, ugly-ass white girl trying to talk black, her idea of it, anyway, from ten years ago.

"Yeah," said Durham, "she looked good."

"She's gettin' her rest," said Foreman.

Foreman took a Cuban out of a wooden box on the glass table before him, clipped it with a silver tool set beside the box, and lit the cigar. He got a nice draw going and sat back.

"Saw your brother, Mario, today," said Foreman casually, as if it had just come into his mind.

"So did I," said Durham. "Just a little while ago."

"This was in the morning," said Foreman. "I had a little transaction with him."

"Yeah?"

"No big thing. Rented him a gun. Traded him five days' worth for a little bit of hydro he was holding."

Walker glanced over at Durham. No one said anything for a while, as Foreman had expected. But he wanted his business with Twigs to be up front, on the outside chance that some kind of problem came up later on.

Durham's eyes went a little dark. "Now why you want to do that? I'd get you some smoke, you needed it."

"Well, for some reason, Mario's always got the best chronic." Foreman chuckled. "The older I get, seems I need the potent shit to get me high."

"What, mine don't get you up?"

"The truth? It hasn't lately. When Mario lays some on me, I trip behind it."

'Cause what I give to Mario, I give to him out of my private stash, thought Durham. And you know this.

Durham exhaled slowly, trying to ignore the ache in his stomach. "What he needs a gun for, anyway?"

"Said he was lookin' to make an impression on someone. I didn't get the feeling he was gonna use it."

"He ain't say nothin' to me."

"Boy's harmless, though, right?"

Durham cut his eyes away from Foreman. "He ain't gonna do nothin', most likely." He did believe this in his heart.

"What I thought, too. Now look, he didn't want me to tell you. Didn't want to worry you or y'all's moms. But I just thought it might be better if you knew."

"Okay, then."

"We all right, dawg?"

Durham nodded. "Yeah, we're good."

"We better be gone," said Walker, placing his empty pilsner on the table.

"Gotta see the troops get out for the night," said Durham.

"I'll get you a bag for your guns," said Foreman.

Durham pulled a roll of cash from out of his jeans. "Fourteen, right?"

"Fifteen," said Foreman, standing from his chair.

"Why you want to do me like that?" said Durham, but Foreman was ignoring him, already walking toward a side room where he kept his supplies.

❐

FOREMAN stood on the stoop of his house, watching the Benz go down the drive. He was under a pink awning that Ashley loved but he hated. It was a little thing, though, one of them concessions you make to a woman, so he told her that he liked the awning, too.

He had played it right, telling Dewayne about Mario and the gun. Now there wouldn't be no misunderstanding later on. If Dewayne didn't like it, well, next time he'd give him some of that good smoke he kept in the family. Everything was negotiation in this business, nothing but a game.

"It go okay?" said Ashley, coming up behind him with a fresh glass of wine in her hand.

"Went good." Foreman put his arm around her waist, looked her over, then kissed her neck. "Those boys were noticing you."

"You jealous?"

"I don't think you're goin' anywhere."

"You got that right, boyfriend."

"I better keep an eye on you, though. Fine as you look, someone might try to steal you out from under me."

"That's where they'd have to steal me from, too."

Foreman kissed Ashley on the mouth. She bit his lower lip, and they both laughed as he pulled away.

9

Y O U ever been back in there?" said Strange, looking through the windshield to the brick wall bordering St. Elizabeth's.

"Once," said Devra Stokes. "This girl and me jumped the wall when we was like, twelve."

"I interviewed a witness there, a couple of years back."

"Hinckley?"

"Naw, not Hinckley."

"I was just playin' with you."

"I know it."

They sat in the Caprice, across from the institution, eating soft ice cream from cups that they had purchased at the drive-through of McDonald's. Juwan, Devra's son, sat in the backseat, licking the drippings off a cone.

"It was this dude, though," said Strange, "had pleaded insanity on a manslaughter charge, we thought he might have some information on another case. He seemed plenty sane to me. Anyway, we sat on a bench they have on the grounds, faces west, gives you a nice look at the whole city. This is the high ground up here. Those people they got in there, they got the best view of D.C."

"I wouldn't mind getting taken care of like they take care of those folks in there. You ever think like that?"

"It's crossed my mind, in the same way that it would be easy to be old. Walk around wearing the same raggedy sweater every day, don't even have to shave or mind your hair. But I don't want to be an old man. And I wouldn't want to be locked up anywhere, would you?"

"Sometimes I think, you know, not to have all this pressure all the time . . . not to have to think about how I'm gonna make it for me and Juwan, just for a while, I mean. That would be nice."

"I know it's got to be rough, raising him as a single parent," said Strange.

"I got bills," said Devra.

"Phil Wood's not taking care of you and your little boy?"

"Juwan's not his. Juwan's father —"

"Mama!"

Devra turned her head. The boy's ice cream had dripped and some of it had found its way onto the vinyl seat. Devra used the napkin in her hand to clean the boy's face, then wipe the seat.

"Mama," said Juwan, "I spilt the ice cream."

"Yes, baby," said Devra, "I know."

"Don't worry about that," said Strange. "You see that red cushion back there? My dog sleeps on that, and he has his run of the car. So I ain't gonna worry about no ice cream. This here is my work vehicle, anyway."

"I'm sorry."

"Ain't no thing," said Strange. "Look here, what about Juwan's father, then?"

Devra shrugged. "He's in Ohio now. They had him incarcerated out at Lorton, but they moved him a few months ago.

Once a week, me and Juwan used to take the Metrobus, the one they ran special from the city, out there to see him. But now, with him so far and all, I don't think Juwan's even going to remember who his father is."

Strange nodded at the familiar story. A young man fathered a child, then went off to do his jail time, his "rite of passage." Lorton, the local prison in northern Virginia, was slowly being closed down, its inhabitants moved to institutions much farther away. Lorton's proximity to the District had allowed prisoners and their families to remain in constant contact, but that last tie between many fathers and their children was ending now, too. Juwan's future, like the futures of many of the children who had been born into these circumstances, did not look promising.

"Can't Phil help you out with some money?"

"Phil's got no reason to give me money. He had a whole rack of girls. I was just one."

"But he paid you to stay away from court on that brutality rap."

"That was a one-time thing."

"I'm gonna need you to talk about it with me, you don't mind."

"Talk about what?"

"Well, the fact that he was beatin' up on you, for one. Plus, the time you filed the original charges was about the same time some of the murders went down that they got Granville up on. Including the murder of his own uncle. So I need to know, did Phil ever discuss any of those murders with you? Or did you hear anything else about those murders from anyone close to Phil or Granville around that time?"

"I got no reason to hurt Phil."

"It's not about hurtin' Phil. The prosecution's gonna put him up on the stand to testify against Granville. What the defense does, they want to give a complete picture of the prosecution's witness to the jury. If Wood was the kind of man who would take his hand to a woman, that's something the jury ought to know. Throws a shadow, maybe, over the stuff he's saying about Granville."

"How's that gonna change anything? Ain't nobody denying that they were in the life."

"True. But that's how it works. Their side claims something and our side tries to refute it. Or make it more complicated than it really is."

"Sounds like bullshit to me."

"It is. But I'm still gonna need your help."

"I don't know." Devra looked out her open window, away from Strange. "I don't want to get back into all that. I moved away from it, hear? I got my little boy. . . ."

Strange turned his body so that he faced her. "Look here. They're gonna try and put Granville to death. Some folks feel that only God gets to decide that. And a lot of folks in this city, they don't see how killing another young black man is gonna solve any of the problems we got out here."

"Granville did his share of killin', I expect."

"Maybe so, Devra. But this is about something more than just him." Strange touched her hand. "It's important. I need you to talk to me, young lady, tell me what you know."

"I gotta think on it," she said.

"Give me your phone number and the address where you're stayin' at, you don't mind."

Stokes did this, and Strange wrote the information down. He withdrew his wallet and opened it.

"Let me give you my business card," said Strange. "Got a bunch of different numbers on it; you can reach me anytime."

Strange turned the ignition and drove the Caprice off the McDonald's property. An E-series Benz and a beige 240SX followed him out of the parking lot and down the hill of Martin Luther King.

◻

STRANGE dropped Devra Stokes by her old Taurus in the lot of the salon on Good Hope Road. He waited for her to strap Juwan into a car seat and get herself situated and drive away. He noticed the older woman who owned the shop staring at him through the plate glass window. And he noticed the two cars that had been following him since back at the McDonald's idling behind him, about a hundred yards and several rows of spaces back.

Strange drove out onto Good Hope. In his rearview he studied the vehicles, a black late-model Benz, tricked out with aftermarket wheels, and a beige Nissan bomb, the model of which he could not remember but which he recognized as the poor man's Z.

Strange went down Good Hope and cut left onto 22nd Place without hitting his turn signal. The Benz fell in behind the Nissan and they stayed on his tail. He took another left on T Place and did not signal; the other cars did the same. T Place became T Street after a bit, and he took that to Minnesota Avenue. They were still there, about five car lengths back. Okay, so now he knew they were following him. But why?

Down near Naylor Road, Strange slowed down, moved into the middle lane, and came to a stop at a red light. Cars were parked along the curb to his right. The Benz stopped behind him and the Nissan pulled up to his left. He moved his car up into the crosswalk, as there were no cars there to block his exit. If he needed to make a move he could do so now. The Nissan did the same and pulled up even with his driver's-side door.

Could be this was a trap. If that was the case, the rider on the Nissan's passenger side would be the shooter. But Strange wasn't ready to look over at them yet.

In the rearview, Strange could read the front tag on the Benz and he committed it to memory. He said it aloud so that he would get used to the sound of the sequence, and he said it aloud again.

He saw a fat young man in the driver's seat, a ring across the fingers that were gripping the wheel. Another young man, with no expression on his face at all, sat beside him.

He heard a whistle and looked to his left. Two young men with similar features, thick noses and bulgy eyes, were looking straight at him. A bunch of little tree deodorizers hung from their mirror, and music played loudly in their car. The bass of it rattled their windows. The one in the passenger seat grinned at him, raised his empty hand, and made a quick slashing gesture across his own throat.

Strange was startled by the loud beep of a car horn. He looked in his rearview and saw the fat man in the Benz making the gun sign with one hand. He pointed the flesh gun in the direction of Strange. And then Strange realized that the fat man was pointing his finger over the roof of Strange's car, at the traffic light in the intersection. Strange looked ahead at a green light; the fat man was telling him that the light had changed and it was time to move on through.

Strange gave the Caprice gas. He heard the fading laughter of the two on his left under the throb of their music as he went down the road. The Benz and the Nissan pulled out of the intersection as well but turned right on Naylor Road and vanished from his sight.

It might have been paranoia, a middle-aged man thinking negative things about a group of young black Anacostians who had the look of being in the life. Strange was angry at himself, and a little ashamed, for the assumptions he had made. But he had also been living in this very real world for a long time. He wrote down the plate number that he had memorized in the spiral notebook he kept by his side.

❐

STRANGE had first met Robert Gray, not yet a teenager, at Granville Oliver's opulent house in Prince George's County the previous fall. Oliver had pulled Gray out of a bad situation in the Stanton Terrace dwellings and had been grooming him for a role in the business he was still running at the time. When Oliver had been arrested and incarcerated, Strange had promised Granville, and had made a promise to himself, that he would look after the boy and try to put him on the right path.

But it hadn't been an easy task. There was the geography problem, in that Strange lived in Northwest and Gray's people were down in Southeast, so he couldn't see the boy all that much. And Strange wasn't about to take him under his own roof, especially now that he was dealing with having a new family of his own; Janine and his stepson, Lionel, were his first priority, and he was determined to do everything he could to make that work. So Strange had seen that Gray was put up with his aunt, the sister to his mother, who was doing a stretch for grand theft and assault, her third fall. Through Granville Oliver's lawyer, Raymond Ives, Strange had arranged for a monthly payment to be made to the aunt, Tosha Smith, as one would pay foster parents for their services. The money was Granville Oliver's.

Tosha Smith lived in a unit of squat redbrick apartment buildings on Stanton Road. Strange parked on the street and walked up a short hill, across a yard of weed and dirt, past a swing set where young children and their mothers had congregated. One girl, wearing a shirt displaying the Tweety Bird cartoon character and holding a baby against her hip, looked no older than fifteen. Strange navigated around two young men sitting on the concrete steps of Smith's unit and ascended more stairs to her apartment door.

Tosha Smith, fright-time thin with a blue bandanna covering her hair, opened at his knock. Her initial expression was adversarial, but in a practiced, unemotional way, as if this were her usual greeting for every unexpected visitor who came to her door.

"Tosha," said Strange.

"Mister Strange." Her face softened, but not by much.

Strange had visited her many times, but the look of relaxation that came with familiarity did not seem to be in her repertoire.

A grown man, on the thin side, with bald patches in his hair, sat on the couch playing a video game, staring at the television screen against the wall as a cigarette burned in an ashtray before him. He did not look away from his game or acknowledge Strange in any way.

Even in the doorway, Strange could take in the unpleasant odor of the apartment, not unclean, exactly, but closed up, airless, with the smell that always reminded him of an unminded refrigerator. And every time he had come by it was dark here, the curtains drawn over shuttered blinds. So it was today.

"You wanna come in?" said Tosha.

"Robert in there with you?"

"He's out playin' with his friends." Tosha noticed something cross Strange's face and she grinned lopsidedly, showing him grayish teeth. "Don't worry, I always know where he's at. We don't allow him to go more than a block or two away from here."

"We?"

Tosha jerked her head over her shoulder. "I got Randolph stayin' here with me now. Boy needs a man around, don't you think?"

"If it's right."

"You don't have to worry about that. Randolph keeps him in line, tells Robert to mind his mouth when he gets the way young boys get. Randolph'll go ahead and smack the black out him, his tongue gets too bright."

Strange could hear a baby crying from back in the apartment. He shifted his feet. "You say Robert's in the vicinity?"

"You'll find him out there somewheres close, ridin' his bike. Tell him to get in here before dark comes, hear?"

Why don't you drag your junkie ass on out here and tell him yourself? thought Strange. But he only nodded and went back down the stairs.

"I'll be lookin' for my money this month," said Tosha to his back.

Strange kept going, finding relief in the crisp spring air as he made his way outside. The sun had begun to drop behind the neighboring buildings, and shadows had spread upon the apartment grounds.

Strange circled the block in his car, then widened his search to the adjacent streets. He spotted Robert Gray standing around with a group of boys, most of them older, on the corner of another apartment complex. The boys, some wearing wife-beaters with the band of their boxer shorts showing high above the belt line of their jeans, studied Strange as he got out of his curbed Chevy. Gray said something to one of the boys, got on his bike, and rode it over to Strange, now leaning against the front quarter panel of his car out in the street.

"How you doin', Robert?"

Gray's eyes went past Strange to somewhere down the street. "I'm all right."

"Look at me when I talk to you, son."

Gray fixed his gaze on Strange. He had intelligent eyes, and he was polite enough. But Strange could not recall ever seeing him smile.

"How's school going?"

Gray shrugged. "We nearly out. Ain't all that much left to do."

"Your aunt and them treating you okay?"

"I get along with 'em."

"The boyfriend, too? He's not eatin' up your share of the food, is he?"

"Him and my aunt don't eat all that much, you want the truth." Gray cocked an eyebrow. He was a handsome boy, one of those who already had the features of a man. "You see Granville?"

"Saw him today. He was asking after you."

"They gonna kill him?"

"I don't know. Whatever happens, it doesn't look like he's

ever gonna come out of jail. It's important you know this. All that bling-bling you and your friends always talking about and lookin' up to, the whips and the platinum and the Cristal, you get in the life, it always goes away. Forever, you understand?"

Gray half nodded and quickly looked off to the group of boys standing on the corner. Strange felt impotent then. To Gray he wasn't much more than a fool, and an old man in the bargain. This much he knew.

"Look here," said Strange. "You still up for my football camp?"

"Yeah, I'll play."

"I hear you *can* play."

"You *know* I can."

"We're gonna start the camp in August. Now, all the boys who play for me, they need to show me their last report card from the school year. So I want you to finish up strong."

"I'll do all right. But how I'm gonna get over there to where y'all practice?"

"I'll work that out," said Strange, realizing that he hadn't figured it out yet. But he would. "All right then, why don't you get on home before it gets dark."

"I will, in a little while."

"Take care of yourself, young man."

Gray wheeled off on his bike and joined his friends. Strange got back in his car.

Strange phoned Quinn from his cell as he drove across Anacostia. Quinn told him that he was outside the address given on Olivia Elliot, and he was getting ready to confirm. He asked Strange for the son's name. Strange gave it to him and told Quinn that if he needed him he could reach him at Janine's house, which he had not yet gotten used to calling home.

Strange was looking forward to holding his woman and talking to his stepson, sitting at the dinner table, just being with the

ones he loved. Seeing the things he saw out here every day, he figured he deserved a couple of hours of that kind of peace.

He turned the radio on and moved the dial to PGC. The
Super Funk Regulator was on the air, talking to a woman who had
called in from her car.

"Where you at right now?" asked the DJ.

"I'm on Benning Road, headed home from work."

"Who you goin' to see?"

"My son Darius," said the woman giggling, obviously hyped
to be on the radio and live. "He's ten years old."

"You have a good one," said the DJ. "Thanks for rollin' with
a brother."

"Thanks for lettin' a sister roll."

Strange smiled. He did love D.C.

10

It was Terry Quinn's habit to keep a paperback western on the car seat beside him when he was on a job, since there were often long stretches during surveillance when he found himself with little to do. Today he had brought along *They Came to Cordura,* an out-of-print novel by Glendon Swarthout, from the used-book store where he worked in downtown Silver Spring. Sitting in his vintage hopped-up Chevelle, looking at the group of boys playing outside the building where Olivia Elliot had apparently settled, he didn't think he'd have that extra reading time to kill.

He was on a street numbered in the high fifties, in the neighborhood of Lincoln Heights, a residential mix of single-family homes and apartments at the forty-five-degree angle of border close to the Maryland line. This portion of the city, on the east side of the Anacostia River, was called Far Northeast, just as Anacostia was known as Far Southeast by many who lived in that part of town.

Nearby was the W. Bruce Evans Middle School. Administrators there had recently sent a group of "problem students" to the D.C. Jail to be strip-searched in front of prisoners, one of whom had masturbated in plain sight as he watched the kids disrobe. Some District school official had apparently decided to re-enact an unauthorized version of Scared Straight. Quinn wondered how that "strategy" would have settled with the parents of problem kids out in well-off Montgomery County or in D.C.'s mostly white, mostly rich Ward 3. But this controversy would fade, as this was a part of the city rarely seen by commuters and generally ignored by the press, out of sight and easily forgotten.

Lincoln Heights was not all that far from Anacostia, a couple of bus rides away. If Olivia Elliot was trying to put some distance between herself and Mario Durham, she had made only a half-hearted effort. But Quinn wasn't surprised. Washingtonians were parochial like that; even those who were running from something didn't like to run too far.

He grabbed a blank envelope from the glove box and neatly wrote "Olivia Elliot" across its face. He folded a sheet of blank notebook paper, slipped it inside the envelope, and sealed it. Then he got out of his car, locked it down, and crossed the street.

There were plenty of kids, girls as well as boys, out of doors, though the sun had dropped and dusk had arrived. School was nearly done for the year, and if there was any parental supervision to begin with, it was even more lax this time of year. As Quinn went down the sidewalk toward the kids he saw rows of buzzers in the foyers of the attached homes, indicating that these houses had been subdivided into apartments. An alley split the block halfway, leading to a larger alley that ran behind the row of houses. Not unusual, as nearly every residential street in town had an alley running behind it, another layout quirk unique to D.C.

Quinn stopped close to the address Strange had given him, where four boys had built a ramp from a piece of wood propped up on some bricks in the street. A kid on a silver Huffy with pegs coming out of the rear axle circled the group.

"Hey," said Quinn. "Any of you guys know where I can find Mark Elliot?"

A couple of the boys snickered and looked Quinn's way, but none of them replied. The kid on the bike pulled a wheelie and breezed by.

"He might be new in the neighborhood," added Quinn.

They continued to ignore him, so he walked on. He saw some girls on the next corner, one of them sitting atop a mailbox, and he decided to see if he would fare better with them.

He heard, "Hey, you guys!" in a straight, white voice, and then, "He might be new in the neighborhood!" in the same kind of voice, and then he heard the boys' laughter behind him. Quinn felt his blood rise immediately; it was hard for him to handle any kind of disrespect. He wondered, as he always did, if he would have been cracked on down here, like these kids were cracking on him now, if he were black.

"Mister," said a voice behind him, and he turned. It was the kid on the bike, who had followed him down the street.

"Yeah."

"You lookin' for Mark?"

Quinn stopped walking. "Are you Mark?"

The kid pulled up alongside him and stopped the bike. He was young, lean, with an inquisitive face. "Your face is all pink. You all right?"

"I'm fine."

"You *mad*, huh?"

"No, I'm all right."

"Shoot, they're only messin' with you because you're white."

"Y'all think there's something wrong with that?"

"I don't know. It's just, we don't see too many white dudes around here, is all it is. And when we do see 'em, they act like they scared."

"I'm not scared," said Quinn. "Do I look scared to you?"

"Yeah, okay. But why you lookin' to get up with me?"

"You're Mark Elliot, then."

"Yeah, I'm Mark."

"I was looking for your mother." Quinn held up the envelope. "I gotta give her this."

"You a police?"

"No."

"A bill collector, right? 'Cause, listen, she left out of here a while ago and I don't know where she's at."

"She's gonna be back soon?"

"I prob'ly won't see her. I'm gonna be watchin' the Lakers game tonight over at my uncle's. He's fixin' to pick me up right about now."

"Listen, Mark. I'm not looking to hurt her; I'm trying to give her something. She entered a contest. A raffle, you know what that is?"

"Like they do at church."

Quinn nodded. "She won a prize."

"What kind of prize?"

"I'm not allowed to say what it is to anyone but her. And I need to put this in her hand."

"She's out gettin' a pack of cigarettes."

"Thought you didn't know where she was."

"Just give it here," said Mark, reaching out his hand. "I'll make sure she gets it."

"I can't. It's against the rules. I'll drop it by later." Quinn eye-motioned toward a redbrick structure, two houses back. "I know where you live. You're up on the third floor, right?"

"We in two-B," said Mark, and his features dropped then. He knew he had made a mistake. He kicked ineffectually at some gravel in the street. "Dag," he said under his breath.

"I'll come back," said Quinn. "Thanks, Mark."

Quinn began to walk quickly back toward his car. The kid followed on his bike.

"What's your name?" said Mark, cruising alongside Quinn.

"Can't tell you that," said Quinn, who kept up his pace. "It's against the rules."

"I told you mines."

Quinn didn't answer. He went by the group of boys in the street, who appeared not to notice him at all this time, and he put his key to the driver's lock of his car.

"Is it fast?" said Mark, who had stopped his bike and was standing behind Quinn.

"Yeah, it's fast," said Quinn, opening the door.

"You live out in Maryland, huh?"

Quinn figured the boy had made his plates. Quinn kept his mouth shut and started to get into his car.

"You don't want to talk to me no more, huh?"

Quinn turned and faced the boy. "Look, you're a good kid. I'd like to talk to you some more and all that, but I gotta go."

"If I'm good, then why'd you want to go and do me like you did?"

"Like how?"

"You tricked me, mister."

"Listen, I gotta get goin'."

Quinn settled in the driver's seat and closed the door. He looked once more at the kid, who was staring at him with disappointment, something worse than anger or hate.

Quinn cranked the engine and rolled down the block. He found East Capitol and took it west.

Just before Benning Road, Quinn pulled over beside St. Luke's Church and let the Chevelle idle. He found Mario Durham's cell number in his notebook and punched the number into the grid of his own cell. Mario Durham answered on the third ring.

"Mario," said Quinn. "It's Terry Quinn, Strange's partner. I got an address for you."

"Damn, boy, that was fast."

"I know it," said Quinn, his jaw tight. "Write this down."

Minutes later, driving across Benning Bridge over the Anacostia River, he noticed that his fingers were white and bloodless on the wheel.

Quinn knew, as every seasoned investigator knew, that to find a parent you always went first to the kid. Relatives and neighbors rarely gave up another adult to an investigator or anyone who looked like a cop. But kids did, often without thought. Kids were more trusting, and you used that trust. If you were in this game, and it was a game of sorts, this was one of the first things you learned.

So Quinn was doing his job. But he couldn't get Mark Elliot's face, his look of disappointment, out of his head. Quinn should have been up with the buzz of success. Instead he was ashamed.

❐

MARIO Durham noticed that the letter *J* had fallen off the word *Jordan*, printed real big across one of his sneakers, while he was riding the bus down Minnesota Avenue. He had those red, black, and white ones from last year he had bought off this dude said he didn't want the old style in his closet anymore. They had looked good to Durham, but now he realized maybe he had got beat for twenty-five dollars. If he was here now, his brother, Dewayne, would say, That's what you get for buying used shoes. But he had smelled the insides before he bought them, and they were clean, like they still sitting on the shelf at Foot Locker. They had looked all right to him.

Durham took off the shoe still had a *J* on it and worked at the letter with his fingernail until it started to peel at the edge. He tore it off. Good. Now both of his shoes looked alike.

He was still holding this shoe when he heard a girl laughing, and he looked around to see these two girls, sharing one of the seats a couple of rows up. They were staring at him, holding that shoe. A guy who wasn't with them, sitting nearby, was looking around to see what they were laughing at, and now he was looking back at Mario and he was kinda smiling, too.

People had been laughing at Mario Durham all his life. Wasn't anything special about this bus ride right here.

Soon those people went on about their business. He found that this was usually so, that folks would leave him alone after they got over the first thing they saw about him that made them crack on him and laugh: that he was skinny, or funny lookin', or that he was tearing a letter off his shoe. And that was worse than being laughed at sometimes — just being ignored. Feeling that he wasn't even important enough to notice, that's what really cut him deep.

Dewayne said that when someone stepped to you, then you had to step back. But what was he gonna do, even strapped like he was right now? Kill a Metrobus full of people for smilin' at him? But it did make him mad. You came into this life trusting people to be good, and it seemed like they always did you dirt in the end.

Like Olivia. She said she loved him and to prove it she was giving him that good thing, too. So when she asked him, could he ask his brother to front a pound of hydro so that they could sell it, make a little money together, and have some stash to smoke for their own selves, he had to say yes. She was the first woman who had shown some interest in him in a long while.

Dewayne gave him the LB after a lecture about being responsible and shit, and this being his chance to show his kid brother that he could do right. And then Olivia had disappeared with the chronic, just took her son and booked right out of Southeast, and shamed him to his brother. Mario Durham had stood for just about everything, but he couldn't stand for that. Now she was going to have to give the hydro back to him, or the money she'd made from it if she'd gone and sold it already. Because Dewayne had only been half right saying it was his "chance." Really, it was his last chance, and he couldn't let it slip by. He needed to show Dewayne that he could stand tall, that Dewayne could trust him, not just as a brother but also as a man. Maybe Dewayne would even put him on. Finding Olivia, getting back the pound she'd took, that's how he could redeem himself in his brother's eyes. For what she'd done, one way or another, the bitch was gonna pay.

Mario Durham reached up and pulled the signal cord, as his stop was coming up ahead. He needed to transfer over to the Benning Road line and take that bus east. He wasn't far now from where Olivia was at.

Durham walked the aisle toward the door, hitching up his Tommys as he passed the two girls. He heard one of them laugh, and he heard the dude nearby say something about Secret Squirrel, then, "You lookin' good, Deion" from one of the girls, then more laughs. He bit down on his lip and took the steps down off the bus, passing through the accordion doors that opened to the street.

◻

OLIVIA Elliot fired up a joint and sat back on the sofa. She took a good hit off it and held the smoke in, letting it lie in her lungs while she squinted at the TV set, had a rerun going of *Martin*. She thought she'd seen this one before, but she figured on watchin' it anyway. Truth was, wasn't one of these shows all that different from the others. Martin Lawrence was funny, too; he had come up over in Landover or something, which made his show more interesting to watch, 'cause she knew this girl who knew this other girl who claimed she knew his family. It was like Olivia felt she knew him herself.

The sound was low on the set. She had the stereo going, Missy Elliot gettin' her freak on, the remix joint that the Super Funk Regulator played on PGC.

Olivia had another hit of the hydro and then she had to put it down. She'd learned not to take too much of this, to back up off it quick, because it was potent. Must have come from Dewayne

Durham's private stash. She had the feeling when she'd met his funny-lookin' older brother, Mario, that he'd be good for something. This shit right here was what it was.

It was like God had sent Mario down to her, and then the pound of herb with him. She hadn't intended to take it straight off, not exactly, but it came to her, big surprise, when she was high up on it one night, not long after Mario had brought the pound over to her apartment. She had been way up and got to thinking, Why do I need Mario to make some money off this? Why don't I keep it my own self, go somewheres away from here and sell it off? Mario, he wasn't gonna be no problem. And, okay, Dewayne, he was a drug dealer for real, and he had a gang and a rep and all the bad shit that went along with it. But everyone knew those boys didn't leave too far from their neighborhoods, not even to settle a beef, and especially not over some girl and her kid.

So she decided to take the chronic and go away. Not too far, 'cause you didn't have to go that far, but at least into Northeast. And then she'd seen that notice in the newspaper talking about a short-term sublease, fully furnished, and she was gone. Gathered up her clothes, and Mark's clothes, and his bike, and not much else. The furniture she had, she was paying for it on time, and she had stopped making payments on it anyhow. The car she'd bought, a used Toyota Tercel, she was doing that the same way. She moved herself and Mark out of that place in Woodland Mews in a couple of hours, and she'd been living here since.

For the first time since she'd left high school, in the tenth grade, she had some money in her dresser drawer. She'd sold off half of the chronic in one-hundred-dollar bags, just to friends and to people she'd met in the apartments around hers and to people they knew. And now she was flush. She didn't have a job or nothin' like that, but she intended to start looking for one soon. The important thing was, no one had found her or come looking for her, far as she knew, up till now. Mark had mentioned that some white dude had been by that day, and he was all embarrassed and stuff for telling the white dude where they lived, but she told Mark not to worry over it too much. The white dude was probably some bill collector, like from the furniture company or somethin' like that.

It touched her, the way Mark was always trying to please her and protect her. The flip side of that was, the only thing she worried about in her own life was Mark. She did love her boy and she wanted him safe. But he seemed to be adjusting to this new neighborhood. He looked happy most of the time and he made friends easy. She'd never lived in Northeast, but this was east-of-the-river Northeast, not too different from the Southeast side where she'd come up, and it seemed cool.

Mark was smiling when she'd kissed him good-bye. She'd just seen him off a few minutes ago. Her brother, William, had picked him up, was gonna take him over to his place to watch the playoffs, the Lakers against the Sixers, and spend the night. William was going to keep Mark for a couple of days, the way he always did.

Olivia missed him when he was gone, even for a night, but it was good for Mark to be around a man, and William was a strong role model and as straight as they came. He'd always disapproved of her lifestyle, telling her constantly to get herself together, but mostly she'd let it roll off her like everything else, 'specially since she knew deep down that her brother was right. And these nights that William took Mark, it allowed her to kick back, burn some smoke without having to hide it, listen to music by herself, and laugh at whatever was playin' on the TV.

Maybe she could fix this place up some, get an extension on the lease, settle here. Put curtains up or somethin', 'cause the way they had this place painted, it was dark and kinda gray. Get an exterminator out here for the roaches that showed up all over the kitchen when you turned the lights on back there. Some new sheets for Mark's bed. She had the money. It was hid good, too, right in between her mattress and box spring. Along with the rest of the herb.

The buzzer rang from over by the phone. It was that buzzer from downstairs, said that someone was wantin' to get in. She wasn't expecting anyone, so she stayed where she was. Probably someone was down there hittin' all the buzzers, just lookin' to get inside.

She shook a Newport out of her pack and lit it. The menthol, it tasted good after you smoked some get-high. Olivia smiled, looking at the face Martin was making on the TV show. The music sounded good, too, coming from the stereo. She looked at the joint resting in the ashtray and considered picking it back up. But she was already trippin' behind this shit, so she let it lay there where it was.

11

S UE Tracy had met Quinn over at his apartment on Sligo Avenue, in a boxy brick structure near a small convenience market in Silver Spring. When they spent the night together they did it at his place. More often these days, Sue, who had a one-bedroom off Rockville Pike, seemed to prefer to stay on his side of town.

Silver Spring had beer gardens and restaurants within walking distance of Quinn's, and live music if you wanted it, and you could leave the house and go to any of those places wearing whatever you had on without thinking twice. The city was starting to take on the concrete sterility of white-bread Bethesda, and it was getting the same upscale chains, and the fake Mexican cantinas, and the grocery store where people could be "seen" eating overpriced sushi in the window booths and overpaying for vegetables in the checkout lines. But Silver Spring hadn't lost its personality or its mix of working immigrants and blue-collar eccentrics yet. You could still rest your can of Bud on the engine block of your car while you fiddled around under the hood on a sunny day and not get a reproachful look. You could say that you liked women, not just as people but also in bed, and not feel as if you were wearing a swastika band around your arm. If that ever changed, Quinn swore he'd be gone.

Earlier in the evening they'd had dinner at Sue's favorite place, Vicino, on Quinn's street. Then they caught a set of Bill Kirchin's band up at the Blue Iguana on Georgia Avenue. Quinn had suggested it, as the drummer, a guy named Jack who lived in the neighborhood, cooked. They bought a six on the way back to Quinn's place. They could have walked everywhere, but they took Quinn's '69 Chevelle, a 396 with Cregars and Flowmaster pipes. Sue was used to driving her work vehicle, a gray Econoline van, so it was a treat for her to get behind the wheel of something that had some muscle. She especially liked to move the Hurst shifter through its gears.

They were a little high on red wine and beer when they got to his spartan apartment. Sue opened a couple of cold ones while Quinn searched his CDs for something she would like. He was into Springsteen, Steve Earle, and the like, his collection running toward big guitars, male singers, and male concerns. Sue had come up in the fabled eighties D.C. punk movement. Occasionally their tastes converged.

"What do you want to hear?" said Quinn. "Dismember Your Man?"

"It's the Dismemberment Plan," said Tracy. "And you don't own any, so shut up. Why don't you put on the new Dave Matthews?"

"Cute. You know I don't get that guy. Music for old people who look like young people. It's not rock, it's not jazz. What the fuck *is* it?"

"I'm kidding."

"How about some Neil?"

"Neil's good."

Quinn dropped *Everybody Knows This Is Nowhere* into the carousel and let it play. "Cinnamon Girl" came forward as he joined Tracy on the couch. She wore a sky blue button-down stretch shirt out over slate gray pants. Her blond shag-cut hair fell to her shoulders. The shirt was open three buttons down and showed the curves of her breasts, full and riding high. Quinn thinking, This is a sweet night right here.

They drank off some of their beer. Sue removed her Skechers, put her feet up on the table set before the couch, and smoked a cigarette while Quinn told her about his day.

"Anything on Linda Welles?" said Tracy.

Quinn shrugged. "I passed out flyers down at the Metro station in Anacostia."

"I appreciate it."

"Her brother, he called the police, right?"

"Sure, but the police don't get all that mobilized for a missing girl in the city."

It usually was reported to Youth and Preventive Services and pretty much sat. Most were runaway and not criminal cases. The girls stayed local and moved quadrant to quadrant. So families went to people like Sue for help finding them.

"She could be shacked up with some older boy, has drug money, a nice car," said Quinn.

"That's right, she could be," said Tracy, crushing her cigarette in the ashtray. "But we still need to find her."

"I will."

"My hero."

Quinn put his beer bottle down on the table and slipped his hand under the tail of Tracy's shirt and around her waist. "I'm larger than life."

"Don't be so boastful."

Quinn kissed her. He unbuttoned her shirt and kissed the tops of her breasts, then pulled one cup of her bra down to kiss her darkish nipple. It hardened at the lick of his tongue, and he felt her stretch like a cat beneath him. Quinn tried to undo her bra but fumbled it.

"You got oven mitts on or something?"

"I need a manual for this thing."

"It's a back-loader, Terry."

"Oh."

Tracy's chest was flushed pink and her hair was a beautiful mess. She sat up, undid her bra, and pulled it free. Quinn drew her shirt back off her shoulders.

"Gulp," said Quinn.

"You look surprised."

"I always am," said Quinn. "And thankful, too."

They undressed quickly, "Cowgirl in the Sand" filling the room. Quinn laughed as her panties flew past his head. They embraced and were down on the pillows and then knocking the pillows off the couch. They were all over each other and she moved him roughly to her center. She was wet there, and Quinn smiled.

"Damn, girl, where's the fire?"

"You don't know?"

"What I mean is, why the rush?"

"Quit fucking around."

Soon he was all the way in her, her back arched to take it, her mouth cool on his, her damp muscled-up thighs flanking his sides. Quinn thinking, This is something God dreamed up, has to be. Something this good, it can't be an accident.

❏

STRANGE picked up Greco at the office and drove the dog up to the row house on Buchanan Street. Strange had lived here for many years before marrying Janine. He was perfectly content and comfortable at Janine's place and as certain as any man could be that their marriage was going to last. But he still spent time at his old house. The house was paid for, so there weren't any issues with money, and he had not considered selling it.

He told Janine that he needed this place to keep his duplicate case files and to work away from his primary office. But there
were other reasons for his reluctance to give up the Buchanan residence. It had been his first and only real-estate purchase, and the
pride of home ownership was, for him, still strong. And of course
he needed to know that there was always some other place he
could go to, *run to*, some would say, when the space between him
and Janine and Lionel got too close. He had lived with women
briefly, but in those cases there'd always been an exit door. He'd
been a bachelor his whole life and he had married in his fifties.
This new life, this whole new thing, was going to take some getting used to.

Strange went down to his basement and did three sets of ab
crunches, lying on a mat. He then did a dumbbell workout and
put in fifteen minutes on the heavy bag with a pair of twelve-ounce
gloves, more than enough to break a good sweat. Then he show-
ered, fed Greco, and went on up to the second floor to his office.

He tore the shrink-wrap off a couple of soundtrack CDs
he had purchased through the Internet that had just come to this
address in the mail today. A Morricone import called *Spaghetti
Western*, which held six tracks from the film *A Gun for Ringo*, among
others, had arrived in the shipment. He slipped the CD into the
CPU of his computer and sat down behind his desk. The music
came through the Yamaha speakers on his desktop, and he nodded
his head. This was exactly what he had hoped it would be. He had
been looking for this particular soundtrack for some time.

Strange filed that day's Xeroxed records on the Granville
Oliver case into the cabinets that supported the rectangle of
kitchen-counter laminate that served as his desktop. He did some
bills, killed more time listening to his CD, and then went looking for Greco, who was lying by the front door and ready to go.
Strange grabbed some cruising music, locked the house down,
and walked with Greco to his free-time vehicle, a black-over-black
'91 Cadillac Brougham with a chromed-up grille.

He popped some Blue Magic into the dash deck and drove north on Georgia Avenue. The school year had not quite ended, and night had fallen, but there were plenty of kids out, hanging on corners and walking the streets. In fact, he had seen his young employee, Lamar, heading on foot toward the Capitol City Pavilion, a go-go venue the young ones called the Black Hole, on a recent evening. Strange wondered, as he always did, what these kids were doing out so late, and he wondered about the adults who were responsible for them, why they had let them out of their sight.

Janine's house was a clapboard colonial, pale lavender, set on a short, quiet, leafy street called Quintana, around the corner from the Fourth District police station in Manor Park. Lionel's car, a Chevy beater he had recently purchased, was out front, and Janine's late-model Buick was in the drive. Strange used his key to open the front door. He entered the house with Greco beside him, his nub of a tail twitching back and forth.

"It is me," said Strange, his voice raised, not yet used to letting himself into Janine's house.

"That you, Derek?" said Janine from back in the kitchen.

"Nah, it's Billy Dee," said Strange.

"Getting' to look like him, too," said Lionel, tall and filled out, coming down the center-hall stairs and patting his head, which barely had any hair on it at all.

"I know," said Strange. "Didn't have a chance to get that taken care of today. Gonna get to it tomorrow."

"You know that album you got, has those guys with the big ratty Afros hanging out by the subway platform, talkin' about, 'do it till you're satisfied'?"

"B.T. Express."

"Yeah, them. You're lookin' like the whole B.T. Express put together."

"Said I was gonna take care of it."

Lionel reached his hand out as he hit the foot of the stairs. Strange took it, then brought him in for the forearm-to-chest hug.

"How you doin,' boy?"

"I'm good," said Lionel. "You gonna watch the game with me tonight?"

"You know it. What's your mom got on the stove?"

"I think she made a roast or somethin'."

"Was wonderin' what it was," said Strange, "smelled so good."

"Smells like home," said Lionel with a shrug.

Couldn't put my finger on it, thought Strange. But, yeah, there it is.

They ate in the dining room after Strange said grace, and the food was delicious. Lionel was graduating from Coolidge High, and the ceremony was coming up soon. He had been accepted to Maryland University in College Park and would start there in the fall. He had been down on the fact that he would not be able to afford to live on campus, but Strange had bought the old Chevy for him, his first car, and that had somewhat offset his disappointment.

"How's that car running?" said Strange.

"Good," said Lionel. "I took it up to the detail place and had them brighten up the wheels."

"You check the oil?"

"Uh, yeah."

"'Cause you got to do that," said Strange. "You need to change that oil every three or four months, at the outside."

"Okay."

"You want that car to last you, hear?"

"I said okay."

"You don't change the oil, it's like gettin' on with a woman without giving her a kiss."

"Derek," said Janine.

"It might feel real good when you're doing it, but you want her to be there for you the next time you get the urge."

"Derek."

"What I mean is, a woman ain't gonna be stayin' around too long if you don't treat her right. Car's the same way."

Lionel shifted in his seat. "You mean, like, changing the oil on the car is kinda like giving a woman flowers, right?"

"Exactly," said Strange, relieved that Lionel had gotten him out of the woods.

Lionel cocked his head. "You supposed to do that every time you hit it, or every three or four months?"

"Lionel!"

"Sorry, Mom. It's just, *Derek* is getting deep with me here, and I wanted to make sure I understood."

Janine flashed her eyes at Strange.

"Dinner's delicious, baby," said Strange.

"Glad you're enjoying it," said Janine.

The three of them watched the game in the living room. Strange and Janine were for the Lakers, and Lionel was for the Sixers. It was a generational thing, like Frazier-Ali had been thirty years back.

On the television screen, Robert Horry was sinking foul shots like there was nothing on the line, though this was the championship series and the game was close, with less than a minute to play.

"Man is ice," said Strange. "Experience beats youth, every time."

"Girl at school told me today I look like Rick Fox," said Lionel.

"Must've been a blind girl," said Strange.

"Funny."

"I'm playing with you. But what's up with his hair?"

"The girls be geekin' behind it."

"You ever grow your hair like that, you and me are gonna have to have a talk."

"You think all dudes are funny, don't look a certain way."

"He could afford a comb, at least, all that money he's got."

"You're just old-time."

"You think that's what it is?"

"I got news for you. Women love that dude, Pop."

Strange grinned. Lionel had been calling him "pop" more and more these days. He couldn't even put into words the way it made him feel. Proud and happy, and scared, too, all at once.

"All I'm saying is," said Strange, "you don't need to be gettin' any fancy hairstyles for the girls to like you. And anyway, you look good the way you are."

Later, Strange and Janine sat on the couch splitting a bottle of beer. Lionel had gone out to see a girl he liked, who called the house several times a night. He had assured his mother that he wouldn't be late.

"That was pretty smooth tonight," said Janine. "Comparing women to cars."

"Yeah, I know. You got to remember, though, I came to this game late. You had sixteen years of practice with that boy before I even came through the door."

"You're doing fine."

"I'm trying."

"Oh, Derek, I almost forgot. Some man called today asking if he could talk to you about the Oliver case."

"Was it one of the lawyers?"

"No, this was a white guy, and anyway, I recognize those lawyers' voices by now. But this guy hung up before I could get a number."

"Caller ID?"

"It said 'No Data' on the screen."

"He'll call back," said Strange. He turned and kissed Janine on the side of her mouth. "Listen, we got some time before Lionel gets home. . . ."

"I don't feel like going up just yet," said Janine. "I'm happy sitting right here for a while, you don't mind."

"I'm happy, too," said Strange.

And he was. He couldn't think of anyplace he'd rather be. Strange didn't know for the life of him why he was fighting all this. These were the people he loved, and this was home.

❐

SUE Tracy lit a cigarette and got up naked off the couch. Quinn watched her move to the stereo to change the music and felt himself swallow. To have a woman, a woman who *looked* like a woman, all hips and breasts and just-fucked hair, parading around his crib without a stitch like it was the most natural thing in the world to do, this was what he had dreamed of since he was a boy, when he'd found those magazines behind the toolshed in his backyard. Quinn was so stoked now he wanted to phone his friends. But then he thought, Shit, my friend is right here in front of me. He had never figured on this part back when he was twelve years old. The stroke mags never taught you that.

"What?" said Tracy.

"What?"

"You're staring at me and you've got a silly smile on your face."

"You look nice."

"Yeah, so do you. You want another beer?"

"Okay."

He heard her washing herself in the bathroom, and soon she returned with two more beers and a towel for Quinn. She sat on the couch and stretched her legs out, her toes noodling with the hair on Quinn's thighs.

"Good night," said Tracy.

"Really good," said Quinn.

They tapped bottles and kissed.

"You were late getting here," said Tracy.

"I was finishing up something for Derek, over in Northeast. Confirming an address on a woman for a client of ours. It was a bullshit job, but I took care of it."

"Why was it bullshit?"

"I don't know," said Quinn, the self-disgust plain in his voice.

"Why?"

Quinn looked away. "I had to lie to this kid, the son of the woman, to confirm the address. I tricked him, see? The look he gave me afterwards . . . I bet you money he's been told all his life to distrust white people, that in the end white folks are always gonna fuck you over if you're black. And you know how I feel, that it's wrong to plant that kind of seed in any kid's head, no matter what color you're talking about, because it never gets unlearned. So it just got to me, to see that look he gave me, like everything he'd been taught had come true. And you know he's never gonna forget."

"Who's looking for his mother?"

"A loser. That was the other thing that bugged me. That we just found this woman for this client, knowing this client's type, without giving it any kind of thought. 'Cause whoever this client is, he's no good, just a bad one to put anywhere near that boy's life. But Derek and me, we treat it like a game sometimes, who's got the bigger set of balls, like that, without thinking about the consequences. I don't know; I'm just pissed off at myself, that's all."

"You're angry."

"As usual, right? Derek tells me I gotta relax."

Tracy looked down at Quinn's equipment, lying flaccid between his legs. "You look pretty relaxed to me."

"I'm just resting. You want me to rally, I will."

She touched his cheek. "Look, Terry. It's just a job. You agreed to do something for money and you did it. Don't make it more complicated than it is."

"It's wrong when there's kids involved."

"You're probably worried about nothing."

"I'm right about this," said Quinn. "What we did today, it was fucked."

12

THE street was quiet and inked with shadows as Mario Durham moved down the sidewalk, his head low. He shifted his eyes from side to side. On the surrounding blocks there had been some kids hanging out, but on this street there were none. No cars running, either. No kind of drug strip, nothin' like that. Dogs barked in the alleys, and muted television and music sounds came from behind the walls of the apartments and row houses he passed. The nights were still cool, and the windows of the residences were shut or just opened a crack. Durham thinking, That's good.

He went by Olivia's hooptie, that old Toyota Tercel of hers, parked along the curb, then took a few steps up and went down a walkway to the address given him by that white-boy detective. He found the front door locked and was not surprised. There were a couple of rows of buttons outside the door, and he flattened out both of his palms and pushed on all the buttons at once. He had seen this done on TV shows. It always seemed to work on those shows, and it worked now. A click was audible as the lock was released, and he opened the door and went through it and then up a set of wooden stairs.

The second floor was unlit and held two apartments, one that faced the front of the house and one that faced the back. Two-B, Durham decided, would be the one to face the back. Durham went to that door. He could hear both television and stereo noise coming from inside the crib. Had to be Olivia in there, 'cause she liked to get high, watch TV and play her music at the same time. The door was heavy and wooden and had a peephole in its center. Durham knocked on it and stood back. He reached forward and knocked again.

The television sound faded down. He heard footsteps approaching from behind the door. He looked at the peephole and watched as it went dark.

"Open up, Olivia," said Durham, and when he got nothing he repeated his instructions the same way.

"Go away, Mario," was the reply.

They went back and forth for a while, but eventually she did open the door. Durham had known she would, after she'd thought it out. What else was she going to do?

◻

OLIVIA Elliot turned down the television volume and went to see who was at the door. When she looked through the hole and saw Mario, she didn't jump. She wasn't scared, and her heart didn't race inside her chest or nothin' like that. Some people got paranoid when they burned smoke, but it had always evened her out, made her see things more clear.

She let him stand out there and call her name a couple of times, though, while she figured out what her next move ought to be.

"Go away, Mario," she said.

"I ain't goin' *no* goddamn where," said Durham.

"You gonna need some of that Grecian stuff, then, 'cause you gonna go gray, standin' out there, thinkin' you're comin' inside."

"Then I'll go gray. And I'll *go* get my brother, too."

She leaned against the door. This was what she didn't want to hear, but at least Dewayne Durham wasn't out there on the landing with a couple of his boys now. She'd need to handle this with Mario alone, work it out and end it tonight.

Leaning against the door, she put the tip of her finger in her mouth while she let it all bounce around in her mind. Her mother had told her to take her finger out her mouth all the time when she was a kid, that it would buck her teeth. But the habit had never left her.

"Olivia! C'mon, girl."

Finally she opened up the door. And when he stepped in, his fists all balled up at his sides like he was gonna get physical with her, she nearly laughed. Lookin' like Lil' Romeo or sumshit, wearin' a Redskins jersey and a matching cap, like a kid would. Shoot, Lil' Romeo had more heft on him that this little slip of nothin' right here.

"Damn, Olivia, how you gonna let a man stand in the hall all night long?"

She motioned him inside, shutting the door behind him as he entered, one hand in his pocket, bobbing his head in that way he did, like it was mounted on a spring.

"So you found me."

"Didn't you think I would?"

"You want a drink or somethin'?"

"Nah, baby. I ain't here to drink."

Durham had forgotten how fine she was. She wasn't tall, but she was put together right. And she liked to look clean, even just hanging inside her place. She had on a summer dress and some shoes, sandals with heels and no backs, on her feet. On her chest where the dress separated were a few black hairs. Girl had some hairs on her chest and around her nipples, too. But that was the only fault Durham had found in her. Other than that, she was all right.

Olivia walked over to a grouping of furniture and Durham followed. Music, that "Fiesta" joint by R Kelly and Jay Z, was up real loud, and Durham could smell blunt smoke mixed with her cigarette smoke in the room. The blunt smell was sweet, the good stuff, had to be his brother's. Well, maybe she still had some of it left.

"Where your son at?" He moved toward her and she held her place. She was up against the arm of the couch.

"He's stayin' with my brother for a couple of days."

"It's good he's not here. 'Cause you and me need to have a very serious conversation."

"Ain't no big drama to it, Mario."

"Oh, yeah? Guess it wasn't no thing to you. Including the thing we had together, right?"

"I was fixin' to call you and straighten it all out."

"When?"

"Look here, Mario, you gonna let me talk?"

He was nodding his head quickly and his eyes flared. It was comical to her, high as she was, watchin' him act all overdramatic, like he was in one of those old silent movies. She bit down on her lip, but she guessed that her eyes showed that she was amused.

"Somethin' funny?"

"Nah, it's just . . . Look, I shouldn't have left up on you like I did. I'm sorry for that. But it wasn't workin' between us, you know this. You *know* this, Mario."

He was still nodding his head, trying to act hard, but Olivia noticed that the flame had gone out of him. She had wounded him now.

"Mark," said Olivia, "he's funny about having men around our house, and you got to understand, I put my son above every-thing else. I knew you wouldn't understand. I didn't know how to talk to you about it, so I just booked and came over here."

"What about the hydro?"

"I didn't steal it, that's what you mean."

"Explain what you *did*, then."

"I gave it to this dude I knew, said he could sell it for a good price, only take a little off the top. He was a friend of a good friend, so I knew he wouldn't do me dirt. And he didn't. The herb got sold."

"And you were gonna do what with the money?"

"Give half to you, the way we talked about."

"Uh-huh. So you got the money now?"

"It's coming," said Olivia, folding her arms across her chest.

He knew it was a lie. She could see it in his eyes, the way they'd got hot again. 'Cause on top of what she'd done to him, stole from him and shamed him to his brother, now she was telling these stories to him, too.

"So the money's comin'," he said.

"Yeah."

"When?"

"Soon."

"*Bull*shit."

And now what? she thought. More of these one-word sentences, prob'ly, and then he'd just flare his eyes some more and turn around and leave. Get his brother, but not tonight, which would give her time to book, gather up Mark and her personal shit and move on to something else. Wasn't gonna be no fun, but then she'd known what she was getting into from the start. The important thing was, nothing was gonna happen tonight. You got down to it, what was this little man right here gonna do on his own, for real?

She looked down at his shoes and laughed. She didn't mean to, but the chronic, it had fucked with her head. And this really was one sorry motherfucker right here. Couldn't even afford no Jordans, had pair of "ordans" on his feet. And then he looked down and knew right away what she was laughing at. And he got this funny look on. Not *acting* mad anymore but mad for real.

He slapped her square across the face.

It stung her and surprised her. It surprised *him*. For a moment, Durham looked at his hand, the one that had slapped her. He had never hit a woman before. He had never hit a man. But when she had laughed, it was like it was all those people on the bus and everyone else who'd ever cracked on him was standing there before him, laughing. *All* of them, not just her. Well, he damn sure did have her attention now.

No one had ever looked at him before the way she was looking at him this minute. She was showing fear, and something else: respect.

She touched at the spot that had already reddened. Then, slowly, she stood straight and cocked up her chin. That look of fear, it had passed as quickly as it had come.

"That's all you got?" said Olivia.

"I'll give you more, you want it."

"You dare take a hand to me?"

"Bitch, I will close my hand next time, you don't mind your mouth."

She chuckled and looked him over. "Oh, shit. Now Steve Urkel gonna act all rough and tough, huh?"

"Olivia, I'm warning you, you are fuckin' with the wrong man."

"Man?" She looked him over and moved in a step so that her face was close to his. "I don't see no man. You see a man in this room, point him out."

"I'm about to —"

"You about to *what?* Slap me again?" Her eyes caught fire. "Mother*fuck* you, punk."

Spittle flew from her mouth as she spoke those words, and she raised her hand to strike him. Durham grabbed her wrist. She drew her free hand back and he grabbed that wrist, too. He pushed her away, releasing his hold on her, and she backpedaled and hit the couch. She charged him then.

He stepped in as she neared him. Her arms were spread and she was open in her middle, and he punched her in the stomach with all he had. He was trying to stop her, but he realized as his fist sank into her doughy flesh that he had caught her good. He felt a power then that he had never known before.

Olivia hinged forward at the waist. Her sour breath hit him as it was expelled. Her eyes bulged in pain and surprise. And as she jacked forward he drove his fist up into her jaw, putting everything into it. The uppercut lifted her off her feet. The noise it made was like a branch snapping off a tree.

Olivia staggered and found her feet. She lowered her head and put her hands on her knees. She retched and spit out blood. She spit out a tooth. A thread of mucus ran from her nose and hung in the air.

"Oh, sweet God," she said.

The revolver from the pocket of his Tommys appeared in his hand. He gripped it by its barrel.

She looked up at him, at the gun, and her eyes went wide, humble and afraid. He liked the way it made him feel. He was strong, handsome, and tall, everything he had never been before. He wished Dewayne were here to see him now.

"Nah," said Olivia, standing out of her crouch, unsteady on her feet. A glaze came to her eyes and she spread her hands. She wanted to plead to him but couldn't get the words. She was thinking of her son.

The gun in his hand was electric, and he swung it like a hammer. The butt of it connected to her face. She turned her face and a sprinkle of blood jumped in the same direction, and while she tried to keep her feet he whipped her there again, harder this time. Her body spun. She tumbled over the couch. Her legs dangled off the arm of it and one of her sandals dropped to the floor.

Olivia wasn't making any kind of noise now. The music was still playing, and so was the television. But it seemed real quiet in the room.

Durham walked around to the front of the couch and looked down at her. Her face was all fucked up. The socket was caved in around one of her eyes, where he guessed the gun had connected. It was a mess, but through the blood and bone he could see that the eye had popped out some and was layin' down low. It seemed the way the eye was pointed that she was lookin' off to the side. The eye was an inch or so lower than where it should have been, and it was exposed nearly all the way around. Nerves and muscles and shit was the only thing still holdin' it on her face. Her jaw had turned color and was set off to the side kinda funny, and it had already swelled up, too. Her hands were bent at the wrists in the center of her chest, like she had arthritis or sumshit like that. If she was breathing, he couldn't tell.

I guess I killed her, thought Durham. I just murdered the fuck out of that bitch.

He dropped the gun back in his pocket.

He walked around the apartment for a little while. How long, he didn't know. He searched her room and took her keys off her nightstand. He searched the room where her son slept. He looked under the boy's bed and through his drawers. The usual kid shit was thrown around the room: CD cases and game cases and wires and controllers coming from the PlayStation he had hooked up to a small TV. Ticket stubs from a Wizards game. He had a Rock poster and a magazine picture of Iverson taped up on his wall, too. But no chronic and no money. He went to the kitchen and then the bathroom and searched through the cabinets and all but found not one thing. In the bathroom mirror he saw his face and noticed the dirt tracks on it. His forehead had sweat bullets across it and his eyes were bright.

He sat down on the toilet seat and wrung his hands.

He couldn't just leave her here, that much he knew. Take her somewhere else, dump her body, let her go missing for a while until he figured out what to do. When they did find her it would look like she got herself killed at random. She'd said her boy would be with his uncle for a couple days, and that would give him some time.

He took the shower curtain down off its rings. Out in the living room he spread the curtain on the floor and picked Olivia up off the couch. She hadn't gone cold yet and she wasn't stiff like he'd thought she'd be. Blood trailed on the wood floor as he carried her and dropped her roughly on the curtain's edge. He rolled her up in it and looked at the mess she had left behind.

He couldn't take her down the front stairs. He went to the back door that led to a rickety old porch overlooking the alley. It was quiet back there, except for the dogs. A light from down the way showed that below the porch was a narrow yard of dirt. He knew what he'd do, but he wasn't ready yet.

He found some Comet or something like it in the kitchen, wet some paper towels, and shook some of the cleanser on the couch where most of the blood was. He rubbed at it and it got soapy and also turned the brown couch to beige. Must've had some bleach in it or somethin', and anyway, didn't look like the blood was coming out. He got up what she'd spit out and all and used more cleanser on the floor, and that came out all right. But the couch was going to be a problem. He couldn't bring the color back to it, that was a fact. He had fucked that up good. But he rubbed at it some more as if he could. Then he flushed all the paper towels down the toilet, one by one so they wouldn't clog it, and waited to make sure they had disappeared.

He started to talk to himself as he worked. "You all right, Mario," and "You okay, boss," like that. He noticed he was sweating right through his jersey. His hands were slick with sweat.

Durham found a rag under the sink and went around the apartment wiping off his fingerprints at the places he could remember he'd touched. He must have touched damn near everywhere, he knew. Still, he did the best he could. He put the rag in his pocket, then went back out to the living room. The shower curtain was red where Olivia had bled out. He bent down over what had been Olivia and picked her up, lifting mostly with his legs. He had no bulk on him and little muscle, so it was hard. He felt his back strain as he carried her out to the porch. He looked around but not too carefully, as he knew now that the rest of it would run on luck.

He dropped Olivia off the back porch. She came out of the curtain halfway down. When she hit, the sound was dull, like she wasn't nothin' but a bag of trash. He thought he heard her moan for a second, but he knew that it had to be in his mind. There wasn't no sounds out there, not really. The dogs that had been barking all night were still barking, and that was all.

❐

AFTER turning off the television and stereo, and the lights, Mario Durham got Olivia's Tercel and drove it back into the alley with its lights off. He rolled her back up in the curtain, noticing that one of her arms was bent funny and most likely had got broke from the fall. He had to fold her some to get her body in the trunk of the car. She still hadn't gone stiff.

Durham drove into Southeast. He knew a place he could dump her there.

It surprised him, how calm he was. He was sorry he had killed Olivia and all, but he couldn't take it back now, and anyway, he had done this thing for Dewayne. What else was he gonna do, go back to his brother with empty hands, tell him that Olivia had given his chronic to someone else and it was just gone? Dewayne had always taught him that when someone stepped to you, you had to step back. And when Mario had promised to square it, Dewayne had said, "Don't tell me, *show* me," and this is what Mario had done. Now, finally, Mario would be a man in his kid brother's eyes.

He turned the radio on and kept the volume soft.

The thing he had to look out for now was the police. He didn't want to go to no prison for this. That was the only thing that scared him right there. Fuck all that rite-of-passage bullshit he heard the young ones talkin' about. He knew he wouldn't last in no kind of lockup.

He'd get rid of Olivia and lay up with his best boy Donut for a while. Let his mother and Dewayne know where he'd be at, but only them. Dewayne would front him cash, he needed it. The underground time, it wouldn't be all that long. The police didn't waste too much clock on murder cases down here. And once those cases got cold, they stayed cold; this much he knew.

He stopped the car on Valley Avenue, near 13th Street in Valley Green, along the Oxon Run park. Donut lived only a few blocks away; Durham could walk to his place from here.

Oxon Run was a long, deep stretch of woods controlled by the Park Service, cut by one of those concrete drainage channels down the middle. The Park Service had signs posted warning trespassers to stay out, trying to discourage the dealers and their runners from using the woods as an avenue of escape. Kids weren't even supposed to play back in there. Durham knew they did, he saw kids back up in there all the time, but he hoped those signs would work to keep some of them out.

It was late and the street was quiet. Durham waited a few minutes to get his nerve. Then he got out of the car and opened up the trunk. He had parked close to the woods. It wouldn't be easy to carry her, but it wasn't all that far.

It was tricky getting her out, trickier still to close the trunk lid with her in his arms. But he did it, and he walked like a man cradling a bundle of wood across the unmowed field and into the woods. He could smell his own sweat by the time he hit the trees.

He went deep in. He was talking to himself again, saying that everything was all right, because he was afraid of animals and especially snakes. Was a moon out, and he managed to make a kind of path by that light and ignore the thin branches that were swiping at his face, and he went on. He dropped Olivia on the ground when he couldn't walk no more.

Durham had hoped to dig a shallow grave with his hands, but he broke a fingernail on the hard earth as soon as he tried. He decided to cover her up with leaves and stuff instead. That would work just as good.

He unrolled her from the shower curtain, 'cause the curtain was light in color and in daylight maybe it could be seen by some kid just walking by. He did this, and she tumbled out. He heard more air come out her and figured that was natural, like how they said people still breathed sometimes in those funeral homes and shit, even though they was dead. And then he heard her moan some and knew that she had not died after all.

He stood over her and tried to make her out in the little light that came down through the trees. She wasn't moving. But her good eye was open, and it was fixed straight up on him.

He couldn't stand to hit her again with a rock or nothin' like that, so he brought out the pistol and shot her three times in her chest. It was louder than a motherfucker, and the bullets made her body jump some from where it lay. Smoke kind of moved slow through the moonlight and its smell was strong. Well, he thought, she is dead now.

He didn't bother with covering her up. The gunshots had unnerved him, and anyway, she seemed protected enough back here. He dropped the gun in his Tommys and gathered up the shower curtain and folded it as he walked in the direction he'd come. He stumbled here and there and heard his own voice saying something about God and Please, and he felt the sweat drip down his back.

He went back to the street and stuffed the curtain down an open sewer near the car. He wiped the car down good, the steering wheel and everything, with the rag he'd kept in his pocket. Then he locked the car and threw the keys down the same sewer slot. Far as he could tell, wasn't no one had been around to see a thing.

He got his bearings, trying to figure where Donut lived from here. Wasn't all that far, just a few blocks south and then east. He started walking that way, keeping his head down low.

13

T HAT same night, on the other side of Oxon Run, near an elementary school in Congress Heights, Dewayne Durham sat in his Benz, parked on Mississippi Avenue, surveying his troops. Next to him sat Bernard Walker. Walker had the new Glock 17, purchased from Ulysses Foreman, resting in his lap. His head was moving to that Ja Rule he liked, "I Cry," as he finger-buffed the barrel of the gun.

"We did some business tonight, Zu," said Durham. "Made a whole rack of money out here."

"Weather's good," said Walker. "People want to get their heads up when it's nice out."

"Thinkin' of adding some bodies to the army."

"We could use it."

"That kid, the one ridin' the pegs on that bike this afternoon, back by Atlantic? The one I tried to tip some money to?"

Walker nodded. "Quiet boy, gets respect."

"Him. He got a father you know of?"

"Ain't even got much of a mother, what I've seen. He's out all hours of the night."

"We'll put him on the crew. That'll be his new family right there. I'm gonna start him as a lookout down here, soon as school lets out."

"That ain't gonna be but another week or so."

"We'll start him then."

Durham looked up at the school from their position on the street. Boys stood around the flagpole, holding the portioned-out mini-Baggies of marijuana and some similarly portioned, foiled-up units of cocaine. The dope went hand-to-hand from the runners to the sellers, who stood on the midway and corner of the strip. Lookouts rolled up and down the street and on surrounding streets on their bikes. They carried cells with them to phone and warn the workers positioned around the school in the case of any oncoming heat.

The elementary school sat on a rise, and behind it were a couple of boxy apartment buildings and some duplexes going up the block, all backed by a series of alleys. Across the street was a field leading to the woods of Oxon Run.

Dewayne Durham had chosen this spot because of the many avenues of escape. The police from 6D rolled by regularly, and once in a while they stopped, using their mikes and speakers or sometimes just yelling from the open windows of their cruisers for the boys to get on home. On rare occasions they got out of their cars in force and gave half-assed chase, but they never followed the troops into the woods. Every so often the police would roll in with a major shakedown and make a few arrests, but it did nothing to slow down the business. Marijuana possession, up to half a pound, was a misdemeanor in the District, so if the kids did draw an arrest, priors or not, they generally did no time. They were also out on the street in a very short period; in D.C. a bond was as easy to come by as a gun.

Dewayne's choice of location had to do with the convenience of the school grounds as well. You could hide drugs in several spots, especially around the flagpole, where holes had been dug out and re-covered with turf for just that purpose. Or you could just drop the goods in the grass if you had to, things got too deep.

So this was a good spot. Horace McKinley and the Yuma Mob had one almost like it on the southern side of the park.

Up by the flagpole, Durham could see Jerome "Nutjob" Long and Allante "Lil' J" Jones standing around, giving occasional orders to the troops.

"I need to drop by my moms," said Durham. "Maybe we'll see my brother somewhere if we drive around, too."

"Where he's stayin' at now?"

"I don't know. He shows up at my mother's from time to time, but he ain't been there lately. Probl'y with that friend of his, calls himself Donut, down around Valley Green."

"The one be sellin' dummies?"

"That's the one."

"You worried?"

"I don't like that fool havin' a gun."

"You wanna book out now?"

"Sure. Nut and J can take care of things. We'll swing by again later on. Give Nutjob the gun."

"You sure?"

"He needs to get used to holdin' it. And get the money from 'em while you're there."

"Right."

Walker slid the Glock under his waistband as he got out of the car. He crossed the street and went up the rise to the flagpole, chin-signaling one of the sellers, who held the money, as he passed. The seller followed Walker up the hill.

Walker had a look around the street before passing the gun over to Jerome Long.

"Here you go, Nut. Take care of things."

Long glanced down at the gun as he weighed it in his hand. "It's live?"

"Yeah, you all set."

Long took the automatic and slipped it under his shirt and behind the belt line of his khakis. He wore the flannel shirt tails out. Though it was already too warm this time of year to have flannel on his back, he favored the material for three seasons because he liked the way it looked on him. It went nice with his khakis and his Timbs.

"I'll hold it down, chief," said Long.

The seller handed Walker a thick wad of cash and jogged back down the hill.

"We'll roll on back in here in a while," said Walker, stashing the money in his jeans. He turned and went down to the idling Benz.

Long and Jones watched the Benz pull off and move down the street.

"That gun looked new," said Jones.

"They went to see Foreman this afternoon," said Long. "So I guess it is."

"Why Zulu show you all that love just now?"

"What you mean?"

"Why he give that gun to you and not me?"

"Gave it to the first one of us he came up on, I guess. Anyway, we *both* in charge, you know that."

"Can I hold it?"

"Nah, uh-uh."

"Why not?"

"Dewayne and Zulu wanted you to hold the gun, they would've put it in your hand."

"Damn, boy, why you do me that way?" Jones looked over at his friend. "Feels good to have it, though, right?"

"Yeah," said Long. "I dare a motherfucker to start some shit out here tonight."

◻

JAMES and Jeremy Coates had been drinking and smoking hydro since the afternoon, and now James was getting stupid behind it, daring other drivers at stoplights with his eyes, flashing that kill-grin he had, shit like that. Jeremy had seen him get like this too many times before, but he knew better than to comment on it, and anyway, Jeremy's head was all cooked, too.

James called himself J-1 and Jeremy called himself J-2. They had argued briefly over who would get the number one designation at the time they had come up with the names. James had won the argument, since he was the older of the two.

They had been driving around for an hour or so, looking for girls, rolling up in the usual spots, the Tradewinds and other places in PG, but as yet had found no luck.

The cousins had not done well with D.C. women. They were not attractive in any way, though they did not know this or would not admit it, and they had not yet found their sense of city style. So if they had women at all, they usually had to buy them with money or drugs. Sometimes, if the girl was game, and sometimes even if she was not, they would share a girl or scare one enough to give herself up.

Often they couldn't even tempt a girl into the car with cash or cocaine. This had been one of those nights. James and Jeremy looked an awful lot alike: Both were small and wiry, with bulbous noses and thyroid-mad eyes, and when they were high and sweaty like they were now, it scared girls some to look at them. Scary or no, the Coateses didn't like to be turned down. James especially, when he wanted some of that stuff and couldn't get it, he got mean.

They were driving through Washington Highlands on Atlantic, going over the drainage ditch of Oxon Run. Jeremy was under the wheel of their beige-over-tan '91 240SX, shifting into third on the five-speed as he pushed the car up the hill. It was a four-cylinder rag, but they hadn't known that or even asked about it when they'd bought the car. It had a spoiler on the back of it, and it looked kinda like a Z, so they had figured the ride was fast.

"Boulay bookoo chay abec moms, ses-wa," sang James as he turned the radio up high.

"Turn that bullshit down," said Jeremy. He reached for the volume dial and heard a horn sound as the 240 swerved into the oncoming lane. He brought the car back to the right of the line.

"That's French, yang," said James. "Talkin' about the Moo-long Rooge. They be sayin', Do you want to fuck with my moms? or sumshit like that."

"I don't give a fuck what they be singin' about. Sounds like they're screamin' more than singin', you ask me."

"Which one of them bitches from the video you like the best?"

Jeremy Coates screwed his face up into a grimace as he thought it over. "Not the white bitch, I can tell you that. No-ass bitch, looks like a chicken with those legs comin' out her like they do. I guess Maya, I had to choose."

"I like Pink. Pink has got some ass on her, yang." James smiled. "I bet it's pink inside, too."

"Shit, even a mule is pink inside."

"You ought to know. Remember that time I came up on you on the farm, back in Georgia?"

"*Shut* the fuck up. I was just cleanin' that mule off."

"I ain't see no brush."

"I was washin' it."

"Yeah, looked like you was waxin' it, too."

"Aw, *fuck* you, man."

James laughed. He punched his cousin on the shoulder and got no response. Jeremy turned right on Mississippi. As he did, the batch of little tree deodorizers hanging from the rearview swung back and forth.

"We goin' to see the Six Hundred boys?" said James.

"Thought we'd drive by and see what's what."

"I saw that Jerome Long outside a club last night with a girl. Girl was laughin', lookin' at him like she was lookin' up at Taye Diggs or sumshit like that."

James had a beef with Nutjob Long, who had looked at him the wrong way and smiled one night at a club. Long was known to be good with the women. James Coates hated Long for that, too.

James pulled a gun up from under the seat. It was a 9mm Hi-Point compact with a plastic stock and alloy frame, holding eight rounds in its magazine. The gun was a starter nine, popular with young men because of its low price. James had traded a hundred and twenty dollars' worth of marijuana to get it. He fondled the gun as he held it in his lap.

Jeremy looked down at the gun, then back at the road. "Damn, boy, you ought to be ashamed to be holdin' some cheap shit like that."

"It shoots."

"And a Geo gets you from place to place, too. You don't see me drivin' one, do you?"

"I'm gonna get me one of those Rugers next."

"Sure you are."

James looked through the windshield at the elementary school, coming up on their left. "Slow this piece down, yang. I want them to see us while we pass."

They cruised slowly by the school. They ignored the kids who were selling on the street and the lookouts riding their bikes, and they stared hard up the hill toward the two young men standing by the flagpole. James made sure the young men could see his smile.

"That's Long," said James. "That's his boy Lil' J up there beside him, too."

"So?"

"So keep on going a few blocks, then turn this motherfucker around and bring it back. Drive past 'em a little faster this time."

"Tell me what you doin' before you do it, hear?"

"We're in their house, right?"

"Yeah, we in it."

"We're just gonna announce ourselves, then."

Jeremy gave the Nissan gas. James pulled back the receiver on the Hi-Point and laughed. They were having fun.

❒

"THAT'S them," said Jerome Long as the Nissan went down the block. "That's those cousins from the Yuma."

"They be tryin' to mock us," said Allante Jones.

"They can try."

"You see all those little trees they got swingin' from their mirror?"

"And that spoiler, too."

"Like it's gonna make that hooptie go faster. Next thing they gonna do is paint some flames on the sides."

"'Bamas," said Long.

The taillights on the Nissan flared as the car slowed down.

Jones squinted. "Looks like they're stopping."

"They ain't stoppin'," said Long. "They turnin' around."

The Nissan had U-turned and was now accelerating back in the direction of the school. Long could hear the driver, the one named Jeremy, called himself J-2, going through the gears. And then he saw James Coates, ugly like his cousin but crazier by an inch, leaning out the window of the passenger side, smiling at them, laughing, as they came up on the school. And then he saw the gun in his hand, and saw a puff of smoke come from it just about the time he heard the pops. Long froze; he couldn't make his hand go to the Glock and he couldn't move his feet. He felt his friend Lil' J tackle him to the ground.

As he went down it looked all jittery, like one of those videos where the camera can't sit still. Long saw the troops diving for cover, a lookout on his bike pedaling like it was the devil behind him, and he heard more shots and it was as if he could feel them going by. There was a metallic sound as a round sparked off the flagpole, and Long put his head down and covered his ears. When he uncovered them, there was just the laughter of James Coates and the music they were listenin' to. Under all that was the sound of their four-banger struggling up the street as they sped away.

The troops were slow getting up.

Jones released his hold on Long and rolled off of him, standing to his feet. Long brushed the dirt off his clothes as he stood. He locked hands with Jones and pulled him in for the fore-arm-to-forearm hug.

"My boy," said Long, his voice sounding high to his own ears.

"You know I got your back."

"Better tell everyone to pull it off the street for a while. All those shots, you know someone's bound to call up the police."

"I'll do it. We could use a break our own selves, too."

It shamed Long that his hands were shaking. It shamed him that he had frozen up the way he had. He buried his hands in the pockets of his jeans. He was embarrassed now, standing next to his friend, as he'd just been bragging about daring a motherfucker to come by here and start something tonight. And here he was, trembling like a kid. He hadn't even been able to pull his gun.

"They surprised us," said Jones, as if he could read Long's mind. "You didn't even have no time to think on it."

"I knew they was stupid," said Long. "But I didn't know they'd be so bold."

"They need to be got," said Jones.

"They will be."

"You know where they stay at?"

"I know this girl who does," said Long. "And I'm gonna re-member that car."

⌐

ARNICE Durham lived in a nice town house her son Dewayne had bought for her in the Walter E. Washington Estates near the Maryland line. She had given birth to Mario when she was sixteen, and Dewayne came, by another man, when she was twenty-six. Arnice was now creeping up on fifty but didn't feel it. Her friends told her she carried her age good.

She had always took care of her body. Though many of her men smoked and used drugs and alcohol, she did not. She was also a regular at church. It was true that she had been poor and looked ghetto most of her life, but that changed when Dewayne started earning the money that he had been bringing in the past two years or so. With Dewayne's cash she bought furniture for her new house, and clothes and jewelry, and she made two trips a week to the hair salon and had her nails done while she was there. Money kept you young. Anyone who said different ain't never had none.

She let Dewayne and his friend Bernard into the house. Dewayne kissed her on the cheek, and she said hello to Bernard and asked if he was wanting on something to drink. She had told Dewayne that his friends were always welcome here.

They went past the slipcovered furniture and wide-screen TV of the living room into the dining room, where a scale was set in the corner along with a cash counting machine. Durham used his mother's place for work — bagging up, scaling out, packaging, and counting — at night, mostly, when it wasn't smart to burn the candles in that house on Atlantic. She knew to let his troops in whenever they came by, long as they went and called ahead first. And she knew not to talk to the police about anything, anytime.

Arnice Durham never questioned her son about his business, and she didn't question her own involvement in it, either. Wasn't any opportunity where Dewayne had come up, and the people in those schools where he went had barely taught him how to read. He was out here now, making his way the best he could, and he was doing fine.

She did worry about Dewayne's safety, though, and she prayed for him regular, not just on Sundays, but every night before she went to bed. She prayed for her first son, Mario, too, but for different reasons. The Lord would watch over both of her sons, because at bottom they were good. This was something she believed deep in her heart. Sometimes, also, she said prayers of thanks for the life Dewayne had given her. She knew she was blessed.

Dewayne was seated at the dining-room table, running money through the cash counter. When he was done he read the number on the display and handed Bernard some bills. He stood and backed away from the table.

"You hear from Mario, Mama?"

"No," said Arnice. "He's all right, isn't he?"

"Oh, yeah, I saw him today; he looked fine. Just checkin' is all; thought he might have rolled on by."

"He might be stayin' up with that boy Donut."

"All right then. Let me get on back to my place."

Dewayne smiled at his mother. She had deep brown, loving eyes. She wore a new dress and she had a necklace on, spelled "Arnice" out in diamonds, all of the letters hanging on a platinum chain.

"You driving me to church this Sunday, Dewayne?"

"I'll pick you up like always."

He kissed her good-bye and left the apartment with Walker.

Dewayne tossed Walker the keys to the Benz as they walked across the lot.

"Drive me home, Zu. You can check on everything when you come back into the city, hear?"

Walker said, "Right."

Walker drove into Maryland on Branch Avenue, headed toward Hillcrest Heights. Durham kept an apartment there, near the Marlowe Heights shopping center. The building he lived in looked kinda plain, but inside his crib Durham had it all: stereo and flat-screen TV, DVD, everything. It was real nice.

The rule was, you kept your business in the city, in the neighborhoods you came up in, but you lived outside of town. You needed to get out of the city to breathe, but you couldn't get no love in Maryland or Virginia on the business side. There wasn't no good way to get a bond, and you got charged with somethin' there, you'd do long time. Plus, there was the PG County police, who had a rep for being ready on the beat-down and quick on the trigger. The only thing those states were good for, on the business tip, was to buy a gun. So you lived in the suburbs and you did your dirt in town.

Durham's cell rang and he answered it. Walker made out that Dewayne was talking to Jerome Long, and when Dewayne was done, Walker asked him what was up. Durham told Walker about the drive-by over at the school, and who had done it.

"What you want to do about that?" asked Walker.

"Nothing now." Durham slid down low in his seat. "I don't want to think on it tonight."

He tried not to, and closed his eyes.

❏

STRANGE got up out of bed without waking Janine and went to the window that fronted the street. He knew he had dozed some and he could not remember hearing Lionel come in the house. There was his old Chevy, though, parked along the curb. Strange felt his hands relax. He reached down and patted Greco, who was standing by his side.

Lionel had detailed the car out, like he said, and it looked nice. The chrome wheels shined under the street lamp, and the tires had been sprayed with that fluid, made them look wet. Strange wondered when the last time was that Lionel had checked the oil.

Well, anyway, the boy was in the house.

Strange thought about Robert Gray, if anyone listened for his footsteps coming through the front door, or if that junkhead aunt of his or her hustler-looking boyfriend looked into Robert's bedroom at night to see if he was covered up. And then he got to thinking about Granville Oliver, and if anyone had ever thought to show that kind of concern for Oliver when he was a kid.

It was hard to imagine that a killer and kingpin like Oliver had once been a boy. Strange couldn't picture that hard man in manacles as one in his mind. But everyone started out as an innocent child. It's just that the poor ones didn't come out of the gate the same way as those who had money, a set of loving parents, and everything that went along with them. It was like those kids were crippled, in a way, before they even got to run the race.

Strange ran his hand through his beard and rubbed at his cheek.

"Derek," said Janine's groggy voice behind him.

"I know," he said. "Come to bed."

"Lionel get in?"

"Yes, he's here."

"You're done working for today," said Janine. "Whatever you're thinking about, stop."

He got back into bed. Because Janine was right. He wasn't going to do anybody any good just standing by that window, and there wasn't anything more he could do tonight. His day was done.

14

THE Granville Oliver trial was being held in Courtroom 19 at the U.S. Courthouse on Constitution Avenue and 3rd Street, in Northwest. Strange passed by the nicotine addicts standing outside the building in the morning sun. The air was still, and the smoke from their cigarettes hung in the light. It would be a hot spring day, a reminder that the dreaded Washington summer was not far behind.

Strange passed through a security station and caught an elevator up to the fourth floor. All of the courtrooms were active, with attorneys, clients, and the clients' relatives and friends standing out in the hall. Outside of one room, a mother was raising her voice to her sloppily dressed, slouching son, and Strange heard a clap as she slap-boxed his ear. Most of the activity was down around 19, where a portable metal detector had been set up. Strange went through it, was thanked by a man in a blue uniform, and entered the courtroom.

The spectator section in the back of the room was half filled, with the first two rows of seats left unoccupied by rule. There were several young ladies, pretty, made up, and nicely dressed, seated on the pewlike benches. A couple of tough young men wearing suits, whom Strange pegged as being in the life, were among them, along with a woman who had the age on her to be a mother or an aunt. A young journalist, a small white male wearing black-rimmed eyeglasses and punkish clothes, sat alone.

FBI agents and other types of cops were scattered about the room. They were there to ensure that there would be no spectator intimidation directed at witnesses in the courtroom. Their hair-styles went from crew cut to flattop, and many of them wore facial hair, mustaches for the veterans and goatees and Vandykes for the young. Some had just made the height requirement, and Strange noted mentally that the shortest ones had bulked themselves up to the monkey-maximum. All of them filled out their suits. A few gave Strange the fish eye as he found a seat. They knew who he was.

In the body of the courtroom there were two tables for the defense and the prosecution. The defense team, from Ives and Colby, was all black, per the request of Oliver, though many of the firm's white attorneys had been working the case from behind the scenes. Raymond Ives had already made eye contact with Strange, as it was Ives's habit to watch the spectators as they entered.

Granville Oliver sat at the defense table wearing an expensive blue suit. He wore nonprescription eyeglasses, a nice touch suggested by Ives, to give him a look of thoughtfulness and intelligence. Underneath the suit he wore a stun belt, by decree of the court.

The jurors had entered the courtroom and were seated. The selection process had taken months, and its progress was heavily monitored in the local news. Nearly two hundred District residents had been excused because they had admitted on a questionnaire that they were unlikely or unable to render a death sentence. Prosecutors had been allowed to continue the process until they were satisfied that they had a "death-qualified" jury. So the jurors who were ultimately selected were hardly an accurate representation of the D.C. community, or its sentiments.

In the jury box were four whites. Two of them were bookish and rumpled and the other two wore unfashionable sport jackets with long, wide lapels. The remaining jurors were black and mostly elderly or nearing retirement age. From the looks of them, they appeared to be upstanding citizens, on the conservative side, lifelong workingmen and -women. Not the type to sympathize, particularly, with an angry young man of any color who in the past had publicly flashed his ill-gotten, blood-smeared gains.

The U.S. attorney for the prosecution began his opening remarks, telling the jury what the case was "about." As he spoke of greed and power and the notion of "street respect," a series of photographs of Granville Oliver were presented on several television monitors placed about the courtroom. These were stills from a rap video Oliver had produced to promote his recording career and recently founded company, GO Records. The origin of the stills was not mentioned. When the prosecutor was done with his speech, he showed the video in its entirety for the jury.

The images would be familiar to anyone under the age of thirty: Oliver in a hot tub with thong-clad women, Oliver behind the wheel of a tricked-out Benz, Oliver in platinum jewelry and expensive threads, Oliver holding twin .45s crossed against his chest. The usual bling-bling, set to slow-motion female rump shaking, drum machine electronica, Fred Wesley–style samples, and a monotone rap coming from the unsmiling, threatening face of Granville Oliver. Any kid knew that the images contained props that were rented for the shoot. Perhaps these images would be less familiar, though, in this context, especially to the older members of the jury.

Strange had come down to speak to Ives because he felt he needed to brief him today. And he also thought he'd sit and hear the opening statement for the defense, describing Oliver's early

life in the Section 8 projects. Ives would detail his fatherless up-
bringing, his crack-dealer role models, his subpar education, and
how, as a youngster, he had learned to shoot up his mother with
cocaine to bring her up off her heroin nod.

It was all propaganda, from both sides, when you got down
to it. But something about the prosecution's presentation that morning had stretched the boundaries of dignity and fairness, and it had
angered Strange. He stood, made the telephone-call sign to Ives
with two fingers spread from cheek to ear, and left the courtroom.

An FBI agent followed him out the door. Strange didn't look
at him or acknowledge him in any way. He kept walking and he
kept his eyes straight ahead. He was used to this kind of subtle intimidation.

Down on the first floor, he ran into Elaine Clay, one of the
public defenders known as the Fifth Streeters, who had been
in the game for many years. Strange had bought countless LPs
from Elaine's husband, Marcus Clay, when he'd owned his record
stores in Dupont Circle and on U Street before the turnaround in
Shaw.

Elaine stopped him and put a hand on his arm. He stood eye
to eye with her and relaxed, realizing he had been scowling.

"Derek, how's it going?"

"It's good. You're lookin' healthy, Elaine."

"I'm doing my best."

She was doing better than that. Elaine Clay was around his
age, tall, lean, with strong legs and a finely boned face. She had
most definitely kept herself up. Elaine had always commanded respect from all sides of the street, a trial lawyer with a rep for intelligence and a commitment to her clients.

"Marcus okay?"

"Consulting still, for small businesses opening in the city.
Complaining about his middle spreading out and the new Redskins stadium. Wondering why he still watches the Wizards. But
he's fine."

"Y'all have a son, right?"

"Marcus Jr. He's college bound."

"Congratulations. I got a stepson starting next fall my own self."

"Heard you finally pulled the trigger and settled down."

"Yeah, you know. It was time. Glad I did, too."

She looked him over. "You all right?"

"Just a little perturbed, is all. I been working the Granville Oliver thing for Ives and Colby, and I was just up at his trial. Some bullshit went down in there that, I don't know, got to me."

"You got to roll with it," said Elaine.

"I'm trying to."

"So that means you been prowlin' around Southeast?"

"That's where the history is," said Strange.

"You need any kind of insight to what's going on down there, give my office a call. I've got an investigator I use, he's been on the Corey Graves Mob thing for me down there for a long time."

"Corey Graves? I was down in Leavenworth a couple of weeks ago, interviewing an enforcer for Graves, used to be with Granville. Boy named Kevin Willis."

"I know Willis. You get anything out of him?"

"He talked plenty. But I got nothin' I could use."

"Call me if you want to speak to my guy."

"He got a name?"

"Nick Stefanos."

"I've heard of him."

"He knows the players, and he does good work."

"That's what I heard."

"Feel better, hear?"

"Give love to your family, Elaine."

"You, too."

Strange watched her backside move in her skirt without guilt as she walked away. He had to. Didn't matter if she was a friend or that he was married and in love. He was just a man.

Outside the courthouse, Strange phoned Quinn at the book-store as he walked to his Chevy. When he was done making arrangements, he placed the cell back in its holster, hooked onto his side.

Strange's temper had cooled somewhat talking to Elaine Clay. But it hadn't disappeared. By showing that video, the prosecution was presenting Granville Oliver as a scowling young black man with riches, cars, and women, everything the squares on that jury feared. The Feds wanted the death penalty, and clearly they were going to get it in any way they could. Their strategy, essentially, was to sell Granville Oliver to the jury as a nigger. No matter what Oliver had done, and he had done plenty, Strange knew in his heart that this was wrong.

❐

In Anacostia, Ulysses Foreman's El Dorado idled on MLK Jr. Avenue, a half block up from the Big Chair. Foreman wheeled the thermostat down on the climate control and let the air conditioner ride. It was a hot morning for spring.

Mario Durham sat in the passenger seat beside him, fidgeting, using his hands to punctuate his speech when he talked. Foreman noticed that Durham still wore that same tired-ass outfit he'd had on the day before. And those shoes, too, one of them had the J missing off the Jordan, read "ordan." Forman studied them and saw that Durham had done them both now the same way. And then he saw the blood smudge across the white of the left one.

Had to be Mario Durham's own blood, 'cause he couldn't have drawn no blood from anyone else. Somebody must have given the little motherfucker a beat-down, and he went and bled all over his own shoes. Foreman didn't ask about it, though. Far as he cared, Durham could just go ahead and bleed hisself to death.

"Wanted to turn this in," said Durham, patting the pocket of his Tommys, where it looked like he held the gun.

"What you said on the phone."

"You don't mind, do you?"

"Why would I mind?" Foreman chin-nodded at a brand-new Lexus rolling up the hill of the avenue in their direction. "You see that pretty Lex right there?"

"Sure."

"I been seein' that Lex all over Southeast these last few weeks. And every time I do see it — same car, same plates — a different motherfucker is under the wheel, drivin' it."

"So?"

"It's a hack. Someone done bought that car just to rent it out. For drugs, money, a gun, whatever. This rental business is the business of the future in D.C. Shit, white people been doin' it to us with furniture and televisions and shit forever. We're just now gettin' behind it our own selves."

"What's your point?"

"Why would I mind if you give me back my merchandise early? I'll just go ahead and turn it over to someone else, 'cause I got the market locked up. The question is, though, why would you give it up so early? You had five days on it, man."

"I was done with it. Thought I'd get some kind of credit on the time I *didn't* use, sumshit like that."

"Yeah, well, you were wrong about that. You want to turn that gun in early, that's your business, but we don't do no store credits up in here. Anyway, I done smoked up all that herb you gave me for it."

"Damn, boy."

Foreman's eyes went to Durham's pocket. "Let me have a look at the gun."

Durham passed it low, under the sight line of the windows, to Foreman. Foreman looked in the rearview and glanced though the windshield, then turned his attention to the Taurus. He broke the cylinder and saw that it had been emptied. He smelled the muzzle and knew that the gun had been fired.

"You shot some off, huh?"

"A few."

"To make that impression you were talkin' about?"

"Nah, I didn't need it for that, turns out. I just shot off the gun in the air a few times, late last night, like it was New Year's or the Fourth of July. I was high and I wanted my money's worth, is all it was."

"Okay, then." Foreman slipped the Taurus under the seat. "Pleasure doin' business with you, Twigs."

Foreman watched with amusement as Durham's eyes flared and his bird chest filled with air.

"I don't like that name," said Durham, his voice rising some. "I don't want you callin' me that anymore."

"You don't want me to, I won't." Foreman looked him over. "You need a ride somewhere?"

"Nah, man, my short's just down the street."

"Where you stayin' now?"

"I'm up with a friend, why?"

"Just like to know where you're at, case we need to hook up." Foreman smiled. "Man returns his strap after one day on a five-day rent, he might just become my best customer."

"Yeah, well, you need me, you can reach me on my cell."

"Take care of yourself, dawg."

"You, too."

Foreman watched Durham walk down the hill, going in the direction of his "short." The only cars he'd be headin' toward was the ones parked outside the Metro stop. 'Cause that's where he was going, any fool knew that.

Still, raggedy as Mario Durham did look, there was something different about him today. Stepping up and saying that he didn't want to be called by that bitch name no more, for one. And his walk was different, too. He wasn't puttin' on that he was bad; he *felt* bad for real. Like he'd just got the best slice of pussy he'd ever had in his life, or he'd stepped to someone and come out on top.

Foreman was curious, but only because he liked to have all the street information he could. Knowing where the little man was staying, that was a bone he could give his brother, Dewayne, and get some points for it, if it came up. It was real useful to be holdin' those kinds of cards, if you could. Mario had said something about laying up with a friend. Had to be that boy they called Donut.

Donut was a "dummy" dealer down by where he lived in Valley Green. He sold fake crack, wasn't nothin' but baking soda dried out, to the drive-though trade from Maryland. Those kids got fucked over, then were too afraid to come back into town for some get-back. Still, Donut was gonna get his shit capped someday for what he was doin'. Foreman had seen him and Mario together a few times, walking the streets.

Foreman's cell rang. He unholstered it and hit "talk."

"What's goin' on, boyfriend?"

"Ashley, you up?" Her gravelly voice told him she still hadn't wiped the sleep out of her eyes.

"Got woke up by a call. It was that dude, Dewayne Durham?"

"Talk about it."

"Says he needs something from you, if you got it."

"Boy's on a buying spree."

"He says he don't want nothin' fancy. And no cutdowns or nothin' like that. Says he doesn't want to pay too much, 'cause it's not for him. It's for this kid he's got, they call him Nutjob."

"Jerome Long," said Foreman, knowing him as a comer in the 600 Crew. He hung tight with his partner, a boy named Allante Jones, a.k.a. Lil' J.

"Dewayne says he wants somethin' today."

Foreman thought it over. He had the Calico, the Heckler & Koch .9, and the Sig Sauer, and that was about it. He was low on product now. The H&K and the Sig would retail for more than Dewayne wanted to spend. That left the Taurus under the seat. Dewayne didn't have to know that this was the gun Foreman had rented to his dumb-ass brother. Wasn't like it had a body hangin' on it or nothin' like that. The gun had been fired, but it wasn't hot. Foreman would just need a little time to clean it up.

"Call Dewayne, baby. Tell him to have his boy meet me at the house in an hour or so. And get yourself dressed, hear?"

"Why don't you come back here and undress me first?"

Foreman felt himself getting hard under his knit slacks. He did like it when she talked to him that way.

"Tell Dewayne to make it an hour and a half."

"I'll be waitin' on you."

"Want me to pick up some KY or somethin' on the way?"

"We won't need no jelly. I'll get it all tuned up for you; you don't have to worry none about that. Hurry home, Ulee."

"Baby, I'm already there."

Foreman figured an hour and a half was plenty. He could knock Ashley's boots into the next time zone and have the gun like new by the time Nutjob and his shadow came by.

Foreman pulled down on the tree, swung his Caddy around, and headed for the Maryland line.

15

Bright and sunny days did nothing to change the atmosphere of the house on Atlantic Street. The plywood in the window frames kept out most of the light. The air was stale with the smoke of cigarettes and blunts, and there was a sour smell coming from the necks of the overturned beer and malt liquor bottles scattered about the rooms.

Dewayne Durham and Bernard Walker sat at a card table with Jerome Long and Allante Jones. The four of them had been discussing the shooting by the school and what needed to be done next.

"Those cousins just came up on us, Dewayne," said Long. "James Coates was poppin' off rounds and smilin' while he was doing it. Wasn't like we provoked 'em or nothin' like that."

"That's how it was," said Jones.

"The cousins," said Long, his lip curling, "they sittin' on the back steps of the house on Yuma, across the alleyway, right now."

Long and Jones had been watching them from the kitchen window moments ago. They were over there, getting high with others from the Yuma, on the porch steps. James would look over toward the house on Atlantic now and again, and do that smile of his. Long hated that the Coates cousins were so bold, knew that in part he was hating on himself for his cowardice the night before. It was eating at him hard inside.

"Why you ain't fire back last night?" said Walker. "I *gave* you my gun. You just want to look like a gunslinger or you want to be one?"

"I ain't had no time, Zu," said Long. "They came up on us so quick. I was about to reach for it when Lil' J tackled me to the ground."

"That's how it was," repeated Jones.

"We could make it happen right now," said Long, "you want us to."

"I ain't lookin' for no full-scale war in broad daylight," said Durham. "This here is between you two and the cousins. You representin' Six Hundred, don't get me wrong. But it's up to y'all to make it right."

Dewayne Durham stared across the table at the two young men. He knew them better, maybe, than they knew themselves. Allante Jones was loyal to his bosses and his friend, fearless, and on the dumb side. Jerome Long was handsome, a player, and, considering his lack of education, smart. What he was missing was courage. He had always avoided going with his hands and he had never killed. This here was a test and an opportunity, to see if these boys were ready to go to the next level, and to reduce the numbers of the Yuma Mob by two, thereby weakening them and Horace McKinley. So it would also be good for business.

"You tell us what to do, D," said Long, "and it's done."

"You need to roll up on those cousins out on the street," said Durham.

"We gonna need a gun," said Long. "I gave the Glock back up to Zulu."

"Are you gonna use it?" said Durham.

"I'm ready to put work in," said Long. He was assuring Durham that he was willing to make his first kill.

Durham phoned Ulysses Foreman from his cell. He got Foreman's woman, the big white girl, on the line. He told her what he needed and what he wanted to pay for it, and they all sat around and talked some more about the business and cars and girls. A short while later, Ashley Swann phoned him back with instructions. He thanked her and cut the call.

"Give him about an hour and a half," said Durham, "then tip on over to his house."

"I won't let you down," said Long.

"It's all over to y'all," said Durham. "I'm gonna be out today, so I'm countin' on you two to get it done."

"Where you gonna be at?"

"I'm taking my son to King's Dominion."

"Thought we was goin' to Six Flags," said Walker.

"Whateva," said Durham, who saw his son, Laron, a beef baby he had fathered four years ago, once or twice a year. "Point is, I might not be back in town till late."

"We're gonna take care of it," said Long, Jones nodding his head in agreement.

"Go on about your business," said Durham, officially ordering the hit. He flipped some cash off his bankroll for the gun purchase and handed it to Long. He and Walker watched them walk from the room and listened for the door to shut at the front of the house.

"Think he can do it?" said Walker.

"I don't know. What do *you* think?"

"Boy's a studio gangster, you want my opinion."

"One way or the other," said Durham, "we gonna find out now."

◻

TERRY Quinn was seated behind the glass case of the used-book-and-record store where he worked, reading a Loren Estleman western called *Billy Gashade*, when Strange phoned him from his cell. He was headed down into Southeast and was looking for company, wondering if Quinn would like to ride along. Strange said that they could hook up at his house. Quinn said he would ask Lewis if he could cover for him, and Strange said, "Ask him how to get the dirt stains out of my drawers while you're at it. I bet he's an expert at that." Quinn told Strange he'd meet him at his row house on Buchanan and hung up the phone.

Lewis was back in the sci-fi room, rearranging stock. His thick glasses were down low on his nose, and surgical tape held them together at the bridge. His hair was unwashed and his skin was pale. He wore a white shirt with yellow rings under the arms. Strange called it his trademark, the Lewis Signature, the look that made all the "womenfolk" fall into Lewis's arms.

"That record came in you were looking for," said Lewis.

It was *Round 2*, by the Stylistics. Quinn had ordered it from his contact at Roadhouse Oldies, the revered vinyl house specializing in seventies funk and soul, over on Thayer Avenue.

"Don't sell it," said Quinn. "I got it for Derek but he doesn't know about it. He's got a birthday coming up."

Lewis nodded. "I'll put it in the back."

"I'm going out for the day," said Quinn. "All right?"

Lewis had recently bought half the shop from the original owner, Syreeta Janes, and he was more than happy to cut Quinn's hours whenever possible.

"Go ahead," he said.

Out on Bonifant Street, Quinn went up toward the Ethiopian coffee shop beside one of his neighborhood bars, the Quarry House, to grab a go-cup for his drive down Georgia. He walked by a group of young men who were headed into the gun store, a popular spot for sportsmen and home-protection enthusiasts. It was also a hot destination for those D.C. residents who wanted to touch the guns they had seen in magazines and heard about in conversation. Though it was illegal for them to purchase guns in this shop, they could buy or trade for these same models later on the black market or rent them very easily on the street. The store was conveniently located just a half mile over the District line in downtown Silver Spring.

❐

SITTING at his desk in his house, listening to a new CD, Strange stared at the tremendous amount of paper spread before him. He had been on the Oliver case for some time, and it had been easy to forget, busy as he'd been, just how much work he had done.

He had started with the original indictment and set up dossiers on all the codefendants and the government witnesses who were scheduled to testify against Oliver. He had studied the discovery, which was everything the government had seized on the case: autopsy files, bullet trajectories, and coroner's reports among the data. He'd read the 302, the form the FBI used to describe the debriefing of its cooperating witnesses. The names of those witnesses had been blacked out; it was Strange's job to identify them through careful reconstruction. He'd used the PACER database to turn up previous charges on the witnesses. By law, these charges did not have to be mentioned in the reports provided by the government prosecutors.

All of this was office work, the first phase of the process. The second phase was done out on the street.

Here Strange took his research and went out to the civilian population, looking for character witnesses and witnesses for the defense: those who had direct knowledge of the actual "events" referred to in the indictment. In court jackets he looked for assault cases, complainants in domestic disputes, and codefendants who might have a beef against his client. He was looking for any kind of background that could be used during cross-examination. Most of the people he spoke to would never make it to the stand.

Strange looked at it all as a stage play with a large cast of characters. In the beginning, he had written Oliver's name on a large sheet of paper and connected lines, like tentacles, from it to the names of those who had known him or had been affected by his alleged deeds. These included the current drug dealers who had stepped into Oliver's abandoned territory. All of this was an awful lot of work, but by doing it, he found that the various relationships and their possible ramifications sometimes became more graphic, and evident, to him.

Many of the leads he'd gotten were false leads, and though he suspected them to be from the get-go, he still went after anything he could. He had even traveled down to Leavenworth, on the nickel of Ives, to interview a former member of Oliver's gang, Kevin Willis, who had later gone to work for the Corey Graves Mob in another part of Far Southeast. Willis had talked on tape about everything he knew: who was "hot" on the street and who would or would not most likely flip. He had talked freely about charges still pending against him. Strange had the tapes in his office off Georgia and duplicates here in his house. But, as with many of the interviews he'd done, the tapes had given him nothing.

But Strange had a feeling about Devra Stokes. He sensed that Stokes, one of Phillip Wood's former girlfriends, had more to tell him. He had phoned the hair and nail salon and been told she was working today. He had gotten Janine to start the process to obtain a Federal Order of Subpoena, in the event that he would need her to testify.

Greco's sharp bark came from the foyer down on the first floor. When Strange went out to the landing and saw Greco's nose at the bottom of the door, his tail twitching, he knew that this was Quinn.

Quinn, a folder under his arm, came up to the office and waited as Strange gathered up the papers he needed for the day.

"What the hell is this?" said Quinn, chuckling, holding up a CD he had picked up off the desk. "*My Rifle, My Pony and Me?*"

Strange looked down at his shoes. "Meant to put that away before you came by. Knew you'd give me some shit about it if you saw it."

"It's a song from *Rio Bravo*, right?"

Strange nodded. "Dean Martin and Ricky Nelson sing it in that scene in the jail."

"*What* scene in the jail? Christ, half the movie's set in the jail."

"I know it. But look, they got another twenty-five tracks just like that one on there, too. Title tunes with vocals from old westerns."

"Okay. You haven't actually seen all these, have you?"

"Most of 'em, you want the truth. But I got a twenty-year jump on you."

"Seen *The Hanging Tree* lately?" said Quinn, reading off the CD.

"No, but I saw a damn good one the other night on TNT. I forgot the name of it already, but I been meaning to tell you about it. Italian, by that same guy did *A Bullet for the General.*"

"I liked that one."

"Anyhow, in this movie, they're gettin' ready for the big gun-fight at the end. The hero gets off his horse and faces a whole bunch of gunmen standing in this big circle of stones, like an arena they got set up."

"That's been done before."

"Well, they do that Roman Coliseum thing for the climax of these spaghetti westerns all the time. They're Italians, remember?"

"I'm hip."

"So they're all starin' at each other for a while, like they do. Squintin' their eyes and shiftin' them around. Then this hero says to these four bad-asses, before he draws his gun, 'What are the rules to this game? I like to know the rules before I play.' And the main bad-ass, got a scar on his face, he smiles real slow and says, 'It's simple. Last man standing wins.'"

Quinn grinned. "I guess that put a battery up your ass, didn't it?"

"I did like that line, man."

"You need to get out more, Derek."

"I'm out plenty." Strange stood, slipping the papers he needed into a manila folder. He undid his belt, looped it though the sheath of his Buck knife, moved the sheath so that it rested firmly beside his cell holster on his hip, and refastened the belt buckle. "You ready?"

Quinn nodded at the knife. "*You* are."

"Comes in handy sometimes."

"You had a gun, you wouldn't need to carry a knife."

"I'm through with guns," said Strange. "Let's go."

Down the stairs, Strange put a bowl of water out by the door and dropped a rawhide bone to the floor at Greco's feet.

"He gonna be all right here all day?" said Quinn.

"Too hot to have him in the car," said Strange. "He'll be fine."

◻

DRIVING down Georgia in the Caprice Classic, Strange had the Stylistics' debut playing in the cassette deck; "Betcha By Golly, Wow" was up, symphonic and filling the car. Strange was softly singing along, closing his eyes occasionally as he tried to hit the high notes on the vocals.

"Careful, man," said Quinn. "You keep shutting your eyes when you're gettin' all soulful like that, you're gonna get us killed."

"I don't need my eyes. I'm driving by memory."

"And you're gonna bust a stitch in your jeans, the way you're trying to reach those notes."

"Tell me this isn't beautiful, though."

"It's dramatic, I'll say that much for it. Kinda like, I don't know, an *opera* or something."

"Exactly. What I was trying to tell you yesterday."

"The singer's really got a nice voice, too." Quinn's eyes smiled from behind his aviators. "What's her name?"

"Quit playin'. That's a dude, Terry! Russell Thompkins Jr."

"Produced by Albert Belle, right?"

"Funny," said Strange.

"You got all of this group's albums?"

"I'm missin' *Round Two.* You asked me the same question last week."

"I did?" said Quinn.

They got down into Anacostia. They drove the green hills as the sun came bright and flashed off the leaves on the trees. Generations of locals were out on their porches, talking on the sidewalk, and working in their yards.

"Just another neighborhood," said Strange.

"On a day like this one, it does look pretty nice."

"I was just thinking, looking at these people who live here . . . The world we run in, all we tend to see is the bad. But that's just a real small part of what's going on down here."

"Maybe it is a small part of it. But a mamba snake is small, and so is a black widow spider. Doesn't make those things any less deadly."

"Terry, when you say Far Southeast, or Anacostia, it's like a code or something to the rest of Washington. Might as well just add the words 'Turn your car around,' or just 'Stay away.'"

"Okay, it's a lot nicer here than people think it is. It's an honest-to-God neighborhood. But the reality is, you're more likely to get yourself capped down here than you are in Ward Three."

"True. But there's also the fact that Anacostia's damn near all black. That might have a little somethin' to do with the fear factor, right?"

"Absolutely."

"Yeah," said Strange, "absolutely. And it's bullshit, too. But you can almost understand it, the images we get fed all the time from the papers and the television news. Listen, I had this friend, name of James, who lived down here. Still does, far as I know. He was a cameraman, worked for one of the network affiliates. So this network was doing a story down here, one of those segments on 'the ghetto,' and they found out that my buddy James lived in this part of the city. So the producer in charge got hold of him and said, 'Take your video camera and go get some tape of black people down in Anacostia.'"

"He said it like that?"

"Exactly like that. This was about fifteen, twenty years back, when you could still say those kinds of stupid-ass things and not worry about gettin' sued. So James does his thing and takes the footage back to the studio. They run it for the producer and it's not exactly what he had in mind. It's images of people leaving their houses to go to work, cutting their grass, dropping their kids off at school, like that. And the producer gets all pissed off and says to James, 'I thought I told you to get some footage of black people in Anacostia.' And James says, 'That's what I got.' And the man says, 'What I meant was, I wanted shots of people standing outside of liquor stores, dealing drugs, stuff like that.' And James said, 'Oh, you wanted a *specific kind* of black person. You should have said so, man.'"

"What happened to your friend?"

"I don't think he got any work out of that producer again. But he's doin' all right. And he says it was worth it, just to make that point."

Strange pulled into the parking lot of the strip shopping center on Good Hope Road. He fit the Caprice in a space near the hair and nail salon and had a look around the lot. Strange didn't see Devra Stokes's car, though the woman he had talked to on the phone had said she would be working today.

Quinn picked up his folder off the seat beside him. "I brought some flyers for Linda Welles, that girl went missing."

"That's all your doin' on that is passing out flyers?"

Quinn hesitated for a moment before answering Strange. He had spent some time on a rough stretch of Naylor Road, knocking on doors, talking to people on the street. And he had tried to speak to a group of hard young men who seemed to gather daily on the steps of a dilapidated apartment structure that had been visible in the Welles video. But the young men had given him blank kill-you stares and implicit threats, and he hadn't hung with them long, despite the fact that he felt they had to know something about the girl. In the end, he had walked away from them with nothing but shame.

"I've interviewed her family," said Quinn. "I've talked to her friends and I went down to the neighborhood that shows up on the video. I got nothin', Derek, so I'm down to doing this."

"Sue's gonna keep you hard on the case, huh?"

"It's not just Sue. I'm trying to do something positive for a change. That Mario Durham thing left a bad taste in my mouth, you want the truth."

"Mine, too, I can't lie about it. But I'm running a business, and I got employees like you to support, not to mention a new family. It was quick money and I took it."

"It stunk, just the same."

"We can talk about that over a beer later on, you feel like it."

"All right. In the meantime, maybe I'll go over to that grocery store and pass some of these out while you talk to Stokes."

Strange reached for the handle on the door. "I'll meet you back at the car."

16

THAT was Inez, over at the shop," said Horace McKinley, flipping his cell closed. "That police, or whoever he is, came by to see Devra."

"Same one we tailed yesterday?"

"He's drivin' the same car. He showed Inez some kind of badge, told her he was an investigator for D.C., some bullshit like that."

"He leave his name?"

"Said it was Strange." McKinley, in fact, had known Strange's name for some time now.

"The girl ain't there, though, right?" said Michael Montgomery.

"Nah, Inez sent her home for a couple of hours when that man called, said he was rollin' on down."

"Guess he shouldn't have called ahead."

"Yeah, we one step ahead of the motherfucker, for now. He

gets her to testify against Phil Wood, we got us a serious problem we got to fix. I'm talkin' about the girl."

Montgomery nodded without conviction. He wasn't into the way McKinley roughed up the women. Gettin' violent on women didn't sit well with him; he'd seen a whole lot of men — if you could call them men — beat on his mother through the years when he was a kid. One of them finally beat his mother half to death. Years later, that man had got his brains blown out across an alley by a gun in Montgomery's hand. Montgomery's mother and his younger brother were staying with some relatives now in a suburb of Richmond. He hadn't seen his mom or the little man for some time.

They stood in the house on Yuma, McKinley's great girth filling out the fabric of his warm-up suit. "Monkey Mike" Montgomery's arms hung loosely at his sides, his hands reaching his knees.

"What you want to do, for now?" said Montgomery.

"Grab the Coates cousins off the back stoop," said McKinley. "Tell them to get over to the apartment where Devra Stokes stays at. Strange told Inez he knew where she stayed, so that's where he's off to next. Tell 'em to make sure this Strange knows they're around."

"They took a few shots at the Six Hundred boys last night. You knew about it, right?"

McKinley nodded. He had heard them bragging on it out back, and he was down with what they had done. Once in a while you had to let the rivals know you were out here and still alive. Except for Dewayne and Zulu Walker, the 600 Crew was light. The one they had shot at, called himself Nutjob, like the name would mean somethin' just by saying it, he wasn't nothin' but a punk.

"I musta knew somethin' when I took those cousins on." McKinley smiled, showing the three silver "fronts" on his upper teeth. "Those boys are ready."

"You want them to talk to Stokes, too?"

"Nah," said McKinley. "Those two are like a couple of horses, man. I don't want to be ridin' them too hard. You and me, we'll visit the bitch when she gets back to work. In the meantime, let's roll over to that barbecue place on Benning Road and get us some lunch."

Montgomery left the house to give the Coateses their orders for the day. McKinley walked toward the front door, where he'd be far enough away from the others. He dialed a number, got a receptionist, gave her a name that was a code, and was transferred to the man he had asked to speak to.

"Strange is still on it," said McKinley. "But you don't have to worry about nothin', hear?"

McKinley ended his call and mopped some sweat off his forehead with a bandanna he kept in his pocket. All this weight he was carrying, it was starting to get to him. He'd been meaning to lose some, 'cause lately he'd been feeling tired and slow all the time.

McKinley could think about that later, though. Right now, all he could get his head around was lunch.

AN elderly man wearing a straw boater sat on a folding chair in the shade outside the hair and nail salon, smoking a cigarette. Strange passed by him, nodded by way of a greeting, and received a slow nod in return.

Strange entered the salon and saw that Devra Stokes was not in, or at least was not in the front of the shop. He went over to the older woman who had been giving him the cold looks the day before, and who seemed to be in charge. Strange guessed her height at four-foot-ten or four-eleven, straddling the line between short and dwarf. Her face was unforgiving, without laugh lines or any other evidence that she knew how to smile.

"Devra in?" said Strange.

"She is not."

Strange flipped open his badge case and showed it to her for a hot second. His private detective's license read "Metropolitan Police Department" across the top. It was the one thing that most people remembered, especially if it was shown and put away in a very short period of time.

"Investigator, D.C."

This was his standard introduction. Officially, the description was correct, intended to give the impression that he was with the police. Anyway, it wasn't a lie.

"That supposed to mean somethin' to me?"

"My name is Strange. I spoke to you on the phone a little while earlier. You said Devra would be in today."

"I sent her home early."

"But you knew I was comin' by."

"So?"

"You're interfering with an investigation."

"So?"

Strange stepped in close to the woman. He had more than a foot of height on her, and he looked down with intimidation into her stone-cold face. She didn't back up. Her expression didn't change.

"Yesterday," said Strange, "when I came by here, I got followed on my way out. You know anything about that?"

"Why would I? And if I did know, why would I care? And why would I care to tell you?"

"You got a name?"

"I got one. But I got no reason to give it to you."

"I know where Devra lives," said Strange, realizing it was childish the moment the words left his mouth. "I'll just go over there now."

"You mean you ain't gone yet?"

Strange left the shop, muttering something about a tough-ass bitch under his breath.

He heard the old man in the chair chuckle as he headed toward the parking lot. Strange stopped walking, stared at the old man for a second, then relaxed as he saw the friendly amusement in the old man's eyes.

"Little old girl stonewalled you, right?"

"That's a fact," said Strange.

"You a bill collector? 'Cause if you are, you ain't gonna get nary a penny out of Inez Brown."

"I can see that. She the owner of that shop?"

The old man dragged the last life out of his cigarette and dropped it to the concrete. He ground the butt out with the sole of his black leather shoe as he shook his head.

"Drug dealer owns that shop," said the old man.

"You know his name?"

The old man continued to shake his head, smoke clouding around his weathered face. "Big boy, wears jewelry. Got this ring that covers his whole hand. Has silver teeth, too. It ain't unusual for his kind to put money into these places. Those young boys like to hang out where the young ladies do."

Strange nodded slowly. "Can't blame them for that."

"No. You can blame 'em for a lot, but not for that."

"You have a good one," said Strange.

"Gonna be hot today," said the old man. "Hot."

Back in the Caprice, Strange eyeballed Quinn, who was outside the grocery store, his face close to the face of a young man, both of their mouths working furiously. Even from the distance, Strange could see that vein bulging on the left side of Quinn's forehead, the one that emerged when he got hot.

Strange found what he was looking for in the small spiral notebook by his side. He phoned Janine and asked her to run the plate numbers from the Mercedes that had tailed him the day before. He had her look into any priors on an Inez Brown, and he gave her the address of the salon and its name so that she could check on who it was, exactly, who held its lease.

"Anything else?" said Janine.

"I got some shirts hangin' back in my office, need some cleaning."

"Thanks for the opportunity to serve you. You want those shirts pressed, too?"

"Not too much starch, baby."

"When you need 'em by?"

"Yesterday."

"Consider it done. Now, maybe you got something else you want to say to me."

"You mean about how much I appreciate all your good work?"

"Thought you were just gonna imply it."

"You don't give me a chance, all that sarcasm."

"Okay, go ahead."

"I do appreciate you. Matter of fact, you're the backbone of my everything. And I've been thinkin' about you, you know, the other way, too. Haven't been able to get you out of my mind all day."

"For real?"

"I wouldn't lie."

"You'll be home for dinner, right?"

"I'll call you. Me and Terry were gonna stop and have a couple beers."

"Let me know."

"I will."

"I love you, too, Derek."

Strange picked up Quinn outside the grocery store. They drove out of the lot.

"Everything all right back there?" said Strange.

"Yeah. Guy was wondering how he could join the Terry Quinn fan club. I was, like, giving him the membership requirements. How about you?"

"Well, Tattoo's sister wasn't no help. But I did find out a thing or two."

"Must have been that quality detective work you're always going on about."

"Not really. Old man I never even met just went and volunteered all sorts of shit."

"Good day at Black Rock," said Quinn.

"It happens once in a while," said Strange. "I didn't even have to ask."

Devra Stokes lived off Good Hope Road in an apartment complex where "Drug-Free Zone" signs were posted on a black wrought-iron fence. Strange pulled into the lot and cut the engine.

"You coming?" said Strange.

"I'm not really into the Free Granville Oliver movement," said Quinn. "So I think I'll hang, you don't mind."

"I'll leave the keys," said Strange, "case you want to listen to some of my music."

"You got that one about lame men walkin'?"

"It's in the glove box. Help yourself."

Quinn watched Strange cross the lot and disappear into a dark stairwell.

❐

JUWAN Stokes sat on the floor of Devra Stokes's apartment, playing with some action figures, while Strange and Stokes sat at the dining-room table. The apartment, filled with old furniture and new electronics, was in disarray and smelled of marijuana resin and nicotine. Devra apologized, explaining that her roommate, a young woman who worked in another salon, had recently brought an inconsiderate, no-account man into the place against Devra's wishes. This man was unemployed, liked to burn smoke and drink at all hours, and was responsible for the mess.

"Not too good for the boy, I expect," said Strange.

"We're looking to get out." As she said it, she looked out the apartment's large window.

"I can help you, short-term."

"How you gonna do that?"

"Defense has witness relocation capabilities, same as the prosecution."

"Like Witness Protection?"

"Not really. You don't change your name, and you don't have anybody looking after you. Basically, they have funds set aside that can get you into a place, an apartment like this one, in another part of town."

"The Section Eights, right?"

"Sometimes."

"I'm not movin' Juwan into no Section Eights."

"Maybe we can do better than that. We can try." Strange leaned forward. "Look, I think you know things that would help out our case. You were with Phil Wood back when the murder of Granville's uncle went down. Phil must have talked to you about it then."

"He talked about a lot of things," said Devra. "But listen, Phil and Granville and their kind, all of 'em been into some serious shit. None of them's innocent. This is the Lord, now, giving them their due. I don't want to get in the way of that. I don't want to be involved."

"I can subpoena you, Devra."

"Nah, hold up." Devra Stokes raised one hand and her lovely eyes lost their light. "I don't like to be threatened. That's something you're gonna find out, you get to know me better. When Phil started taking a hand to me, that's when we broke up. But it wasn't the physical thing so much as it was what was coming from his mouth. 'Bitch, I will do this' and 'Bitch, I will do that.' I was like, Do it, then, motherfucker, but don't be threatenin' me. That's when I filed charges against him. I just got tired of all those threats."

"But you dropped the charges."

"He paid me to. And I had no reason to hurt him that bad. It was over for us anyway by then." Devra looked down at her son. "That life is behind me, forever and for real. I got no reason to go back there. None."

"Mama," said Juwan, "look!" He was flying an action figure, some hillbilly wrestler, through the air.

"I see, baby," said Devra.

"This isn't personal," said Strange. "But you need to understand: I am going to do my job."

"Ain't personal with me, either. But I'm not lookin' to get involved, and I've told you why. Now, I need to get back to work."

"Thought Inez gave you the day off."

"Not the whole day. She told me that it was slow and to take a couple of hours of break and then come back."

"I see," said Strange. "Inez doesn't own that place, does she?"

"No."

"Do you know who does?"

Devra nodded, cutting her eyes away from Strange's. "Horace McKinley."

"McKinley. Wears one of those four-finger rings, got silver on his teeth?"

"Yeah."

"He's a drug dealer, right?"

"That ain't no secret. Plenty of these salons down here got drug money behind them. Same way with the massage parlors all over this city, too." Devra stood, picked up Juwan, and held him in her arms. "Look, I gotta clean him up and get back to work."

"There's plenty you haven't been telling me, isn't there?"

"Seems like you're doing all right without my help."

"Go ahead and take care of your son," said Strange. "I'll walk you out."

Strange went over to the large window that gave to a view of the lot. A beige Nissan with a spoiler mounted on its rear was driving very slowly behind the Caprice, where Quinn waited in the passenger seat. The bass booming from the vehicle vibrated the apartment window. Strange studied the Nissan, sun gleaming off its roof, as it passed. He knew that car.

c h a p t e r

17

I T took Devra a while to get herself and the boy ready. Strange waited for her to do whatever a woman felt she had to do and saw Devra and Juwan to her Taurus. As he walked back to his Caprice, he noticed that the car seemed to be in the general area where he had left it, but there was something off about how it was parked. Strange guessed it was the way it was slanted in its space; he didn't remember putting it in that way.

Quinn was impassive, leaning against the passenger door as Strange got behind the wheel.

"You see that Nissan," said Strange, "was cruising slow behind you, little while back?"

"Saw it and heard it," said Quinn. "They passed by twice. I could see them smiling at me in my side mirror. My pale arm was leaning on the window frame the second time they went by. They must not have liked the look of it or something. That's when they split."

"You make the car?"

"Early nineties, Nissan Two Forty SX. The four-banger, if I had to guess."

"You could hear the engine over the music?"

"The valves were working overtime."

"Okay. How those boys look to you? Wrong?"

"All the way. But that could just be me, profiling again."

"Once a cop," said Strange.

"Tell me you know 'em," said Quinn.

"I do. Those two rolled up on me at a light yesterday. Both of them had those bugged-out eyes."

"Like Rodney Dangerfield and Marty Feldman got together and made a couple of babies."

"They could be brothers. One of 'em made the slash sign across his throat. Another car, a Benz, was trying to hem me in from behind."

"Sounds like it was planned."

"A classic trap," said Strange. "And you know that gangs hunt in packs. Anyway, I thought I was imagining this shit at the time, but I don't think so anymore. They're trying to warn me off of talking to Stokes."

"You want me to, I can show you where they went."

"You followed them, didn't you?"

The lines around Quinn's eyes deepened, star-bursting out from behind his aviators. "I figured, loud as they were listening to that music of theirs, they wouldn't make me, that is if I played it right. And if they did make me, so what? I stayed behind other vehicles, five or six car lengths back, the whole way. Just like you taught me, Dad."

"Thought there was something different about my car from where I'd left it."

"I parked it one space over."

"Knew it was something."

"Was wondering if you were gonna catch it. They stopped at another apartment complex, not far from here."

"Nice work," said Strange, pulling his seat belt across his chest. "Let's run by the parking lot of those apartments."

"I need to eat something," said Quinn. "And I could use a beer."

"I could, too," said Strange.

❒

MARIO Durham took a shower at Donut's apartment, then dressed again in the clothes he'd been wearing the past two days. He had some fresh clothes over at his mother's house, but he didn't want to go there just yet. The Sanders jersey and his Tommys, they were a little ripe but not awful. He had put his nose to them and they didn't smell all that bad.

Mario needed to talk to Dewayne when the time was right, kind of ease him into the events of the night before, then wait for Dewayne's instructions. But not yet; he'd just hang back for today. He was looking forward to seeing that shine in Dewayne's eyes, though. He was thinking Dewayne was gonna be proud to have a big brother who finally went and stepped up.

Mario Durham's whole outlook had changed since he'd killed Olivia. He had taken a life, done what he'd only heard others talk about. Sure, Mario was scared of getting caught, but he was high on the fact that he now belonged in the same club as his brother and Zulu and all the others who bragged about killing around the way. The gun in his hand had changed everything he'd been before. It had made him a man. He was happy to be rid of that gun, but it would be good to get another. He'd do that in time, too.

Mario hadn't told Donut why he needed to lay up with him for a few days, and Donut hadn't asked. But he was itchin' to tell somebody, and he needed some advice. Donut, who got that name 'cause he loved those sugar-coated Hostess ones so much when he was a kid, was his boy from way back.

Donut was on the couch, holding a controller, playing NBA Street. Over the television was a rack, plywood on brackets, holding Donut's blaxploitation and exploitation video collection. He favored Fred Williamson's and Jim Brown's body of work, and also the low-budget, high-grossing B films from the seventies: *Macon County Line, Jackson County Jail, Billy Jack*, and the like. He had his pet actors from that period, too. He liked Carol Speed and Thalmus Rasulala, and especially Felton Perry, played in the second Dirty Harry movie and the first one in that series about the redneck sheriff. There was a time when Donut had fantasized about being an actor his own self, but every mirror he looked into told him different, and eventually reality had beaten down those dreams.

The remains of a fatty sat in an ashtray on the table before him, as did a can of beer. Donut was small like Mario and close to ugly, and he hadn't ever held any kind of payroll job. But he did all right. He sold marijuana to his network of friends and dummies to the suckers drivin' by out on the street.

Donut's window air conditioner rattled in the room.

"You feel better?" said Donut.

"Shower did me right," said Durham.

"I'm goin' out in a little bit, need to pick up some shit."

"I'll just rest here, you don't mind. Kinda hot to be walkin' around."

Donut looked over at his skinny friend, standing by the couch looking at him like a dog waitin' on a treat, one hand in his pocket, jingling change. Long as Donut had known him, that was the way Mario stood: slouched, his hand in his pocket, needy eyed, always wanting something.

"What's up?" said Donut.

"Need to talk to you, Dough."

Donut's eyes went to the couch, then back to Durham. "Then sit your ass down and talk."

Durham sat down beside Donut as Donut put some fire back to the joint. They passed the marijuana back and forth.

Slowly, building it up with drama, Durham told Donut what he'd done. As he related the murder of Olivia Elliot, he began to embellish the story, making her an all-out bitch, making himself stronger, more heroic, and more justified than he had been. His head had gotten up quick from the chronic, and the tale sounded good to his ears.

"Damn, boy," said Donut, "you did it for real."

"She took me off, and my brother, too. What was I supposed to do, let it ride?"

"They gonna find that girl. You know this, right?"

"I put her deep in the woods. But yeah, eventually they will. After that, shit, I get by a few days without no one pickin' me up, maybe I'll be all right. Seems like the whole police force is out there lookin' for that white girl was fuckin' that congressman, so maybe they'll just forget. Cases get cold quick down here anyway; you know that. If the police *are* lookin' for me, well, everyone knows who my brother is. Ain't nobody gonna point me out. But maybe they won't come lookin' for me. I done fixed all the evidence, I think."

"What about that gun?"

"It was a hack. I rented it from that dealer does business with Dewayne. Ulysses Foreman, lives over in PG? I already gave it back."

"You tell him it was a murder gun?"

"Sure," said Mario, still embellishing, still bragging. "I mean, he took one look at me, he knew what I'd done. You can't hide something like that."

"What you gonna do now, then, just wait?"

"I guess."

Donut nodded his head, his eyes pink from the chronic. Durham could tell that Donut was just trying to think things out.

"You can lay up here for a little while, I guess. But not forever, hear? You my boy, but I can't be no accessory to no homicide. With my priors, I'm looking at long time."

"I won't stay long. The thing of it is, I could use some money to stake me, so I can move on out of Southeast for a while."

"I'm light right now."

"Oh, I wasn't askin' for you to give me no cash. I got some in my pocket, my brother gave me. What I was thinkin', I could double it, maybe triple it, with your help. I'll give you what I got for some dummies I can sell out there on the strip. I can make a quick rack of money like that. The quicker I do, the quicker I'm gone."

"Yeah, but you need to be careful behind that shit."

"You don't have to worry about me, Dough," said Durham, shaking his friend's hand. "I'm harder than you think I am. I'll be all right."

Donut looked down at Durham's feet. "You get some money, first thing you need to do is buy you some new sneaks."

"I do need to get myself into the new style."

"Looks like some of that bitch's blood got on 'em, too."

"I guess it did." Durham looked stupidly at the PlayStation 2 controllers lying on the floor. "You wanna play some Street before you tip out?"

"I will, if you're ready to lose."

"I'm done with losin'," said Durham. "Do I look like I could lose to you?"

◻

HORACE McKinley snapped the lid down on his cell as he crossed the parking lot with Mike Montgomery, walking toward the hair shop. He was moving slow, and his stomach hurt some. He had eaten too much barbecue at lunch, but it had tasted too good for him to stop.

"That was James," said McKinley. "Him and Jeremy circled around that Strange's car a couple of times, then went back to their place."

"They make an impression?"

"Some white boy was in the car. But they say they got their point across. I told them to stay where they're at for a while. Sun ain't down yet, and James sounds like he's all fucked up on somethin' already."

"He usually is."

"Yeah, but those two earned it. They done enough for today." McKinley tipped his large head in the direction of Devra Stokes's Taurus. "She's in there. There go her car."

They went into the shop. Devra was painting the nails of a woman her age, a goosenecked lamp throwing light on the table between them. Juwan sat at Devra's feet, his plastic wrestlers in his lap and on the linoleum floor. Inez Brown was seated behind a desk, reading a magazine. She stood and smoothed out her skirt as McKinley lumbered through the door.

Devra and the young woman had been talking, but they stopped at the sight of the fat man and his long-armed companion. The new Eve was coming from the store stereo, and it had become the only sound in the room.

McKinley took a half-smoked cigar and a silver lighter from the pocket of his warm-up suit and flamed the cigar's end. When he was satisfied with the draw he replaced the lighter in his pocket. He looked at the cigar lovingly as he exhaled, then gazed at the young customer as if he were noticing her for the first time.

"Sorry to interrupt your session, baby," said McKinley, "but you're gonna have to leave for a while, come back later on. Me and my employee need to discuss some business up in here."

"She ain't even done with my nails," said the young woman.

McKinley lodged the cigar in the side of his mouth, reached for his wallet, withdrew a ten, and dropped it on the table. "Go on, get yourself some Mac-Donald's, sumshit like that."

"I ain't hungry."

"You look hungry to me."

Her eyes went up and down his rotund body. "How would *you* know what hungry looks like?"

McKinley leaned down and put his face close to hers. "Go on, now," he said. "Before I lose my composure."

She looked away from him and stood quickly. She gathered her possessions and left the shop.

"All right, girl," McKinley said to Devra, smiling pleasantly, showing her his fronts. "Let's have a talk in the back."

"I need to look after my son," said Devra.

"Mike'll look after the boy," said McKinley. "He's good with kids." To Inez Brown he said, "Lock that front door."

Devra got up from her chair and Juwan stood up with her. She danced her fingers through his short, tight hair. "Mama's just going in the other room. I'll be out in a while. Stay out here and play."

The boy sat back down but kept his eyes on his mother as she walked through a doorway behind the register desk. He watched the fat man with all the jewelry follow her. He watched his mother's boss, that little lady who wasn't never nice to him, put her key to the lock of the front door.

"What you got there, little man?" said Montgomery, who had crouched down beside the boy, his forearms resting on his thighs. "Who's that, the Rock?"

"That's Afro Thunder!" said Juwan, pointing to one of the action figures. He didn't mind talking to this man. His eyes told Juwan that this man was all right.

"My mistake," said Montgomery, gently tapping the boy's shoulder. "Tell me the names of the other ones you got, too."

The back room, cluttered with supplies and lit with a forty-watt naked bulb, was little more than a narrow hall leading to a dirty bathroom. A door near the bathroom had a small window, barred on both sides, that gave to a view of an alley.

"Stand over there," said McKinley, pointing to the door.

Devra went to the door, crossed her arms, and leaned her back against the bars.

McKinley drew hard on his cigar and walked toward her. Smoke swirled off of him as he approached. It settled in the dim glow of the naked bulb. He stood three feet from her and smiled.

"You lookin' fine, baby."

"Thank you."

"You makin' some money here, right?"

"I'm doin' okay."

"That's good," said McKinley. "Good to remember why you doin' okay, too."

"I do," said Devra.

"I know you do. I know you remember when you lost your other job, how that felt. I know you remember that it was Phil Wood who asked me to put you on. How it was him who was lookin' out for you."

"I remember."

"Sure you do. So my question is, why you want to go and do him dirt now?"

Devra's palms had begun to get sticky. She dropped her hands to her sides.

"You been talkin' to the police, haven't you?" said McKinley. "That man they call Strange."

"He's not police," said Devra. "He's private. Gathering evidence for Granville's defense. They be trying to talk to everyone knew Phil and Granville."

"They tryin'. Except for some dry snitches they got inside, though, they ain't had too much success. What we got some concern about is you."

"You don't need to worry."

"Strange took you out somewhere yesterday, ain't that right?"

"He bought some ice cream for my boy and me, is all."

"What about over at your apartment, a little while back? He buy you some ice cream there, too?"

"We talked," said Devra, hating the sound of the catch in her voice. "But I didn't talk to him about the case. He asked me to, but I didn't. Everything he knows he already knew, or he found out his own self. We just talked. Wasn't anything more than that."

McKinley nodded slowly. He dragged on his cigar. The smoke reached her and it was foul. He looked at the cigar and then put it behind his back. Smoke coiled up over his broad, round shoulders.

"I'm sorry, baby. This bothering you?"

"It's all right."

"You know," said McKinley, "I'm glad we're straight on this. Seems like you got your priorities together, I mean, with your little boy and all. Seems like a good kid."

"He is."

"I know you want to be a good mother. Seein' as how you had some problems with your own mother and all that. See, Phil told me about her. Granville and him knew her some around the way, when you wasn't but a slip of nothin'. She goes by the name of Mattie, right?"

"She don't have those problems anymore," said Devra. "She's good now."

"But she did have some problems while you was growin' up. Phil says she was one of those rock stars, from back when they had that, what do they call it, *epidemic* here in the city."

"She's good now," repeated Devra.

"But she wasn't back then. Heard she was a real chicken-picker. Would give up her face for ten dollars."

Devra said nothing.

"Was she pretty like you?" said McKinley. "Probably not when she was geekin' behind that shit. They lose their ass at that point. But I wonder, at one time, if she was as fine as you. If she had the ass on her that you got on you now."

McKinley stepped in and put his free hand, thick as a mitt, on Devra's hip. Then, suddenly, he moved it to the crotch of her slacks. He rubbed her clumsily through the fabric. She pushed herself against the door and felt the bars of the windows press into her back. She wanted to cry out. She wanted to look away, but she kept her eyes on his.

"You are fine," said McKinley, his voice soft and raspy.

"Don't," said Devra.

He pressed harder at her objection, and she said, "Uh."

"That hurt you? I didn't mean to." McKinley inspected her body. "Let's see what else we got here."

His hand slid up and over her shirt and went to her right breast. He kneaded it and found her nipple. His forefinger made small circles there. Her nipple grew hard. He pinched it between his thumb and forefinger and it grew harder still.

"There you go," said McKinley, smiling silver. "Your body is betrayin' you now."

He pinched her nipple harder and heard her breath catch. Devra's eyes filled with tears and one broke free and rolled down her cheek. He tightened his fingers more, pinching her there until she closed her eyes completely. He got very close to her face.

"I know you'll stand tall," said McKinley. "You gonna do this for your son. Make sure he has the kind of childhood you never had. Boy needs his mother, right?"

Devra's lip trembled. She couldn't bring herself to speak. She nodded instead.

McKinley released her and stepped back. He brought the cigar around and put it to his mouth. He drew on it and backed up toward the doorway. At the open frame he stopped and looked at her.

"We understand each other, right?"

Devra said, "Yes."

But in her mind she said, You have made a mistake.

18

THAT afternoon, a boy was cutting through the woods of Oxon
Run and came upon a body lying on its back in a small clearing beside an oak. The body was bloated and ripe from the heat.
If not for the smell and the sound of the flies, the boy might have
missed it.

He picked up a stick. He approached the body cautiously
and touched the stick to its side. It was a woman. She was dead,
and he was frightened, but he had the curiosity of a boy, and even
as he trembled he knew that this would be a story to tell his friends
later on.

Flies buzzed all around him, some scattering momentarily
as he bent down to inspect the body. There were three bullet holes
he could count, two in her stomach and another in one of her
breasts. The blood around the holes was close to black and looked
thick, like syrup. The thing that made him run was her face: The
bottom part of her jaw was set off from the top part, and her lips

were drawn back over her teeth so it looked like she had died trying to smile. Also, one of her eyes had come out some and was lying on her fat purple cheek. In the empty socket, maggots clustered and writhed where the flies had laid their eggs.

The boy, who was named Barry Waters, bolted from the woods, saying things like "Go, boy" and "Go now" under his breath as he ran. He realized that the woman was beyond the need of help, but he went directly to Greater Southeast Community Hospital, which he knew to be close by. He tried to tell the woman behind the desk of the ER what had happened, and as he did she tried to calm him down. Barry Waters would be a celebrity of sorts in his neighborhood for the next few days. For years he would dream about the maggots, and in those nightmares he would see that anguished thing that looked something like a smile.

Sixth District police officers and homicide detectives were dispatched to the scene. For the next couple of hours a forensics team and photographers worked over the body before it was moved by ambulance to the D.C. morgue. Neighborhood people watched as "the white shirts" — lieutenants and the like — arrived in their unmarked vehicles. Obvious gang-related killings and hits on young men did not usually draw this kind of official attention; murders of women and children brought out both suit and uniform heat.

It wasn't long before the investigation became focused on a Toyota Tercel, one of two cars parked on the street closest to the entrance to the woods. Blood was visibly smudged on its driver's door handle. In a nearby sewer police found a shower curtain stained with blood along with the keys to the car.

The Tercel was dusted for prints. The car had been wiped down but not thoroughly. Its glove box yielded a registration in the name of Olivia Elliot, with an Anacostia address. Prints on the car would be matched to the prints of the corpse, and a photo ID of Elliot, in the system, would be matched to her body as well. When this was done, a homicide detective would notify family and next of kin. The notification would also serve as the initial investigation into the case.

This would fall to homicide cop Nathan Grady, formerly of the Fourth District. His territory now, in the aftermath of the recent duty realignment, was citywide. Grady, like most of the men and women who shared his kind of shield, hated this part of the job. It would be a while, but not too long, before the final identification was made, but his gut told him that the woman found in the woods was the owner of that Tercel. Once he knew for sure, he'd go tell the husband, or the kid, or whomever, that their loved one was forever gone.

◻

ULYSSES Foreman had scored Ashley Swann a real nice gun for Christmas, a piece she had been wanting for a long time. The revolver had come from that retail gun store down in Virginia, his most frequent source. As was his usual practice, he had paid a commission to a clean Virginia resident to make the buy.

Ashley sat on the edge of their bed in her pajamas, having changed back into them after Long and Jones, Dewayne Durham's boys, had come, bought that pretty blue Taurus .38, and gone. She had taken her gun out of the drawer of her nightstand, which is where she kept it all the time. Ulysses had instructed her that this would be its most useful spot; he kept his, the 9mm Colt, the one with the custom bonded ivory grips, in his own nightstand on his side of the bed.

She was giving the gun a good inspection. She liked the weight of it in her hand.

It was the Smith & Wesson 60LS, the LadySmith, a .357 stainless-steel revolver with a speed-loader cutout and smooth rosewood grips, specially contoured to fit a woman's hand. The grips were smooth and carried the S&W monogram; Ashley oiled them often, and she used her Hoppes kit to clean the chambers and barrel at least twice a month. It was a beautiful gun. She had her eye on a similar model, the 9mm auto, manufactured in frosted stainless with matching gray grips.

"Ulee?"

"Huh." He was lying on his back on the bed, his head propped up on pillows, his eyes on their flat-screen Sony.

"You know that LadySmith nine, the pretty one I seen in the magazine, all gray?"

"Yeah."

"I want one."

"Yeah, okay."

Foreman was watching ESPN Classic. Ashley didn't know how men could stand to look at some old basketball game, had been played years before, when they knew how it was gonna end. But she did like to see him lying there, one arm behind his head, his bicep rounded, that rug of tight, curly hair covering the upper part of his chest.

"I'm thinkin' on goin' to see my daddy down in Port To-bacco," said Ashley.

"Go ahead."

On the tube was game 6 of the Bulls-Jazz finals from '98, played in Salt Lake. He watched Karl Malone take a dish from Stockton — white boy had to do something about those tight drawers, but he could orchestrate the shit out of some ball — and go underneath for a one-handed reverse dunk.

"The Mailman," said Foreman with admiration.

"Ulee?"

Foreman thought about how Malone was wastin' hisself out there in Morman land. Handsome man like him, going home to his dull-ass family after the games, listenin' to country music and shit, when he could be playing in a real city like New York, spending his dollars in clubs, gettin' fresh pussy every night. To Foreman it seemed like Malone wasn't having any fun. Playing with Stockton and his short shorts, and that other white boy, wiped his face like there was somethin' runnin' down it every time he got to the foul line. Lack of fun was probably the reason why Malone had never won the ring.

"Ulee, come with me."

"Huh?"

"To Port Tobacco!"

"Maybe I'll meet you down there," said Foreman. "I got business to attend to."

The truth was, he was a city boy and wasn't cut out for no farm. Also, her father, had one of those lantern-holdin' negroes set on his lawn, made Jesse Helms look like Jesse Jackson. Pop wanted to bite right through his tongue every time Foreman came to visit. There was this other thing, too, bothered him some. Black men down there, deep in southern Maryland, some of them acted like they was back in 1963. Yessirin' and all that, walkin' down those country roads in the summertime, scratchin' at the top of their heads.

Ashley put the gun back on the nightstand. She picked up the glass that was sitting there and had a sip of chardonnay.

"I'm thinkin' of heading down there tomorrow."

"Tomorrow? Baby, I need to stay home. I got some serious demand for low-end product right now, and I am light."

"What about that boy goes to Howard? I thought he was coming up from Georgia."

"He is. He's bringing a load up Ninety-five in that trap car of his. But he's not due up in here for a few more days."

"What you gonna do, then?"

"I got that kid stays in Virginia, keeps a bunch of girls down there, over in Alexandria? I don't know where he gets these girls, but he gets 'em. Anyway, the girls he finds, they got no priors."

"They old enough?"

"Course they are; I wouldn't waste my time they weren't of age. He's gonna come by tomorrow so I can give him the cash to make the buy."

"I wish you could come with me."

"So do I, baby, but work is work. Maybe I'll have him see if they got one of those LadySmith nines in stock while he's down there."

"For real?"

"Why not?"

Foreman heard her place the glass of wine back on the nightstand. He heard the rustle of cloth and her gutter-girl giggle. When he looked over at her she had peeled her pajama top off her shoulders and was crawling toward him across the bed. The bedsprings were crying on account of her weight. Her titties hung low, and those silver-dollar nipples of hers were grazing the sheets.

Foreman didn't have to watch the rest of the game. He'd seen it. And anyway, four minutes to go, Jordan on the court with that look in his eye, any fool would know how it was going to end.

Ashley lowered herself upon him, her greenish-blond hair tickling his face, and kissed him deep. Her nipples felt hot on his chest. Her tongue was hot, too. Lord, could she kiss. He closed his eyes so he didn't have to look at her. She wasn't good-lookin' or nothin' close to it, but he did love her. And the woman could buck like a horse.

"Uh," she said. "Uh-huh."

The way she was on him now, making those sounds she liked to make? His dick was so hard a cat couldn't scratch it. He'd had her earlier that day, but that was hours ago. She kept playin' like this, he was just gonna have to go ahead and toss the shit out of her again.

❏

"GIMME some of that," said Jerome Long.

"You sure?" said Allante Jones. He had just put fire to a joint, double rolled in EZ Widers.

"Gimme it. I need that shit to calm my nerves."

"Shaky, huh?"

"A little."

"You'll be all right, after. You'll feel good then."

They were in their car, purchased for them by Dewayne, a plush 2000 Maxima with seventeen-inch tires and custom alloys, with a V6 under the hood. Jones sat behind the wheel, and Long was beside him. The Taurus .38 was under Long's seat.

The Maxima sat on the street, facing the lot of the apartments where the Coates cousins lived. This girl Long knew from the clubs, who mentioned once that she'd been with one of the cousins before, had told him where they stayed.

Their hooptie, the old 240SX with the spoiler, was parked in the lot. It was dark out now, and they'd been waiting on the street for an hour or so. But so far the cousins had not come out.

Long got the joint from Jones and hit it. He took the herb into his lungs, watching a man in a wheelchair roll down the sidewalk toward their car. The man was dressed in black and wore a black skully on his head. Not far behind him were two young girls, smiling, elbowing each other, having fun.

"Boy musta caught one in the spine," said Jones.

Long closed his eyes. When he opened them the man in the wheelchair was gone. The young girls were alongside the car, laughing as they walked by. Long hit the chronic again, wondering what those girls had to laugh at, and passed it back over to his friend. Sometimes Long didn't know how anyone could laugh, the way they lived.

"You know that Muslim dude," said Long, "always be sellin' *Final Call* newspapers and shit down by the Metro?"

"Young dude wears the dark suit?"

"They all young. This one's light-skinned, got a real faint mustache."

"I seen that dude, yeah."

"He was talkin' to me the other day, tryin' to tell me about the life I was livin'. How I wasn't doin' nothin' but playin' into the white man's plan of a black holocaust."

"You mean like how they done to them Jews."

"Except he was sayin' that we're doin' this to ourselves. Killin' each other like we do."

"Whateva."

Long took the joint but didn't hit it. "Man said it was like we were in some kind of circus down here."

"He did, huh?"

"And we in the ring, performing like the white man expects us to. One big ring of souls, killin' each other while Mr. Charlie claps. You think it's like that?"

"I don't know if it is or if it isn't. But take a look around you, boy. What else we gonna do? 'Cause there *ain't* nothin' else." Jones shook his head. "Nothin'."

Long was high. He stared through the windshield. He saw nothing and no way out. Though the night air was warm, he felt a chill run through him. The cold feeling went all the way down to his feet.

"Don't you ever get scared?" said Long.

"Not really," said Jones. He looked away from Long then. He did get scared sometimes. But he couldn't tell his friend that he did.

The cousins emerged from a stairwell in the apartment complex, crossed the parking lot, and walked toward the Nissan.

Jones chucked up his chin. "There they go, Nut."

"I see 'em."

Jones turned the ignition. "Time to go to work."

19

STRANGE and Quinn had some barbecue at a place Strange liked, around 18th and U, then went over to Stan's, near Mc-Phearson Square, for drinks. The crowd was unpretentious, mixed race and class. The house signature was a full glass of liquor with a mixer side. The music was always tight. This was Strange's idea of a bar.

The tables in the main area were full, so Strange and Quinn found stools at the stick.

Strange drank Johnnie Walker Red with a soda back. Quinn had a Heineken. *Here, My Dear* was on the house stereo, and the bartender was letting it roll from front to back.

"Marvin's masterpiece," said Strange.

"He was local, right?"

Strange nodded. "He came back to sing at Cardozo once, after he got huge. But they say he wasn't really into being back in D.C. All those memories with his old man, I guess. Course, he had all sorts of demons, not just family stuff. I remember back in the seventies, cats were walkin' around sayin', Is Marvin gay?"

"It bothered you, didn't it?"

"Yeah, sure. I'm not gonna lie. And I'm not sayin' he was or he wasn't, 'cause I don't know. But I couldn't understand the concept then and I still can't get all the way comfortable with it today. You get old enough, you're gonna see young people doin' shit you can't get behind, either. Y'all's generation is all right with a man being with a man. I'm not exactly against it, but don't expect me to embrace it, either. In my time, it's not the kind of thing we were taught to accept."

"All of these hatreds get taught," said Quinn.

"Sure they do," said Strange. "We get schooled by the people around us, and it stays inside us deep."

"Yesterday, when I tricked that kid into giving me his mother's apartment number?"

"Olivia Elliot's boy.

"Him. You should have seen the way he was looking at me, Derek. Like he should've known from the get-go that the white guy was gonna fuck him."

"That's like blaming the meter maid's color for the ticket she wrote. You were just doing your job."

"The job stinks sometimes."

"You took those kinds of looks regular when you were a cop. Like you were part of the occupying army or something. On my side, when I wore the uniform, I caught that house-nigger rap all the time. Again, it's part of the job."

Quinn finished his beer and asked Strange if he wanted another drink. Strange put his hand over the top of his glass. Quinn signaled the bartender and was served another Heineken.

"So anything we do," said Quinn, "it comes under the heading of just another job."

"If you accept it going in, yes."

"Like Granville Oliver?" said Quinn. "That just a job to you, too?"

Only Janine knew the truth: that Strange had been responsible for the death of Granville Oliver's father, back in 1968. That Oliver had spared the lives of two killers at Strange's request, in exchange for Strange's help, less than a year ago.

Strange looked into his drink. "It's more complicated than that."

"You were making a living before you took Oliver's case. You didn't have to take it."

"I know you think it's wrong."

"Damn right I do. Piece of shit killed or had killed, what, a dozen people. He infected his community and he ruined the lives of all the young men he took on, and their families."

"Most likely he did."

"Then why shouldn't he die?"

"It's not him I'm working for. For me, it comes down to one thing: I don't believe any government should be putting its own citizens to death. Here in D.C. we voted against it, and the government's just gonna say, We don't give a good goddamn *what* you want, we're gonna execute this man anyway. And that's not right."

"Maybe it will make some kid who's thinking about getting into the life think twice."

"That's the argument. But in most civilized countries where they don't have the death penalty, they've got virtually no murders. 'Cause they've got the guns off the street, they've got little real poverty, and they got citizens who get involved in raising their own kids. The same people who are pro–death penalty are the ones want to protect the rights of gun manufacturers to export death into the inner cities. Hell, we got an attorney general sold on capital punishment and at the same time he's in the pocket of the NRA."

"Well, yeah, but he doesn't think people should dance, either."

"I'm serious, Terry, shit doesn't even make any sense. Look, an active death row doesn't deter crime; ain't nobody ever proved that. It's all about some politicians lookin' to be tough so they can get reelected the next time around. And that makes it bullshit to me. I'd do this for anyone who was facing that sentence."

"What about McVeigh?"

"You know what they do in prison to people who kill kids? McVeigh got off easy, man; that boy just went to sleep. They should've put him in with the general population for as long as he could live. Trust me, wouldn't have been long. But they did him to get the ball rolling on this wave of executions we got coming. Wasn't nobody gonna object, for real, to McVeigh's death. A week later, they put that cat Garza down, and nobody even blinked an eye. Now that the ice got broke, next thing, a line of black and brown men gonna go into that chamber in Terre Haute, and bet it, it'll barely make the news."

"Here we go."

"Look here, Terry. Out of the twenty men they got on federal death row right now, sixteen are black or Hispanic."

"Could be they did the crimes."

"And it could be they got substandard representation. Could be they found a death-qualified jury that's more likely to find guilt than the other kind. *Could* be the prosecutors used those Willie Horton images to convince the jury that what they had was another nigger needed to be permanently took off the street. And I'm not even gonna talk about where these men came from, the opportunities and guidance they *didn't* have when they were coming up. You gonna sit there and tell me that this isn't about class or race?"

"It's about Granville Oliver, to me. Everything you're saying, it makes some sense. But it all comes down to the simple question: Did Oliver do what they say he did?"

"That's off the point."

"It is the *whole* point, way I look at it. If he did those things, then I wouldn't want to do anything to help him get off. I'm looking to stay on the right side from now on. You keep on the Oliver thing, you want to. But it's not for me."

Strange and Quinn noticed that their faces had become close

and their voices had risen. They both moved back and sat straight. Strange looked down the bar and nodded to a man he knew, a Stan's regular.

"What's goin' on, Junie?"

"I'm makin' it, Strange."

Strange sipped at his scotch while Quinn had a pull off his beer and set the bottle on the bar.

"I'm gonna use the head," said Quinn.

"That vein of yours is standin' out on your face."

"So what?"

"Don't get up in anyone's shit, is all I'm sayin'."

"Yeah, okay."

Quinn walked toward the men's room. At a large table near the hall, a man wearing sunglasses sat with a group of six. As Quinn neared him, the man's white cane, which had been leaning against his chair, fell to the floor. Quinn picked it up and replaced it.

"Thank you," said the man.

"No problem," said Quinn.

Junie moved down a stool so he could get closer to Strange. When they ran into each other, the two of them generally talked about local sports, who was coming out of what high school and where they were headed, and the 'Skins.

"That friend of yours is wound up a little tight, isn't he?" said Junie.

"He's okay." Strange smiled over Junie's shoulder at a nice-looking woman who was smiling at him. It was a habit he would never break.

"You two were arguing about something?"

"My boy just gets passionate about shit sometimes. So do I, I guess."

Junie took a sip of his drink. "What you think about Jeff George and the new coach? He gonna listen to Schott?"

"George don't need a coach," said Strange. "You ask me, man needs a shrink."

Quinn came back and finished his beer. As they settled up their tab, Quinn's cell vibrated in the pocket of his jeans. He answered the phone and the lines in his face smoothed out. Strange figured it was Sue on the line.

"What's up?" said Strange when Quinn was done.

"Sue's all stoked. She's over at the Black Cat at some show."

"On Fourteenth?"

"Yeah. Says she was up front, center stage for this guy Steve Wynn. She's fired up and wants to see me."

"We better get going, then. All that piss and vinegar you got in you, you don't want to waste it on me."

They put down twenty on fifteen and crossed the room. Quinn nudged Strange and directed his attention to the man in the black sunglasses.

"What the fuck is he starin' at?" said Quinn with a scowl.

"He ain't starin' at nothin', Terry. The man is blind."

"I'm just fuckin' with you, man."

Out in the night they moved toward the Caprice. Strange held out his keys.

"You feel like driving?"

"Why, you got drunk on one scotch?"

"Nah, just tired."

"I better not," said Quinn. "I can't see for shit at night."

"You got driving glasses, don't you?"

"I didn't bring 'em. And I probably wouldn't wear them if I had."

"Afraid someone might mistake you for your boy Lewis?"

"Something like that."

They stopped at the car.

"We all right?" said Strange.

Quinn shook Strange's hand. "You know it, Derek."

"Always interesting with you around, buddy."

"Yeah," said Quinn. "You, too."

20

T URN this joint up right here, yang."

"Missy?"

"It's got Jay-Z and Ludacris on it, too."

"I ain't like that song."

"Why not?"

"She be talkin' about not wantin' no one-minute man. Cuttin' on some dude 'cause he busts a nut in her too quick."

"So?" said James.

"That's what I'm sayin'," said Jeremy. "She's complainin' when she ought to be thankin' him. What the fuck's up with that?"

The Coates cousins were rolling down the road in their Nissan to one of those Chang markets where they knew they sold the cheapest White Owls. James wanted to smoke a fat one while they watched that new Bokeem Woodbine movie, called *BlackMale,* they'd bought off the street. All they had was rolling papers around the crib; James said that papers weren't good enough when you wanted a long-player smoke. Plus they could pick up more beer at the market while they were there.

They'd been goin' hard at the hydro and alcohol since the afternoon. They didn't have other relatives or girlfriends in the area, and neither of them had made any friends. There wasn't anything to do but hang together and get their heads up when they weren't working. They were high now, and knew that they could get higher still.

❑

WELL behind the Nissan, under the cover of other vehicles, Long and Jones cruised in the Maxima. They had been listening to 95.5 on the radio for a while, because they had one of those blocks of music goin' without commercials. They were letting it play.

"How you want to do it?" said Long.

"It's on you, Nut. You got to call it."

"We could trap 'em at a light."

"I don't like it," said Jones. "Too many witnesses like that."

"Yeah, you right." Long's thumb rubbed the barrel of the five-shot Taurus revolver in his lap. He had been rubbing at it, the sweat from his thumb oil-streaking the gun, for the past couple of miles. "Ain't no good place to do it, right?"

"You want me to, I'll pull the trigger."

Long wanted nothing more. But he said, "It's my time."

"Let's just see where they goin'," said Jones.

Long reached over to the radio and hiked up the volume.

"You like that song?" said Jones.

"Missy? It's somethin' to listen to."

Jones shook his head. "I don't know what that bitch is complainin' about, though. Do you?"

❑

JEREMY Coates pulled over in front of a small neighborhood market in Congress Heights.

"You got your gun on you?" said Jeremy.

"Right here," said James, indicating that the 9mm Hi-Point was wedged behind the belt line of his trousers, under his shirt.

"Leave it," said Jeremy.

"I don't go nowhere without this shits," said James. "You want a gun, you need to buy one your own self."

"Whateva. Go on, then."

"Want to listen to the rest of this song."

"They playin' the remix, man, this shit's gonna go on forever!"

"All right, I'm goin'."

"Get me some rinds while you're in there, too."

"Get your own got-damn rinds, boy."

"Get me some."

"Gimme some money then, yang."

"WHAT they doin'?" said Long.

"Talkin', I guess," said Jones. "Decidin' what to buy. *I* don't know."

"Pull back," said Long. "They gonna see us, we sit here too long."

They were on the cross street, looking at the Nissan idling, smoke coming from its pipe. Jones backed the Maxima up so that they were out of the Coateses' sight. He kept the engine going and turned the radio off.

"Now they can't see us," said Jones, "but we can't see them."

"I can hear their car," said Long, a shake in his voice. "They still there."

It was true. They could hear the motor knocking on the cousins' car, and the same music they'd been listening to coming from its open windows.

"Go on, then," said Jones. "You gonna do it, do it now, cause now's the time."

"I will."

"Just walk right up to that car and fire inside it. Head shots if you can. You got five in that motherfucker, right?"

Five's all I need, thought Long, intending to say it, wanting to be loose and cool, but unable to because his mouth was so dry. It was like those dreams he had sometimes, when he'd be tryin' to speak and couldn't get his lips unglued.

"Go ahead, Nut," said Jones, his voice gentle. "I'll pick you up there."

"Lil' J," said Long.

"You don't have to say nothin'. You know I got your back."

Long got out of the car and closed his door without force. His legs were weak as he crossed the street. He held the blue revolver tight against his leg and he made it to the side of the market, where he flattened his back against its brick wall. He looked back at his friend for a moment, then pushed away from the wall. He turned the corner and stepped off the sidewalk. He walked toward the Nissan idling along the curb.

❏

IN the market, James Coates unrolled some cash as the woman behind the counter bagged up his shit.

"Put them rinds on top," said James.

She was some kind of slope. He didn't know which kind and he didn't care. All of them who had these stores looked the same to him. This one had a kid, had one of those big-ass heads with a flat face. He was sitting near the entrance to the back room, playing with some toy cars and shit.

The woman placed a six-pack of beer in the bag, along with a pack of White Owls and a large plastic bag of pork rinds up top. She took his money, gave him his change, smiled, and thanked him.

James Coates said nothing. He took the bag off the counter and cradled it under his left arm. He heard gunshots from outside and turned his head.

◻

LONG approached the Nissan. The music was coming loud. Still the same song, Long thinking, How long can this motherfucker play? He could see the head of one of the cousins, bobbing as he sat low in his seat. He could see the cluster of little tree deodorizers hanging from the rearview. He could see no one on the passenger side. The other one must be in that store, thought Long. But he didn't look at the store. He needed to keep moving. His pace was steady, and his adrenaline was pushing him toward the car.

The cousin behind the wheel turned his head some as Long came up on him. His expression was like nothing as Long shot the gun directly into his face. The cousin's blood came back at Long in a spray, and Long fired again and one more time as the cousin pitched over to the side. The cousin's face was all over the interior of the car, and Long dropped the Taurus to the asphalt and puked up what he'd had for lunch.

He felt something like the stab of a knife between his shoulder blades and he heard a gunshot at the same time and knew he'd been shot hisself. He fell onto his back and kind of turned his head to the side and saw the other cousin walking toward him. The other cousin had a bag of groceries or sumshit in one hand and a gun in the other, and he was smiling and tears were going down his face.

Long tried to get to his feet, but he couldn't move at all. He could feel the puke chunks on his lips and it felt warm on his behind where he'd shit hisself.

The cousin was standing over him now. His eyes were mad-bulged as he pointed the gun at Long's face.

"Aaah," said Long.

Long saw the cousin's gun hand shake. He saw the cousin's finger pull back on the trigger. He tried to scream but never got it out.

❒

JAMES Coates fired three rapid shots — face, neck, chest — into the jumping body of Jerome Long. He heard the cry of tires on asphalt and turned.

A Maxima was fishtailing around the corner. He could hear the engine roar as the driver pinned the gas. The car was coming right at him.

Coates fired into the windshield. He stayed where he was and he kept firing and he felt himself lifted off the street and a shower of beer and pork rinds around him. The world spun crazily, and he heard himself gurgle and felt nothing but confusion. His back had been broken and so had his neck. His eyes saw nothing forever.

The Maxima sideswiped two parked cars down the block and came to a stop near the next corner when it crashed into a telephone pole. Behind the wheel, Allante Jones sat low, his jaw slack, his eyes fixed. Had he been able to see, he would have seen a spidered windshield and upon it his own blood. A bullet had entered his forehead, tumbled through his brain, and ended his life.

Outside the market, the street was quiet, except for a Missy Elliot song coming from the open windows of a Nissan 240SX.

Inside the market, a woman named Sung locked the front door, extinguished the lights, and sat down on the floor with her little boy. His name was Tommy. She held him tightly and told him not to cry.

21

WHILE Quinn went into a market on Georgia for a six, Strange idled the Chevy along the curb and made a couple of calls on his cell. He talked to Janine, found out what she had learned from his requests earlier in the day, and told her he'd be home after picking up Greco at the row house on Buchanan. Then he found attorney Elaine Clay's card in his wallet and punched in the number to her pager. He talked about the private investigator she used and learned how to reach him.

"He straight?" said Strange.

"He's got his ghosts, if that's what you mean," said Elaine. "He's trying to beat drinking, and I think it's a long fight. But on the work side of things, there's no one more straight."

"*Stef*anos," said Strange, reading aloud what he'd written.

"*Stef*anos," said Elaine, putting the accent on the correct syllable. "These Greeks get touchy about their names."

"I heard *that*," said Strange, knowing then where he would

try to meet this Stefanos face-to-face. "Thanks, Elaine. Say hello to Marcus for me, hear?"

Ten minutes later, Strange and Quinn stood beside Quinn's Chevelle on Buchanan Street.

"Can you get out tomorrow?" said Strange.

"Every day, you want me to. Lewis is cutting me back."

"Phil Wood's taking the stand tomorrow, so my time is getting short. I could use the company and the help."

"And you can help me on the Welles runaway thing."

"Right. I'm gonna try and get us a meeting with this PI, knows all the players down in Southeast."

"Okay. Call me in the morning."

"Bring your eyeglasses, man. Maybe I'll let you drive some."

Quinn nodded toward the row house, where they could both hear Greco alternately barking and crying from behind Strange's door. "You better see to your dog."

Strange watched Quinn's car turn left onto Georgia as he walked up the steps to his house. Nearing the door, he noticed that a section of its window had been shattered and the jamb was splintered. The door was closed, but Strange knew he'd been burgled. The door opened without a key.

Stepping into the foyer, he found Greco lying on his belly, rubbing his eyes with his front paws. His tail was twitching at the sound and smell of Strange's entrance, but he was crying.

"All right, boy," said Strange softly, "let me get a look at you."

Strange lifted the paws away from Greco's face. His eyes were pink and nearly red at the rims. The intruders had used something, pepper spray most likely, to immobilize him.

Strange went to his second-floor bathroom and got some Murine eyedrops out of the medicine cabinet. As he passed the doorway to his office, he noticed that the room had been completely tossed. It was the only room he had seen so far that had been misarranged. He did not stop but went directly down the stairs to Greco.

Strange put drops in Greco's eyes and then got spring water from the refrigerator and flushed his eyes further, splashing the water from a juice glass. Greco stood after a while and shook himself, then touched his nose to Strange's calf. Strange patted the top of his head.

"You're like that one-eyed fat man, boy," said Strange. "You got what they call true grit."

Strange was angry that anyone would do this to a good animal. But he was thankful that the dog was alive.

Strange went up to his office. The Granville Oliver files, including paper and audio tapes, were gone. Other files were missing as well. Some of the cases on his western CDs were broken into pieces. Everything atop his desk, except for his telephone and message machine, had been swept onto the floor.

He had duplicate files and tapes in his daytime offices. He guessed that the storefront on Buchanan had been inspected and found to be wired for security. It wasn't as if they couldn't beat his simple alarm system if that was what they wanted to do. But the home break-in was deliberate in that it carried a deeper meaning.

The message light blinked 2 on his machine. Strange hit the receive bar.

Devra Stokes had called. She said she wanted to talk.

The next message was from a white man: "You interviewed a Kevin Willis in Leavenworth. In your conversation, Mr. Willis talked about a pending capital case. Obstruction of justice in a capital case is the highest form of obstruction and carries the most severe penalty. Eight to ten years, medium security. The loss of your license forever. How much are you willing to lose?"

The message ended there. Strange listened to the message again and transcribed it exactly. He saved the message and checked the directory on the readout of the phone. The call following Devra's said "No Data." Strange phoned Raymond Ives at home and got the attorney on the line. He read the message to Ives.

"You save it?"

"Yeah."

"You'll never be able to trace that call."

"I know it."

"Call the police, report the burglary, and have them come to the house. Get a record of the event."

"What else?"

"Nothing."

"What?"

"Nothing."

Strange listened to Ives breathe. He was telling him that he would talk no further about the subject, not on this line. So Ives suspected that Strange's phone was bugged.

"I'll speak with you later," said Strange.

"Right," said Ives.

Strange phoned the police. He was told that some officers would be dispatched to his place in the next half hour.

He phoned Janine on his cell. If the home phones were tapped, then surely his cell calls were being monitored as well. He didn't care. If the government was after him, FBI or whoever, there wasn't all that much he could do. He wasn't going to spend his time making pay-phone calls and worrying about conversations indoors. He was getting angrier by the moment. All that talk about loss of license and eight-to-ten. He didn't take to threats. This was bullshit, was what it was. They had misjudged him, thinking he would cave to their office-toss and phone messages. And they shouldn't have fucked with his dog.

He got Janine and gave her the facts without conjecture. She asked him if he was sitting down.

"I just watched the news, Derek. Someone found the body of Olivia Elliot in Oxon Run late this afternoon."

"Lord," said Strange.

"You better call Lydell," said Janine.

"I will," said Strange, rubbing at his face. His anxiety shifted from thoughts of himself and the government to his role in this girl's death. And then there was Quinn and Mark Elliot, Olivia's son. The hardest part would be telling Quinn.

"Derek, you there?"

"Yes. I'll be home in a couple of hours. I'm waitin' on the police."

"I'll save you dinner."

"You got anything special for Greco? Some bones, maybe?"

"I'll find something."

"I love you, baby."

"See you soon."

Strange phoned his friend Lydell Blue, a lieutenant in the Fourth District, at home. He told Blue that he was calling about Olivia Elliot, the woman whose murder had made the TV news. He gave Blue Mario Durham's name and cell phone number, and told him what Durham had paid him to do.

"That's your man right there, I expect."

"No address?"

"What I gave you is what I have."

"You better come in tomorrow morning. I'll find out who's got the case in Homicide and have him meet us at the Gibson building. Say nine o'clock?"

"I'll be there. I'll bring Quinn, too."

"All right then, Derek. Thanks for the call."

Blue hung up on his end. Strange heard the police knocking on the door on the first floor and went down to let the two uniformed cops in. He spent some time with them, then left them to do their job. He went to the living room, sat on his mother's old couch, and stared at the cell phone he still held in his hand. There wasn't any way to put it off any longer. He phoned Quinn.

❐

DEWAYNE Durham had gotten the cell message on the way back from Six Flags amusement park informing him of the deaths of Jerome Long and Allante Jones. One of his young men at the elementary school had made the call. Word of the quadruple homicide had spread quickly on the street.

Durham and Bernard Walker dropped off Durham's son, Laron, at his mother's place in Landover. Durham hugged Laron without feeling and sent him into his apartment holding balloons and candy. Durham watched him, thinking, That boy has grown some, not realizing or caring that it had been six months since he had seen him last.

There were still a couple of balloons in the backseat of the Benz as Durham and Walker drove back into the city. Walker tried to look around them in the rearview as he changed lanes.

"Boy who called me said Nutjob shot first," said Durham.

"I guess Jerome did have that fire in him after all," said Walker.

"He ain't had enough to save his life."

"We lost two to get two of theirs. Makes us even, right?"

"That's not the way it works; you know that. Some young boy now in Yuma is gonna see this as a way to prove he can put work in. All's this is gonna do is make the killin' start."

"We'll be ready, then."

"We gonna have to be." Durham shifted in his seat. "Go on over to Mississippi Avenue. Let's see what's up, get the rest of the story from the troops."

When they got to the elementary school in Congress Heights, there were few of their people around. Durham could see a kid up by the flagpole, standing back in the shadows, and another boy, a lookout no older than twelve, up there on a bike. The kid rode his bike down the rise to the Benz, which Walker had put beside the curb. He wheeled around to the passenger side of the car as Durham's window glided down.

"Wha'sup, youngun?"

The boy's face was streaked with sweat, and excitement lit his eyes. A cell phone in a holster lay against his hip. "It was me called you up."

"I'll remember it, too."

"Five-O already came by twice, askin' after you. Same car both times."

They heard the whoop of a siren blast then, as if on cue, as an MPD cruiser came down Mississippi.

"Here they come again," said Walker.

"Book, little man," said Durham, and the kid took off on his bike. He went up the cross street, past the elementary school, and disappeared into an alley.

"What you want me to do?" said Walker.

"Kill the engine. You don't got your gun with you, do you?"

"You told me not to bring it, 'cause of your son."

"We all right, then." Durham moved to the left so that he could see the Crown Vic cruiser in the rearview, idling behind them with its headlights on, radioing in for backup. He could read the car number, but he suspected that this was more than a routine stop.

The Maryland-inflected, deep female voice on the cruiser's loudspeaker told them to put their hands outside the open windows of the car. They did this, then were approached by two officers. One of them had drawn his sidearm, a Glock 17, and was holding it out and pointed at the driver's window with his elbow locked.

"Why they're not waitin' on more cars?" said Walker.

Durham said, "They want to talk to me first."

The officers separated them outside the car. Walker was led to the side of the cruiser by a tall officer with a thick black mustache. Durham was frisked against the Benz by an eight-year veteran of the force, a wide-bottomed woman with short bottle-blond hair. Her name was Diane Beard.

Beard pushed on Durham's head until it was bowed and got close to his ear. "We're taking you in for questioning soon as the backup gets here."

"For what?"

"The shooting tonight."

"I don't know nothin'," said Durham, his standard response to any police question.

"Course you don't," said Beard.

"Why you here?" said Durham, lowering his voice.

"Jerome Long and Allante Jones are dead. The Coates cousins, too."

"Tell me somethin' I don't know."

"Your brother, Mario, is hot."

"What?"

"A woman named Olivia Elliot was found murdered in Oxon Run this afternoon. Mario's the number one suspect. It just came out over the radio."

Durham said, "God*damn.*"

His first thought: Couldn't be. He didn't believe Mario had murder in him. But then, it fit together. Dewayne had told Mario to find the woman for some get-back. He had only meant be a man. He didn't mean for the fool to kill the bitch.

Durham's second thought: Mario would be hidin' out with that boy Donut. And the police would be talking to their moms straightaway. But she wouldn't give Mario up. No one would. They knew who his brother was, after all.

More squad cruisers converged on the scene. Officer Beard yanked up on Durham's arms, which she held behind his back, and pulled him away from the hood of the Benz.

"Little rough, ain't you?"

"Gotta make it look good," said Beard, a small degree of pleasure in her voice.

"I ain't payin' you to make it look *that* good," said Durham.

Beard pushed him along. Pocket-cops, thought Durham. They hate everyone. Most of all, they hate themselves.

22

T HE police gonna want to talk to us," said Mike Montgomery.

"I ain't hidin'," said Horace McKinley.

And I ain't worried, neither. The police can't touch me.

"Too bad about the cousins, though."

"Find that boy we see down by the liquor store. The one makes them T-shirts?"

"I know his sister."

"Find him. Get some T-shirts made up for the cousins. 'RIP, We Will Not Forget,' sumshit like that. You know what to do."

"They ain't had no family or friends."

"It ain't for them. We need to show the street, the Yuma honors their own."

"I'll get it done."

They sat in the abandoned house at a card table, beer and malt bottles strewn about the scarred hardwood floor and the stairs

leading to the second floor. The lights were on in the house. Mc-
Kinley smoked a cigar.

"Gonna be a war for a while," said McKinley, admiring the
Cuban in his hand. "We gonna need some guns."

"We'll go see Ulysses, then."

"Six Hundred gonna want to have some go. You know this."

"They ain't but across the alley."

"Then that alley's gonna be one of those DMZs you hear
about."

"Right," said Montgomery. He didn't know what McKinley
was talking about. He didn't know if McKinley knew.

"Phil Wood's takin' the stand tomorrow," said McKinley.

"You told me."

Montgomery reached into his pocket. He had walked out of
the hair salon with one of those little wrestling figures by mistake.
He'd been using the figure to play one of those hide-and-go-seek
games with that boy Juwan. It had been fun hangin' out with him.
Relaxing. He was tired of this life he was leading, and that boy
had reminded him, in a pure kinda way, that not everyone out here
was involved in this drama that always ended in death. That boy
had been friendly, and not because he was afraid of Mike or knew
who McKinley was or nothin' like that. That boy was nice.

"Phil's gonna be up there for a couple of days." McKinley
drew on his cigar and exhaled a cloud of smoke that further fogged
the room. "So we need to watch the Stokes bitch for a little while
longer."

"Okay."

"I think she got the message today, but you never know. Girl
had some fire in her eyes, I'll give her that. She don't respond to
the way I put it to her, next thing is, we gonna have to squeeze her
little boy."

Montgomery fingered the plastic wrestler in his pocket.

"Mike?" said McKinley.

"What."

"You heard me, right?"

"I heard you," said Montgomery.

But I ain't gonna do nothin' to hurt that kid.

◻

STRANGE drove uptown in his Cadillac, Greco beside him on his red cushion, War's "Lotus Blossom" coming from the box. War was one of those groups Strange always went back to when he wanted to think and breathe. They were known as a jam band, but it was their ballads that really cooled him out.

Kids were out on Georgia's sidewalks, like they always were. There wasn't any curfew anymore, like there had been for a while in D.C. The curfew hadn't worked because the responsibility for the children had been put in the wrong hands. It never should have been up to the police to raise other people's kids.

Strange thought of Mark Elliot, now an orphan. And he thought of Robert Gray, living with that junkie aunt of his and her equally damaging boyfriend.

Strange drove by a church set back on Georgia. He saw a banner outside of it, read, "Member: One Kid, One Congregation." He knew of the program and had once met the man who ran it. He made a mental note to give that man a call.

Lionel was out on Quintana, standing under a street lamp, the hood up on his car, as Strange parked the Brougham. Lionel had a rag in his hand and he was using it to wipe oil off a dip stick.

Strange got out of the Caddy. He waited for Greco to jump out before he closed the door. Greco stayed with him every step of the way as Strange came up on Lionel.

"Hey," said Strange.

"Pop. Rough night, huh?"

"I'm still standin'."

"Mom kept some food on."

Strange brought Lionel to him and held him close.

"Don't stay out here too long, hear?"

Lionel nodded, somewhat embarrassed by the affection, somewhat confused. Strange let him go and walked toward the house, Greco's nose bumping at his calf. Janine was waiting for him behind the screen door. Strange wondered where he had found the luck to have all this, when others had none at all.

◻

DURHAM and Walker were taken to the Sixth District substation on Pennsylvania Avenue, Southeast, and interviewed separately by homicide detectives working the shootings outside the market. Predictably, both said that they knew nothing about the event. Detective Nathan Grady entered the interview room where Dewayne sat and asked him about the whereabouts of his brother, Mario. Dewayne gave him nothing except for the address of his mother, which he knew they could easily find or already had. There was nothing to hold them on, so Dewayne and Walker were told they could leave. Their car was waiting for them out on Pennsylvania.

Back in the Benz, Dewayne called his mother. She was crying and said that the police had already been to her town house. She told Dewayne that she didn't know where Mario could be. Their mother was smart enough not to mention Mario's friend Donut while talking on the cell.

Dewayne Durham told his mother not to worry. He'd stop by later and bring along some sweets that he knew she liked, truffles he could get in a late-night market by her place.

"Drive over to Valley Green, Zu," Durham said to Walker. "Make sure we don't get followed."

Down in Valley Green, near the hospital, they cruised a cluster of streets: Blackney Lane, Varney Street, and Cole Boulevard among them. Durham was looking for Donut's car, a silver blue Accord, as he didn't know exactly where Donut lived. But then they saw Mario, wearing that stupid-ass Redskins getup, standing on a street corner up ahead. Mario stood with one hand in his pocket, slouched, just looking around. Looked like he was waiting for something, he didn't know what. Just like he'd been doin' his whole sorry life.

"Fool," said Dewayne under his breath. "Pull over, Bernard."

Dewayne got out of the car and crossed the street to the corner where Mario stood. Mario kind of puffed out his chest then, like he was one of his brother's kind. But he saw Dewayne's eyes and deflated himself quick.

"What you doin' out here, huh?" said Dewayne.

"Nothin'," said Mario.

He had some fake crack in his pocket, a whole rack of dummies, but he hadn't sold a dime's worth yet. He didn't think his brother wanted to hear about it now.

"Don't you know you wanted on a homicide?"

"They found her, huh?"

Dewayne took a deep breath and let it out slow. "Who you stayin' with? Donut?"

"Uh-huh."

"Where he live at, man?"

Mario told him.

"You got your cell on you?" said Dewayne. At Mario's nod, Dewayne said, "Give it to me."

Mario handed Dewayne his cell. Dewayne dropped it on the concrete and stomped on it savagely, breaking it into pieces. He kicked the various shreds into the worn grass and street.

"They can find you like that, trace your ass right through your phone when you be usin' it. Don't you know *nothin'?*"

Mario looked up into Dewayne's eyes. "Don't be mad at me, D." Dewayne didn't respond.

Mario said, "You *told* me the bitch needed to be got."

"Stupid motherfucker," said Dewayne. His hand flew up and he slapped Mario's face.

The blow caught them both by surprise. Mario rubbed his

cheek and slowly turned his head back to face Dewayne. Mario's eyes had welled up with tears and his bottom lip shook.

"Why'd you do me like that?" said Mario, a tremor in his voice. "You my kid brother, man."

Dewayne brought him into his arms. Mario was right. He had punked his brother, shamed him in front of Walker, who had surely seen it from his spot in the Benz. And that was wrong.

"Come on," said Dewayne, leading Mario across the street, one arm around his shoulders. "We got to put you underground."

"Where I'm goin'?"

"To stay with this girl I know who owes me."

"That gonna be all right with her?"

"It'll be all right if I tell her it will. C'mon."

From behind the wheel, Bernard Walker watched as Dewayne led his retard, no-ass, no-job-havin' brother toward the car. As they neared, Walker noticed the blood-stained shoes on Mario's feet. Yesterday he had had one "ordan," and today he had him a whole pair. Walker thinking, That's progress, to *him*.

◻

TERRY Quinn and Sue Tracy were fucking like animals in Quinn's bed when Strange called. Quinn reached over and swept the phone off the nightstand without missing a stroke. Fifteen minutes later Strange called again. Quinn had put the receiver back in its cradle, and Sue was in the bathroom washing herself when the phone rang. Quinn sat up naked on the bed and answered the call.

"What's goin' on?" said Tracy, coming out of the bathroom, seeing Quinn's pale, drawn face.

"It was Derek," said Quinn, nodding toward the phone. He repeated, briefly, the details Strange had given him. She asked some questions, but he waved her off and got up from the bed. He dressed in jeans and a white T-shirt, and got into his leather.

Quinn stood dumbly in the center of the room and stared at his bureau. His Colt was in there. He took a step toward his dresser and stopped. What would he do with his gun now? The gun was his crutch, he knew. Violence was his answer, had always been his answer, to every conflict, threatened or imagined, he'd ever had. But there wasn't even a target now. Not unless you counted that pathetic little man in the Deion jersey. No, it was Quinn who had gotten that boy's mother killed.

He walked from the bedroom. Tracy heard him pacing the living room and then a crash. It was the sound of a toppled chair. He came back in, and the vein was up on his face.

"I'm going out."

"Where?"

"For a walk."

"I'll come."

Quinn's eyes cut away from Tracy's. "No."

He walked up Sligo Avenue, past houses and apartments and the Montgomery County Police station, the 7-Eleven and the bus station on Fenton, and then along the car repair garages and auto parts stores lining the strip. The closed-mouth kiss of gentrification and the replacement of mom-and-pops by national chains had not yet reached this far south in Silver Spring. Quinn generally stayed in this part of town.

He turned left on Selim, crossed the street at the My-Le, the Vietnamese restaurant there, and went over the pedestrian bridge spanning Georgia Avenue that led to the commuter train station and the B&O and Metro tracks. He stood on the platform and looked down Georgia, his nearsighted eyes seeing only the blur of headlights, street lamps, and streaks of neon. He turned toward the tracks, hearing the low rumble of a freight train approaching from the south. It reached him eventually. When it did, he reached his hand out so that he almost touched the train and could feel its wind. He closed his eyes.

Now he was away from his world. Enemies and allies were

easily distinguished by hats of black and white. Honor and re-
demption were real, not conceptual. Justice was uncomplicated by
the gray of politics and money, and, if need be, achieved at the
point of a gun.

Quinn knew he was out of step. He knew that his outlook
was dangerous, essentially that of a boy. And that it would catch
up to him in the end.

He opened his eyes. The train still rumbled by. Up on Selim,
his Chevelle was idling outside My-Le. He crossed back over the
bridge and went to the open passenger window. He leaned into the
frame. Sue Tracy was behind the wheel, her right hand moving the
Hurst shifter through its gears.

"Thanks for checkin' up on me, Mom."

"Look, I don't know what you dream about up here, cowboy,
but it doesn't get anything solved."

"In my mind it does."

"Okay. But it sounds to me like you've got some work to do
tomorrow. I just wanted to make sure you got some sleep tonight."

"What you wanted was to drive my sled."

"There was that."

"I'll be home in a little while."

"C'mon, Terry," said Tracy, reaching across the bucket and
opening the door. "Get in."

23

S TRANGE and Quinn sat at a table on the second floor of the Brian T. Gibson Building, the Fourth District station, in the office of Lieutenant Lydell Blue. Homicide detective Nathan Grady sat with them. Four Styrofoam cups holding coffee were on the table, along with a file. There were no windows in the office, no rays of sun, no bird sounds, no indication at all that it was a beautiful morning late in spring. It could have been any time of day. The fluorescent lights in the drop ceiling above gave them all a sickly pallor.

"So where we at?" said Strange.

"You first," said Grady.

"I gave Lydell everything I had."

"Tell *me*," said Grady.

Strange repeated the story of Mario Durham's visit to his office. He left out no detail of their meeting, except for one. He relayed the particulars of the subsequent investigation, including the conversations with his interviewees and those of Quinn. Quinn interjected to give further recollections as needed.

"Some man matching your description," said Blue, "talked to a neighbor of Olivia's at her old address. He used some ruse about being a football coach, called himself Will Sonnet. Like that old TV show with Walter Brennan. You know, 'No brag, just fact.'"

"She came forward, huh?" said Strange.

"Soon as she saw on the TV news that they found the Elliot woman," said Blue.

"Nice to know we got some good citizens out there."

"I figured that was you."

"And you told the son that his mother had won a raffle," said Grady, addressing Quinn.

"Yes," said Quinn.

"Tricky."

Quinn ignored the editorial remark. "How'd he connect me?"

"The boy got a partial on your plates." Grady stared at Quinn for a moment, then looked down at a small lined pad, where he tapped his pen. When he looked back up at Quinn he said, "You were a patrol cop here in Four D, weren't you?"

"That's right."

Next thing you'll tell me I look familiar, but you already know who I am. I'm the cop that shot that other cop two years ago. Never mind that I was cleared. All of you will never forget. And now I'm private, a joke, tricking kids so that I can get their mothers killed. The opposite of what a cop does. Why don't you just say it so we can move on?

"We had no reason to think we were going to cause that woman any harm," said Strange.

"True," said Grady.

"Mario Durham looked less than harmless."

"I appreciate your cooperation on this. I really do."

"Anything we can do to help."

Strange knew Grady by reputation and by sight, a tall man with gray-blond hair and ice blue eyes, looked like an older version of that Scandi actor, played in the later *Walking Tall* movies, Bo something. Blue said that Grady was all right. Odd, but all right. He was known to keep crime-scene photos of victims mounted on the walls of his apartment, where he lived alone. Cops who'd been by his place described them: There was one of a young man lying on his back on a Capitol Hill street, his hands still tented in prayer from before he had been shot. Another showed a woman who had hung her cat from the basement pipe, then hung herself beside it. That one was framed above the mantel. Outsiders would say that Grady was disturbed to keep such photos on display. Cops knew that this was Grady's way of dealing with his job.

"Y'all are positive it was Mario Durham who killed her, right?" said Strange.

"As positive as you can be. He left prints all over the apartment and her car. His prints were on her car keys, the shower curtain he wrapped her in, everything."

"Any idea on motive?" said Strange.

Grady shrugged. "They found cash between her mattress and box spring. There was marijuana in there, too, looked like it might have been a little more quantity than for personal use. Mario's got a connection to a dealer —"

"What connection?" said Quinn.

"I'm gonna get to that," said Grady. "So maybe this had something to do with a drug debt unpaid. Or it was one of those crimes of passion. The way you described him, Mario must have been a real player."

"How's the son doing?" said Quinn.

"He's staying with his uncle, William Elliot. It's where he was when she was killed, and why she wasn't reported missing right away. The way I understand it, the arrangement's going to be permanent. The uncle's about as straight as they come. A government employee, married, secure. Doesn't tolerate knuckleheads or any kind of foolishness. Loved his sister but hated her lifestyle, all that."

"Sounds like a really fun guy," said Strange.

"Let's be honest," said Grady. "The boy's never gonna get over the death of his mother. But from my point of view, he's going to have a more secure environment now than he had before." Grady's eyes went from Strange's to Quinn's. "I'm not tryin' to make you two feel good about yourselves, either. Just giving you my opinion."

Strange nodded. "You get anything from Durham's cell number yet?"

"Nothing yet," said Grady. "If he uses it, we'll get a trace. If he's smart, he's destroyed the phone by now, or dumped it somewhere to throw us off."

"He's not smart," said Quinn.

"Shouldn't be too hard to find him, either," said Strange.

"You'd think it'd be easy, even if he did move from place to place. And you know he's not going far. Anacostia's a small town. Talk to his mother, find out who he hangs with, all that. But there's this connection he's got, the one I was mentioning before."

"Go ahead," said Strange.

"Mario's younger brother is a guy named Dewayne Durham. Leads a gang called the Six Hundred Crew. Marijuana sales, primarily, with cocaine in the mix. Dewayne's got priors, was a suspect in several murders in his younger days, the typical profile. He's the big Magilla in his corner of the world."

"So nobody's gonna flip on his brother," said Quinn.

"Exactly," said Grady.

"You bring Dewayne in?" said Strange.

"Yeah," said Grady. "He gave us jack shit."

A brief silence fell.

"The gun he used is in the river right now, I expect," said Strange.

"No," said Grady. "Here's where it gets interesting. You guys hear about that quadruple homicide in Southeast last night?"

"I read about it in the Metro section this morning," said Strange. "They withheld the names of the victims."

Grady leaned forward and issued a joyless show of yellowed teeth, meant to be a smile. "One of the guns used in the shooting was the same gun Mario used to shoot Olivia Elliot."

"What the fuck?" said Quinn.

"How'd you get that so quick?" said Strange.

"There was an alert officer on the crime scene, remembered the caliber of the murder gun in the Elliot case. They sent one of the slugs and a casing out and ran them through the IBIS program, you know, with the ATF?"

"IBIS?" said Quinn.

"Inter Ballistics ID System," said Grady. "You been away."

"Not too long."

"The slug from the shooting matched the slugs taken out of Olivia Elliot. A Taurus thirty-eight. It wasn't just the same model of gun. The markings made it as the same exact piece."

"Keep talking," said Strange.

"Two of the victims of the shooting were known employees of Dewayne Durham. Jerome Long and Allante Jones. Allante. Christ, someone named their kid after a Cadillac, you believe it? And not even one of the good Caddies."

"And?"

"One of them used the Taurus before he died."

"Who'd he use it on?" said Quinn.

"Jeremy Coates. He and his cousin James worked for a rival dealer, this fat cat named Horace McKinley."

McKinley. Strange's blood ticked through his veins. James

and Jeremy Coates owned the beige Nissan that had been tailing him the past two days; Janine had gotten him the information from her MVA contact after Quinn had taken their plate numbers off the 240.

"Funny," said Grady. "Right?"

"If all else fails," said Strange, "I guess you can follow the gun."

"Oh, we're already on that. We did a trace, the ATF again, God love 'em. The serial number was still on there, which tells us the gun came from a pro middleman. It was purchased in a gun store down in Virginia, way down off Route 1, called Commonwealth Guns. It'll be a straw buy, we're pretty sure. Probably went to an intermediary dealer who works the District. Anyway, we're looking into it."

"So the gun sale was legit," said Quinn.

"Most likely. Purchased at an FFL — that's federal firearms licensee to you, Quinn. Since you been away so long."

"And that makes it legal?"

"Legal, not moral. But so what? Legal's enough. Hard to stop straw buys, anyway, even if you wanted to. Sixty percent of the crime guns recovered in D.C. come from legitimate stores in Maryland and Virginia. In Virginia you can buy a gun, do an instant background check, and walk out of the store, that day, with the gun in your hand. Nice, huh?"

"If you're buying a gun for protection or sport, then it makes sense," said Quinn. "So I guess it depends on how you look at it."

"Maybe you ought to ask Olivia Elliot's son," said Grady. "How he looks at it, I mean."

"Anything else?" said Lydell Blue, cutting the tension that had come to the room.

"Yeah," said Grady. "Anything else you two can tell *me?*"

"I've given you everything, I think," said Strange.

But he hadn't mentioned Donut, Mario's friend. He and

Quinn had agreed: They were saving that bit of information for themselves.

"You think of anything else, let me know," said Grady, pushing two business cards across the table. "I've got to get down to the substation in Six D. They just brought Dewayne in for another go-round. I wanna see his face when we tell him about the gun."

"If I run into Mario," said Strange, sliding his own card in front of Grady, "I'll mention you're looking for him."

"Oh, I'll probably run into him first."

The two men smiled cordially and shook hands at they stood.

"Where you off to?" said Blue.

"Running down to check on the Granville Oliver trial," said Strange.

"Another solid citizen," said Grady. Strange didn't respond.

"I talk to you a minute?" said Blue.

Strange nodded as Quinn and Grady left the room.

"Anything more on that break-in last night?" said Blue.

"I don't expect I'll be hearing anything," said Strange. "It was a professional burglary. I'm not gonna let it interfere with what I'm doin'."

Blue stroked his thick gray mustache. "You mean you're not going to take the warning."

"I've pretty much decided I'm just gonna keep doing my job."

"You can't fight the government, if that's who it is."

"True," said Strange. "But I don't know what else to do."

Strange and Blue, friends for thirty-some-odd years, shook hands.

Quinn was waiting for Strange out in the hall. They took the stairwell down to the first floor.

"Interesting meeting," said Quinn.

"I'm thinking about it," said Strange.

Strange's Caprice was beside Quinn's Chevelle in the lot behind the station. Strange motioned for Quinn to come with him.

"Where we headed?" said Quinn.

"Gotta get myself lookin' right first. Then the office, then downtown."

"We're gonna need two cars today. You and me got different things planned."

"We'll pick yours up later. We're swinging back up here for our lunch appointment anyway."

They settled onto the front bench of the Caprice.

"That Grady guy," said Quinn, "he's the one keeps death photos, like art or something, hanging in his crib."

Strange turned the ignition. "Yeah, that's him."

"Man looks like that actor played in *Walking Tall*. Not Joe Don Baker. Parts two and three, I mean. The ones that sucked."

"Bo something or other," said Strange.

"Derek?"

"Funny."

"It's Svenson, dude."

"That's it. *Damn*." Strange pulled out of the lot. "Was killing me, looking at Grady across that table. I just could not remember that cat's name."

❒

STRANGE had his hair cut and his beard trimmed at Hawk's, then walked to the office, where he met Quinn, who had been making some calls and gathering equipment and files. Greco greeted Strange as he entered the storefront, settling back onto his red cushion after receiving a rub on the head. Lamar Williams was up on a ladder, changing a fluorescent bulb, and Janine was seated behind her desk, tapping the keyboard of her computer.

"Good morning," said Janine. "You look nice."

"My neck itches," said Strange, picking up his messages off Janine's desk. "I'll be right back out."

In his office, Strange looped his belt through the sheath of his Buck knife and retrieved a sand-filled sap from his top desk drawer. He slipped the sap into the back pocket of his jeans and pulled his shirttail out to cover it. He made a phone call, then grabbed some files and other items, and went back out to the front of the shop.

"Here you go," said Janine, handing him a PayDay bar, his favorite snack. "In case you miss a meal."

"Thank you, baby," said Strange. "Stick to your desk if you can today. I'm gonna need to keep in contact with you, hear?"

Strange looked up to Lamar, on the top step of the ladder.

"What's goin' on, boss?" said Lamar.

"What's goin' on with *you?*"

"Keepin' this place clean. Taking care of my mother and my baby sister. Studying for my final tests. Same old same old."

"Were you studying for your tests when I saw you walkin' down Georgia toward the Black Hole the other night?"

"Dag, Mr. Strange, you got eyes everywhere? I was just checking out some go-go they had up in there, wanted to see if I could run into this girl I wanted to get to know. I'm allowed to have some fun, ain't I?"

"Long as you take care of that other stuff you claim you're doing, too."

"I am."

"You keep it up, then."

Quinn got up from his chair, a file in one hand and a fresh pack of sugarless gum in the other.

"Can I get one of them Extras, Terry?" said Lamar.

Quinn handed Lamar a stick of gum. "You ready, Derek?"

Strange nodded. "Let's go."

Out on the street, walking to Strange's car, Quinn said, "You're a little rough on him, aren't you?"

"He thinks I am now," said Strange. "When he's older and he understands what I was trying to do, he'll think of me different."

"The kid's trying, Derek."

"I know he is," said Strange. "Lamar's good."

⊓

ON the way downtown they stopped at the offices of One Kid, One Congregation, below Massachusetts Avenue, where Strange had made a short introductory appointment with Father John Winston, the nonprofit's director. Winston was a former police officer, now a minister, out of a large metropolitan area in the Midwest, who had brought his program to D.C. Strange talked with Winston briefly in the office and knew right away that he liked the man and what he was trying to do. Both were ex-cops, so there was that connection as well.

Back in the Caprice, Strange drove down toward 3rd and Constitution.

"What was that about?" said Quinn.

"Robert Gray," said Strange.

"That boy you inherited from Granville Oliver."

"He's in a bad place right now. I'm gonna try and get him into this program, where a church kind of adopts a kid. It's a citywide thing, and I've heard it works. Might be just what Robert needs. This guy Winston, he's started a similar program for addicts here, too."

"Sounds good."

"If I can swing it, we'll get him into a family up near us, so we can have him on the football team, too."

Quinn looked at his friend across the bench. "Derek Strange, always looking to save the world."

"A kid or two, maybe," said Strange. "That would be enough for me."

c h a p t e r

24

STRANGE and Quinn entered courtroom 19, where the Oliver trial was in progress, after a thorough security check. The heads of a few spectators and several law enforcement types turned as they walked in and took their seats. Strange and Quinn did not return their stares.

Judge Potterfield, rotund and jowly, had asked attorneys from both sides to approach the bench for a consultation. Phillip Wood, sharply dressed and freshly shaved, was on the stand. Granville Oliver sat placidly, his stun belt beneath his blue suit, staring at Wood through nonprescription glasses.

The prosecution's questions for Wood resumed. His testimony had been rehearsed and came off that way. It could have been recorded as a primer for the life, D.C.-style, complete with name checks of familiar clubs, go-go bands, motels, skating rinks, favorite models of automobile, brands of champagne, Calico autos and AK-47s. Wood was asked about Bennett Oliver, and if Granville had ever discussed killing his uncle or having him killed.

"Granville told me he suspected his uncle Bennett was gettin' ready to flip to the Feds," said Wood. "They had his uncle talkin' about a buy on a wiretap and they were gonna send him up. Granville thought his uncle was gonna cut a deal."

"What were Granville's thoughts about that?" said the prosecutor.

"Objection," said Ives. "Mr. Wood's interpretation of the defendant's thoughts calls for speculation."

"I'll rephrase, your honor. Did Granville Oliver ever *say* that he would in any way try to stop his uncle from talking to federal agents?"

"He said it was time for Bennett to be got."

"To be got?" said the prosecutor.

"To be killed. Next thing I heard, Bennett Oliver was dead."

"I see." The prosecutor paused for effect and softened his tone. "Do you love Granville Oliver, Mr. Wood?"

"Yes," said Phillip Wood, looking straight at Oliver. "That's my main boy right there. I love Granville like my own blood."

Oliver's expression remained flat and unreadable.

Judge Potterfield called a short break in the proceedings. Strange caught the eye of Raymond Ives, Oliver's primary defense attorney, and head-motioned him to follow.

Strange and Quinn met Ives, immaculate and trim in a William Fox pinstripe, outside the courthouse. They stood on the sidewalk of Constitution where the bus and car sounds would serve to mute their conversation. A man who looked like a federal cop watched them, standing near the building's front steps among the cigarette smokers, not smoking himself.

"Maybe we should discuss this alone," said Ives.

"I don't have a problem with him being here," said Strange, speaking of Quinn.

"Okay," said Ives. "I went over the message left at your house. You say the voice was the voice of a white man."

"Same one, probably, who called my office on Ninth and spoke to my wife. This is no gang member leaving me death threats. Those boys in Southeast want to fuck with me, they'd do it direct. This here's not their style."

"The voice spoke of your conversation with Kevin Willis down at Leavenworth."

"I got nothing from Willis on the Oliver case."

"Right. I reviewed the transcripts of your tapes."

"And?"

"At several points Willis talks about people in protective who are hot or who are about to flip. He's referencing potential witnesses who have nothing to do with the Oliver trial. These are cases that are still pending, Derek."

"Make your point."

"They have grounds for an obstruction charge."

"You should have warned me about that."

"I did warn you."

"I don't remember you sayin' anything."

"I went over it with you before you left town; it's in my notes of our meeting. Now, understand, if the government wants to go after your license or prosecute you further, they're within their rights to try."

"The Feds had Willis set me up."

"Maybe. That would be damned hard to prove."

"You want me off the case?"

"If you dropped out now, I'd understand. But I need you more than ever. What I'm telling you is, you've got to be aware of the possible situation you have here. Let's assume we're talking about the FBI. They can bug your office, your house, your bedroom, even your car."

"I know all that."

"They can monitor your phone conversations, including

your cell. At the very least you ought to be communicating with your people through pay phones."

"Whatever," said Strange.

"You don't seem too concerned."

"I'm staying on this."

"Okay. Good. When the time comes to resolve your problem, I'll represent you, gratis."

"I was counting on that."

"In the meantime," said Ives, "you heard the testimony in there. I need something from the Stokes girl, if there is anything, right away. Something to refute Phil Wood's testimony that Granville hit his own uncle or had him hit."

"I'm working on it," said Strange.

He asked Ives about what they could do for the girl and her son. Ives described the arrangements that could be made. When he was done he said, "I don't need to tell you to watch your back."

Strange and Ives shook hands. Quinn and Strange walked toward the Caprice.

"Hope you're hungry," said Strange.

"It depends."

"The Three-Star Diner."

"That Greek place where your father worked," said Quinn.

"We're meetin' a Greek," said Strange. "So it makes sense."

❐

THEY sat in a booth, its seats covered in red vinyl, along the window of the Three-Star on Kennedy Street. Quinn had a cheeseburger with mustard and fried onions only, and a side of fries. Strange ate eggs over easy, grilled half smokes, and hash browns, his usual meal.

Sitting across from them was Nick Stefanos. He had the half smokes and hash browns like Strange, but took his eggs scrambled with feta cheese. Both of them had scattered Texas Pete hot sauce liberally atop the dish.

"I remember this place," said Stefanos. "My grandfather knew old man Georgelakos. They went to the same church, St. Sophia. And they were in the same business."

"Your grandfather had a lunch counter?"

"Nick's."

"Fourteenth and S, in Shaw. I can picture the sign out front."

"Right. He used to run up here from time to time. 'I'll be right back; *Kirio* Georgelakos needs a few tomatoes, I'm gonna run some up to him.' Like that."

"That's his son," said Strange, pointing behind the counter to Billy Georgelakos, wide of girth and broad of chest, nearly bald, working with a Bic pen wedged behind his ear. "My father worked here, too. He was the grill man in this place."

"Small town," said Stefanos, smiling pleasantly at Strange.

Stefanos wore a black summer sweater over a white T-shirt, simple 505 jeans, and black oilskin shoes. He kept his hair short and distressed. His face was flecked with scars, white crescents and tiny white lines on olive skin. He wasn't handsome or ugly; his looks would have been unremarkable except for his eyes, which some would have called intense. His height and build were medium, and he kept his stomach reasonably flat for his age. Strange put him in his early forties. He looked as if he had lived a life. Strange could almost see this one as a younger, reckless man. He sensed that Stefanos had been about good times in his youth, and wondered if drugs were his thing today, and if not, what had replaced them. Maybe it was the adrenaline jolt from the job, or something else. Elaine Clay had said that he had his problems with drink.

"Elaine told me you had a wire on the gang situation in Southeast."

"I've been working RICO cases and the Corey Graves thing for a long time. You just naturally pick up a ton of information, and misinformation, when you're canvassing those streets."

"Like any cop," said Quinn.

"Exactly," said Stefanos, looking Quinn over.

"I interviewed Kevin Willis down in Leavenworth recently," said Strange. "Willis was an enforcer with Granville Oliver before he went over to Corey Graves."

"Be careful with Willis. Kid talks so much, you lose track of what he's sayin'. He's charming, but he's got those long teeth, if you know what I mean."

"I got bit, too." Strange told Stefanos about being burgled, and the phone call, and its relation to the Willis tapes.

"So he talked about hot wits in pending cases," said Stefanos. "That's where the obstruction could come in."

"I know it. *Now.*"

"You fucked up."

"Thanks for all your support," said Strange, a dry tone entering his voice. But he liked Stefanos's candor.

Billy Georgelakos's longtime waitress, Ella, came to the table with a pot of coffee and refilled their cups with a shaking hand. Stefanos thanked her as she poured, tapping unconsciously on the hardpack of Marlboro reds set on the table beside his plate.

"Tell me what you know about Horace McKinley," said Strange.

"Yuma Mob," said Stefanos. "You remember that Cary Grant movie *Mr. Lucky?*"

"Was there a horse in it?" said Quinn.

"If they were gonna remake that movie," said Stefanos, "they'd put Horace McKinley in the title role. He's got that rep. Been hard-busted a few times, but nothing seems to stick."

"Why's that?" said Strange.

"Could be he has good attorneys; could be no one can get any wits to post. Could be he's connected in others ways, too."

"As in, some kind of law with juice has the finger on him."

"I can't say." Stefanos pointed his fork at Strange. "You don't know too much, huh?"

"I know some. My wife, Janine, she works for me. She dug

up plenty of good information since yesterday. But I'm trying to piece all the players together down there. You know I'm working the Granville Oliver trial."

"For Ray Ives."

"Uh-huh. So keep in mind that everything I'm looking for, it's got to go back to Granville."

"Most things do in that part of the world. Granville was the king for a good while down there, and he went deep into the community. Take McKinley. He got put on and brought up by Granville when Horace wasn't much more than a fat kid."

"That would mean McKinley knew Phil Wood, too."

"Phillip Wood," said Stefanos. "As in the cat who's flipping on Granville as we speak."

"The same."

Stefanos closed his eyes as he took in a forkful of half smoke and chewed. "*Damn,* that's good."

"My father's signature," said Strange. "Keep talking about McKinley."

"What I hear, Horace is standing tall with Phil Wood. He figures that Granville is gonna get the needle or life without parole, so there's no upside with him. McKinley runs Yuma, but his loyalty's with Phil. Like I say, this is only what I hear."

"That would explain his intimidation," said Strange.

"It could explain it," said Stefanos. "You'd have to go deeper than you been going to find out for sure."

"How do you know all this?" said Quinn.

"I keep my ears open all the time. Stand by the pay phones and talk into a dead receiver, shop in those neighborhood markets for nothing. Ride the Green Line once in a while and listen. Young men down there talk about the day-to-day rumors of gang business every day, the way other young men talk about sports."

"That's your secret? Take the Green Line train and keep your ears open?"

"My main secret? My snitches. I can ride the Metro all I

want, but without informants I wouldn't have shit. I hand out a lot of twenty-dollar bills, Terry."

Stefanos returned his attention to his plate.

"What about Dewayne Durham?" said Quinn.

They waited for Stefanos to swallow another mouthful of food. He started to speak, then raised one finger to hold them off and finished his meal. He pushed the plate away from him and centered his coffee cup where the plate had been.

"What was the question?"

"Dewayne Durham."

"Yeah, Dewayne. Runs the Six Hundred Crew. Same kind of business, marijuana sales mostly. The two gangs work different strips. I hear they even work out of abandoned houses, one on Yuma and one on Atlantic, and stare at each other across the same alley. Once in a while they cross paths and shots get fired."

"Like last night," said Strange.

"I heard. Four dead — over nothing, most likely. A hard look, or someone walked down the wrong street, whatever. Just another war story to tell around the campfire. Like boys coming home from battle, wearing the medals and the uniforms, getting the eyes from the ladies. That little window of glory. Something to show that they were here. That's all this is, you know? It doesn't have a goddamn thing to do with drugs."

"In my time," said Strange, "they would have met somewhere and gone with their hands to see who could take who."

"Guns make the man now," said Stefanos.

"Nothing wrong with guns," said Quinn. "It's the ones using them make the difference."

"You don't have to tell me," said Stefanos. "I'm a man. I like the way a gun feels in my hand and I like the way it feels when I squeeze the trigger. I've used guns when I had to. But we're not talking about hunting or target practice, and this isn't the open country. It's an East Coast city with plenty of poverty. Guns don't belong here."

"That's why they're illegal in D.C., I guess."

"You'd never know it, with all the pieces on the street. All these fat-shit congressmen, blaming culture and rap music for the murder rate while they got their hands out to the gun manufacturers and their lobbyists. Don't you think that's wrong?"

"I guess we've got a difference of opinion."

Strange cleared his throat. "Let's get back to Dewayne Durham. Dewayne's got an older brother. Little guy, looks like a beaver, goes by Mario?"

"I don't know him," said Stefanos.

"We're kinda lookin' for him on something else," said Strange. "No one's gonna help us out, on account of who his brother is, and I figure by now Dewayne has put him underground."

"The cops'll get him."

"We want to get to him first. It's crazy, I know. But it'll make us feel better if we do."

"Go out and find some rumors, then," said Stefanos. "You guys ever used to congregate at a liquor store or a beer market when you were younger, to find out where the action was for the night?"

"Country Boy in Layhill," said Quinn.

"For me it was Morris Miller's," said Stefanos. "In Anacostia it's Mart Liquors, at Malcolm X and Martin Luther King. Or any bank of pay phones. The gas stations are good for that. Bring plenty of cash, and don't forget the diplomacy. And humility, too."

"Fuck humility," said Quinn.

"Suit yourself. Me, I want to be around at the end of the race." Stefanos looked from one man to the other. "You guys are busy."

"The gun in that shooting last night," said Strange, "it matches a gun used by Mario Durham in another killing."

"Like I say, I don't know him." Stefanos shrugged. "My advice would be to follow the gun."

"I've been thinking the same way."

Stefanos picked up his pack of 'Boros, then put it back down.

He looked at Quinn, back at Strange, and back at Quinn once more, squinting his eyes. "You're the cop who shot that other cop a couple of years ago, aren't you?"

"I got cleared," said Quinn, his own eyes narrowing. "You're pretty direct, aren't you?"

"People say I am. To a fault sometimes."

Quinn leaned back in his seat. "It's better that way, I guess."

"You look like you could use a smoke," said Strange to Stefanos.

"I've got to get going anyway."

"I'll walk you out."

Stefanos slid out of the booth and shook Quinn's hand. "Nice meeting you, man."

"You, too."

Stefanos stopped and looked at the photograph mounted on the wall by the front door. In it, a tall black man stood by the grill beside a short Greek, both of them in aprons. Stefanos saw the resemblance of the Greek to his larger son behind the counter; in the tall man he saw Derek Strange.

"That's him," said Strange. "That's my father right there."

"*Yasou,* Derek," said Billy Georgelakos from across the store.

"*Yasou, Vasili,*" said Strange, pointing to the booth where Quinn still sat. "Give the check to my son over there, hear?"

"You speak Greek?" said Stefanos.

"A few key phrases. I know what you folks call a black man — the nice word, I mean. I know how to call someone a jerk-off, and I know the word for, uh, pussy."

"Prove it."

"*Mavros, malaka,* and *moonee.*"

"The three M's. You're just about fluent."

"It'll come in handy, I happen to get over to Athens for the Olympics."

Out on Kennedy, Stefanos put fire to a smoke. He took the first drag in and held it deep. Strange stood beside him, watching.

"Tastes good, huh?"

"After a spicy meal like that? Damn right." Stefanos gave Strange the once-over and smiled. "Strange Investigations. I drive by your place all the time."

"You know my sign?"

"Magnifying glass over half the letters. How'd you ever come up with that?"

"That logo with the guy smoking the pipe, wearing that hat's got two bills on it? It was taken."

"Maybe I'll stop by sometime."

"If the light in the sign's turned on, I'm in. You're welcome anytime."

"How about your partner? Think he wants me around?"

"I think he liked you, to tell you the truth. Terry's carrying some baggage with him, is what it is."

"Aren't we all." Stefanos dragged on his cigarette, looked at it, and hit it again.

"Just so you know, you and me got some similar opinions about guns. I figure, we sat down in a bar together, we might have a lot to talk about."

"I'm trying to stay out of bars. But I wouldn't mind hooking up with you sometime."

"You know, I'm working this death penalty case for a reason."

"Another thing we agree on. It's why I'm on the Corey Graves thing. The federal prosecutors were looking to make it a capital case and they just got the go-ahead from the attorney general."

"I heard."

"There's been too much death in this city already, Derek. I've had enough of it."

"I have, too."

"The neighborhoods you guys work, your partner's gotta be careful, with that personality of his. He shows some smarts and less emotion, he's gonna live longer."

"I tell him all the time."

"I remember what that guy went through, with the news-papers and television and all, after he shot that other cop. He's got some shit flying around in his head; it's understandable. For what it's worth, I liked him, too."

"Don't forget to stop by. Ninth and Upshur."

"I'll be around."

"Thanks for your help, Nick."

Stefanos shook Strange's outstretched hand and said, "Right."

Strange watched him walk toward a Mopar muscle car, a white-over-red Dodge with aftermarket Magnum 500 wheels. He listened to the cook of the Detroit engine and went back into the diner. Quinn was dropping money on the table, a toothpick rolling in his mouth.

"You ready?" said Quinn. "I need to pick up my car."

Strange nodded. "Let's go to work."

25

BERNARD Walker waited in the idling Benz as Dewayne Durham walked out of the Sixth District substation on Pennsylvania Avenue in Southeast. He could see that screwed-up look on Dewayne's face, which meant confusion. Trouble, something to do with his family. Often it was his mother, always needin' something. Money, jewelry, clothes, a ride to church. But today it was that brother of his, who'd fucked up big with that girl. When the police had called him into the station that morning — "You wanna come in, Dewayne, or should we send a car to pick you up?" — they said it had to do with Mario. Somethin' about an "interesting" new development they had in the case.

"Everything all right?" said Walker, so tall in the driver's seat that his hair was touching the headliner of the car.

"Mario," said Durham, as if that were explanation enough. He reached to the radio and turned down the sound.

"Well?"

"The gun he used to kill that bitch? It was the same gun Jerome used on that Coates cousin."

"Same model?"

"Same exact *gun.*"

"Foreman's woman said that gun was clean."

"I know it. Foreman told her it was. He took a gun had a body on it, a murder gun attached to my own brother, and sold it to Long. Why you think he'd want to put me in that kind of situation?"

"Maybe he didn't know."

"Could be he didn't. Or maybe someone wanted to see me get jammed up."

"You think Foreman would set you up like that? Why?"

"That's what I need to find out."

"We better go talk to your brother," said Walker.

"Nah, uh-uh. I don't trust what he'll tell me, scared as he is. And I don't trust myself to be around him right now. I'm tellin' you, Zu, I'm about to kill a motherfucker today. I see him and he starts to lie, I might just go ahead and dead my own brother. I don't want to do that to my moms."

"We could talk to his fool friend, see if Mario said anything about it to him."

"Yeah," said Durham. "Let's do that."

❐

DONUT'S apartment was dirty and it smelled like resin and cigarettes. A window air conditioner ran low and kept the smell in the two-bedroom unit. Donut sat on the couch, wires and controllers around him from the PlayStation 2 connected to his TV. Normally these things were on the living-room table in front of the couch, along with his ashtray and other smoking paraphernalia, his cell, and his CD and game cases. But Bernard Walker had kicked the table over on its side as soon as Donut had let him in, and now Donut's shit was scattered about the room.

"I don't know nothin'," said Donut. His hands were between his thighs, and he was scissoring his knees together compulsively while staring straight ahead.

Walker bent his long torso forward so that he could speak softly to the ugly man on the couch. "We ain't asked you nothin' yet."

"Go ahead and ask me whateva. I got no call to lie."

"Just wanted to come by and thank you for looking after my brother like you did," said Dewayne Durham, standing beside Walker, his voice friendly and calm.

"This how y'all thank me?" said Donut, his hands spread toward the mess on the living-room floor.

"I got a couple of questions for you, is all," said Durham. "Answer straight, and we'll be gone."

"I'm listenin'."

"That gun my brother had, the one he used on that girl. He tell you where he got it from?"

"That Foreman dude," said Donut.

"Good. You doin' all right. Keep answering fast like that and don't think too hard before you do. Now, Mario say anything about his conversation with Foreman? When he returned the gun to him, I mean."

"Like what?"

"Like, did Foreman know that Mario had used that gun on the girl?"

Donut nodded quickly. "He said Foreman knew it was a murder gun. He knew."

Durham looked over at Walker, who nodded one time. They stood there for a while, saying nothing. Donut guessed they were deciding what to do with him. He knew a lot of shit. He prayed they wouldn't kill him for what he knew. And now he had put the finger on Foreman, too, that big horse, used to be a cop. But he could worry about Foreman later. First thing was, he needed to get out of this situation right here.

"Donut?" said Durham.

"Huh?"

"Listen close."

"I am."

"You know where Mario's at?"

Donut knew. He knew the address of that girl he was stayin' with and he knew the phone number, too. It was written down on a pad of paper, lying somewhere on the floor with everything else. Mario had called him that morning, talkin' about the girl and how her ass looked in her jeans, and also about the trouble he was in. But Donut wasn't about to tell Dewayne Durham all that.

"No," said Donut. "I ain't talked to him since he left out of here."

"That's good for you," said Walker. "You need to keep it that way."

"You know I will."

"And you do see him again," said Durham, "you don't want to be getting him involved in that dummy bullshit you peddlin' out on the street."

"I wouldn't do that."

"Aiight, then," said Durham. "You got my cell number, case you remember anything else?"

"Mario wrote it down. I know where it is."

"Let's go, Zu."

Walker stepped on Donut's case for NBA Street and broke it on the way out the door.

In the Benz, Dewayne Durham used his cell to phone Ulysses Foreman. Walker listened to Durham question Foreman about the gun. Durham's voice was cool and controlled. He never raised it once, not even at the end, when he said to Foreman, "We ain't settled this yet."

"What'd he say?"

"Said he knew the gun had been fired, but Mario told him he was just testin' it, like it was the Fourth of July, sumshit like that."

"So he says he didn't know."

Durham nodded. "That's what he says."

❐

DONUT looked through the slots of his venetian blinds, waiting for the Benz to leave his parking lot. When he was sure they were gone, Donut phoned his friend.

"Mario."

"Dough?"

"Your brother was here, askin' about some shit. That gun you used? Maybe it got used in another murder or somethin' after you turned it in."

"I ain't know nothin' about that."

"I ain't say you did."

"Why was he buggin', then?"

"I don't know. He was just *agitated* and shit."

Donut listened to dead air. He could almost see Mario, his mouth open, staring into space, walking around the room with the cordless in his hand, the other hand in his pocket, jingling change.

"What else is goin' on?" said Mario.

"What else? Mario, you wanted for *murder.*"

"I know it."

"Look here, Mario, those rocks I gave you? Throw that shit away, man. The vials, too, everything. Your brother don't want you fuckin' with no dummies."

"Yeah, okay. Dewayne didn't rough you or nothin', did he?"

"Nah," said Donut. "That Bigfoot-lookin' motherfucker of his, though, he broke my game case. Just, like, *stepped* on it."

"Madden?"

"NBA Street."

"That shits was already broke."

"That ain't the point." Donut rubbed his finger along his jawline. "So how's that girl Dewayne put you in with?"

"She's at work."

"How *is* she, though? Is she fine?"

"Yeah," said Mario. "I already told you, she got a nice round onion on her, man."

"I just like thinkin' about it."

"Donut?"

"What?"

"Don't give me up. You know I can't do no time."

Donut said, "You're my boy."

◘

STRANGE sat behind the wheel of his Caprice in the parking lot of the St. Elizabeth's McDonalds, the Aiwa minirecorder in his hand barely making a sound as the tape whirred, recording the conversation in the car. Devra Stokes was beside him on the bench. Her son, Juwan, sat in the back, diligently working on a cup of soft chocolate ice cream, humming to himself from time to time. It was hot inside the car; Strange had kept the windows rolled up most of the way in an effort to reduce the ambient noise.

"And he said this where?" said Strange.

"This one time?" said Devra.

"This time you distinctly remember."

"Me and Phil were in his car, the Turbo Z. The one Granville had bought him? We were out in the lot of Crystal Skate. Back around then, that used to be where the mob liked to hang. I liked to roller-skate then, and so did Phil. Phil was good."

"Do you have a date on this?"

"Not exactly. It was, like, a few days before Bennett Oliver got murdered in his Jag."

"Why do you remember that so clearly?"

"'Cause when it happened, I thought of Phil right away."

"Why?"

"This night at the skating park, Phil had drunk some wine and had a little smoke. We was in his Z that night, just talkin'. Phil said to me that Bennett had been caught on a wiretap. He said that Granville believed his uncle was gonna flip on him to the Feds, one of those plea-outs they do."

"And?"

"Phil said that Bennett needed to be got."

"To be murdered, right?"

Devra nodded.

"Answer for the tape, please, Devra."

"Yes, to be murdered."

"Did Phil say he was going to do it himself?"

"Yes. Phil said he was the one that would put the work in."

"Clarify, please."

"Phillip Wood told me that he was gonna kill Bennett Oliver."

"Why him? Why not Granville?"

"Phil said it would be good for him to do it. Good for his career, I mean. It would remove another person above him, make him closer to Granville. In Granville's eyes, it would make him his main boy."

"Were there other instances where Phil talked about this plan?"

"I guess. But I don't remember, like, specific. The night at Crystal Skate, it sticks in my mind."

"And what happened next?"

Devra shrugged. "Bennett got shot."

"Did Phil Wood say he'd done it?"

"No. After, he never said nothin' about it again. And I didn't ask. I just thought, you know, since he'd told me he was gonna do it, that he'd been the one. I figured it was better I didn't know for sure. I'd seen what happened to some other people, knew too much."

Strange shut off the recorder. "Thank you, Devra. That's good. That's exactly what we need."

"Will I testify?"

"Yes, I think you will. My wife will have the subpoena today. It's not that we're against you; it's only to make it official."

"And then what?"

"I talked to Ray Ives. They're going to get you and Juwan into an apartment, probably over in Northwest. Not the Section Eights. A step or two up."

"What, I get a new name or somethin'?"

"No, it's not like that. You keep your name and you're not under any kind of guard. Witnesses are relocated in this city all the time. Long as you're in another quadrant and you go about your life quietly, usually it's fine."

"Usually."

"Right."

"You know, living here in Southeast, you hear all about what happens to people who are hot. That Corey Graves thing?"

"I'm familiar with it," said Strange.

"They got him charged with a whole lot of stuff besides the drug business he was runnin'. Witness intimidation. Hiding witnesses. Not to mention all the beef murders he did."

"I'm not gonna lie to you. I know it's risky, and so do you. Question is, why are you being so courageous?"

Devra looked out the window. "'Cause that motherfucker threatened me. He threatened my *son*, Mr. Strange. He talked mad shit about my mother, too. And he did things to me he shouldn't have done."

"Horace McKinley."

"That's right."

"*What* did he do?"

Devra turned her head so that she faced him. "He put his hand on my privates and rubbed it there. He pinched one of my nipples until it hurt so bad I wanted to cry out. But I didn't cry out. I kept it in. That fat man with his *ci*gar breath, up in my face. I could have killed him then, I had a way. I had so much hate in me."

"Where does he stay at?" said Strange. He heard a catch in his voice and swallowed, checking his anger.

"I don't know. He hangs with his boys over on Yuma, the six hundred block, in a house, looks like a crack house with all that plywood in the windows, during the day."

Strange touched Devra's forearm. "I'm sorry you had to go through that. I admire you, the way you stood strong."

"I'm ashamed for what I did when I was younger. Who I hung with, too. But that will never be me again. Just to do nothing, try to put it behind me, it's not enough. I figure, sometimes you got to *do* something. Isn't that right?"

"You're a brave young woman."

"Not really. Maybe I'm just foolish, like I always been."

"I don't think so."

"Anyway, what should I do now? Just go back to work?"

"Yes, for right now. How long you on for?"

"Till closing time. She stays open till ten o'clock."

"You don't want anyone to think anything's wrong. I'll call you later at your place and tell you about the next step and the arrangements we've made."

"Mom," said Juwan, "this ite cream's good."

"I know it, baby," said Devra, looking over the seat and smiling at her son.

"You're keeping him with you?" said Strange.

"Yes."

"What did you tell Inez today when you left?"

"That I was taking a break."

"She wouldn't follow you?"

"She was the only one in the shop. She wouldn't leave it for nothin'; that shop is everything to her."

"That's a bad little woman right there. My wife works for me, and she did some checking on Inez Brown. Assault priors, check kiting, everything."

"I'm not surprised." Devra's eyes took all of him in. It was an unexpectedly uncomfortable moment, and Strange shifted in his seat. "So you're gonna look after me yourself?"

"Me and my partner. A guy named Terry Quinn."

"Where's he at?"

"Here in Southeast. We're workin' on a couple of things today."

"You ever lose a witness?" said Devra.

"I've made mistakes," said Strange, thinking of Olivia Elliot. "But I'm not gonna lose you."

❐

FROM her car on the street, a forest green Hyundai, Inez Brown watched the parking lot of McDonald's. She had put the Hyundai along the curb just right, so she could see the white Caprice, its tail facing her. She could see Strange and the girl, and the top of the boy's head in the backseat. But she figured, the way she was behind him, way back on the street, he'd be awfully lucky to notice her car, if Strange even knew what kind of car she drove.

Devra had said she was goin' out for lunch and some ice cream for the boy. That's where she'd fucked up. 'Cause Inez knew the little kid, ran that mouth of his all day long, liked that Golden Arches ice cream best.

Inez sat on a couple of cushions so she could see over the wheel. She had good eyes. She could see the two of them, the fake cop and the girl, lippin' in the front seat of his car. That's all the fat man had asked her to do: find out if these two were still talking, even after she'd been warned. Stupid little bitch, with her young ass, too.

Inez checked her watch. She'd done her job and now she needed to get back. She didn't like to be away from her business, not even for a few minutes. No telling the customers she'd lost, doing this thing right here. She'd head back to the salon now. Phone Horace when she got there, tell him what he wanted to know.

26

QUINN put time in out front of Mart Liquors, talking to some of the men and women who were entering and leaving the shop. He spoke to the regulars who hung outside the place as well. Quinn asked them about Mario Durham and a guy named Donut. He showed them the flyer of the missing teenager, Linda Welles. Some answered politely and some were bordering on hostile, and a few didn't bother to respond to his questions at all. He got nothing from any of them. They had made him straight off as some kind of cop.

He tried the Metro station. He tried the phone banks at the gas stations and accompanying convenience marts. He received the same nonresponse.

Quinn drove the neighborhoods next. He had no plan. He cruised Stanton Road, passing liquor stores and squat redbrick structures surrounded by black iron fences. He went down Southern Avenue, then got on Naylor Road. On Naylor were more liquor stores, Laundromats, and other service-oriented businesses. Around 30th Street, on a long hill, were the Naylor Gardens apartments, a complex as well tended and green as a college campus. Farther along, up past Naylor Plaza, the apartments abruptly went from clean and pampered to ghetto grim. And farther still were a couple of stand-alone units like those Quinn had visited several times before.

He slowed his Chevelle and idled it on the street. This was the complex that Linda Welles's brothers had recognized in the sex video. The party had been held in one of these units. It was where she had last been seen.

Quinn looked up a rise of dirt and weeds to a three-story bunker of brick. On the stoop sat several young men wearing wife-beaters and low-hung jeans revealing the elastic bands of their boxers, skullies and napkin bandannas. They were passing around a bottle in a brown bag. They looked down at the street, where Quinn's engine rumbled. One of them, a heavyset young man with blown-out hair, looked directly at Quinn and smiled.

Quinn pulled off from the curb. He had tried to interview that group earlier, remembered the smiler and his hair. He had had the sense then that they knew something about the fate of Linda Welles, but he hadn't pushed it. He hadn't done his job. He remembered feeling weak and punked as he'd driven away from them the last time. And he felt that way now.

Quinn drove over to the area of Valley Green. He pulled the Chevelle up along some street-side kids on their bikes. He asked about Mario Durham and "a dude named Donut." He got some shrugs and smart remarks, and watched impotently as the kids rode away, doing wheelies, laughing, cutting on one another and the white man in the old car.

He parked at a small market and went inside. He questioned the woman behind the counter and got a shrug. He bought a pack of sugarless gum and thanked her for her time. Then he walked next door, into a Chinese carryout, where a thin man with fat freckles across the bridge of his wide nose stood in a small lobby in front of a Plexiglas wall with a lazy Susan in it. A Chinese woman stood behind the Plexiglas; her smile was welcoming, but her eyes were not. She looked friendly and frightened, both at once. Quinn got the woman's attention and talked into a slotted opening above the lazy Susan.

"I'm looking for a guy named Mario Durham," said Quinn.

"I don't know."

"How about a man they call Donut?"

"You want food?"

Quinn looked down at the linoleum floor and shook his head.

"*I* know Donut," said the man with the freckles. "Boy owes me ten dollas."

Quinn turned. "You know where he lives?"

"The building he lives in ain't but two blocks from here. I don't know the apartment number where he stays at, though."

"The building's good enough. He owes you ten?"

"Boy took me for a Hamilton, like, a year ago. He thinks I forgot. But I'm gonna get it someday."

"You'll get that ten sooner than someday," said Quinn, "you give me the address."

"Make it twenty," said the man, "and I'll give it to you now."

⌐

HOMICIDE Detective Nathan Grady got a break soon after meeting with Strange and Quinn. A young man named Richard Swales, picked up on an intent-to-distribute beef, had offered his help, in exchange for some "consideration," in locating Mario Durham. He told the arresting officer that he knew from talk on the street that Durham was wanted in a murder. From the substation, where they were keeping Swales in a holding cell, Grady was called and told of the lead. Grady said he'd be right in.

In the interview room, Swales admitted that he did not know Mario Durham personally or his whereabouts. But there was a guy folks called Donut, Durham's "main boy," who most likely could point the police in the right direction. Grady learned that Donut's real name was Terrence Dodson. He asked Swales where he could find Dodson. Swales said that he didn't know, but he knew the "general area he stayed at."

"Can I get some love?" said Swales.

Grady said that if the information he'd given him was correct, and if it led to an arrest, yes, it could help Swales's case.

That's all Grady had been looking for. Someone less afraid of Dewayne Durham than he was of prison. A two-time loser about to strike out. It was how most cases were solved.

It took a hot minute to find Terrence Dodson's address in Valley Green and get a record of his priors. Grady took his unmarked and, accompanied by a cruiser and a couple of uniformed officers, went to the address. One of the uniforms stayed out on the street with the cars. The other uniform went with Grady into the building, where they found Dodson's apartment door. Grady knocked, the uniform behind him, and the door soon opened. As it did, Grady flashed his badge.

"Terrence Dodson?" said Grady, looking down on the small, ugly man who stood in the door frame, one eye twitching, trying to manage a smile.

"That's my given name. Ain't nobody ever call me that, though."

Grady slipped his badge case back into his jacket. "Donut, then, right?"

"That's right."

"You know a Mario Durham?"

"Why?" said Donut, chuckling weakly. "He done somethin'? What, that fool spit on the sidewalk, sumshit like that?"

"Mind if I come in?"

"You got a warrant?" Donut barked out a laugh. "I'm just playing with you, officer, *I* got nothin' to hide."

Donut stepped aside to let the white man pass. Big motherfucker, too. Looked like that man played in the sequels to that movie with Felton Perry, about the redneck sheriff with the bat. The ones that weren't no good.

❐

HORACE McKinley sat in a vinyl nail-studded chair meant to look like leather in what used to be the living room of the house on Yuma. He talked on his cell as Mike Montgomery paced the room.

McKinley flipped the StarTAC closed. His forehead was beaded with sweat. There was sweat under his arms and it ran down his sides.

It had been a busy morning. He had learned from his own boys that Mario Durham was wanted in a murder. He had spoken to Ulysses Foreman, who had taken a call from Dewayne Durham, angry that the gun used by Mario had also been Jerome Long's murder gun in the Coates killings. Foreman had called McKinley to give his condolences on the cousins, and also to assure him that he hadn't known, of course, that one of his guns would be used against the Yuma Mob. McKinley saw an opportunity for an alliance with Foreman, and maybe to gain a favor or something free. He told Foreman that this was simply the cost of doing business for both of them and that no offense had been taken. And now that little old girl, ran his salon, had phoned with some disturbing news.

"That was Inez," said McKinley. "The Stokes girl's been talking to that Strange again."

"What're we gonna do?"

McKinley breathed in deeply and heard a wheeze in his chest. He was carrying too much weight. Now would be a good time to give up on those Cubans, too.

"Ice her down for a while, I guess."

"Kill her?"

"No, I don't want to kill the bitch 'less I have to. I was

thinkin' we'd hide her until she comes around. I figure, we separate her from her little boy for a few hours, she'll change her mind about talking anymore."

"We could use some help."

"The troops been depleted, Mike. I got everyone on the street and I told them I needed a big cash night. It's just you and me."

"You want me to stay with the kid?"

"You'd do better with him than I will. Me, I'm better with the girls." McKinley smiled at Montgomery, who was frowning. His long hands were jammed deep in the pockets of his jeans. "You gonna hold that boy tight? I don't want you gettin' soft on me now. This is business here; that's all it is. We got to protect our own and what we got."

Montgomery nodded. McKinley was only a couple of years his senior, but he was the closest thing to a father he'd ever had.

"I'm behind you, Hoss. You know this."

"No doubt. You my right hand, Mike."

"We gonna do this now?"

"No. We can get over to the salon later, take care of the girl. She ain't goin' nowhere else today."

"What we gonna do now, then?"

"Let's roll over to Foreman's first and buy us another gun. I spoke to him, and he's still got this Sig I had my eye on for a while. He's expecting another piece later on today, too, case we need it. He's got a boy he uses, gonna make a run."

Montgomery pulled the keys to the Benz from his pocket and twirled them on his finger. "I'm ready."

"We gonna have us our little war, I guess."

"Might not happen too soon. Durham's got his head turned around, lookin' after that fool brother of his."

"That might be the time to hit him," said McKinley, rising laboriously from the chair. "While he's weak."

◫

ULYSSES Foreman stood on the back deck of his house, smoking a cigar. Ashley was back in their room, packing for her trip down to her daddy's in southern Maryland. She had the stereo on in there, Chaka Khan singin' about "I'm every woman," Ashley singing along. She loved Chaka. So did Ulysses, back when she was with Rufus. That was a fine motherfucker right there.

Foreman held one arm out and flexed as he drew on his cigar. He needed to get over to the gym, looked like he was starting to atrophy. Man had to pay attention to his body, especially in times like these.

It had been a morning. A call from Dewayne Durham about that brother of his and that goddamn gun. That was his own fault, renting the Taurus to Twigs. Once a fuck-up, et cetera. Foreman should have known. Apparently Mario had claimed that he knew about the gun being hot, too. Foreman had told Dewayne that this wasn't so, but he wasn't sure it had registered all the way. Now he'd have to do something for Dewayne just to keep his fire down. A gift, *that* would work; he could lay a gun on him, nothing too expensive, but no cheap-ass Lorcin, either, nothin' like that. The kid from Alexandria was making a run for him today; he'd have him pick something up.

Then he'd talked to Horace McKinley, who had acted all unconcerned that he had sold that gun to Durham's boy Jerome Long, who'd gone and used it on the cousins. The fat man *acting* unconcerned, but always strategizing. Foreman wondered what he'd want in the end.

Foreman moved his head around some, back and forth, trying to get the ache out his neck. Shit was just building *up*.

"I'm ready," said Ashley, behind him.

He hadn't heard her, with all that thinking he'd been doing. But he could smell that body spray she liked, raspberry, from that "collection" of Nubian Goddess fragrances she bought at the CVS.

Foreman turned. She had on some shorts-and-top thing, looked like pajamas to him. When he'd said so she'd laughed and told him that it was a daytime outfit she'd bought at Penney's. She was carrying a glass of chardonnay in one hand, had one of her Viceroys in the other.

"You done packing?"

"Said I was ready, sugar. I was wondering, should I take my gun?"

"Leave it," said Foreman. "You won't need it down on that farm, anyway. And the way you drive with that lead foot of yours, you might get pulled over. No reason to risk that."

Ashley moved forward, held her cigarette away so that the smoke didn't crawl up into his eyes. He could smell the wine and nicotine on her breath as she kissed him deep. The woman could hoover a man's tongue. He had hit it that morning, just a couple of hours ago, but he felt himself growing hard again. He reached down and stroked the back of her thighs, felt the ridges and pocks there. He liked everything about her, even those marks.

"I love you, Ulee."

"I know you do."

"Couldn't you just say it back?"

"I show you every day, don't I?"

"Wish you could come with me."

"So do I, but I got business to attend to. Keep your cell on, hear?"

"I will."

"You always *say* you will, but then I get that voice says, Leave a message."

"I'll keep it on."

"I'll call you later."

From the front steps, he watched her pull away in that Cougar of hers, feeling strange as she turned onto Wheeler Road, like maybe he should have gone with her this time, just gotten the fuck away. But this house, the woods, the seclusion, it had all been bought with sweat and hard work; none of it came easy. You needed to remember how much you loved your lifestyle when it came time to protect it. That's why, despite the funny rumbling in his gut, he was hanging back here today.

A car soon came down the drive, that boy was gonna make the buy and some girl he knew. A little while from now, Foreman figured, McKinley and that sidekick of his, one with the long arms they called Monkey, they were gonna be rollin' in here, too.

◻

DETECTIVE Nathan Grady stood over Donut, who sat on the couch. Donut had invited Grady to have a seat with him, but Grady had said that he preferred to stand. Always look down on the person you were interviewing, and crowd them when you could.

Donut's legs were scissoring back and forth, and sweat had formed on his upper lip, betraying his friendly, accommodating smile.

"So you don't know about the whereabouts of your friend Mario."

"Nah, uh-uh."

"And you weren't aware that he was wanted on a murder?"

"No, I wasn't aware of that situation right there."

"Seems like everybody in Anacostia's heard about it but you."

"Now that you tell me, though, I feel real bad about that girl got herself dead."

"You haven't heard from your friend in the past few days, have you?"

"Been a long while. I was just wonderin' today where he been at."

"I suppose we could go into your phone records. Ask around with your neighbors, too. Maybe they've seen him coming in and out of here."

"You should. I'd like to know my own self where he is."

Grady rocked back on the heels of his Rocksports. He looked back at the uniformed officer standing by the door, then lifted his head and made a show of sniffing the air. Donut watched him, thinking, Here it comes.

"That marijuana I smell, *Dough*-nut?"

"I don't smell nothin'."

"You got some priors, so it made me think, you know, you might still be dealing."

"That was the old me. I been rehabilitated. And I go to church now, too."

"So you wouldn't mind if I looked around?"

Donut shrugged. This motherfucker did find something, it wouldn't be but an ounce or so. What they call personal-use stuff. He'd be on the street in an hour, and the charge would get thrown out, anyway, come court date. He knew it, and so did this bobo with a shield. As for the stuff he had that looked like crack, shit, that wasn't nothin' but baking soda cooked hard. Make them all look stupid when they got it back to the lab.

"You know what an accessory-to-homicide conviction would do to you, with your history?"

"I got an idea. But, see, I don't know where Mario is."

"We're gonna talk again. You're holding out on me, it's not gonna go your way come sentencing time."

"You find Mario," said Donut, "let me know. He borrowed a shirt from me and didn't return it. A Sean John — wasn't cheap, either."

"Anything else?" said Grady, his jaw tight.

"Boy owes me five dollas, too."

❐

QUINN drove down the block, saw the unmarked with the GT plates and the 6D cruiser outside Donut's building, and kept his foot on the gas. He turned the corner and idled the Chevelle against the curb. He phoned Strange on his cell.

"Derek."

"Terry, what's going on?"

"I found the building where Mario's friend Donut lives. But I think Grady or some other cop might have found him first. They got cars outside the place now."

"We can visit him later on."

"Where are you?"

"I'm tailing Horace McKinley as we speak. I waited for him near his place on Yuma after I finished up with Devra Stokes. I followed him and his boy when they drove out in their Benz."

"And?"

"They're headed out of the city, going onto Wheeler Road right now. Passing a Citgo station . . ."

"Stay several car lengths back and try not to get made."

"Funny," said Strange.

"Want me to meet you?"

"I'll call you in a few minutes. There they go, they're turning."

"Into where?"

Quinn waited. He could almost see Derek's face, intense, as he watched the car up ahead.

"Looks to me," said Strange, "like they're driving right into the woods."

27

STRANGE parked his Caprice beside the Citgo station, near the rest rooms and out of sight. He grabbed his 10 × 50 binoculars from the trunk, locked the car down, jogged around a fenced-in area holding a propane tank, and ran into the woods. He went diagonally in the direction that McKinley and his sidekick had gone, hoping that they were headed for a house set back not too far off Wheeler Road. He crashed through the forest like a hooved animal, unconcerned with the noise he made, and saw brighter light about a quarter mile in. He slowed his pace, approaching the light, which he knew to be a clearing, with care.

Strange took position behind the trunk of a large oak. A brick rambler, looked like it had some kind of deck on the back of it, stood in the clearing at the end of a circular drive. Parked in the drive were a late-model red El Dorado, McKinley's black Benz, and a green Avalon with aftermarket alloy wheels.

Strange looked into his binos. McKinley and his sidekick,

young dude with some long-ass arms, were getting out of the Benz. McKinley, big as he was, and with a strained look on his face, tired from all that weight, was getting out more slowly than the other young man.

There were three people standing at the top of the rambler's steps, on a small concrete porch under a pink awning. The color of the awning told Strange that a woman lived in the house. Two of the three people, a handsome young man and an attractive woman, were in their early twenties. The third was a bulked-up man heading toward the finish line of his thirties. The older man, smoking a cigar, wore a ribbed shirt highlighting his show muscles. He descended the steps to greet McKinley. With that barracuda smile of his, the bulked-up man looked like some kind of salesman.

Strange lowered his binoculars. Was this McKinley's drug connect? Probably not. Most of the major quantities sold down here came from out of town. But this here looked like more than a backyard barbecue. The muscleman was selling something.

Strange stepped back about twenty yards and phoned Quinn. He told him to park beside the Citgo station, and where he could find him, approximately, in the woods.

❏

HORACE McKinley shook the hand of Ulysses Foreman, taking the pliers-like strength of his grip, Foreman always eager to show off what he had.

"Damn, big man, you ain't lost nothin'."

"You the big man, dawg," said Foreman, nodding at Mike Montgomery but not bothering to shake his hand.

McKinley wondered where that white rhino of Foreman's was. She was usually here to greet them, too, trying to talk like a black girl, coming off like some strand-walking ho, showin' off her big pockmarked ass cheeks.

"Where your woman at?" said McKinley.

Foreman dragged on his cigar. "She went off to see her daddy down in southern Maryland."

"I'll catch her next time, then. You got somethin' for me?"

"C'mon in."

McKinley and Montgomery went up the steps to where the young man and woman stood. It was crowded up there, and the woman backed up as McKinley introduced himself, extending his hand to her, ignoring the man.

"Couple of associates of mine," said Foreman from behind them, not bothering to state their names.

"Horace McKinley. Pleased to meet you, baby." Horace turned to the young man, then made a gesture to the Avalon with the Virginia plates parked in the drive.

"That you?"

"Yeah," said the young man, smiling with pride.

"Why don't you get you a real car? Avalon ain't nothin' but a Camry with some trim on it, and a Camry ain't nothin' but shit."

The young man didn't know how to react. He had been disrespected in front of the girl, but he wasn't going to step to this Horace McKinley. Probably a dealer, 'cause that's who Foreman did business with. Looking at him, wasn't no *probably* about it; with all that ice, the four-finger ring and the necklace, he was a drug dealer for sure. Wouldn't do any good to his health to show the fat man any kind of defiance.

"I got my eye on a Benz I like," said the young man, but McKinley had already moved his attention back to Foreman, standing at the bottom of the steps.

"Where we goin'?" said McKinley.

"Down to the rec room," said Foreman.

"Nah," said McKinley. "Nice day like this? Why don't you get me one of them good cigars you smokin', and a cold beer or two, and meet us out on the back deck. We can do our business out there."

"Fine. Go on through the house and I'll see y'all out there."

McKinley and Montgomery went into the house. Foreman came up to the porch, reached into his jeans, and extracted a roll of bills. He peeled some money off and handed it to the young man.

"Let me give this to you now," said Foreman, "lighten up this wad I got."

"What you want me to get?" said the young man, taking the money and slipping it into his khakis.

"I got to think on it," said Foreman. "Come down to the basement while I take care of him. You and your girl can kick back and shoot some pool, or just watch some TV, while I'm working things out with the fat man."

The young man grinned sheepishly. "Can I get one of them *ci*gars, too?"

◻

"THAT didn't take long," said Strange.

"I followed your scent," said Quinn. "Fill me in."

"Nothin' for a while now." Strange looked at the house. "Dude with muscles, between your age and mine, lives there. He met McKinley and his boy out front. That's their Benz, the one followed me the other day. The Toyota with the chrome on it belongs to a young man, has a nice-looking girl with him."

"And?"

"Muscled-up dude gave the young man some cash and they all went into the house. I moved around some and saw McKinley on the back deck. Came back here to meet you so you wouldn't get lost. You remember the path you took?"

"I dropped some bread crumbs on the ground on my way in, just in case." Quinn reached for Strange's binoculars, took them, and looked at the house through the glasses. "You get what you needed from Stokes?"

"Yeah. Right after I talked to her I went to the post office and mailed the tape to Ives. Then I drove over to Yuma, the six hundred block, and watched this shit-hole-lookin' house where McKinley hangs."

"Stokes gonna be okay?"

"Long as we keep an eye on McKinley." Strange gave Quinn the details of McKinley's assault on Devra Stokes.

"Guy's a real gentleman."

"Man does that to a woman is a coward. I'd like to get him alone and see how he holds up."

"Maybe you'll get your chance."

Strange looked Quinn over. "Nice work finding that boy Donut."

"Like your boy Stefanos said, just hang out and listen." He handed the binoculars back to Strange. "What do you think's up with all this?"

"They got me all curious now," said Strange. "Let me get closer and take the plate numbers off that Caddy and the Avalon. You got a pen on you, something to write on?"

"Yeah."

"I'll read the numbers out to you, unless you want to read 'em off to me."

"Your eyes are better than mine."

"I know that, man. Just didn't want you feeling like my lackey, is all."

When Strange had gotten the numbers off the plates closer in, they moved back to their spot in the woods.

"Now let's move around to that place I found before," said Strange. "Get a better look at that deck."

❒

WHILE the young man shot some pool, smoked a cigar, and tried to impress his girl, Foreman put some red felt over one of those trays he used to rest his food on while he watched TV. Then he laid the rest of his inventory, the Sig Sauer .45, the Heckler & Koch .9, and the Calico M-110, atop the tray. He placed bricks of corresponding ammunition above the guns, a couple of beers with pilsner glasses on the side, and two cigars laid out just so. Presentation was everything in this business. It was his trademark, setting him apart from the other arms dealers in town.

"Don't be drinkin' none of my beer while I'm gone," said Foreman to the young man. "I want you together when you go down to that store."

"I don't drink no beer nohow," said the young man, winking at the girl. "My drink is Cris."

Foreman could have guessed. These young studio gangsters were all the same. "I won't be too long, hear?"

Foreman carried the tray up the stairs and out through the sliding doors to the back deck. McKinley had made himself comfortable on one of the deck chairs, came with two others and a lounger, recently purchased at one of those outdoor-furniture stores. Looked like McKinley was testing the weight limit on it, the way the cushion was riding low. Montgomery stood with his back against the wooden rail.

"Here we go," said Foreman, placing the tray on a circular glass table Ashley had insisted they buy with the set.

McKinley managed to get himself out of the chair. Foreman handed him a cigar and lit it for him, holding the flame so that McKinley could get a good draw. He offered a cigar to Montgomery, who declined. Foreman almost double taked checking out Montgomery's arms. Boy was a knuckle-draggin' motherfucker. Wasn't no mystery why they called him Monkey Mike.

"Let's see what you got," said McKinley.

Foreman lifted the Heckler & Koch off the tray and handed it butt out to McKinley.

"H and K nine," said Foreman. "Ten-shot magazine, stainless, got a roughed-up stock so it don't slip out your hand. German engineering."

"Like my car."

"High quality. You know how they do."

"How much?"

"Seven fifty."

McKinley returned the gun to Foreman. "Let me see that other one right there."

Foreman picked up the Sig Sauer. He turned it so it caught the sunlight. He admired it before handing it over, stroking the checkered black grip, making a show of its beauty. He knew Mc-Kinley liked the gun and had deliberately waited before giving it to him.

"That's the deluxe Sig right there," said Foreman. "Forty-five with the eight-shot magazine. Double action, slide stays open after the last shot so you know to reload. Trigger guard's squared off, like them combat guns. I got it tricked out with all the options. Nickel slide, and those Siglite sights for the nighttime."

"Nice," said McKinley. "What you want for it?"

"Nine hundred, for you."

"For me? Shit."

"I could sell you a Davis for a lot cheaper, I guess. I figured, you driving a Mercedes, you don't want to be carrying the kind of gun be in the glove box of a Neon."

"True. But that don't mean I'm gonna take my money and burn it in the street."

"Nine hundred is damn near close to my cost. And I'm gonna throw in another brick of bullets for you, like I always do."

"What about another magazine?"

"I got one. But you're gonna have to purchase that."

"Just the bullets, then, man."

McKinley sighted down the barrel, then inspected the piece. The truth was, he knew as little about guns as he knew about cars. But he always ordered the most expensive item on the menu. Man had to show off the rewards of his hard work, otherwise none of it meant shit.

McKinley placed the gun back on the tray. He poured some beer into a pilsner glass and had a long swig. "That young boy downstairs, he makin' a buy for you today?"

"Yeah, he's leaving soon."

"I'm lookin' for somethin' on the low-end side. A revolver, maybe, for one of my troops."

Foreman had planned to lay a cheap piece on Durham, to simmer him down over the mix-up with Mario. Now he'd have to think of something else.

"I can do that," said Foreman.

"Might have some trouble coming up; want to make sure all my people are ready."

Foreman nodded. He didn't want to talk about Dewayne Durham if that's where this was going. He had always stayed at a distance during these wars, and he was determined to remain neutral in this latest conflict.

"Might need you to deliver it to me, later on," said McKinley.

"Prefer to do it right here," said Foreman in a friendly way. "You can always send one of your boys, you don't want to come back out yourself."

"You don't want to get involved, huh?"

Foreman shrugged. He looked over at Montgomery, who was kind of staring off, not paying much attention to the two of them.

"You ain't afraid of Dewayne Durham, are you?" said McKinley.

"I sell to everyone," said Foreman. "I told you that the first time I met you. The thing is, I wouldn't want anyone thinking I was taking sides. Someone like Durham might see me over at your place on Yuma, get the wrong idea. And why wouldn't he see me? He ain't but across the alley. Wouldn't be good for my business."

"He's gonna go down," said McKinley. "When he does, I'm gonna remember who stood next to me. That might be good for your business."

As you'll go down, too. You all do. And you ain't all that special, ei-
ther, thinkin' you're the only one's gonna keep me in business. There's
never a shortage of young men down here to take your place.

"I'll keep it in mind."

"Or maybe I should tip on back here," said McKinley,
"seein' as how I missed your woman. I do like to look at her."

Foreman felt his face grow warm at the implied threat. He
knew of McKinley's violent reputation with women.

"You're always welcome," said Foreman, forcing a smile.
"I'll call you later, soon as my boy comes back with that piece."

"Here's your money," said McKinley. He rested the beer
glass on the tray and peeled off nine hundred-dollar bills from a
roll. He holstered the Sig in the waistband of his warm-up pants
and dropped the matching top out over the band. Montgomery
picked up a box of bullets without asking if he should.

"I'll meet you out front with that brick," said Foreman.

"Nice doin' business with you."

Foreman shook McKinley's sweaty hand. "You too, dawg."

McKinley head-motioned Montgomery. "Let's go, Mike."

◻

STRANGE and Quinn walked through the woods to their original
vantage point, where they could see the front of the house. Soon
they watched McKinley and his sidekick emerge from the door,
pass under the pink awning, and stand by the Benz in the circular
drive.

"They're leaving," said Quinn, keeping his voice low.

"Fat boy got his new gun," said Strange, "so I guess they're
done. Least we know now what's going on in that house. I'll be
giving Blue the plate numbers off muscleman's Caddy. If I'm
guessing right, that's his ride. I'm sure the MPD and the PG
County boys, not to mention the ATF, will be happy to get a local
arms dealer off the street."

"Why are they hanging around?"

"Maybe that salesman's gonna give them a good-bye kiss. I wonder what that young man and his girlfriend are doing for this guy."

Quinn watched as the man in the muscle shirt walked out of the house. "What now?"

"McKinley and his boy know my car. I got away with tailin' him a little while ago, but I was lucky. I'm gonna need you to follow McKinley, you don't mind. Shame you got that car says, Look at me, but you play it smart and don't get too close to him, you'll be all right. When you're satisfied he's not going after the Stokes girl, get over to the nail salon where she works and sit tight in the lot. I'll meet you there later on."

"What are you gonna do about the girl then? You can't watch her all night."

"I was thinkin' I'd take her home, to Janine's, I mean, for a couple of days. Until me and Ives can get her someplace else."

"Look, I got some business to take care of," said Quinn, thinking of Linda Welles and the boys at the apartment house on Naylor Road. His reluctance to talk to them earlier had been eating at him since.

"Still looking for Sue's runaway?"

Quinn nodded. "I want to check out a lead."

"Fine. I know you don't want to get involved in the Granville case. But this here is something else; you'll be doing one of those good things you been wanting to do. Just make sure Devra's all right."

"What're you gonna do?"

"Follow that young couple, they move out of here. Like I said, I'm curious."

"Leave your cell on," said Quinn.

Strange shook Quinn's hand. Quinn turned and booked through the trees.

LOOKING at the needle on his gas gauge, Strange began to worry that he was going to run out of fuel. He'd been driving for a half hour now, following the Avalon, and as yet the young man behind the wheel had shown no signs of nearing a destination.

The Avalon was on Route 1 in Virginia, heading south. Strange had tailed him and the woman on the Beltway, over the Wilson Bridge, and onto 1, at that point called Richmond Highway.

To Strange, Virginia's Route 1 looked the same as Maryland's stretch of Route 1 from Laurel to Baltimore, a blacktop badland now dominated by chain and family-style restaurants and big-box retailers but still littered with trick-pad motels, last-stand truck stops, and drinker's bars. Confederate flag stickers appeared on some cars the farther south he drove, "Tradition, Not Hatred" written below the stars and bars. Strange realized just how far off his turf he had come.

The road had stoplights but was straight and heavily traf-
ficked, the easiest kind of tail job. Being made wasn't the problem,
though. The problem was keeping up, as the boy was a lane changer
with a lead foot.

Strange listened to *Let's Stay Together,* front to back, on the trip.
The one had Green looking like a high school kid on the cover,
"How Can You Mend a Broken Heart" a highlight of the set. Or-
dinarily he'd enjoy a drive like this, the window down, the Rev-
erend Al at his peak on the box. But he was worrying about the
gas gauge, and the Stokes girl, and Quinn. And wondering if the
boy in the Avalon was ever going to slow down.

Down below the Marine Corps base in Quantico, on a
stretch of deep forest–lined highway absent of any commercial
enterprise, he saw the Toyota's right turn signal flash. The car
pulled off on the shoulder and then went into a graveled lot cut
out of the woods. Strange stayed behind a Chevy pickup and kept
his foot on the gas, glancing over at the Avalon as he kept his
speed. The boy was parking in front of what looked like an old
house, standing alone well back off the road. A sign, going the
width of the house's porch, said "Commonwealth Guns."

Strange drove for another mile or so, found a cut in the me-
dian strip intended for official use only, and made an illegal turn.
He drove north and made the same kind of turn a mile past the
store. He drove into the graveled lot and parked beside the
Avalon. These were the only two cars in the lot, and anyway, there
wasn't any place to hide his car. If the young man hadn't made him
yet, he'd be all right.

Strange walked about fifty yards up a path to the house. He
stepped onto the front porch, where a Harley Softail was chained
and padlocked to a post. He entered the shop.

It had the feel of a sportsman's store at first glance. The dis-
plays showed rods, bows, and knives, in addition to rifles and shot-
guns. Signs supporting gun ownership and gun owners' rights

were hung on all the walls. Accessories, holsters, and cleaning kits crowded the aisles. The aisles led to the destination point, a glass case in the back of the store.

Strange went directly to the case. The young man and his companion were there, looking down at the handguns housed under the glass. A little white man stood behind the case. He greeted Strange and told him he'd be with him as soon as he finished with these folks. Strange told him to take his time. The young man glanced over, perhaps only registering Strange's size, gender, and race, and returned his attention to the guns.

Strange stayed to the right side of the case and examined its contents. The guns seemed to be arranged by type and caliber, with brands kept together and graduated by price. Davis and Lorcin went to Taurus, S&W, and Colt; Hi-Point went to Beretta, Glock, Browning, Ruger, Sig Sauer, and Desert Eagle. Derringers moved into revolvers and then on to automatics. The highly priced, coveted Dan Wesson revolvers, long-barreled .357s and .44 Mags, were set off from the rest.

The young man was holding a Taurus revolver, hefting it in his hand.

"It's meant to be heavy," said the little man. "Thirty-four ounces, most of it's in the barrel. Soft rubber grip. Good stopping power. Similar to what the police used to use before they went over to autos. Your basic thirty-eight special. This here is one of my most popular models. Perfect for protection. All those home invasions you hear about — in the city, I mean. I can't keep these in stock."

Strange knew the police pitch was intended to sell the young man. The rest was just bullshit. The little man wore an automatic holstered on his waist. It looked large on his narrow hips. Strange figured that big motorcycle outside was his, too. Big gun, big bike, little man. Wasn't anything surprising about that.

"How much?" said the young man.

"Two ninety-five for the blue finish. The stainless will run you another fifty."

"I'll take the blue."

"It's for you?"

"Nah, it's for her."

The young woman smiled. She was pretty and looked innocent enough. Strange wondered if she knew, exactly, what she was doing. If she thought this was just a favor for her boyfriend, or if she imagined herself to be a player in some kind of adventure.

"You're a Virginia resident, right, sweetheart? Over twenty-one?"

"Yeah," said the girl.

"You'll need to fill out a form, and then I have to call it in. Instant check. I can have you out of here in ten minutes. The government hasn't screwed that part up yet, not in the commonwealth, anyway."

The little man got the form, and while the young woman was filling it out, he approached Strange.

"Can I answer any questions for you quick?"

"I'm lookin' for some home protection myself. But right now I'm just scouting around."

"I'll be finished up here soon and we can talk."

Strange resumed his browsing. The little man was right. Didn't take but ten minutes after the girl had filled out the form, and the transaction was nearly done. The part left was the money. The young man removed some large bills from his wallet and handed them to the girl, who paid the merchant and got a receipt. Then they walked out of the shop with a handgun and a box of ammunition.

Obviously the gun was for the young man. He had paid for it with his own money in plain sight. But the form had been filled out by the girl, who was of age and had no prior convictions. That was all that was required for the two of them to make the straw purchase. The merchant had done nothing illegal and technically had obeyed every law. Another handgun would now be circulated in D.C. It would end up being used, most likely, in some kind of violent crime.

"Now," said the little man, coming back to Strange. "What can I do for you?"

"Nothing," said Strange, looking into the man's eyes.

Strange left the shop.

QUINN tailed McKinley to the house on Yuma and kept driving as the Benz came to a stop. There wasn't a turnoff nearby, and he had gotten too close to their car. The only option was to keep moving, just plow straight on ahead.

Passing by the Benz, Quinn did not look their way. But he felt the eyes of McKinley and his sidekick on him as he went by. It wasn't a surprise to Quinn that he'd been made. Strange had been riding him to get a work vehicle less conspicuous than his Chevelle for some time now. And he was white. Unless he was some kind of cop, or buying drugs, there was no good reason for him to be in this part of town. Still, he was angry at himself for not paying full attention to the street layout as he'd neared their house.

Quinn looked in his rearview as he prepared to make a left at the next corner. McKinley was getting out of the passenger side of the vehicle, staring at the Chevelle.

Quinn punched the gas, going up 9th. He headed for the salon off Good Hope Road.

The strip center was quiet as Quinn entered the lot. He parked his car two rows away from the salon, facing it. From this space he could look through its plate glass storefront. Even with his poor long vision, he could make out the tiny owner, talking on the phone. The Stokes girl was there, looked like she was working on a customer. He could see her son, walking around and then dropping to the floor, in there, too. All of them were secure in the shop. It didn't look to Quinn that the girl or her boy was in any kind of danger.

Those couple of hours of weekday activity, people getting off work and grabbing groceries and fundamentals on their way home, had come and gone. Until now, Quinn had not even noticed that the day had passed. The rumble in his stomach told him that he had not eaten anything since the meeting at the diner. The sun was dropping fast, lengthening the shadows in the parking lot as it fell.

The customer came out of the shop, examining her nails in the last light of day before dusk. She walked out into the lot and got into an old green Jag. Quinn sat for a little while longer, then phoned Strange.

"Derek here."

"Where you at?"

"Someplace on Richmond Highway, near the city. I'll tell you where I been when I see you. I'm gonna catch the Beltway and come around now. Where are *you?*"

"Baby-sitting Stokes, like you told me to. McKinley's at his place on Yuma."

"*Three-Ten to Yuma.*"

"Was wondering when you were gonna make that connection."

"I'll be there in about a half hour."

"I'm gonna roll over to Naylor, check on that Welles lead."

"Your call. You think the girl's okay, go ahead."

"Looks like business as usual in there. She looks fine."

"I'll meet you back there, then," said Strange. "In the lot."

❐

"THERE he goes," said McKinley, talking into his cell, watching through the windshield of the Benz as the Chevelle backed out of its space and drove from the parking lot.

"That Strange's boy?" said Montgomery, his cell to his ear, sitting behind the wheel of his late-model Z in the lot near the Benz.

"His partner."

"How you know?"

"The Coates cousins said some white boy was in Strange's car while he went to talk to Stokes at her apartment."

And I been told.

"Oh, yeah."

"Boy's stupid, too. Trying to be all undercover and shit, driving a loud-ass car. Anyway, we better hurry up. Man's prob'ly just going to take a pee."

"We gonna go in the back?"

"Like we said. Let me get off here and call Inez. You follow me then, behind the store."

In the salon, Devra sat at her work station, watching as Inez Brown went to the phone. She spoke to the caller briefly, then ended the call. Inez went around the counter, taking her keys with her, and locked the front door.

Devra looked out into the parking lot. It had begun to get dark.

"Come here, Juwan," said Devra. The boy got up from where he was playing, his action figures scattered around him, and walked to her. She brought him into her arms.

"What's wrong, Mama?" said Juwan. He could see something funny in his mother's eyes.

"Nothin'. You just stay here *with* me, now."

Inez Brown went into the back room, then quickly returned to the front of the shop, coming over to where Devra sat in a chair, holding the boy.

"Why you lockin' the door?" said Devra. "It ain't closin' time."

"It is for you," said Brown, showing a little row of white teeth. It was the first time Devra could remember seeing her smile. The smile scared her some.

"Why you doin' this?"

"You don't *know?* Girl, you fucked up. Runnin' that pretty-ass mouth of yours."

"I never did you no wrong."

"I just don't like you, is what it is. Did I mention that you were fired, too?" Brown laughed from somewhere shadowed and deep. As she laughed, Horace McKinley walked in from the back room.

"Let's go," said McKinley. "Out the back."

"Where?" said Devra, her voice catching as she stood, keeping her hand on her son's shoulder.

"You're coming with me," said McKinley. "The boy's gonna stay with Mike."

"No."

"No *nothin'*. I got no time to argue with you. You didn't listen, and now we got to do somethin' else. We're just gonna put you somewhere, let you think about the things you did that I told you *not* to do. See how quick you get to missing your little boy."

Devra backed up a step. McKinley reached over and grabbed her arm. She flinched as his fingers dug into her flesh. He pulled her toward him and she let him, grabbing her purse off the table as she went past. Her knees were weak, but she moved and brought the boy along. They stopped to pick up a few of the wrestling figures and kept on. It felt like she was floating as they made their way to the back room. The back door was open, and they stood in the frame. McKinley's Benz was in the alley and a black Z was idling behind it. The one named Mike, who had kind eyes and played nice with her son, was standing beside the driver's door.

"I don't want to hear no screamin' or nothin' like it," said McKinley. "Say good-bye quick."

Devra got down on her haunches so that she was close to her son. He was crying, but trying not to.

"Baby," said Devra, "I want you to go with that man. The one you were playing with before?"

"I want to go with *you*."

"You know where home is, right?" said Devra. She whispered the street name and apartment number in his ear, and the name of Mrs. Roberts, who lived on their floor.

"I know."

"We gonna be there together, real soon. I'll catch up with you, hear? It's gonna be all right."

She kissed him roughly and smelled his scalp. She turned him then and pushed on his back until he took a few steps. She watched him walk toward the black car. Mike opened the passenger door for him, and he got inside the Z.

Devra moved toward the Benz. Nearing the car, she caught the eyes of Mike Montgomery and held his gaze. Looking at Montgomery deep, she wasn't so afraid for her son anymore. But she wondered if she'd ever hold him again.

❏

THE girl had come home from work, taken a shower, and then was just gone. She'd left without telling him where she was going. Said something about some sodas in the refrigerator and a key in a bowl by the front door, that was it. He heard the door close, and that was how he'd known she'd left out the place. He hadn't said nothin' out of line to her or nothin' like that. Girl just wasn't *social*, is what it was.

Mario was bored. He hadn't talked to no one since Donut had called him that last time, and his brother hadn't called all day. He had turned on the TV, but there wasn't anything on worth watching. Bitch didn't even have the cable. Who the fuck didn't have cable these days? Even the no-job-havin' motherfuckers he knew paid for the service. If she had it, at least he could sit and watch some of those joints they ran on *106 & Park*, that video show they had on BET.

He decided to go out on the street and try his luck, sell a couple of vials of that fake crack.

He was off his turf. Somewhere in Northeast — he hadn't bothered to take notice of the particulars when Dewayne drove him to the woman's place. Truth was, he didn't know *where* he was. No idea. But that was cool. An opportunity, since no one around here knew who he was. He could sell some of these dummies and then disappear. Move on, soon as the heat died down. All he had to worry about was the police.

He gathered up his shit and went out the door. Going down the stairwell of the apartment house, he could smell himself, and it wasn't pretty. It was the clothes he'd been wearing these past few days, that's what it was. He could put some deodorant on; he'd seen some in that girl's medicine cabinet. Or take a shower, like he'd done at Donut's, if he had the time.

He went down to the corner. It had gotten dark out. Not full dark yet, but near to it. There was some kids out playin', but nobody else. A market was on the corner, but wasn't anybody hanging outside of it. And on the corner was a street lamp that hadn't been broken. That would be a good place to stand, under that light.

He went there and assumed the position. One hand in his pocket, kind of staring out into the street. Like he was waiting for a ride but in no hurry to get it. He'd seen enough of these boys to know how they did it.

Some cars passed. A white car turned the corner, and Mario stepped back into the shadows. It was a Crown Victoria with big side mirrors, but it wasn't the police. Just some kids who liked to drive the same kind of car the Five-O drove. Stupid-ass kids.

A gray Toyota hooptie slowed down nearing the corner and came to stop in the middle of the street. Two hard-looking young men were in the front seat. The driver had marks on his face, looked like he'd been cut.

"You sellin'?" said the driver in a dry, raspy voice.

"I might be," said Mario.

"Come closer, man. I can't hear shit with you standing there."

Mario walked out to the car and leaned his elbows on the frame of the open window. He could smell that the driver and his friend had been drinking beer, and they were wearing fucked-up clothes. These two couldn't be undercover or nothin' like that. No one could make themselves look that ghetto 'less they *were* ghetto for real.

"I got some rock."

"Talk about it."

"What you want, a dime?"

"Do I look like a dime-smokin' motherfucker to you? Gimme a fifty, man."

Mario looked around and reached into his pocket. He brought out some vials Donut had given him and found one that he had filled with what looked like fifty dollars' worth of rock. He put it in the hand of the driver while the one in the passenger seat checked the mirrors for any signs of law.

The driver scowled. "Fuck is this shit?"

Mario's heart beat hard in his chest. "What's wrong with it?"

"This looks like a hundred dollars' worth, not fifty. Fuck you tryin' to pull?"

"I'm new on this strip," said Mario. "Just tryin' to be generous so I can get some of that repeat business."

The driver studied Mario's face. "This shit better be right."

"It is," said Mario, nodding his head quickly.

The driver paid Mario with a ten and two twenties. The bills were damp.

"Pray you ain't fuckin' with me, *Deion*," said the driver. His friend was laughing as the Toyota pulled away.

Yeah, okay, thought Mario. I'll fuck with you anytime I want. 'Cause I am gone up out of this piece, soon as things cool down. And you ain't never gonna see my face again.

"Bitch," he said under his breath.

He puffed out his chest, feeling bold right about then. But soon he began to lose his nerve and he walked back toward the woman's apartment, his head down low. He could come out later, he wanted to, and sell a little bit more. In the meantime, he'd go and kick back on that girl's couch. See if there was anything worth watching on the box. Maybe take a shower, he had time.

29

QUINN pulled over on Naylor behind a new red Solara, tricked out with gold-accented alloys. He let the car idle as he looked up to the three-story, bunkerlike structure that sat atop a rise of dirt and weeds. The pipes on his Chevelle were sputtering and loud, and the young men on the front stoop all turned their heads at the sound. Quinn cut the engine and let himself relax, but not to the point of inaction. He knew if he deliberated too long, if he was sensible, he'd just pull away.

Do your job.

He grabbed the manila folder on the seat beside him and got out of the car. He locked it down and walked up the steps to the apartment unit.

There were chuckles and comments as he neared. All of them were staring at him now. He sensed that they hadn't moved since the afternoon. A halogen light that hung from the building cast a yellow glow on the stoop. The light bled to nothing as the hill graded down. Quinn stopped walking ten, fifteen feet away from the group.

A couple of them were drinking from brown paper bags. The air smelled of marijuana, but none was going around; a faint fog of smoke hung in the light. The young men's eyes, pink and hooded, told him they were up.

"Terry Quinn." He flashed his license, which looked like a badge. "Investigator, D.C."

A couple of the young men looked at each other, smiling. He heard someone mimic him, "Terry Quinn. Investigator, D.C.," in the voice of a game-show announcer, and there was low laughter then, and movement as several of them adjusted their positions. One of them, wearing a napkin bandanna and smoking a cigarette, leaned forward, his forearms on his thighs. He was bone skinny, no older than thirteen, with the flat eyes of a cat.

"I remember you," said a heavyset young man with a blown-out Afro, his shirttails out over his jeans. Quinn remembered him, too. He was the smiling one from earlier that afternoon.

"I was looking for a girl named Linda Welles," said Quinn. "I'm still looking. Last time she was seen was in this neighborhood. Her family's worried about her. She's fourteen years old."

He removed a flyer from the folder and held it out to the heavyset young man. The young man looked at it, and his eyes flared, but just as quickly lost their light. Quinn knew with certainty then that this one could help him find the girl.

"Take it," said Quinn, still holding out the flyer. But the young man left his hands at rest. He hadn't moved at all since Quinn had come up on the group.

It was quiet now. They were all staring at Quinn, and even the drinkers were holding their bags still between their knees.

"You know where the girl is, don't you?" said Quinn.

The young man said nothing.

"You don't tell me now, I'm gonna come back."

"Why you gonna come back?" said the young man. "You here *now*."

"I'm gonna come back," said someone in that same announcer's voice, and another voice said, "With the cavalry and shit." Quinn heard chuckling and an "Oh, shit."

The heavy young man pulled back the tail of his shirt and let it drop back against his waist. The butt of an automatic, stainless with black grips, rose out of his waistband and lay across the elastic of his boxer shorts. Quinn couldn't seem to move. His face was hot. He was frozen there.

"You know why I remember you?" said the young man. "Wasn't because of no girl."

"What was it, then?" said Quinn.

"I remember you 'cause you were so little, and so white. Mini-Me, comin' up here, acting so tough. 'Cause you knew that we wouldn't hurt no white boy down here, bring all sorts of uniforms to our neighborhood. And you were right, the first time around. I don't want to do no time over some miniature motherfucker like you, don't mean shit to me *no* way. But you keep on standing around here, I might just go ahead and take my chances."

Quinn could feel his free hand shaking and he balled it up to make it stop. He stood straight and kept his eyes locked on the heavy young man's.

"You want somethin' else?"

"I'm comin' back," said Quinn.

"Yeah, okay. But for now? Walk while you still can."

Quinn turned and headed back toward his car. He heard someone say, "Mini-Me," and a burst of laughter, and the slapping of skin. It was like he was a kid again, cutting through the woods at night. His humiliation was chasing him like something horrible, a screaming, maggot-covered corpse with an upraised knife. He was ashamed, and still he wanted to run.

Quinn dropped into the bucket of his car. It would be different if he still had the street power of a cop. But he knew he'd never have that kind of power again. He turned the ignition key and drove away from the curb.

Quinn wished he'd brought his gun.

❐

THE salon was dark inside when Strange arrived. On the glass door was a hand-painted sign that gave the store hours. That Inez Brown had gone and closed the store up two hours early, but Devra had said she'd be working till closing time.

Strange paced the sidewalk while he phoned Devra from his cell. She wasn't in, or wasn't answering. He left a message on her machine.

Strange looked around. Where was that old man, the one who'd given him the information yesterday, when he needed him? The real question was, where the fuck was Quinn?

Even as he was thinking it, he watched the Chevelle pull into the lot, easing into a space beside the Caprice. Strange dropped off the sidewalk to the asphalt and walked to the driver's side of the car. He put his palm on the roof as he leaned in the open window.

"Where's Devra?"

"She's not in there?" said Quinn. He looked through the windshield at the darkened shop.

"God*damnit,* Terry, I told you to keep an eye on her."

"You said it was my call," said Quinn, his face pale and taut. "Looks like I shit the bed."

Strange studied Quinn's troubled eyes and doughy complexion. "What's wrong with you, man?"

"I found some guys who know where the Welles girl is, but I got nothin' out of them. Matter of fact, I let myself get punked out."

"Shit, that's all this is?" Strange shook his head. "Terry, I let people out here disrespect me every *day.* It's part of how we do our job. Let them have their little victory and get what you can."

"It was worse than disrespect."

"Besides, you come down here gettin' violent on people, how long you think you'd be able to work these neighborhoods? You'd be a marked man, and it doesn't even matter if the people you fucked with got put away. They have friends and relatives, and those people never forget. I started shakin' down people like I was wearin' a uniform again, I'd be out of business. Get it through your head, man, you're not a cop."

"This was something else," said Quinn. He stared straight ahead, unable to look at his friend. "It never would have happened, I had my gun."

"Nah, see, you don't even want to be considering that. You had your gun, you'd a killed someone and got yourself some lockdown, or got your *own* self killed. Either way, you'd be fucked." Strange put his hand on Quinn's shoulder. "Look, man, I don't have time for all this now. I got to find that girl and her kid. Time to visit McKinley. You with me?"

"Let's go," said Quinn.

"I'll follow you," said Strange.

◗

BERNARD Walker lit the candles on the first floor of the house on Atlantic and put a couple on the steps going up to the second floor. He came back into the living room, where Dewayne Durham sat at a card table ending a call. Durham flipped the cell phone closed and placed it on the table.

The house was oddly quiet. Dewayne had sent out all his people to work the school on Mississippi. He had told Walker that he didn't want him playing that beat box tonight like he liked to do, and Walker had complied. So it was just the two of them and the silence now.

Dewayne nodded at the cell. "I just called my brother at the girl's place. He ain't there."

"Maybe he's taking a shower," said Walker.

"He better be. What he better *not* be is out. I told him to sit tight."

Durham rubbed his face and stood, walking into the hall that led to the galley kitchen and the door at the rear of the house. Walker followed. They stood beside each other and looked across the darkened alley at McKinley's house on Yuma. All of McKinley's people, it looked like they were out working, too.

McKinley had the lights on all over the first floor. Though the front of the house had wood in its windows, there wasn't any plywood on the back windows, only curtains, and most of those had been torn down. They could see McKinley walking around in there slowly, gesturing to someone who was half his size.

"There go the Candyman right there," said Walker. "Looks like . . . Shit, he's got a woman with him."

"Ain't like him to be *any* goddamn where without that boy Monkey," said Durham. "Much less with a woman."

"He don't know how to treat a woman *no* way," said Walker.

Durham squinted. "Zu? Why is it we're in here lightin' candles and shit, worried about the police, when fat boy is over there with all the lights burning bright?"

"He's bold, I guess."

"Right," said Durham. "He is bold. Just ain't right, how bold he is."

Walker felt his stomach rumble. "I'm hungry. Thirsty, too. You want to go out for a while, pick up somethin'?"

"Need to rest, think some," said Durham. "I'm gonna go upstairs and lay out on that mattress for a while."

"Aiight, then."

"Swing by Mississippi, get the money from the troops while you're there."

"Anything else?"

"Bring me back a couple of sodas," said Durham, "and a Slim Jim."

❐

"DAMN, boy, I am hungrier than a motherfucker." McKinley punched in numbers on his cell, got the pizza joint on the line, was put on hold. "Girl, you want anything?"

"No."

"We gonna be here awhile."

"I don't want no pizza."

"Suit yourself." The sucker who worked at the pizza place got back on, and McKinley ordered two pies with meat and a rack of super-sized sodas. He didn't think he could eat two pizzas by hisself, but they had a special on, saved you money when you bought two. And you never could have too much soda round the house.

McKinley gave the sucker his address.

Devra was sitting on the hardwood floor of the living room, her back against the chipped plaster wall. Her purse was beside her; McKinley had checked it out and found nothing but her keys that she could hurt him with, and he had reasoned that she would never try. McKinley shut his phone down and put it in a holster he kept clipped to his side. He walked to Devra and stood over her. He noticed she had coiled up some as he approached.

McKinley's warm-up top was zipped down and open, showing the wife-beater he wore underneath. He'd let his chains hang out. His new gun, the Sig .45, was under the waistband of his pants, the grip slanted and tight on his belly. The girls liked ice and automatics, this he knew.

Devra met his eyes, then took in the rest of him. He was sweating, and his fat belly was spilling out over his drawers, looked like dough was gonna swallow up that gun of his.

"You could sit in a chair," said McKinley.

"I'm fine."

"You don't have to make it too hard on yourself, girl. Ain't like I got you chained up or nothin' like that. You free to walk around. We just gonna sit tight together for a while till you come to your senses."

"I want my son."

"You'll get him, too. Tell me you're not gonna talk to that man no more, and I'll put y'all back together. Tell me for real, though, 'cause I won't take no more lies. I'll keep you here for a couple of days, till they're done crossing your old boyfriend Phil, and you can go free."

"All's we was doin' was havin' some ice cream."

"That again? Shit. Fine as you are, I don't believe you even eat ice cream." McKinley smiled again, showing her his teeth. The girls liked that, too. "Look here, I'm sorry for touchin' you rough yesterday. That don't mean we can't be friends *today.*"

"Mother*fuck*er," said Devra, feeling her eyes get teary and trying to hold it in. "Why can't you just . . . just leave me alone."

"Damn, girl, you don't have to get all upset." McKinley rolled his shoulders. "Just sit your ass there, then. Don't say nothin', you can't say nothin' nice."

McKinley walked away, wondering why the women did him like that. The only girls he'd had lately he'd had to pay for. Didn't make any difference to him. Pussy was pussy. One way or another, it cost you money.

A half hour later, the pizza delivery boy arrived. McKinley undid the chain, flipped the dead bolt, and opened up the door. Boy was wearin' some stupid-ass-striped shirt, looked like a barber pole. He put the pizzas and the sodas inside the door while McKinley counted out some money. He gave him two quarters on top of the bill. Boy didn't even say thank you or nothin'. He had been staring kind of wide-eyed into the house the whole time he was standing out there on the stoop. Prob'ly looking at the girl, like any girl could go for him. Looked like a scared animal or something. Sucker with a minimum-wage job, out here armed with nothin' but pizza, risking his neck at night with everything going on. Maybe he was seeing his future, why his eyes were wide. Boy was right to be scared.

McKinley closed the door and picked up the boxes that had been laid at his feet.

"Sure you don't want none of this? It's better when it's hot."

The girl didn't answer, hugging herself against the wall.

McKinley said, "Suit your *own* damn self."

◻

STRANGE and Quinn were in the Caprice on Yuma, a half block down from the McKinley house, parked behind Quinn's Chevelle. They watched the pizza boy deliver a load to the house and they watched him go back to his car, a rusted-out Hyundai.

As he pulled away, Strange ignitioned the Caprice and followed the delivery boy down to 9th. The Hyundai cut right on Wahler and headed toward Wheeler Road. At the stop sign at Wheeler, as the delivery boy slowed down, Strange goosed the gas and pulled up alongside the Hyundai on its left side. Strange honked his horn to get the driver's attention. Quinn was already leaning out, his license case flipped open, holding it face out so the driver could see.

"Investigators," said Quinn, "D.C."

"What I do?" said the driver.

Strange's Caprice looked like a police vehicle, down to the heavy chrome side mirrors. He slanted it in front of the Hyundai, as a cop would do, and kept it running. He and Quinn got out and went to the Hyundai. Quinn took the passenger side and Strange stood before the open driver's-side window. Strange flashed his license.

"That house you just delivered to," said Strange. "Tell me who you saw."

"Some fat dude paid me."

"Anyone else?"

"Girl was sittin' in there on the floor, too."

"Describe her, please."

The delivery boy did, his hands tight on the wheel.

"The fat man, he have a bunch of locks on that front door?"

"Heard him turn somethin' and slide a chain, is all."

"You don't need to be talkin' to anyone about this, hear?"

"I won't." The delivery boy looked up at Strange. "You lookin' at that fat boy for somethin'?"

"Nothing to concern yourself with."

"I ain't concerned. I hope you get him if he's wrong, though." The driver wiped his face. "Wearin' all that ice, and all he could see to give me was fifty cents."

"You have a good one," said Strange. "And thank you for your time."

AFTER getting out to move some debris blocking the entrance, Strange and Quinn cruised slowly down the alley between Atlantic and Yuma. Strange had killed his headlights and was navigating by his parking lights. There didn't seem to be anyone out, not even kids. On the Atlantic side of the alley he saw houses, some bright, some dark, one lit dimly by the flicker of flames, all partitioned by chain-link fences in various states of disrepair.

"There it is," said Quinn, looking at the back of a house on the Yuma side. "I counted back from the corner. That's the one, with the lights. I don't see anyone, though."

"Pizza boy said it was just McKinley and the girl, what he could make out. McKinley's down on his big-ass haunches now, wolfin' that pizza, I expect."

"Be a good time to hit him."

"I guess we better do that, then, before we change our minds."

Strange turned onto the street at the head of the alley and parked behind Quinn's Chevelle. Strange went over what they had already discussed.

"It's not much of a plan," said Quinn.

"Ain't no plan at all," said Strange. "I'm countin' on that girl having the stones I think she does. I figure that McKinley's partner has the boy, and she's gonna be focusing on getting back with him. I know how much she loves her son."

"What if it goes wrong?"

"One of us goes down, the other one's got to get the girl out quick. Take her to her apartment and figure it out then."

"You know he's got a gun." Quinn looked at Strange's hip, where his knife was sheathed. "You gonna take him on with that?"

"I got somethin' else for him, I get close enough. You remember his gun, too, Terry. Don't stay back there too long and get your ass shot."

"I'll do my best."

"You got your cell?"

"In my pocket."

Strange looked at Quinn's bright, jacked-up eyes. "Look, man, you don't have to do this. You don't owe anybody anything."

"When you side with a man, you stay with him," said Quinn. "And if you can't do that, you're like some animal. You're finished."

"Oh, shit," said Strange with a low chuckle. "You are something."

They shook hands. Quinn got out of the car and closed the door behind him. He bolted across the sidewalk, up a rise, and moved into the shadows between two duplexes farther down the block.

Strange got a coil of rope out of his trunk and patted his back pocket. He walked up toward the house.

30

H ORACE McKinley was in the living room, eating a slice of pizza topped with hamburger and pepperoni, when he heard someone banging on the back door. His heart skipped as he swallowed what was in his mouth. Couldn't be Mike; he always came in through the front. He dropped the slice into the open cardboard box at his feet. Neighborhood kids, most likely, pullin' pranks and shit, like they liked to do.

"Don't you move now," said McKinley, standing out of his chair, talking to Devra, who was still against the wall, hugging her knees. "I'll be right back."

McKinley pulled the automatic from his waistband and racked the slide.

Devra watched him walk into what would be the dining room in a normal house. He went through an arched cutout there, barely fitting through it, and back into a hall. The hall led to the galley kitchen and the back door, she knew. When he got into the hall she heard him curse and then start to run, his heavy steps vibrating the wall at her back. And then she heard him opening the back door and yelling something out, his voice fading now 'cause he was outside.

Devra looked at the front door. Only thing stopping her was a dead-bolt latch and a chain. Thinking, If I am going to see my baby again, now is the time to try.

QUINN stood on the back porch, knocking on the window and its frame, talking to himself, saying, "Come on, fat man, come and get it," and then smiling right into the man's sweaty face as he turned sideways to get himself through an opening and appeared in the hall. Quinn heard his muffled curse as he raised the gun in his meatball hand. Quinn held his position and his smile, knowing he was firing up the fat man, watching him run straight toward him through the kitchen to the door.

Quinn turned and leaped off the porch. His feet scrabbled for purchase on the dirt as he made it to the chain-link fence that surrounded the patch of backyard. He put his hand on the rail of the fence and was over it clean as he heard the back door swing open. The fat man was yelling at him now, and Quinn ducked his head. He zigzagged combat style down the alley and heard the first shot, thinking, I am not hit, and he heard himself humming as the second shot sounded and a whistle of air passed his ears. And now he just hit it, dug deep for speed and ran straight. He came to the end of the alley where it dropped onto the street, cut left, and slowed to a jog. His short bark of laughter was all relief, a burst of pressure release with the knowledge that he had cheated death.

He looked back toward the alley, wondering if he had given Derek enough time.

◻

IT was that white boy, Strange's partner. Had to be.

McKinley slipped the Sig back inside his drawers. He rolled his shoulders and looked around. A light came on in one of the houses, and a dog, that rott two doors down, was barking fierce. Wasn't but two shots. No one in this neighborhood was going to call the police 'cause of that. And if they did, wasn't no police gonna bother to respond.

McKinley walked across the dirt, stepped up to the porch, and entered the house. He closed the door behind him, mumbling as he locked it. He heard himself wheezing and felt the sweat dripping down his back as he walked through the kitchen into the hall. He went by the arched cutout, not wanting to squeeze through it again, and straight into the living room, where Devra Stokes was standing, one hand kind of playing with the fingers of the other.

"I tell you to get up?" said McKinley, standing before her.

"Heard gunshots, is all."

"Girl, *sit* your ass back down."

He looked over the girl's shoulder and saw the chain hanging free on the front door. He said, "What the *fuck?*" just as he felt the presence of someone behind him and turned.

What he saw in that last second was a man with size, and McKinley reached for his gun. He had his hand on the grip when something whipped up toward him fast, a blur of flat black. When the flat black thing hit him under the chin, the pain was cold electric and the room spun crazy. His feet weren't holding him up, and he was floating, could almost see himself, like a balloon in one of those parades. The spinning room was the last thing he saw as his world shut down.

◻

WHEN McKinley opened his eyes and his vision cleared, there were a couple of men in the room with the girl, all of them standing over him, talking about him like he wasn't there. It was Strange and the white boy, the one he'd chased down the alley. McKinley burped and smelled the garlic and meat on his own breath.

"Look who woke up," said Quinn.

"Told you he was all right," said Strange.

McKinley was propped up against the plaster wall. His hands were together behind his back, and he moved to separate them. They were tied. He went to move his feet, and they were tied, too. McKinley turned his head to the side and spit out some blood. He rolled his tongue in his mouth. His teeth ached and one of the side ones he chewed with was loose. It was just kind of sitting in there, connected by threads. He could move it all around with his tongue.

Strange had fucked him up. That thing in his hand, looked like a sap, it must have been what he'd hit him with. He was slipping it into his back pocket now. And there was his own new Sig sticking out the waistband of the man's pants. This man has no idea what I can do to him, thought McKinley. None. But the thinking made him tired, and he closed his eyes.

"He's going out again," said Quinn.

"He's just resting," said Strange.

"What now?"

"We make a trade."

Strange took McKinley's cell phone off his belt holster, getting down in front of him. He grabbed McKinley by the chin in the spot where he had laid the sap up into him. It opened McKinley's eyes.

"That doesn't smart too much, does it?" said Strange.

"Motherfucker," said McKinley sloppily.

"Mind your language," said Strange. "What's your boy's cell number?"

"His name is Mike," said Devra, her arms crossed with her purse clutched tight, looking down hard at McKinley.

McKinley gave Strange the number and Strange had him

repeat it, knowing it hurt McKinley to talk. He punched the number into the cell.

"He gets on the line," said Strange, holding the phone to McKinley's ear, "I want you to tell him to bring the boy here. Tell him the condition you're in, and how important it is that he not even dream about doin' anybody any violence. Because you will be the first one to suffer. Do you understand?"

McKinley nodded. He listened to the phone and said, "Mike ain't pickin' up."

"Leave a message when it tells you to. We'll try again."

They did, with the same response. And tried again, ten minutes later. McKinley left his third message, and Strange stood.

"Get her out of here," said Strange to Quinn. "Take her back to her apartment. I'll be in contact with you by phone. We'll meet up in a little while."

"What are you gonna do?"

"Talk to our friend here alone," said Strange. "We got a few things to discuss in private."

Devra Stokes spit on McKinley on her way out. Neither Strange nor Quinn moved to stop her.

❐

AFTER Quinn and Devra left, Strange shut down most of the lights in the house and returned to the living room. On the floor was a lamp with no shade, holding a naked bulb, and he picked it up and carried it over to McKinley. He placed it beside him and left it on. The bulb threw off heat, and its glow highlighted the bullets of sweat on McKinley's forehead and the tracks of it moving down his face.

Strange got back down on his haunches and pulled up McKinley's wife-beater, exposing his chest and belly.

"What you doin'?"

Strange drew his Buck knife from its sheath. He held it upside down and pressed the heavy wood-and-bronze hilt against the blackened area of McKinley's jawline. McKinley recoiled as if shocked.

"That hurts, I expect," said Strange. He moved to press the spot again but did not make the contact. "What's your partner Mike's full name?"

"Montgomery."

"And where's he stay at?"

McKinley gave him the address. Strange asked him to repeat it so he could remember, and McKinley complied.

Strange rested one knee on McKinley's thigh and put his weight there. He touched the edge of the blade to the area below the nipple of McKinley's right breast.

"You got titties like a woman," said Strange. "You know that?"

"Man, what the fuck you *doin'?*" said McKinley in a desperate way.

Strange moved the knife so that the blade now rested with its edge above the purple aureole of McKinley's nipple.

"You put your hands on that girl, right about where I'm touchin' this blade. *Didn't* you, boy?"

"I didn't mean to hurt her. I didn't *cut* her, man."

"You like the way this feels, *Horace?*"

"Don't."

"You tellin' me?"

"God*damn*, don't be cuttin' on me with that knife."

"You gonna leave the girl alone, right?"

McKinley nodded.

"The boy, too."

"Both of 'em, man."

"'Cause I don't want you gettin' near her at all. Her or her son, you understand?"

"I hear you, Strange. We good, right?"

Blood splashed onto Strange's hand as he sliced into McKinley's flesh, sweeping the knife savagely across his breast.

McKinley bucked and screamed. The tendons stood out on

his neck as he writhed from the pain. The scream became a sob that McKinley could not stop. Strange found it odd to hear a big man cry so free.

"Now we're good," said Strange, wiping the Buck off on McKinley's shirt and sheathing it. "You just sit there and try to relax."

❐

STRANGE moved the lamp as close as it would get to McKinley. The heat from the bulb, he guessed, was now hot on his face. Strange then dragged a chair over and set it before the fat man. He had a seat.

McKinley had stopped sobbing. His breathing had subsided to a steady wheeze. The dirty flap of nipple, nearly severed and dangling off McKinley's chest, had begun to turn from purple to black. The blood had stopped flowing from the cut Strange had made.

"What now?" said McKinley, elbowing the lamp away from him as best he could. "Ain't you done enough?"

Strange drew the Sig from his waistband. He pointed it at McKinley's face and moved his finger inside the trigger guard. McKinley's lip trembled as he closed his eyes.

Strange lowered the gun. He turned it and released its magazine, letting it slide out into his palm. He checked to make sure a round had not been chambered.

"Just wanted you to experience what you put that girl through," said Strange. "That kind of helplessness."

"*Fuck* you, man."

"I'll just keep this." Strange stood, the magazine in his hand. "You can have the rest."

He dropped the body of the .45 onto McKinley's lap. McKinley was cut, bleeding, and beaten. Worst of all, a piece of his manhood was forever gone. McKinley was past being frightened now. One eye twitched, and a thread of pink spittle dripped from his mouth.

"What makes me so different?" he said.

"What's that?"

"You out here trying to save Granville Oliver, and at the same time lookin' to harm me? Shit, him and me, we're damn near the same man. He ain't no better or different than me. I *worked* for him when I was a kid."

"I know it," said Strange. He had been thinking the same thing himself, trying to separate it out in his mind.

"So why?"

"Cops, private cops, whatever, they got this saying, when one of y'all kills another one like you: It's the cost of doing business. What it means is, you got your world you made, and we're in it, too. And no one outside that world is gonna shed tears when you go. But it's an unspoken rule that you don't turn that violent shit on people you got no cause to fuck with." Strange slipped the magazine into a pocket of his jeans. "You shouldn't have done what you did to that girl."

"What, you don't think Granville's ever done the same?"

"I don't know for sure," said Strange. "But he's never done it to anyone I knew."

McKinley looked down at the body of the Sig lying in his lap, then back up at Strange. "Why didn't you kill me? I'd a killed you."

"I'm not you," said Strange. "And anyway, ain't enough left of you to kill. You're through."

"You don't know nothin', Strange," said McKinley, grimacing horribly, showing his bloody teeth. "You the one's through. One phone call from me is all it's gonna take. You and everyone you know, all a y'all gonna be under the eye. You gonna lose everything, Strange. Your license, your business, your family. Everything." McKinley tried to smile. "*You* the one's through."

The fat man's threats rippled through him. Strange stared at him but said nothing more. He redrew his knife, bent down, and cut the bindings on McKinley's feet. Then he severed the ropes that held his wrists. McKinley brought his arms around and dropped his hands at his sides.

Strange walked from the house.

❒

McKinley found his cell on the floor. He grunted and got himself up on his feet. He went around the house turning lights on as he dialed Mike Montgomery's number. But he only got the message service again. He hit "end" and dialed the number for Ulysses Foreman.

"Yeah."

"McKinley here."

"What's goin' on, dawg?"

"I need you out here to my place on Yuma. Bring that extra magazine for the Sig with you, man. I lost the one you sold me. I'm alone right now; I'm not even strapped."

"I can get it to you tomorrow. Or you can send someone out here —"

"I wanted it tomorrow I would have *called* you tomorrow. Now, you gonna damage our business relationship over this?"

"You got no call to take a tone with me."

"Just bring it, hear? Or maybe your woman would like to bring it out herself."

McKinley listened to dry air. Foreman's voice, when it returned, was strangely calm.

"Ain't no need for you to bring my woman into this, big man."

"You gonna bring it?"

"Yeah, I'll come out."

"And stop by the CVS store for some gauze, and that surgical tape stuff, too. I'll get you for it later."

"You have an accident?" Foreman's tone was almost pleasant.

"Never mind what I had," said McKinley. "I expect to see you soon."

McKinley cleaned his chest up over the sink. The cut started to bleed again, and he pressed a rag to it to make it stop. While he held it there, he tried Mike Montgomery again.

"Goddamn you, Monkey," said McKinley when he got the recording. "Where the fuck you at?"

❐

ULYSSES Foreman got his leather shoulder holsters from out of the closet and put them on. He found his 9mm Colt with the bonded ivory grips, checked the load, and slipped it into the left holster. From the nightstand he withdrew Ashley's .357 LadySmith revolver holding jacketed rounds. He holstered the LadySmith on the right. He stood in front of the bedroom's full-length mirror and cross-drew both guns. He holstered the weapons and repeated the action. The revolver was a little light.

Foreman got into a leather jacket. It was warm for any kind of coat, but necessary to wear one in order to conceal the guns. In the basement he found the Sig's extra magazine and put it into a pocket of his leather. He clipped his cell to his side, got a few cigars out of the humidor, and a cold beer out of the refrigerator, and went outside to the back deck. He lit a cigar, drank off some of his beer, and looked up into the sky. It was a clear night, with most of a moon out and a whole burst of stars.

Foreman phoned Ashley Swann on her cell. She answered on the third ring.

"I've been waiting for you to call," she said.

"Told you I would," said Foreman. "Wanted to get up with you, 'cause I got to go out and do some business for a while."

"Everything all right?"

"Fine," he said, closing his eyes. "Tell me where you're at."

"I'm out beside the soybean field. My daddy hasn't cut the grass yet. It's tickling my toes, long as it is. It's wet from the dew."

Foreman tried to imagine her then. In his mind she had on that pair of salmon-colored pajamas and she was barefoot, holding a glass of chardonnay in one hand, holding a Viceroy with the other. Smiling 'cause she was speaking to her man. Standing under the same moon and stars he was standing under right now. Not beautiful like a model or nothin' like it, but his. And he was smiling now, too.

"I love you, baby," said Foreman.

She chuckled. "That wasn't so hard now, was it?"

"No," said Foreman. "Wasn't hard at all."

"Can you come down here? Daddy would like to see you."

"I will," said Foreman. But even to his own ears his voice sounded unsure.

"Tell me you love me again, Ulee."

He told her so, and ended the call. He stood there for as long as he felt he could, thinking of all he had and what he'd do to keep it. Smoking, drinking, and admiring the sky.

❐

WHEN Strange had cleared out of the immediate neighborhood, he pulled the Caprice over to the curb and phoned Quinn.

"Terry, it's Derek. You at Devra's place?"

"I am."

"I got Montgomery's address. I don't know how we're gonna handle this —"

"Derek, it's all right."

"What is?"

"Mike Montgomery's right here, in Devra's apartment. So's the boy. Everything's all right."

Strange felt his grip loosen on the wheel. "I'll be right over. Don't let Montgomery go nowhere, hear?"

"Figured you'd want to talk to him," said Quinn. "We're waitin' on you now."

31

Q U I N N met Strange at the door and let him into the apartment. Quinn was smiling and so was Devra, the boy at her side. He was holding on to the tail of her shirt and did not let go of it when she moved to embrace Strange.

"Thank you," she said. "You okay?"

"I'm real good now," said Strange. "We alone here?"

"My roommate hasn't been home for a couple of days. She's been layin' up with her boyfriend ever since I told her I don't want that man burning smoke in front of my son."

"Montgomery's in the kitchen," said Quinn. "Devra hooked him up with a soda."

"What happened?" said Strange.

"Montgomery said he took Juwan to his place, but the boy couldn't stop crying. Montgomery figured, he brought the boy back here, he could pick up some of his toys, might make him feel better."

"He could have bought the boy some toys at a store," said Strange.

"True," said Quinn.

"How'd they get in?"

"Lady across the hall, a Mrs. Roberts, has a key. Devra reminded Juwan of that before they got split up."

"Smart boy," said Strange, and Juwan smiled.

"I've been getting our things together," said Devra.

"Good," said Strange. "I'm gonna call my wife, have her get a bed ready in our guest room and a sleeping bag for the boy. You can stay with us for a few days until Ray Ives figures out a better arrangement. You'll like Janine, and she'll like having a woman around for a change. I got my stepson, Lionel, he's kid-friendly, too. And a dog. You into dogs, Juwan?"

"Will he bite me?"

"Nah, old Greco's a boxer. Boxers love kids."

"I'll just finish packing up," said Devra.

Quinn and Strange watched her walk down a hall, Juwan holding her shirttail tight.

"Let's go talk to Montgomery."

"Don't be too hard on him," said Quinn. "He doesn't want to admit it, all that bullshit about picking up some toys here. He was bringing the kid back. He did a good thing."

"I know," said Strange. "I want to thank him, is all."

Quinn looked at the dried drops of blood on Strange's shirt and the blood still on his hand.

"You cut yourself?"

"Not *my* self, no."

"You come down here, get all *violent* on people, Derek, it's gonna be bad for business."

"Come on, man, let's go."

Mike Montgomery was in the kitchen sitting at a small table, leaning back, his long hand around a can of Coke. Strange said, "Mike," and extended his hand, but Montgomery did not move to take it, and Strange had a seat. Quinn leaned against the counter.

"I just wanted to tell you," said Strange, "you did a real good thing tonight."

Montgomery nodded but did not meet Strange's eyes.

"You like kids, don't you, Mike?"

Montgomery shrugged.

"How about football, you into that?"

Montgomery swigged from the Coke can and set it back down on the table.

"I got a football team for young men, just getting close to their teens. I could use a guy like you to help me out."

"Shit," said Montgomery, shaking his head, smiling but without joy. "I don't think so, man."

"Okay, you're tough," said Strange. "But you don't have to be so tough all the time."

"What else I'm gonna be?" said Montgomery, now looking at Strange. He wore his scowl, but it was a mask. His eyes told Strange that he could be, *was,* someone else.

"You can be whatever," said Strange. "It's not too late."

Again, Montgomery said nothing. Strange slipped a business card from his wallet and dropped it on the table between them. Montgomery made no move to pick it up.

"You hurt him?" said Montgomery, his eyes moving to the blood across Strange's shirt.

"Took him down a few notches, is all." Strange leaned forward. "Tell me something: Who's protecting McKinley?"

Montgomery shifted his weight in his seat. "I don't know what you're talkin' about. And if I did know I wouldn't say. I already betrayed him once tonight. Don't be askin' me to do it again."

"You're better than you think you are," said Strange.

Montgomery looked away. "Tell the little man I said good-bye, hear?"

He got up from the table and left the kitchen. Soon after, Strange and Quinn heard the front door open and close.

"You tried," said Quinn.

Out in the parking lot, Mike Montgomery got into his Z, a car McKinley had paid for in cash and given him as a gift. He hit the ignition and drove over to Suitland Road, taking that out of D.C. and into Maryland. The cell phone on the seat beside him began to ring. He had programmed it to go to messages after six rings, but three was enough for his ears, and he reached over and turned the power off. McKinley had been trying to get him all night, and that ringing sound was like someone screamin' in his head. Horace was his father and older brother, all in one. But he shouldn't have hurt that girl like he did. And he shouldn't have fucked with no kid.

Montgomery had no job and no way to get one. He could hardly read. Would be hard to punch a clock, have some boss in his face all the time after sitting high where he'd been these past couple of years. Trying to be straight, knowing he'd killed. But he'd have to figure all that out. For now, he had around fifteen hundred cash he'd saved and a full tank of gas. A gym bag, holding a change of clothes and his toothbrush, was in the trunk.

Montgomery followed Suitland Road over to Branch Avenue, which was Route 5. He knew that 5 connected with 301 when you took it south. And 301 went all the way to Richmond, you stayed on it long enough.

His mother was down there, and his baby brother, too. He was looking forward to throwing a football around with the boy. The little man loved football, and Montgomery did, too.

Mike hadn't seen them for quite some time.

❐

IN the salon parking lot, Quinn and Strange carried Devra's bags to her car. Strange had phoned Janine, and after some discussion and debate, the plans had been made. Strange gave Devra the directions to the house on Quintana and strapped the boy into his car seat while Devra said good-bye to Quinn.

"Aren't you gonna follow me?" said Devra to Strange.

"I'll be along in a little while. Me and Terry got some more business to take care of tonight."

She kissed him on the cheek and got into her car. They watched her drive away.

"So what did you do to McKinley?" said Quinn.

"You been dyin' to know, haven't you?"

"You had that look in your eye."

"I just cut him some. Nothin' a good brassiere won't hide."

"What was that shit in there about who he was working for?"

"I'll tell you later. Still rolling it around in my mind." Strange shifted his shoulders. "Can you handle a little more work?"

"I'm hungry."

"I'm about to chew on my arm, too."

"Donut doesn't live too far from here."

"I'll follow you," said Strange. "We find Mario, maybe we can end this day right."

32

WHEN Mario Durham woke up on the couch, the television was still showing something he didn't want to watch, and he was still alone. Quiet as it was, he guessed the girl Dewayne had put him up with hadn't come home. He wouldn't be surprised if she spent the night somewhere else. She wasn't the friendly type, or maybe she was afraid of him, or afraid of what she'd do if she got around him too long. Dewayne prob'ly told her not to think about gettin' busy with him, that he had too many women problems as it was. On the other hand, she could be one of them Xena bitches, didn't like men.

Compared to most, Olivia had been a good woman, except for that one mistake she'd made. Shame she'd done him dirt, made him have to do her like he did. Anyway, he couldn't change nothin' about that now.

Durham washed his face and rolled on some of the girl's deodorant from out of the medicine cabinet. He went to the kitchen and looked around for something to eat, but he couldn't find nothin' he liked. Then he thought of that market on the corner. He could get a soda and some chips down there, couple of those Slim Jims that his brother liked to eat and that he liked, too. And then he thought, While I'm down there, might as well do a little more business, put some cash money in my pocket. It had gone pretty smooth the last time.

He gathered up the rest of the dummies, and some cash to make change, and dropped the vials in a pocket of his Tommys. He fitted his knit Redskins cap on his head, adjusting it in the mirror so it was cocked just right, and left the apartment.

Mario walked down the darkened street to the corner where the market was still open and the streetlight stood. It was quiet out now. He didn't wear a wristwatch and hadn't thought to check the time. But he knew it must be late.

He stood on the corner, one hand in his pocket, his posture slouched.

A car came and went, and it was nothing. Then another came, five minutes later, and slowed down. The driver rolled his window down and Mario went there and they caught a rap. It was even easier this time, knowing when to listen and what to say. He was busy selling the driver a couple of dimes, so he didn't notice the old gray Toyota as it passed.

Mario did his business and the car drove away. He pocketed two twenties for a double dime and walked back to the corner and stood under the light. He put one hand in his pocket and jiggled the vials he had left. He looked furtively around the street.

Mario heard light footsteps behind him. Before he could turn, he felt something hard and metallic pressed against the base of his skull.

"*Deion,*" said a dry, raspy voice.

He didn't hear the shot or anything else. The bullet blew his brains and some of his face out onto the street.

33

So you got no idea where your boy is," said Strange.

"None," said Donut, sitting on the couch, his knees scissoring back and forth. "I told the other cop all this already. How many of y'all they gonna send over before someone believes what I got to say?"

Quinn was standing by the shelf holding Donut's video collection. He picked *The Black Six* out of the row and had a look at its box.

"Hey, Derek, you know Carl Eller starred in a movie?"

"*Black Six,*" said Strange. "Mean Joe Greene, Mercury Morris. Gene Washington was in it, too."

"Like a *Magnificent Seven* with black guys, huh?"

"Except they didn't need seven. Eller counted as two."

"Don't mess with that," said Donut. "Please."

Quinn returned the tape to its space. He was just killing time while Strange worked the ugly little man. It had taken them a while to find his apartment. This time of night, Donut's neighbors had been reluctant to answer the knocks on their doors. But an old man on the first floor had given them Donut's unit number.

"Donut," said Strange. "You don't mind I call you by your nickname, do you?"

"Ain't nobody call me anything else."

"We'll leave right now, you tell us where Mario is."

"Believe me, if I knew, I would."

Strange stared down at him, all sweat and nerves. "Maybe you could put us up with his brother."

"That wouldn't be such a good idea."

"We got time. We could sit around here, see if the phone rings. Mario calls you, we'd all know you been lying to us. That's obstruction in a homicide. I'm guessing, and it's just a guess, mind you, that you might have some priors."

"Shit, y'all just enjoy fuckin' with a man, don't you?"

"Dewayne's number?"

"I got it somewhere in this mess," said Donut. "But don't tell him where you got it from, hear?"

After they'd left, Donut watched from his window as the salt-and-pepper team walked across the parking lot.

Donut smiled, pleased with himself. All these police trying to get him to talk, and not one of them had. He could hardly wait for Mario to call him, so he could tell his boy that he hadn't gave him up.

◻

STRANGE and Quinn walked toward their cars.

"Surprised he even let us in," said Strange.

"You impersonating a police officer had something to do with it."

"I only told him I was with the police. As in, I'm *behind* them one hundred percent."

"Okay. You gonna call Dewayne?"

"I don't know what I'll say to him. But I can't think of anything else to do."

Strange's cell rang. He unclipped it from his belt. The caller ID read "Unknown."

"Derek Strange here."

"It's Nathan Grady. Where you at?"

"Southeast."

"Mario Durham's been shot to death. I'm at the crime scene right now. Thought you and your partner would want to know."

"Damn."

"He went cleaner than the Elliot girl. You can come over if you want to have a look at him. I'm gonna be here awhile."

"Give me the directions," said Strange.

Strange told Quinn the news, then followed him into Far Northeast.

❐

DEWAYNE Durham was sleeping on the mattress in the second-floor bedroom when his cell rang and woke him. He had not heard or even been subconsciously aware of the two shots McKinley had fired out in the alley. Durham had been in a very deep sleep, and he had been dreaming. As he reached for the phone, he tried to bring back pieces of his dream. Something about his mother, but he couldn't recall what it was.

That homicide detective, Grady, was on the phone. He was calling to tell Dewayne that his brother, Mario, had been shot dead over in Northeast. One bullet to the head, close range. "What kind of gun?" said Dewayne. Grady found the question odd but told him that it had most likely been a .45, as a spent shell casing had been found near Mario's body. Dewayne asked him how they knew it was Mario, and Grady described his Redskins getup, telling him that the clothing description coming over the radio was what had sent him to the scene.

Dewayne shook his head. Fool never even thought to change his shit.

Grady told Dewayne that he'd called him first as a courtesy. That he would call his mother next if he wanted him to. Dewayne said he'd prefer to go to her place, give her the news in person. Then he could come to the scene and identify the body if that was what the detective wanted him to do. Grady said fine, and not to rush, since the ME crew and photographers would be there for some time. He gave Dewayne the address and cut the line without saying good-bye.

Dewayne Durham sat on the edge of the mattress and rubbed at his face. If he was gonna cry, then now would be the time. Get it done up here, alone, then go down and tell Zulu what was going on. But he couldn't even will himself to cry.

He'd shed tears with his mother later on, he supposed. Seeing her cry, that would be what would set him off. But for now all he could think of was the get-back. Wondering who hated him enough, and who was bold enough, to do something like this to a member of his family. Because that person had to know that he'd signed his own death certificate tonight.

Dewayne picked up the stainless Colt .45 with the rosewood checkered grips that lay on the floor and got up off the mattress. He slipped the gun under his waistband and slanted it so that the butt was within easy reach of his right hand. Then he went down the stairs.

Bernard Walker sat at the card table in the soft glow of the candlelight. There were a couple of Slim Jims and an open bag of chips lying on the table, along with Walker's Glock. Walker was listening to some go-go, the new 911 PA tape he'd bought off a street vendor, on his box, but the volume was way down low.

"I kept it soft," said Walker, looking up at Durham, "so you could sleep."

"I'm up now," said Durham. "And I got some news."

◻

ULYSSES Foreman handed Horace McKinley a full magazine. McKinley slapped the clip into the butt of his Sig.

"There we go," said McKinley, smiling. His gums were spiderwebbed red, and some of the blood had seeped into the spaces between his teeth. "Don't feel so naked now."

"Brought you that first-aid shit you asked for," said Foreman, eyeing the big man's saddlebag chest. There was a damp burgundy stain on his wife-beater, where his right tit was.

"Gimme it," said McKinley. He holstered the Sig in his warm-up pants and reached for the white plastic bag that held the gauze and tape. "What I owe you for that?"

"Nothin'," said Foreman.

"You can take your jacket off, you want to."

"I'll just leave it on."

"Got your shit on underneath, right?"

"You *know* I do."

"Have a seat," said McKinley. "I'll be right back."

Foreman watched McKinley go into a hall toward the kitchen. It was shorter to go through the dining room, but McKinley would have trouble squeezing through the space. Fat motherfucker must have stock in McDonald's, Burger King, and KFC all at the same time, thought Foreman. He couldn't understand how a man could let his body go like that.

In the kitchen, McKinley washed himself over the sink. He had water and electric, unlike those Little Orphan Annie motherfuckers across the alley. As he thought of them, he glanced through the back-door window and saw the house on Atlantic, lit by candlelight. Looked like Dewayne Durham and Bernard Walker were having one of those romantic dinners and shit. Now would be a good time to interrupt him.

McKinley made a pad from the gauze and tape. He grunted, holding his flap of nipple flat as he stuck the gauze on his chest.

He was still bleeding some. He'd have to go to the clinic tomorrow, maybe get some stitches put on there to hold it tight. But that was tomorrow. He needed to find Mike, warn him to move the boy someplace safe. And he had some business with Foreman, too.

He phoned Monkey Mike but got a dead line.

He went back out to the living room where Foreman sat. He had a seat himself and smiled at the man with the show muscles who, after all those years out of uniform, still looked like a cop. Being a cop was like having those grass stains he used to get on the knees of his jeans when he was a kid. You could never get those out.

"I feel better now," said McKinley.

"You want a cigar?"

"Never turn down one of your Cubans."

McKinley slid two out of the inside pocket of his leather, handed one to McKinley, lit his own, lit McKinley's. They sat there in the living room in the light of the bare-bulb lamp, smoking, getting their draws.

"Nice," said McKinley. "Look here, I didn't mean to give you the wrong impression on the phone a while back. I was just *agitated* at the time."

"Ain't no thing," said Foreman, looking at the spot, still leaking, on McKinley's chest. "What happened?"

"Someone took advantage of the fact that I was alone here, unarmed, and made the mistake of tryin' to step to me. I'm gonna take care of that situation my own self."

"Where's your boy at?"

"Mike? I'd like to know myself." McKinley chin-nodded in the direction of Foreman's leather. "What you holdin', man?"

"My Colt."

"That's a pretty gun, too, got those ivory handles. What else?"

Foreman reached into his jacket and slid the revolver from one of the shoulder holsters. He handed it butt out to McKinley, who weighed it in his hand. He turned the gun, admiring the contrast of the polished rosewood grips against the stainless steel.

"LadySmith Three fifty-seven," said Foreman.

"It's light."

"Yeah, but you could put your fist through the hole it makes. 'Specially on the exit. It's light 'cause it's made for the hand of a woman. That's Ashley's gun right there."

McKinley handed the gun back to Foreman, who holstered it.

"How is your woman?" said McKinley.

"She's good."

"Bet that pussy's good, too. I ain't never had a white girl I ain't paid to have. It's all pink anyway, right?" McKinley laughed, reached over and clapped Foreman on the arm, watching his narrowed eyes. "Oh, shit, c'mon, big man, we just talkin' man-to-man here. I mean you no disrespect."

Foreman sat back and dragged on his cigar. "Say why you brought me out here, for real."

"Okay, then. This situation we got, you sellin' to my competition, I come to the conclusion it ain't workin' for me. Two of my boys just got deaded by one of your guns; you *know* this."

"And they lost two of theirs the same way. I'm sorry those boys had to die, but it ain't none of my concern. I didn't pull those triggers, any more than the dealer plunges the needle into a junkie's arm."

"Like I said, it ain't workin' for *me*. You tryin' to stay neutral, all right, you've made yourself clear. But Durham's done, man, finished. All's that's left is for someone to come along and throw some dirt on him. I'm gonna take over his territory soon, you can bet on that like the sunrise."

"That ain't none of my business, Horace."

"I'm gonna be *all* your business, man. 'Cause eventually it's just gonna be me and my troops down here, understand?"

"So?"

"What we gotta do now is make that happen tonight. Cement our relationship so we can move forward, man."

Foreman tapped ash off his cigar. "No."

"What you mean, *no?*"

"I mean I won't do it. You askin' me to cross a line that I won't cross."

"It's gonna be good for your future, man."

Foreman kept his tone friendly. "Thanks for thinkin' of me, but I'm already doin' all right."

"I'm not talkin' about you doing better. I'm talkin' about you makin' the right decision here so you can keep what you got."

Foreman stared through the roiling smoke at McKinley. He nodded slowly, his dark eyes shining wet in the light.

"You should have got straight to the point from the get-go. I understand you now, Horace."

"Good. It's just a short walk from here to there."

"Who we talkin' about, exactly? And how many?"

"Dewayne. Zulu, I expect."

"You got some kind of plan?"

"Simple. We walk on over there, cross that DMZ, and knock on their door. Tell 'em we want to give them, what do you call that, one of them olive branches. Tell 'em we want to talk. There's been too much killin' lately, can't we all get along, some bullshit like that. They let us in the house, we take 'em down. Like I said, simple. We outnumber their guns, and we got surprise on our side. Shouldn't be a problem."

"When?" said Foreman.

McKinley said, "They're over there right now."

Foreman stood out of his chair, dropped his cigar to the scarred hardwood floor, and crushed it under his shoe. He released the safeties on both of his guns, reholstered the revolver, racked the slide on his Colt .9, reholstered it, and straightened out his leather.

"We gonna talk all night," said Foreman, "or we gonna do this thing?"

"Damn, big man," said McKinley, "you make a decision, you don't fuck around."

"You the one made the decision, Hoss. I'm just a man with a couple of guns."

◻

MARIO Durham lay on his back. The bullet had taken out the bridge of his nose and one of his eyes. His hat was still fitted to his head, which rested on the street in a river of blood.

"He looks real casual, doesn't he?" said Nathan Grady. "Like he just laid down in the street to take a nap. I like the way he's got his hand in his pocket, too, don't you? Except for his face, you wouldn't even know he was dead."

Strange and Quinn were inside the yellow crime tape, standing beside Grady. Kids and adults from the neighborhood were behind the tape, some talking to uniformed officers, some laughing, some just staring at something that would give them bad dreams later that night. The photographers and forensics team were still working over the body and had not yet covered Mario up.

"Why is he like that?" said Quinn.

"My guess is the bullet severed his cerebral cortex," said Grady. "When that happens it freezes the victim at the moment of death. I've seen it before. Mario was probably standing on the corner, his hand in his pocket, when he took the bullet. He died instantly, I'd say."

"Standing on the corner doing what?" said Strange.

"Well, one of the locals said they saw little Mario there earlier in the evening, looked like he was selling something, or trying to. When we get into his pockets we'll find out."

"He got killed over drugs?"

"Could be. Looks like an amateur killing. A pro wouldn't put a forty-five to a man's head. I mean, a twenty-two would have been sufficient, right? One thing's for sure: He didn't get killed for his sneakers. You see 'em?" Grady laughed. "My man here is sportin' a pair of 'ordans.' Or maybe I'm missing something and that's the rage these days."

Strange and Quinn did not comment.

"Anyway, he's dead. Justice in Drama City, right? Thought you guys would want to see him. For closure and all that."

"You call his kin?" said Strange.

"His brother, the drug dealer. He's coming down in a while to ID the body. I'm gonna let him tell their mother."

"Thanks for calling us," said Strange.

"Yeah, sure. Take care."

Grady motioned to the photographer, indicating that he should take another picture of the corpse. Strange guessed that the photograph of a bloody Mario Durham, "sleeping" in the street with his hand slipped into his pocket, would soon be hanging on Grady's wall.

Strange and Quinn ducked the crime tape and walked to their cars.

"Get in for a minute, Terry," said Strange, nodding at his Caprice. "I want to talk to you before we go home."

□

DEWAYNE Durham looked out the back window at the alley and the house on Yuma. The house was all lit up inside, and McKinley was standing in the kitchen with a man, big like him but muscular, not fat.

"Foreman," said Durham. He raised his voice. "Bernard, better get in here."

Soon Durham felt Walker behind him, looking over his shoulder.

"That's Foreman, right?"

"Yeah."

"What the fuck's goin' on?"

"I don't know. But they're leavin' the house."

"Maybe they're just goin' to their car."

"You see either one of their cars out in that alley?"

Durham heard Walker pull back the receiver of his Glock and ease a round into the chamber of the gun.

"They're comin' over here," said Walker.

Durham watched them cross the alley. His fingers grazed the grip of his gun. "He ain't hidin' nothin', either."

"I can smoke 'em both, they get close enough."

"Before you do that," said Durham, "let's see what they got on their minds."

c h a p t e r

34

T H E overheads of cruisers flashed the crime scene and threw colored light upon the faces of Strange and Quinn. A meat wagon had arrived for Mario Durham, and its driver was leaning against the van, smoking a cigarette. The neighborhood crowd had begun to break up and many were walking the sidewalks back to their homes. Some kids had set up a board-and-cinder-block ramp in the street and they were taking turns jumping it with their bikes.

"Same old circus," said Strange, looking through the windshield from behind the wheel of the Caprice. He was holding his cell phone, flipping its cover open and closed.

"You feel robbed?"

"A little. In my heart I know I shouldn't, but there it is."

"*I* do," said Quinn. "Everything we did today, all the running around and all the sweat, and I feel like we didn't accomplish jack shit. Like we were one step behind everyone else."

"Well, we're not the law. They do have a little bit of an advantage on us. Anyway, we got the girl and her kid to a safe place. That was something."

"Not enough for me. I'd feel a whole lot better if I'd accomplished something."

"There's always tomorrow."

"I was thinkin' you'd come with me over to Naylor before we head back to Northwest. Talk to those boys about Linda Welles."

"Tonight?"

"Damn right."

"Nah, man, my day is done. I'm gonna go home and have a late dinner with Janine, see my stepson, make sure Devra and the boy got settled in all right. Pet my dog. You need to go home, too."

"Yeah, okay."

"Look at me, Terry. Promise me that's what you're gonna do."

"I'm going home," said Quinn.

"Good man," said Strange.

Quinn listened to the click of the cover, then looked at the cell in Strange's hand. "You gonna use that or just wear out the parts?"

"I been debating on making a call."

"To who?"

"Dewayne Durham. I got his number from Donut, remember?"

"And what would you tell him?"

"It would be an anonymous call. I'd tip him that his brother got done by Horace McKinley or one of his people. I was thinkin', a call like that, it might speed along McKinley's demise."

"Why would you do that?"

"McKinley threatened me, Terry. Threatened my family. Talked about me losing my license, my business, everything."

"Wouldn't be the first time you been threatened. You said it earlier, you let yourself get disrespected like that every day."

"This was a different kind of threat. Boys like that don't

concern themselves with licenses and businesses. They want to take you out, they take you *out*. Got me to thinkin', it was the same kind of threat I got on my answering machine the night my office got burgled."

"He's working for the same people broke into your place."

Strange nodded. "Would explain for real why he was so interested in hiding this witness. And he got all emotional back there, implied that he was protected. Which is why he goes about his business down here and doesn't take the long fall."

"Protected by who? The FBI?"

"Whoever. The government. Mr. Big. I don't know for sure, and I never will know, most likely. You get the general idea."

"But you're not gonna make that call, are you, Derek?"

"No. I'm not in the business of killing young men, no matter who it is. Anyway, McKinley's gonna die or be locked up soon enough, I expect, without my help. They can't keep him out of jail forever."

"And then you'll be out here defending him."

"Could be. But not defending *him*. Defending his *rights*. And yeah, there's a difference. McKinley himself called me on that one earlier tonight. And I've been trying to work it out."

"So have you?"

"Not entirely. It's an ongoin' process, I guess."

"What are you going to do about the ones watching you?"

"Nothin'. Just keep doing my job. I already decided I'm not gonna let them fade me."

Strange made a call to Lieutenant Lydell Blue. He told him about the house in the woods off Wheeler Road, gave him the license plate numbers off the red El Dorado and the Avalon, relayed what he'd seen and some of his suspicions, and reported on the death of Mario Durham. Blue thanked him, said that they'd get the local branch of the ATF involved, and commented that Strange and Quinn had had a full day. It prompted Strange to remind Blue about a full day they had both had together, thirty years earlier, involving two Howard girls, a bag of reefer, and a couple bottles of wine. Strange laughed with his friend and ended the call.

"Well, let me get on my way," said Strange. "I'm about ready to go to sleep right here."

"I'm gone, too," said Quinn, touching the handle of the door.

"Terry," said Strange, holding his arm. "Thanks for your help today, man. You know I couldn't have done any of this without you."

"No problem."

"*Go home,*" said Strange, staring into Quinn's eyes.

Quinn pulled his arm free. "I will."

"Always interesting with you around, man."

Quinn smiled. "You, too."

Strange watched him walk across the strobing landscape to his car. Head up, strutting, with that cocky way of his. He wanted to scream out Terry's name then, call him back, tell him something, though he didn't know what or why. But soon Quinn was in his Chevelle, cooking the big engine, and driving up the block.

Strange started the Caprice and slid an old O'Jays, *Back Stabbers*, into the deck. That nice ballad of theirs, "Who Am I," with Eddie Levert singing tender and tough like only he could, filled the car, and Strange felt himself unwind. He put the car in gear and headed for home.

❐

"YOU crossed that line," said Dewayne Durham. "Might give me the impression you want to do me some harm."

"I wanted to talk to you, is all," said Horace McKinley. "Didn't think it would work too good, us shoutin' at each other across the alley."

"Ain't nobody here but me and Zulu."

"My troops are all out workin', too. What with all this talk I hear about us goin' to war, thought it'd be a good time to sort some shit out."

"What about you?" said Durham, looking at Foreman. "You always talkin' about stayin' neutral. Why you out here, Ulysses? Why you standin' next to *him?*"

"Horace called me," said Foreman. "Asked me if I'd mediate this discussion. Said y'all would need someone in the middle, someone who wasn't gonna take no sides. It's in my interest that the two of you work this out. So here I am."

Durham and Walker stood on the back steps of the house on Atlantic, looking down at McKinley and Foreman, who stood in the weedy patch of yard. On McKinley's ribbed wife-beater, high on his cowlike chest, was a wet purple stain. The butt of his gun rose from the waistband of his warm-up suit. He wasn't trying to hide that he was strapped, and neither were Durham or Walker. Durham guessed that Foreman was wearing his iron, too. They all knew. But to mention it would be akin to admitting fear. And this was something none of them would ever do.

"We gonna stand out here all night?" said Foreman.

"C'mon in," said Durham.

Durham and Walker gave them their backs and walked through the door, electing to lead rather than step aside to let the others pass. They were followed by McKinley and Foreman into a dark kitchen lit by a single votive candle and then a hall, where they found their way by touch against the plaster walls. Then they were all in a living room furnished with a card table and a couple of folding chairs. Candles had been set and lit on the floor, on the card table, and on the stairway. Drums and bass played softly from a beat box on the floor.

Durham and Walker stopped walking and turned. McKinley and Foreman also stopped and faced them, the card table between them. They stood with their legs spread and their feet planted. The big men filled the room. Candlelight danced in their faces and the flames from the candles threw huge shadows up on the walls.

"Go ahead and talk," said Durham.

McKinley spread his hands, keeping them in the area of his gun. "We just need to slow down some, think before we let our pride go and start some kind of drama we can't take back."

"Keep talking."

"Want you to know, straight away, that I didn't tell the Coates cousins to fire down on your boys at the school that night."

"They did it anyway."

"Those 'Bamas was just wild like that," said McKinley, searching out the corner of his eye for movement from Foreman. But Foreman was just standing with his shoulders squared, looking straight ahead.

"New gun?" said Durham, nodding at the grip of the automatic, tight against the folds of McKinley's belly.

"Sig forty-five," said McKinley.

Durham felt heat come to his face. "My brother, Mario, was shot dead tonight."

McKinley nodded solemnly, thinking that it had happened about thirty years too late. Someone should have shot the motherfucker when he'd popped out his mama's pussy, much good as he'd been to anybody his whole sorry-ass life.

"Too bad he died," said McKinley.

"You wouldn't know nothin' *about* it, then."

"I guess the po-lice caught up with him. Heard he had some trouble with a girl."

"Nah," said Durham, his lip trembling. "Wasn't the police."

"Who it was, then?"

"Oh, I don't know. Prob'ly just some fat motherfucker with a forty-five."

The four of them stood there, staring at one another, saying nothing, watching the light shift in the room.

"Well, Zulu," said Durham, "I guess we done talked too much."

Foreman reached and cross-drew his guns just as Durham and Walker went for theirs. They never touched their guns. They dropped their hands to their sides, knowing they had been bested, looking at their own deaths down the barrels of the .357 and the .9. McKinley pulled his Sig and held it on the men.

"You did talk too much," said Foreman, snicking back the hammer of the revolver, disgust on his face. "*Too* got-damn much. For a minute there I thought you were gonna try and talk us to death. You had the draw on us, too. Motherfuckin' kids out here playin' gangster. Shit."

McKinley laughed shortly. "Do it, big man."

"Yeah," said Foreman. "Okay."

Foreman turned the LadySmith on McKinley and squeezed off two quick rounds. McKinley's blood blew back at him and Foreman kept firing, moving the gun from McKinley's belly to his chest, plaster exploding off the wall as the bullets exited his back. McKinley grunted, reached out for something, and lost his feet. As he fell, Foreman shot him in the groin and chest. Then the hammer fell on an empty chamber with an audible click.

Foreman still had the Colt trained on Durham and Walker. He holstered the revolver expertly, without looking for the leather, and faced them. Smoke was heavy in the candlelight. Foreman's ears rung from the boom of the Magnum. He did not squint, looking at them, and he kept his voice even and direct.

"Hope you learned a lesson here tonight," said Foreman. "I was a cop. Still am in my mind. You punk-ass motherfuckers out here, think you can threaten a police officer. You are wrong. Tellin' me what's good for my business. I don't give a good fuck about him, or you, 'cause there's always gonna be someone to come along and take y'all's place. You who think you're so special. Y'all ain't shit. Think about that the next time you get the idea you're gonna rise up."

Durham said nothing. He had raised his hands in defense and they were shaking. He wanted to lower them, but he couldn't move them in any direction at all.

"I hear sirens," said Walker.

"Police gonna have to respond to this one," said Foreman. "That gun does make some noise. Anyway, it's your problem, not mine. I know you won't mention I was here."

"We'll take care of it," said Walker.

Foreman stood over McKinley and fired two shots from the Colt into his corpse. The force of the rounds lifted him up from the hardwood floor. Then the body settled in the mix of plaster and blood.

"That's for talkin' shit about my woman," said Foreman, holstering the Colt.

He walked off, disappearing into the darkness of the hall. Durham lowered his hands, hearing the back door open and shut.

"D," said Walker, "I'm gonna need some help to drag Hoss out there to the alley."

But Durham did not answer. He was staring at his shaking hands.

35

STRANGE parked the Caprice on Quintana, killed the engine, and looked at the house he shared with his wife and stepson. Janine and Lionel were standing on the front lawn with Devra Stokes, in the light of a spot lamp Strange had hung above the door himself. Strange smiled, seeing the puff Lionel put in his chest as he talked to the girl. Juwan was playing with Greco, throwing him that red spiked rubber ball the tan boxer loved, then chasing him around the yard. Greco allowed the boy to catch up, letting him put his hand in his mouth, trying but failing to get the ball free.

Strange got out of the car. Greco's nub of a tail twitched furiously as he heard the familiar slam of the Caprice's door, but he stayed with the boy. Strange crossed the sidewalk and met the group in the light of the yard.

"What's goin' on, family?" said Strange. He hugged Lionel,

then Janine. He kissed her and kept his arm around her shoulder after breaking their embrace.

"We're just getting acquainted," said Janine, smiling at Devra.

"Everyone's nice," said Devra.

"Yeah, they're all right," said Strange.

"Where you been, Pop? Keeping the streets safe for democracy?"

"While the city sleeps," said Strange.

"Hungry?" said Janine.

"You know I am."

"I saved you some meat loaf."

"Knew there was a reason my car turned down this street on its own."

"You could have stopped at any old restaurant," said Janine.

"It wouldn't be home," said Strange. He kissed her again, and this time did not break away. "Ain't nothin' better than this."

◻

QUINN went home to a quiet, empty apartment. He hadn't heard from Sue Tracy all day and hadn't expected to. She and her partner, Karen, were close to finding a girl they'd been looking for for the past month or so. They'd planned to snatch her off the street that night.

The message light on his machine was blinking and Quinn hit the bar. It was Sue, asking him to call her on her cell.

He took off his shirt, washed his neck and face over the bathroom sink, and washed under his arms. He changed into a clean white T-shirt, went to the kitchen, found a Salisbury steak dinner in the freezer, and put it in his microwave oven. He set the power and time and touched the start button, then moved out to the living room and phoned Sue.

"Sue Tracy."

"Terry Quinn."

"Stop it."

"Where are you?"

"Out at Seven Locks with Karen. We got our girl. We're processing the paperwork with the police, and her mother is on the way."

"Can you come over?"

"It's gonna be a couple of hours."

Quinn looked at his watch. "Christ, it's late."

"Too late?"

"No, no. I want to see you."

"Good. Did you have a productive day?"

"A lot happened," said Quinn. "I don't know about productive."

"What about Linda Welles? Anything?"

"Yeah, plenty," said Quinn, too quickly. "I'll give it to you when you get here."

"You might be sleeping."

"Wake me up."

"I'm going to, believe me. Listen, Terry, they're calling us in. Love you."

"I love *you*," said Quinn.

The line went dead. Quinn stared at the phone.

I'll give it to you when you get here.

He had a couple of hours to kill before Sue would be by. Enough time to go down there, get it, and have it for her when she arrived.

It wasn't about finding Linda Welles. It was about doing something, and in the process, getting back a piece of his pride. He knew this, but he pushed the knowledge to the back of his mind.

Quinn went to the kitchen. He had a few bites of the Salisbury steak and some of the accompanying potatoes and mixed vegetables. Just enough to make his hunger headache fade but not enough to make him heavy and slow. He threw the rest of the dinner in the trash. He drank a large glass of water and walked to his bedroom.

Quinn retrieved his Colt, a black .45 with checkered grips, a five-inch barrel, and a seven-shot load, from his chest of drawers. He released the magazine, examined it, and slapped it back into the butt. He racked the slide. Quinn had bought the piece, a model O, after a conversation in a local bar.

It never would have happened, I had my gun.

Quinn holstered the Colt behind the waistband of his jeans and put on his black leather jacket.

Okay, so he'd been punked. He could fix that now.

He thought of Strange. He hadn't lied to him. He'd gone home like he'd promised.

Quinn grabbed some tapes, a pen, and the Linda Welles file on his way out the door. He walked out into the night air, letting the mist cool his face. He ignitioned the Caprice and put *Copper-head Road* into the deck and turned it up. As he was going south on Georgia, the traffic lights flashed yellow. Quinn's long sight was gone and the lights were a blur. He downshifted coming out of the tunnel under the pedestrian bridge leading to the railroad tracks. A freight train neared the station as he passed. Going up the hill, Quinn punched the gas.

❐

IN Far Southeast, Quinn stopped the Chevelle on Southern Avenue near Naylor Road. He withdrew his Colt and flicked its safety off, then refitted it under his jacket. He turned off Southern and drove up Naylor. He passed the well-tended Naylor Gardens complex, the buildings deteriorating in appearance as he moved on. Up past Naylor Plaza he saw the group of young men sitting on the front steps of their unit at the top of a rise of weeds and dirt. He swung the Chevelle around in the street and parked behind a red Toyota Solara with gold-accented alloy wheels and gold trim.

Do your job.

Quinn was out of the car quickly, walking up the hill. The young men had heard his pipes and were watching his approach. He walked through the mist and the hang of smoke in the halogen light. His blood jumped as he walked, watching the faces of the heavyset young man with the blown-out Afro and the skinny kid with the napkin bandanna and the others who had been there earlier in the day. He reached behind him. His hand went up under his jacket. Finding the grip of the gun, he was not afraid. He pulled the Colt, going directly to the heavyset young man. He grabbed the young man's shirt and bunched it in his left fist, touching the barrel of the Colt under his chin.

"Put your hands flat beside you," said Quinn. "Your friends don't want to fuck with me. Believe it."

The young man did it. No one made a comment or laughed. No one moved.

"I ain't strapped," said the young man.

"I don't *care*," said Quinn. "Linda Welles."

"Who?"

"The girl on the flyer I showed you. You know where she is, who she's with. Gimme a name."

The barrel of the gun dented the young man's skin as Quinn pressed it to his jaw.

"She stayin' with this boy Jimmy Davis, up on Buena Vista Terrace. Up there off Twenty-eighth."

"Where on Buena Vista?"

"He's in this place, got a red door."

"Say it again."

The young man repeated the name and address. Quinn released his shirt and stepped back. He held the gun loosely at his side. He looked around at the faces of the boys on the steps. They stared at him with nothing in their eyes. One of the young men raised a brown paper bag and tipped its bottle to his lips.

Quinn backed up a few steps. He holstered the gun. He

turned and walked down the rise to his Chevelle. He got under the wheel, started the car, and pulled off the curb.

At the next corner, Quinn stopped and wrote down the name and location the young man had given him on the back of one of the flyers. He ejected the Steve Earle tape and slipped *Darkness on the Edge of Town* into the deck. "Adam Raised a Cain" came forward, and he turned it up. Quinn rolled down his window and began to laugh. It was easy. Fire with fire. All it took was a gun.

He drove down Naylor and onto 25th, and looked around at the unfamiliar sights. He didn't know this stretch of road, and anyway, his night vision was for shit. Street lamps and headlights were haloed and blurry. He wasn't lost. He'd come out on Alabama somewhere and from there he could hit MLK. He wasn't in a hurry. He was enjoying his Springsteen, his victory, the night.

He pulled up behind a car at a stoplight. Cars were parked along the curb at his right. In his rearview he saw a red import, tricked out in gold. He looked to his left. A white car with tinted windows rolled up had pulled alongside him. He couldn't see the occupants of the car. He heard Strange's voice in his head: *A classic trap. Gangs hunt in packs.*

Quinn's eyes went back to his rearview. The driver of the red car was heavy and wore his hair in a blown-out natural.

Quinn reached behind him and fumbled under his jacket. He found purchase on the grip of the Colt and began to draw it out. As he did this, he looked out the open window, feeling the presence of someone there.

He saw a skinny boy with a napkin bandanna on his head and a stainless automatic in his hand. The boy's finger went inside the trigger guard just as Quinn freed his gun and cleared it from his waist, seeing the stainless piece swing up, knowing he was far too late.

Quinn thinking, *He ain't nothin' but a kid,* as the world flashed white.

AUGUST

36

GRANVILLE Oliver's biceps pushed against the fabric of his orange jumpsuit. His manacles and chains scraped the table before him as he lowered his hands.

"Thanks for coming by," said Oliver.

"Ain't no thing," said Strange.

"Sentencing's today."

"Ives told me."

"Whichever way it goes, I figure we won't be seeing each other again. So I thought we should, you know, say good-bye, eye to eye."

Strange nodded. The room was quiet except for the muffled voices of attorneys and their clients seated in other cubicles behind Plexiglas dividers. A guard with heavy-lidded eyes sat in a darkened booth, watching the room.

"You did everything you could," said Oliver.

"I tried."

"Yeah, you and that white boy was working with you, y'all did a good job."

Strange leaned forward. "Say his name."

"Quinn."

"That's right."

"You two did all right, bringing that girl in like you did. For a while, seemed like her testimony was really gonna help my case. Sayin' that Phil was talkin' to her about plannin' to kill my uncle and all that. Course, when they crossed her, the prosecutors tried to make her look like a common ho, what with her havin' that boy out of wedlock, and the lifestyle she was into when she was kickin' it with Phil. But she kept her composure up there. She was good."

"She was."

"Where's she at now?"

Devra Stokes was living in Northwest, working in a salon, going to Strayer and taking secretarial classes around her hours in the shop. She and Juwan were renting an apartment, found by Ives, in a fringe but not deadly neighborhood. She and the boy were doing fine. But there was no reason for Strange to give Oliver, or anyone else connected with the trial, her whereabouts.

"I don't know," said Strange.

"Anyway, I guess it's all over now. Relieved to have it behind me, you want the truth."

After the defense had rested its case and closing arguments had been presented, jury deliberation lasted less than two weeks, an unusually short time for a case with this kind of life-and-death ramification. Once the verdict was read, a kind of minihearing had commenced in which Raymond Ives and his team argued mitigating circumstances in hopes of avoiding the death penalty. That phase, too, had concluded, leaving only Judge Potterfield's sentencing to complete the trial.

"Too bad it didn't work out for you," said Strange.

"Aw, shit, I knew how it was gonna end from day one. That jury they handpicked, they decided what they were gonna do the first time they got a look at me. I mean, you get down to it, they didn't even need to go through the trouble of havin' that trial."

"Maybe you're right."

"Ain't no maybe about it. It wasn't no kind of shock to me when they found me guilty. Question now is, will I live or die?"

Strange sat impassively, looking into Granville Oliver's golden eyes.

"You know, it's funny," said Granville. "There was that day, when the Stokes girl was testifyin', that I actually thought that there was a chance I might walk. She had planted that, what do you call it, *seed of doubt* up in that whole courtroom. And I remember thinkin', Wouldn't that be some shit, if it was what she was sayin' that was gonna get me off?"

"Why would that be funny?" said Strange.

"Phil Wood told that girl he was gonna kill my uncle Bennett? Shoot, Phil was just talkin', pumpin' his own self up for the benefit of that pretty young ass. Phil had killed before to get his stripes, but he wouldn't never pull the trigger on my own kin, not unless I ordered him to do it. And I never did."

"What are you telling me?"

"*I* killed my uncle, Strange. Walked right up to the open window of his new Jag and shot that snitch motherfucker to death. Man was about to flip on me, and it was down to that. Him or me, and I wasn't gonna do no long time, not for blood or anyone else." Oliver looked Strange over. "You surprised?"

"Not really. In my heart, I guess I knew all along."

"Didn't make no difference to you, huh?"

"No. I suppose it didn't."

"You knew I was who they said I was and still you kept on it. Why?"

Because I took your father out, thirty-some years ago. Because it was me who put you behind the eight ball, like all these other kids out here, got no fathers to teach them, by example, right from wrong. How to be tough without being violent, how to walk with your head up and

your shoulders square, how to love one woman and be there for your chil-
dren and make it work. Because it was me who put you on the road that
took you where you are today.

"I was just doing my job," said Strange.

"Well, you stood tall," said Oliver.

"I did my best."

"And I appreciate it. Wanted you to know."

Their hands met in the middle of the table. Strange broke
Oliver's grip and stood.

"How's the little man doin'?" said Oliver, looking up, man-
aging a smile.

"Robert's fine. He's with that family affiliated with the church.
I'm going to see him at practice this evening."

"Boy can play, can't he?"

"Yes, he can," said Strange.

"Holler at you later, hear?"

"I'll pray for you, Granville."

And for myself, thought Strange, as he turned and walked
from the D.C. Jail, leaving Granville Oliver in chains.

❒

STRANGE had no live cases on the week's schedule. He was rest-
less and had time to kill before evening practice, so he went about
filling up his day. He visited a technical school in Northwest that
Lamar Williams had mentioned to him as a place that offered
computer training on a noncollegiate level. Strange had promised
Lamar that he would contribute half to the cost of classes if he
thought the school was okay. He picked up a brochure and got
their rates from one of the admission staff, and had a look at the
facilities. Then he called Janine on his cell. He asked her if she'd like
to meet him at the old Crisfield's, up on Georgia, for a late lunch.

After raw oysters, soft-shell crab sandwiches, and a couple of
beers at the U-shaped bar, Strange and Janine went back to the

house on Quintana and made slow love in their bedroom as Greco slept at the foot of the bed. The house was quiet, with only the sounds of their coupling and the low hum of the window air conditioners running on the first and second floors. Lionel was in College Park, having started his freshman orientation.

Strange and Janine held each other for a while, kissing but saying little, after both of them had come. She looked up into his eyes and wiped some sweat off his brow.

"You're troubled."

"Even with all this," said Strange. "I mean, with all I have, with you and Lionel. It's crazy, I know."

"You can't hide it. Especially not in our bed."

"I just feel like doin' something. Making some kind of a difference. 'Cause damn if it don't seem like I been chasing my tail these past months." Strange put his weight on one elbow. "You know, the night Terry got shot —"

"Derek."

"The night he got *shot*, Janine, he told me that all he wanted was to feel like he accomplished something."

"Derek, don't."

"That's what I want to feel now, too."

"Maybe you haven't felt that way lately. But you will."

"I never should have let him go home alone like he did. I should have brought him back here that night to hang with all of us."

"But that's not what happened."

"I know it."

"Lie down," said Janine. "Hold me and let's go to sleep. Can't remember the last time we had an afternoon to ourselves like this, just to do nothing but rest."

"Okay," said Strange. "I need to rest. That sounds good."

But when he awoke, late in the afternoon, his feelings had not changed.

◻

STRANGE drove down to 9th and Upshur. He had not yet read the paper, so he picked up that day's *Post* at Hawk's barbershop and told one of the cutters he would return it.

Going into his shop, he went through the reception area and into his office, where he had a seat behind his desk. The vinyl version of *Round 2*, the Stylistics' follow-up to their debut, was leaning up against the wall, facing out, directly behind his chair. Lewis, from the used-book store in downtown Silver Spring, had mailed it to Strange, and Strange had not yet taken it home. Like the gum wrappers still in the top drawer of Quinn's desk, it was something he had not wanted to deal with just yet.

Strange went right to the Metro section. Between the roundup columns, "In Brief" and "Crime," there had been five gun-related murders reported over the past weekend. Many of the victims had gone unnamed and all were in their late teens or early twenties. One had occurred in east-of-the-park Northwest and the others had occurred in Far Southeast. At the city's annual Georgia Avenue Day celebration, a teenager had been shot by random gunfire, sending some families fleeing in panic and causing others to dive on their children, shielding them from further harm.

Strange went to the A section. Deep inside, a congressman from the Carolinas dismissed the need for further handgun laws and vowed to continue his fight to hold Hollywood and the record industry accountable for the sexual content and violent nature of their product. This same congressman had threatened to cut off federal funds to the District of Columbia, earmarked for education, if D.C. did not agree to change its Metro signs from "National Airport" to "*Reagan* National Airport."

Strange turned his head and looked at the Stylistics album, a birthday gift from Quinn, propped up against the wall.

Do something.

"I will," said Strange, though there was no one but him in

the room. His voice was clear and emphatic, and it sounded good to his ears.

◻

STRANGE turned on the light-box of his storefront, returned the newspaper to Hawk's, and drove north to his row house on Buchanan. From his basement he retrieved a couple of red two-gallon containers of gasoline, one of which was full, and carried them out to the trunk of his Caprice. He went to the Amoco station next, filled up his tank and filled the empty container with gas. He placed it next to the other in the trunk and used his heavy toolbox to wedge them tight against the well. Then he drove down Georgia to Iowa Avenue along Roosevelt High and parked in the lot between Lydell Blue's Buick and Dennis Arrington's import.

The boys were down in the Roosevelt "bowl," doing their warm-ups in the center of the field. The quarterback, Dante Morris, and Prince, another veteran player, were in the middle of the circle, leading the team in their chant. Strange could hear them as he took the aluminum-over-concrete steps of the stadium to the break in the fence.

"How y'all feel?"

"Fired up!"

"How y'all feel?"

"Fired up!"

"Breakdown."

"Whoo!"

"Breakdown."

"Whoo!"

Strange shook hands with Blue and then with Arrington, a computer specialist and deacon who was a longtime member of the coaching staff. The boys were warming up together but would soon break into their Pee Wee and Midget teams, determined by weight, for the remainder of the practice.

"You're a little late," said Blue.

"Had to get some gas," said Strange.

"We got a scrimmage set up for this weekend."

"Kingman," said Arrington.

"They're always tough," said Strange.

"I like the way that boy Robert Gray is playing," said Blue. "Boy runs with authority. He's not much of leader, but he can break it."

"He's just getting to know the other kids," said Strange. "And he's naturally on the quiet side. Plus he's smart; he already learned the plays in just a week's time. Be a change from Rico, anyway, the way that boy runs his mouth."

Rico was the team's halfback, a talented but cocky kid who had a complaint ready for every command.

"Gray'll keep Rico on his toes," said Blue. "Make him appreciate that position he's got, and work harder to keep it."

"I was thinkin' the same thing," said Strange. "And who knows? Maybe Robert'll earn that position himself."

"You gonna take the Pee Wee team alone, Derek?" said Blue, his eyes moving to Arrington's. "'Cause me and Dennis here got our hands full with the Midgets."

Strange nodded. "I'll handle it."

"You could use some help."

"I know it," said Strange, and ended the conversation at that.

After practice, the coaches had the boys take a knee and told them what they had seen them do right and wrong in the past two hours. The boys' jerseys were dark with sweat and their faces were beaded with it. When Strange and Blue were done talking, Arrington asked them what time they should show up for the next practice.

"Six o'clock," said a few of the boys.

"What *time?*" said Arrington.

"*Six o'clock, on the dot, be there, don't miss it!*" they shouted in unison.

"Put it in," said Strange.

They all managed to touch hands in the center of the circle.

"*Petworth Panthers!*"

"All right," said Strange. "Those of you got your bikes, get on home straightaway. If you got people waitin' for you, we'll see you get in the cars up in the lot. For you others, Coach Lydell and Coach Dennis and myself will drive you home. I don't want to see none a y'all walking through these streets at night. Prince, Dante, and Robert, you come with me."

Strange crossed the field in the gathering darkness, Robert Gray beside him, his helmet swinging by his side.

"You looked good out there," said Strange.

Gray nodded but kept his face neutral and looked straight ahead.

"It's okay to smile," said Strange.

Gray tried. It didn't come naturally for him, and he looked away.

"It's a start," said Strange. "Gonna take some work, is all it is."

Strange dropped Dante Morris, Prince, and Gray at their places of residence. Pulling off the curb from his last stop, Strange got WOL, the all-talk station on 1450 AM, up on the dial. The local headline news had just begun. From the female reporter, Strange learned that Judge Potterfield had sentenced Granville Oliver to death.

◻

DRIVING south on Georgia, Strange saw a boy standing in front of his shop on 9th. He swung the Caprice around, parked in front of the funeral home, and walked toward the boy. He wasn't any older than seven. His dark skin held a yellow glow from the light-box overhead. The boy took a step back as Strange approached.

"It's okay," said Strange. "That's my place you're standing in front of, son. I was just coming by to turn off the light."

The boy looked up at the lighted sign. "That your business?"

"That's me. Strange Investigations. I own it. Been in this location over twenty-five years."

"Dag."

"What you doin' out here this time of night all by yourself?"

"My mother went to that market across the street. Said she couldn't hold my hand crossing Georgia with those market bags in her hand, so I should wait here till she comes back."

"What's your name, young man?"

The boy smiled. "They call me Peanut Butter and Jelly, 'cause that's what I like to eat."

"Okay."

"Mister?"

"What?"

"Will you wait with me till my mother comes back? It's kinda scary out here in the dark."

Strange said that he would.

❏

AFTER the mother had come, and after Strange had given her a polite but direct talk about leaving her boy out on the street at night, Strange put his key to the front door of his shop. He had a slight hunger and knew that he could find a PayDay bar in Janine's desk. As he began to fit the key in the lock, he heard the rumble of a high-horse, big American engine, and he turned his head.

A white Coronet 500 with Magnum wheels was rolling down the short block. It pulled over directly in front of the shop and the driver cut its engine. Strange recognized the car. When the driver got out, Strange could see that, indeed, it was that Greek detective who worked for Elaine Clay. As he crossed the sidewalk, Strange could see in the Greek's waxed eyes that he was up on something. And as he grew nearer, he smelled the alcohol on his breath.

"Nick Stefanos." He reached out his hand and Strange took it.
"I remember. What you doin' in my neighborhood, man?"

"I was driving around," said Stefanos. "You said that if the light-box was on I should stop by."

"I was just fixin' to turn it off," said Strange.

"Too late," said Stefanos with a stupid grin. "I'm here."

37

STRANGE and Stefanos walked to the Dodge, parked under a street lamp. Stefanos leaned against its rear quarter panel and folded his arms.

"I heard the news about Oliver on the radio," he said. "I guess it's why I thought of you and took a shot at stopping by."

"They'll give him the needle now, up in Indiana."

"Not just yet. There's plenty of appeal time left. Anyway, you did what you could."

"That's what everyone tells me," said Strange. "So you were just driving around, huh?"

"Yeah, my girlfriend, woman named Alicia, she's out with friends. I got itchy hanging around my crib."

"Smells like you made a few pit stops on your way here," said Strange. "Thought you were staying away from drinking."

"I said I was tryin' to stay out of bars. It's not the same thing."

"You fall off that wagon much?"

Stefanos shrugged. They stood there for a while without speaking. Stefanos lit a Marlboro and tossed the match onto the street.

"You sure did stir up the bees down in Southeast," said Stefanos.

"I guess I did."

"After Horace McKinley was found in that alley, it started the ball rolling, didn't it? The ATF got involved and put together a case against that gun dealer, lived over the line in Maryland."

"Ulysses Foreman. But it wasn't McKinley's death that triggered all the activity. It was Durham's boy Bernard Walker gettin' arrested for an unrelated murder a month later. The Feds flipped him on Durham and got him to detail the Foreman operation — what he knew about it, anyway. Apparently it was Foreman who blew up McKinley's shit. They even indicted Foreman's girlfriend as a coconspirator in the gun trafficking charge. Getting defendants to flip beats good police work every time."

"I guess I ought to thank you for the job."

"What job?"

"The Dewayne Durham thing, the whole Six Hundred Crew operation, it's gonna be a RICO trial now. Elaine Clay was the PD assigned to the case. I'm doing the investigative work for the defense."

"Congratulations," said Strange.

"It's work," said Stefanos. He reached into the open window of his car, pulled free a pint bottle from under the front seat. "What ever happened with that little problem you had with the authorities?"

"Nothing. No more burglaries, no more threats. Never heard another word after McKinley got chilled."

"No reason to go after you anymore. They got their verdict."

"I guess."

Strange watched him unscrew the top and tip the bottle to

his lips. He watched the bubbles rise in the whiskey as Stefanos closed his eyes. The Greek wiped his mouth with the back of his hand when he was done.

"Here you go," said Stefanos, offering Strange the bottle. "Shake hands with my old granddad."

"Crazy motherfucker," said Strange, waving the bottle off.

"Suit yourself," said Stefanos. He dragged deeply on his cigarette and blew smoke at his feet.

Strange looked him over. "Feel like going for a ride?"

Stefanos said, "What'd you have in mind?"

Strange told him.

"Guess you caught me in the right frame of mind," said Stefanos.

"You want to take a pee, wash your face or somethin', before we go? It's a long drive."

"No. But let's pick up a six-pack. I need something cold to go with this bourbon. We can take my ride, you want to."

"I'll drive," said Strange. "You're half blind."

❐

THEY drove out of the city via New York Avenue, took the tunnel to 395, and were soon into Virginia and on Route 1. They spoke very little. Strange listened to his tapes, and Stefanos drank and smoked. He seemed to enjoy the wind in his face.

The road became more barren as they drove south.

Forty minutes later, they passed the Marine Corps base at Quantico and continued on.

"Won't be long now," said Strange.

"What's the plan?"

"No plan. Get in quick, burn the motherfucker down, try to get out without getting nailed."

"Viva la revolution," said Stefanos.

"I need you as a lookout."

"But I'm half blind."

"Funny."

"I got the matches. Don't I get to play?"

"Yeah, okay."

"We gonna wear gloves or something?"

"And ski masks, too. Shit, we get caught, we're gonna get caught on the site. I ain't gonna worry about fingerprints or nothin' else but haulin' ass out of there. Let's just do this thing, all right?"

Deep forest lined both sides of the highway. Strange took his foot off the gas pedal and let a car pass on his left. Soon he slowed the Caprice down and swerved off onto the berm, then he made a right onto a gravel drive where Stefanos had seen a cut in the trees. What looked like a house stood alone back off the road. A sign reading "Commonwealth Guns" was strung along a porch holding barred windows. A light in a glass globe mounted beside the door illuminated the porch.

Strange killed the headlights as he drove the car onto the grass and parked alongside the house. The motorcycle was not on the porch.

"Let's go," he said.

They got out and went to the trunk. Strange opened it and took out the two cans of gas. A car approached on the highway and he closed the trunk lid, extinguishing its light.

"There's gonna be cars from time to time goin' by," said Strange. "Just keep working fast."

"You got a rag in there?"

"Yeah."

"Give it to me. I'll find a stick to tie it around while you do your thing. After I take care of that porch light. Leave some gas for the torch."

"Okay, man. Let's go."

Stefanos waited for the rag, wrapped it around one hand, then went up to the porch and unscrewed the hot lightbulb inside its shield. Then he moved to the treeline in the nearly total darkness and hand-searched the ground until he found a small branch. He wrapped the rag around the top of the branch and tied it tightly so that it would not slip off.

Strange doused the porch with gasoline and continued around the house, flinging the liquid against its walls. When he was done with one can he went back for the other and continued his circular path. Cars sped by on the highway, but none stopped.

Strange met Stefanos at the trunk of the car.

"We all set?" said Stefanos.

"Yeah. It's an all-wood house, should go up good."

"Here," said Stefanos, holding out the branch. Strange poured gasoline onto the rag, careful not to get any near the car.

"That's good. Drive the car up to the road. I'll be right with you, hear?"

Stefanos smiled. "Set 'em off, Jefferson: one, two, three, four."

"You are something. Gimme your matches."

"Here you go, Dad."

Strange felt the book pressed into his hand.

Stefanos took the car up to the road, let it idle on the berm. He looked south and in the rearview took in the northern view. There were no cars coming in either direction. He flipped the headlights on and then off.

Strange lit the rag atop the branch. The light from it was startling and he swung the branch and released it, pinwheeling it onto the porch of the gun store. The porch caught fire immediately and then the rest of the house seemed to explode into a ring of flame. Strange stepped back, feeling the heat of the fire, watching it engulf the house. He heard the sound of his own car's horn but stayed where he was. He admired the power of the fire and the color dancing against the trees. He heard his horn again and he turned and jogged to his car. Stefanos was in the passenger seat, sweat shotgunned on his forehead. Strange got under the wheel and pulled down on the tree. He fishtailed off the berm, pinning the accelerator as he hit the asphalt.

Stefanos unscrewed the top from his pint bottle and had a drink. He handed it to Strange, who tipped it to his lips. The two of them laughed.

Strange handed the bottle back. "Thanks, buddy."

"You feel better now?"

"Yeah, I feel good." He thought of the cleansing warmth of the fire and the beauty of the flames.

"It's a long jolt, we get popped for this. We ruined a man's livelihood. He was running a legal business there."

"He has insurance, I expect," said Strange. "The way I look at it, we just saved a bunch of lives."

Stefanos lit a cigarette. He looked at the white divider lines on the highway, rushing under the car. "I'm sorry about your friend."

"They found that girl he was looking for," said Strange, smiling some, thinking of Quinn. "He had written down her location on the back of a flyer. It was sitting there right next to him on the seat."

Stefanos looked across the bench at Strange. "Not many of us left out here."

"No."

"I guess I'm in it for life."

"I guess I am, too."

"Seems like a long game, doesn't it?"

"Long but simple," said Strange. "Only got one rule."

"Just one?" said Stefanos.

Strange nodded. "Last man standing wins."

Acknowledgments

Thanks to Joe Aronstamn, Russell Ewart, Father George Clements, ATF Special Agent John D'Angelo, ATF Special Agent Harold Scott Jr., ATF Division Director Jeffrey Roehm, Sloan Harris, and Alicia Gordon, for their assistance and guidance in the writing of this book. As always, much love to Emily, Nick, Pete, and Rosa, for their patience and support.

BACK BAY · READERS' PICK

Reading Group Guide

SOUL
CIRCUS

A Novel by

GEORGE PELECANOS

George Pelecanos's film noir favorites

Anyone who has had a look at my website (www.george
-pelecanos.com) knows that I am a fan of '70s crime/action
films, so there is no need to once again talk up those movies (but
if you have not seen *Charley Varrick*, *Rolling Thunder*, *The Outfit*,
or *The Seven-Ups*, seek them out). For a change of pace, here are
some older noirish crime films that deserve a look.

Public Enemy (1931)

William Wellman's tough look at the rise and fall of a criminal
in Prohibition-era Chicago set a template for the gangster film
that has remained relatively unchanged and unimproved for
eighty years. Jimmy Cagney, in a star-making role, plays the
title character. The violence and sexuality are pre–Hays Code
daring. Look for the infamous grapefruit to the face of Mae
Clarke and the powerful final scene. With Edward Woods, Joan
Blondell, and Jean Harlow. An early sound picture that is still
highly watchable today. "I ain't so tough."

Angels with Dirty Faces (1938)

One of the many gangster films of the original, Depression-era
cycle, but this is in a class of its own. Two childhood friends take
very different paths: Jerry Connolly (Pat O'Brien) becomes a

priest; Rocky Sullivan (James Cagney), a hoodlum. When Sullivan is sentenced to death for his crimes, Father Connolly asks his genuinely tough pal to act like a coward in order to turn the young men who worship him away from a life of crime. The ending of this film, Sullivan's last walk to the chair, packs a wallop. Max Steiner's ominous score and director Michael Curtiz's staging caused my heart to pound in my chest and all-out shocked me when I first saw it as a kid. It hasn't left me to this day. *Angels* has been an influence on many of my books, most noticeably *The Big Blowdown, Hard Revolution,* and *The Turnaround.* With nice, naturalistic performances by Frankie Burke and William Tracey (Rocky and Jerry as boys), the original Dead End Kids, and Humphrey Bogart as a villain who gets his comeuppance in lead. "Let's say a prayer for a kid who couldn't run as fast."

Kiss of Death (1947)

Henry Hathaway's direction and all New York City locations are a highlight of this '40s crime film about ex-con turned family man Nick Bianco (Victor Mature), who agrees to work with the DA and bring down a psychopathic criminal (Richard Widmark in his screen debut as the giggling, bonkers Tommy Udo). This is the one where Widmark ties an old lady to her wheelchair and pushes her down a flight of stairs, a scene that has lost none of its power. *Kiss* would be a better than average film even if it had been cast with a bland noir stalwart like Dana Andrews or Dennis O'Keefe in the lead, but the hulking, vulnerable Mature plays Bianco with genuine emotion and lifts this into the realm of top-shelf drama. The climax, played almost wordlessly in an Italian restaurant, is super tense. With a radiant, natural Colleen Gray as Bianco's wife and Brian Donlevy as the law.

Act of Violence (1948)

Many of the films in noir's second cycle concerned themselves with veterans returning from the war only to find that their lives have been irrevocably altered; death has followed them, and its shadow has crept across their hometowns. Of these stories, *Act of Violence*, directed with flair by Fred Zinnemann, is one of the best. Van Heflin plays a former POW with a secret who is stalked by one of his fellow soldiers/prisoners, Robert Ryan. The casting could not be more perfect. Heflin was an everyman, and Ryan (a marine who my father called the McCoy) was always at his best as a sadistic tough guy. Mary Astor (from *The Maltese Falcon*) stands out as a barroom slut. With Janet Leigh as Heflin's luscious young wife. Concludes, Western style, with a shootout by the train tracks. Catch this on TCM.

Force of Evil (1948)

Abraham Polonsky's searing study of corruption and what it does to the relationship between two brothers, played by John Garfield and Thomas Gomez. On-location New York cinematography influenced by Edward Hopper paintings, true noir sensibility, and dialogue that nears poetry in its rhythm and complexity (indeed, a portion of the voiceover narration in the final act is written in iambic pentameter). Here Polonsky linked the numbers racket to the crooks on Wall Street and, among other reasons, was blacklisted because of it; the strain of that witch hunt was reportedly a factor in Garfield's fatal heart attack four years later. He left behind a work of art.

In a Lonely Place (1950)

A melancholy screenwriter (Humphrey Bogart) with violence issues is suspected of a murder until a neighbor (Gloria

Graham) in his garden apartment complex provides his alibi. After they fall for each other, she begins to doubt his innocence. Nicholas Ray's masterpiece, Humphrey Bogart's best performance, and a showcase for the lovely Gloria Graham, who shined similarly in Fritz Lang's volcanic *The Big Heat*. *In a Lonely Place* manages to locate the psychological heart of noir without resorting to the visual self-parody that eventually crippled the genre. Lush black-and-white cinematography by Burnett Guffey. Music by George Antheil. The Smithereeens wrote a song based on the poem recited in this, one of my favorite films.

Gun Crazy (1950)

Joseph H. Lewis's stylish, sexy take on the Bonnie and Clyde legend is a prime example of a talented filmmaker spinning gold with poverty-row funds. John Dall and Peggy Cummins play sharpshooters who meet at a carnival and fall in love. They knock off a series of gas stations, banks, and payroll facilities until their inevitable fall. Dall is willowy and sensitive, while the blond and beautiful Cummins is most alive with a gun in her hand; she gets off when the shooting starts. Inventive camera work by Russell Harlan puts us in the backseat of the car during the main robbery and makes the viewer complicit in the crimes. Written, mostly, by blacklisted Dalton Trumbo under the name of Millard Kaufman. In the noir tradition, the fog that envelops the lovers in the film's climax has been creeping toward them all their lives. One of the very best films of its kind.

Pickup on South Street (1953)

A Cold War thriller about a pickpocket (Richard Widmark) who unwittingly gets tangled up with Commie spies. Sam

Fuller's skillet-to-the-face style is relatively subdued here, to great effect. The New York locations, particularly the waterfront, are as memorable as the story. Brutal and convincing, with damaged characters whose loyalties, motivations, and actions are complex. With Jean Peters as the love interest/punching bag and Richard Kiley as a conflicted heavy. Thelma Ritter, playing a stoolpigeon named Moe, buys a piece of immortality in her shattering last scene. Lovingly restored on DVD by Criterion.

Kiss Me Deadly (1955)

From its stunning opening sequence to its apocalyptic finale, *Kiss Me Deadly* is, visually and thematically, the ultimate film noir. Adapted from the Mickey Spillane novel by the great Greek American novelist and screenwriter A. I. Bezzerides and directed by artist/journeyman Robert Aldrich. Ralph Meeker plays Mike Hammer the way Spillane unintentionally drew him: brutal, destructive, and not particularly bright. Cloris Leachman is the doomed hitchhiker he picks up one night, setting in motion a chain of events that leads to an atomic meltdown. Shocking violence, great L.A. locations, and a gallery of grotesques that includes Jack Elam, Albert Dekker, Paul Stewart, and Gaby Rogers as a blond-haired dish who stinks of death. With Nick Dennis as an auto mechanic who gets under the wrong car. The unorthodox credit scroll tells you that everything you are about to see will be counter to your expectations; you've entered a "world gone wrong."

The Killing (1956)

I love John Huston's *The Asphalt Jungle,* but I give the nod to this similar heist film because of its unbeautiful actors, unsavory characters, and down-and-dirty milieu. Tall country-buck

Sterling Hayden (also from *Asphalt*) leads the team in a race-track robbery that (naturally) goes awry. Director Stanley Kubrick and "Dime Store Dostoyevsky" Jim Thompson adapted the novel *Clean Break* by Lionel White. Kubrick plays with time and structure and comes into his own with the assured style of a maverick in his second feature, but it is in the writing and acting where this one shines. Watch the turns by Elisha Cook Jr., Marie Windsor, Ted De Corsia, Vince Edwards, Jay C. Flippin, and Kola Kwariani. A special place in movie history awaits the legendary Timothy Carey, here playing a racist sniper. Hayden's last line in the film encapsulates the noir ethos perfectly.

Touch of Evil (1958)

Mexican chief of narcotics Vargas (Charlton Heston) and his newlywed wife (Janet Leigh) encounter danger and corruption south of the border when they come up against a dirty American police captain named Hank Quinlan (a nearly unrecognizable Orson Welles). Crime films seem to unleash the outlandish in Welles. As in *The Lady from Shanghai*, the director pulls out all the visual stops, but *Lady* was a trip to the funhouse (literally, in its climax) whereas *Evil* is a twisted ride to the bottom of the gutter. With this one, Welles cut to absolute black, and effectively put an end to the genre. Everything that has been done since has been a parody. R.I.P., film noir.

Look for George Pelecanos's further suggestions for viewing in the reading group guides to his novels *Hard Revolution* and *The Way Home*.

Questions and topics for discussion

1. Pelecanos uses slang and urban dialect to great effect in *Soul Circus*. Each character, regardless of race or ethnicity, has a distinct voice. Discuss what dialogue means to the story, and the way Pelecanos uses dialogue differently with different characters in *Soul Circus*.

2. Morality is a theme that weaves itself throughout *Soul Circus*. Which moral issues stand out the most to you? Which characters face the toughest moral dilemmas, and how do they resolve them?

3. What do you think of the relationship between Mario and Dewayne Durham? Discuss how their feelings for each other alter their actions and reactions throughout the book.

4. Granville Oliver faces a possible death sentence in his trial. How do you feel about the potential use of capital punishment in Oliver's case — and in general?

5. At several points in the novel, Derek recognizes how lucky and happy he is to have a real home and family with Janine and Lionel, yet he still feels the need to keep his row house on Buchanan Street. Why do you think Derek seems uneasy about giving up that part of his life?

6. Do you think Derek and Terry Quinn should feel any responsibility for Olivia Elliot's death?

7. What racial struggles does Quinn face on the job? How does he deal with these tensions, and how do they affect his relationship with Derek? How do they influence his actions?

8. What is Ulysses Foreman's role in the crime chain? How much guilt do you feel he carries by trafficking guns to the gangs?

9. What considerations does Devra Stokes need to take into account before agreeing to testify on Oliver's behalf? Do you think she makes the right decision?

10. What is your opinion of Mario Durham? Do you feel any pity for him and his predicament? Do you feel he is appropriately punished by the novel's end?

11. How are the female characters in *Soul Circus* perceived by the male characters? Discuss the ways in which the women in the novel are vulnerable and influenced by the men in their lives, and the ways in which each woman is strong.

12. What similarities can you find between Derek and Nick Stefanos? Do you think these similarities are important — to the men themselves and/or to the story?

13. Do you feel there is justice in the action Derek and Nick take at the end of the book?

14. What does Pelecanos's writing reveal about urban life in Washington, D.C., and the cultural upheavals in his hometown? In what ways does he succeed in shedding light on the D.C. underworld?

About the author

George Pelecanos is the author of several highly praised and best-selling novels, including, most recently, *The Night Gardener*, *The Turnaround*, and *The Way Home*. He is also an independent-film producer, an essayist, and the recipient of numerous writing awards. He was a producer and an Emmy-nominated writer for *The Wire* and currently writes for the acclaimed HBO series *Treme*.

...and the next Derek Strange novel

In *Hard Revolution* George Pelecanos reaches back to a turbulent period in Derek Strange's early life. Following is a brief excerpt from the novel's opening pages.

ONE

DEREK Strange got down in a three-point stance. He breathed evenly, as his father had instructed him to do, and took in the pleasant smell of April. Magnolias, dogwoods, and cherry trees were in bloom around the city. The scent of their flowers, and the heavy fragrance of a nearby lilac bush growing against a residential fence, filled the air.

"You keep your back straight," said Derek, "like you're gonna set a dinner up on it. You ain't want your butt up in the air, either. That way you're ready. You just blow right out, like, and hit the holes. Bust on through."

Derek and his Saturday companion, Billy Georgelakos, were in an alley that ran behind the Three-Star Diner on a single-number block of Kennedy Street, at the eastern edge of Northwest D.C. Both were twelve years old.

"Like your man," said Billy, sitting on a milk crate, an *Our Army at War* comic book rolled tightly in his meaty hand.

"Yeah," said Derek. "Here go Jim Brown right here."

Derek came up out of his stance and exploded forward, one palm hovering above the other, both close to his chest. He took an imaginary handoff as he ran a few steps, then cut, slowed down, turned, and walked back toward Billy.

Derek had a way of moving. It was confident but not cocky, shoulders squared, with a slight looseness to the hips. He had copied the walk from his older brother, Dennis. Derek was the right height for his age, but like all boys and most men, he wished to be taller. Lately, at night when he was in bed, he thought he could feel himself growing. The mirror over his mother's dresser told him he was filling out in the upper body, too.

Billy, despite his wide shoulders and unusually broad chest, was not an athlete. He kept up on the local sports teams, but he had other passions. Billy liked pinball machines, cap pistols, and comic books.

"That how Brown got his twelve yards in eleven carries against the 'Skins?" said Billy.

"Uh-uh, Billy, don't be talkin' about that."

"Don Bosseler gained more in that game than Brown did."

"*In that game.* Most of the time, Bosseler ain't fit to carry my man's cleats. Two weeks before that, at Griffith? Jim Brown ran for one hundred and fifty-two. The man set the all-time rushing record in that one, Billy. Don Bosseler? Shoot."

"Awright," said Billy, a smile forming on his wide face. "Your man can play."

Derek knew Billy was messing with him, but he couldn't help getting agitated just the same. Not that Derek wasn't a Redskins fan. He listened to every game on the radio. He read the Shirley Povich and Bob Addie columns in the *Post* whenever they saw print. He followed the stats of quarterback Eddie Le-Baron, middle linebacker Chuck Drazenovich, halfback Eddie Sutton, and others. He even tracked Bosseler's yards-per-carry. In fact, he only rooted against the 'Skins twice a year, and then with a pang of guilt, when they played Cleveland.

Derek had a newspaper photo of Brown taped to the wall of the bedroom he shared with his brother. With the exception of his father, there was no one who was more of a hero to him than Brown. This was a strong individual who commanded respect, not just from his own but from people of all colors. The man could play.

"Don Bosseler," said Derek, chuckling. He put one big, long-fingered hand to the top of his head, shaved nearly to the scalp, and rubbed it. It was something his brother, Dennis, did in conversation when he was cracking on his friends. Derek had picked up the gesture, like his walk, from Dennis.

"I'm kiddin' you, Derek." Billy got up off the milk crate and put his comic book down on the diner's back stoop. "C'mon, let's go."

"Where?"

"My neighborhood. Maybe there's a game up at Fort Stevens."

"Okay," said Derek. Billy's streets were a couple of miles from the diner and several miles from Derek's home. Most of the kids up there were white. But Derek didn't object. Truth was, it excited him some to be off his turf.

On most Saturdays, Derek and Billy spent their time out in the city while their fathers worked at the diner. They were boys and were expected to go out and find adventure and even mild forms of trouble. There was violence in certain sections of the District, but it was committed by adults and usually among criminals and mostly at night. Generally, the young went untouched.

Out on the main drag, Derek noticed that the local movie house, the Kennedy, was still running *Buchanan Rides Alone*, with Randolph Scott. Derek had already seen it with his dad. His father had promised to take him down to U Street for the new John Wayne, *Rio Bravo*, which had people talking around town. The picture was playing down at the Republic. Like the other District theaters on U, the Lincoln and the Booker T, the

Republic was mostly for colored, and Derek felt comfortable there. His father, Darius Strange, loved westerns, and Derek Strange had come to love them, too.

Derek and Billy walked east on the commercial strip. They passed two boys Derek knew from church, and one of them said, "What you hangin' with that white boy for?" and Derek said, "What business is that of yours?" He made just enough eye contact for the boy to know he was serious, and all of them went on their way.

Billy was Derek's first and only white playmate. The working relationship between their fathers had caused their hookup. Otherwise they never would have been put together, since most of the time, outside of sporting events and first jobs, colored boys and white boys didn't mix. Wasn't anything wrong with mixing, exactly, but it just seemed more natural to be with your own kind. Hanging with Billy sometimes put Derek in a bad position; you'd get challenged out here when your own saw you walking with a white. But Derek figured you had to stand by someone unless he gave you cause not to, and he felt he had to say something when conflict arrived. It wouldn't have been right to let it pass. Sure, Billy often said the wrong things, and sometimes those things hurt, but it was because he didn't know any better. He was ignorant, but his ignorance was never deliberate.

They walked northwest through Manor Park, across the green of Fort Slocum, and soon were up on Georgia Avenue, which many thought of as Main Street, D.C. It was the longest road in the District and had always been the primary northern thoroughfare into Washington, going back to when it was called the 7th Street Pike. All types of businesses lined the strip, and folks moved about the sidewalks day and night. The Avenue was always alive.

The road was white concrete and etched with streetcar tracks. Wood platforms, where riders had once waited to board streetcars, were still up in spots, but the D.C. Transit buses were now the main form of public transportation. A few steel troughs, used to water the horses that had pulled the carts of the junkmen and fruit and vegetable vendors, remained on the Avenue, but in short order all of it would be going the way of those mobile merchants. It was said that the street would soon be paved in asphalt and the tracks, platforms, and troughs would disappear.

Billy's neighborhood, Brightwood, was mostly white, working- and middle-class, and heavily ethnic: Greeks, Italians, Irish Catholics, and all varieties of Jew. The families had moved from Petworth, 7th Street, Columbia Heights, the H Street corridor in Northeast, and Chinatown, working their way north as they began to make more money in the prosperous years following World War II. They were seeking nicer housing, yards for their children, and driveways for their cars. Also, they were moving away from the colored, whose numbers and visibility had rapidly increased citywide in the wake of reurbanization and forced desegregation.

But even this would be a temporary move. Blockbuster real estate agents in Brightwood had begun moving colored families into white streets with the intention of scaring residents into selling their houses on the cheap. The next stop for upper-Northwest, east-of-the-park whites would be the suburbs of Maryland. No one knew that the events of the next nine years would hasten that final move, though there was a feeling that some sort of change was coming and that it would have to come, an unspoken sense of the inevitable. Still, some denied it as strongly as they denied death.

Derek lived in Park View, south of Petworth, now mostly colored and some working-class whites. He attended Backus Junior High and would go on to Roosevelt High School. Billy went to Paul Junior High and was destined for Coolidge High, which had some coloreds, most of whom were athletes. Many

Coolidge kids would go on to college; far fewer from Roosevelt would. Roosevelt had gangs; Coolidge had fraternities. Derek and Billy lived a few short miles apart, but the differences in their lives and prospects were striking.

They walked the east side of Georgia's 6200 block, passing the open door of the Arrow cleaners, a business that had been in place since 1929, owned and operated by Bill Caludis. They stopped in to say hey to Caludis's son, Billy, whom Billy Georgelakos knew from church. On the corner sat Clark's Men's Shop, near Marinoff-Pritt and Katz, the Jewish market, where several of the butchers had camp numbers tattooed on their forearms. Nearby was the Sheridan Theater, which was running *Decision at Sundown,* another Randolph Scott. Derek had seen it with his dad.

They crossed to the other side of Georgia. They walked by Vince's Agnes Flower Shop, where Billy paused to say a few words with a cute young clerk named Margie, and the Sheridan Waffle Shop, also known as John's Lunch, a diner owned by John Deoudes. Then it was a watering hole called Sue's 6210, a Chinese laundry, a barbershop, and on the corner another beer garden, the 6200. "Stagger Lee" was playing on the house juke, its rhythms coming through the 6200's open door.

On the sidewalk outside the bar, three young white teenagers were alternately talking, smoking cigarettes, and running combs through their hair. One of them was ribbing another, asking if his girlfriend had given him his shiner and swollen face. "Nah," said the kid with the black eye, "I got jumped by a buncha niggers down at Griffith Stadium," adding that he was going to be looking for them and "some get-back." The group quieted as Derek and Billy passed. There were no words spoken, no hard stares, and no trouble. Derek looking at the weak, all-mouth boy and thinking, Prob'ly wasn't no "buncha niggers" about it, only had to be one.

At the corner of Georgia and Rittenhouse, Billy pointed excitedly at a man wearing a brimmed hat, crossing the street and heading east. With him was a young woman whose face they couldn't see but whose backside moved in a pleasing way.

"That's Bo Diddley," said Billy.

"Thought he lived over on Rhode Island Avenue."

"That's what everyone says. But we all been seein' him around here lately. They say he's got a spot down there on Rittenhouse."

"Bo Diddley's a gunslinger," said Derek, a warmth rising in his thighs as he checked out the fill of the woman's skirt.

They walked south to Quackenbos and cut across the lot of the Nativity School, a Catholic convent that housed a nice gymnasium. The nuns there were forever chasing Billy and his friends from the gym. Beyond the lot was Fort Stevens, where Confederate forces had been repelled by the guns and musketry of Union soldiers in July of 1864. The fort had been recreated and preserved, but few tourists now visited the site. The grounds mainly served as a playing field for the neighborhood boys.

"Ain't nobody up here," said Derek, looking across the weedy field, the American flag flying on a white mast throwing a wavy shadow on the lawn.

"I'm gonna pick some *porichia* for my mom," said Billy.

"Say what?"

Derek and Billy went up a steep grade to its crest, where several cannons sat spaced in a row. The grade dropped to a deep gully that ran along the northern line of the fort. Beside one of the cannons grew patches of spindly plants with hard stems. Billy pulled a few of the plants and shook the dirt off the roots.

"Thought your mama liked them dandelion weeds."

"That's *rodichia*. These here are good, too. You gotta get 'em before they flower, though, 'cause then they're too bitter. Let's go give 'em to her and get something to drink."

Billy lived in a slate-roofed, copper-guttered brick colonial on the 1300 block of Somerset, a few blocks west of the park. In contrast with the row houses of Park View and Petworth, the houses here were detached, with flat, well-tended front lawns. The streets were heavy with Italians and Greeks. The Deoudes family lived on Somerset, as did the Vondas family, and up on Underwood lived a wiry kid named Bobby Boukas, whose parents owned a flower shop. All were members of Billy's church, St. Sophia. On Tuckerman stood the house where midget actor Johnny Puleo, who had played in the Lancaster-Curtis circus picture, *Trapeze*, stayed for much of the year. Puleo drove a customized Dodge with wood blocks fitted to the gas and brake pedals.

On the way to the Georgelakos house, Derek stopped to pet a muscular tan boxer who was usually chained outside the front of the Deoudes residence. The dog's name was Greco. Greco sometimes walked with the police at night on their foot patrols and was known to be quick, loyal, and tough.

Derek got down on his haunches and let Greco smell his hand. The dog pushed his muzzle into Derek's fingers, and Derek patted his belly and rubbed behind his ears.

"Crazy," said Billy.

"What you mean?"

"Usually he rises up and shows his teeth."

"To colored boys, right?"

"Well, yeah."

"He likes *me*." Derek's eyes softened as he admired the dog. "One day, I'ma get me one just like him, too."